Also by David Morrell
Published by Fawcett Crest Books:

TESTAMENT
THE TOTEM
BLOOD OATH
FIRST BLOOD
THE BROTHERHOOD OF THE ROSE
THE FRATERNITY OF THE STONE

THE LEAGUE OF NIGHT AND FOG

DAVID MORRELL

FAWCETT CREST • NEW YORK

A Fawcett Crest Book
Published by Ballantine Books
Copyright © 1987 by David Morrell

Library of Congress Catalog Card Number: 86-24185

ISBN 0-449-21371-4

This edition published by arrangement with E.P. Dutton, a division of NAL Penguin, Inc.

The quotation on page 100 is from Heinz Höhne's *The Order of the Death's Head*, copyright © 1966 Verlag der Spiegel, Hamburg, and copyright © 1967 Sigbert Mohn Verlag, Gutersloh; English translation copyright © 1969 by Martin Secker and Warburg Limited.

Manufactured in the United States of America

First International Edition: March 1988
First U.S. Edition: August 1988
Eighth Printing: November 1991

To Paul Seydor
a friend for all seasons

CONTENTS

New evils require new remedies . . .
new sanctions to defend and vindicate
the eternal principles of right
and wrong.

The Times (LONDON)
ON THE
NUREMBERG TRIALS

THE LEAGUE OF NIGHT AND FOG

Prologue

FOUR
SHADES OF
NIGHT

THE NIGHT OF THE LONG KNIVES

A phrase invented by the Nazis, the Night of the Long Knives, refers to the events on the night of June 30, 1934, in Austria and Germany. Hitler, having achieved the titles of chancellor and dictator, still needed to gain the remaining position that would give him absolute power over Germany—the presidency. Determined to remove all obstacles, he flew secretly to Munich... where, accompanied by his personal bodyguards, he arrested at gunpoint his main rival and former friend, Ernst Röhm. Röhm, the chief of the so-called Brownshirts—a terrorist paramilitary unit of the Nazi party, officially known as *Sturmabteilung*...or Storm Troopers, SA for short—had sought to merge his four-hundred-thousand-member force with the German army and consequently (so Hitler alleged) take over Germany. Hitler, anxious not to lose the support of the army, even more anxious to rid himself of competitors, executed Röhm and several ambitious Brownshirt officers.

Not satisfied with half-measures, the Führer decided to eliminate other threats as well. While Röhm and his staff were being shot in Munich, Hitler's close associates Himmler and Göring conducted a similar purge in Berlin. Among those executed were the former chancellor of Germany, unfriendly police and state officials, and dissident executives of the Nazi party. Hitler later claimed that seventy-seven traitors had been killed in order to prevent an overthrow of the German government. Survivors of the purge insisted that the actual number was over four hundred. A postwar trial in Munich raised the total even higher—beyond one thousand.

The significance of the Night of the Long Knives is twofold. As a consequence of the terror that Hitler created, he did gain the final crucial title of president and, as absolute ruler of Germany, steered his nation toward the obscenities of the Second World War. Beyond that, his use of bodyguards in executing his rivals raised the group to a stature that equaled and eventually surpassed the power of Röhm's paramilitary terrorists. In time, the guards numbered more than a million. Just as Röhm's Brownshirts, *Sturmabteilung* . . . or Storm Troopers, were known as SA, so Hitler's Blackshirts, *Schutzstaffel* . . . or elite guard, were known by their unit's initials. But unlike SA, initials remembered today by few, the initials of the Blackshirts remain synonymous with depravity. The hiss of a snake. The rasp of evil.

SS.

THE NIGHT OF
BROKEN GLASS

Also known as *Kristallnacht* or Crystal Night, the Night of Broken Glass refers to events on November 9, 1938, throughout Germany. Two days earlier, Herschel Grynszpan, a Polish Jew, assassinated Ernst von Rath, a minor diplomat at the German embassy in Paris, in retaliation for the deportation of Grynszpan's family and 23,000 other Jews from Germany to Poland. Grynszpan's intended target had been the German ambassador to Paris, but von Rath attempted to intervene and was shot instead. Ironically, von Rath had openly criticized Nazi anti-Semitic attitudes and was scheduled for disciplinary action by the Gestapo. No matter—a Jew had killed a German official, and Hitler took advantage of the incident. Publicly claiming that the assassination had prompted anti-Semitic riots throughout Germany, he privately gave orders for the as yet nonexistent riots to occur.

These "spontaneous demonstrations" were organized by Reinhard Heydrich, second in command of the SS. After Nazi mobs enthusiastically completed their work on the night of November 9, Heydrich was able to give a preliminary report to Hitler that 815 Jewish shops, 171 Jewish homes, and 119 synagogues had been set on fire or otherwise destroyed; twenty thousand Jews were arrested and sent to concentration camps; thirty-six were killed, another thirty-six critically injured. These figures turned out to be drastically underestimated. So widespread was the destruction that everywhere streets were littered with fragments from shattered windows, hence the expression "the Night of Broken Glass."

Concluding his report, Heydrich recommended that

the best course to follow would be for the insurance companies to settle the Jews' claims in full and then to confiscate the money and return it to the insurers. My information is that claims for broken glass alone will amount to some five million marks. . . . As for the practical matter of cleaning up the destruction, this is being arranged by releasing Jews in gangs from the concentration camps and having them clean up their own messes under supervision. The courts will impose upon them a fine of a billion marks, and this will be paid out of the proceeds of their confiscated property. Heil Hitler!

The Night of Broken Glass represents the start of Germany's undisguised state-directed pogrom against the Jews. Though many foreign governments—and even some executives within the Nazi party—objected to the atrocities committed on *Kristallnacht*, no one did anything to stop them or to ensure that they weren't repeated and in much worse degree.

THE NIGHT AND FOG

The *Nacht und Nebel Erlass* ... or Night and Fog Decree, one of Hitler's personal edicts, was issued on December 7, 1941, the same day Japan attacked America's naval base at Pearl Harbor. Directed against "persons endangering German security" and specifically against members of resistance groups in German-occupied territories, it proposed that execution was not itself a sufficient deterrent against anti-German threats. Psychological as well as physical force was necessary. Thus, not all agitators would be killed upon discovery; many instead would be transported to an unknown location, their destiny never to be learned by outsiders. Friends and family members would forever be kept in suspense. As the edict stipulated, "The intimidating effect of these measures lies (a) in the disappearance without trace of the guilty person, (b) in the fact that no kind of information must be given about the person's whereabouts and his fate." Those tempted to participate in anti-German activity would fear that they, like their loved ones, would disappear within the night and the fog.

An example of how this decree was carried out occurred in 1942: the fate of the village of Lidice, in Czechoslovakia. In reprisal for the assassination of Reinhard Heydrich, Nazi soldiers surrounded the village and shot every male within it, ten at a time. It took all day before the executions ended. The women of the vil-

7

lage were transported to the concentration camp at Ravensbrück in Germany, where they died from weakness or were gassed. But the children of the village, ninety of them, simply vanished into the night and fog. Relatives in other villages could not find a trace of them.

THE DARK NIGHT OF
THE SOUL

1

On January 20, 1942, six weeks after the Night and Fog Decree, Hitler ordered his senior SS officers to attend a special conference in Berlin for the purpose of organizing the Final Solution to what the Führer called "the Jewish question." Anti-Semitic riots and laws, intended to force the Jews to leave German territory of their own accord, had been only partially successful—most Jews had been reluctant to leave their homes and businesses. Massive deportations too had been only partially successful—the process took too much time and was too expensive. But now the ultimate extension of Crystal Night was set in motion. Extermination.

Mass executions by firing squad were uneconomical due to the cost of ammunition. A cheaper method, that of cramming victims into trucks and killing them with engine exhaust, was judged unsatisfactory because not enough victims could be asphyxiated at one time. But asphyxiation itself was not at fault. The problem was how to do it efficiently. In the spring of 1942, the death camps began.

These were not the same as concentration camps, where huge numbers of people were squeezed together into squalid barracks from which they were marched each day to factories to work for the German war effort. As a consequence of brutal workloads, insufficient food, and unsanitary conditions, most occupants of the concentration camps did indeed die, but death was not the primary purpose for which prisoners had been sent to these work camps. Slavery was.

The death camps, however, had no other function than to kill with the utmost speed and efficiency. There were killing centers at some concentration camps, Auschwitz and Maidanek for example, but the exclusive death camps numbered only four. All were situated in Poland: Sobibor, Belzec, Chelmno, and Treblinka.

As Treblinka's commandant, Franz Stangl, confessed,

it was Dante's Inferno. The smell was indescribable. The hundreds, no, the thousands of bodies everywhere, decomposing, putrefying. All around the perimeter of the camp, there were tents and open fires with groups of Ukrainian guards and girls—whores, I found out later, from all over the countryside—weaving drunk, dancing, singing, playing music.

In the fifteen months of its existence, from July of 1942 to September of 1943, the camp at Treblinka exterminated one million Jews—a sixth of all Jews murdered in the Holocaust. When the camp was at its most efficient, twenty thousand people were killed each day, a statistic that becomes even more horrible when one realizes that all of these executions occurred in the morning. The rest of the day was devoted to disposing of the bodies by burning them in huge open pits. At night, the flames were allowed to die out, the nauseating smoke to drift away, so the next morning's victims would not be alarmed by the unmistakable stench of incinerated corpses.

2

The victims tumbled from overcrowded cattle cars, relieved to be off the train that had brought them from the Jewish ghetto in Warsaw. Some with whom they'd traveled had smothered or been crushed to death. The survivors tried not to look at the bodies. Instead they squinted at the painful but renewing sunlight, finally able to free their lungs of the poisonous fumes of vomit and excrement.

Signs said TREBLINKA, CASHIER, and TRANSFER HERE FOR EASTBOUND TRAINS. Fear was offset by hope: *this wasn't a camp.* The SS soldiers, with their twin lightning-bolt insignia, were to be expected—though another insignia, a death's head on their caps, aroused apprehension. The clock on the station had hands that were painted on and didn't move. Soldiers blurted commands to enter the railway station, to strip, to proceed to the showers. A shower would be welcome, but the victims wondered why such a luxury was being granted. A guard seemed to read their thoughts: "We can't stand your filthy stench!"

Herded into the station, they took off their clothes and surrendered their valuables. "To protect your keepsakes while you're in the shower," they were told. They were given haircuts, down to the scalp, and this too made them fearful. Guards burst into the station, lashing their victims with whips, chasing them out the back . . . where naked they were urged along a path, which the SS had nicknamed "the Road to Heaven." Other guards struck them with clubs. "Faster! Run *faster!*"

The victims stumbled over fallen companions. At the end of the path, there was only one direction in which to go—to the right, up five concrete steps, through a huge open door. When the last of the group of five hundred had been squeezed inside the chamber, the door was slammed shut and locked. Instead of shower nozzles, there were vents. Outside, an engine roared. Exhaust filled the room. As the victims struggled not to inhale, they didn't realize that they'd been chased so that their lungs would rebel against the attempt not to breathe. They didn't realize that their clothes and valuables would help the Germans fight the war, that their hair would be stuffed inside military mattresses and pillows,

11

that the gold fillings in their teeth would be extracted to pay for guns and ammunition. All they knew was that they couldn't hold their breath any longer. They died standing up.

3

In the pit of brutality, the human spirit managed to triumph. During August of 1943, Jews who'd been forced to do work at Treblinka that even the SS and their Ukrainian assistants couldn't endure—dragging corpses from the gas chambers, arranging them on railway ties in trenches, and setting fire to them—revolted. Using makeshift weapons, they killed their guards and raced toward the nearby forest. Many were strafed by machine guns, but others, possibly as many as fifty, reached the cover of the trees and escaped.

The Nazis abandoned the camp. With the Russians approaching from the east and most of the Jews in Poland already exterminated, the SS hurriedly destroyed the evidence of their obscenities. Treblinka's phony railway station, its Road to Heaven, its gas chambers and incineration pits were all plowed beneath the earth.

A farmer and his cattle were positioned over them. But despite the flames that had charred one million corpses, the victims insisted on bearing witness even in death. The gases from so much decay made the earth heave five feet into the air. The gases dispersed. The earth settled—five feet below its former level. More gases heaved the earth. Again it sank. And rose again.

The cattle fled. So did the farmer.

Book One

SUMMONS

ICICLE

1

CARDINAL'S DISAPPEARANCE
REMAINS A MYSTERY

ROME, ITALY, February 28 (AP)—Vatican officials and Rome police remain baffled five days after the disappearance of Cardinal Krunoslav Pavelic, influential member of the Roman Catholic Church's administration group, the Curia.

Pavelic, seventy-two, was last seen by close associates after celebrating a private mass in the chapel of his Vatican living quarters Sunday evening. On Monday, he had been scheduled to give the keynote address to a widely publicized conference of Catholic bishops on the subject of the Church's political relations with Eastern European communist regimes.

Authorities at first suspected right-wing terrorists of abducting Cardinal Pavelic to protest a rumored softening of the Vatican's attitude toward any communist regime willing to ease restrictions on Church activities. However, no extremist group has so far claimed responsibility for Pavelic's disappearance.

2

St. Paul, Minnesota. March. For the second time that night, the cards Frank Miller held became a blur. Though red and black were distinct, he couldn't tell the difference between a heart and a diamond or a spade and a club. Trying to subdue his concern, he took off his glasses, rubbed his eyes, and massaged his aching forehead.

"Something the matter?" Sid Henderson asked across the table from him. Like Miller, Henderson was in his seventies. Indeed all the bridge players in this room in the St. Paul community service center were either that old or just slightly younger.

Miller strained to focus on his cards. "The matter? Nothing."

"You sure? You look kinda sick."

"It's too hot in here. They've turned up the thermostat too high. Somebody ought to open some windows."

"And give us all pneumonia?" Iris Glickman asked to Miller's right. She *claimed* she was only sixty-seven. "It's freezing outside. If you're hot, take off your suitcoat."

But Miller had already loosened his tie. He couldn't allow himself to ignore decorum completely and play his cards in his shirt-sleeves.

"Maybe you should go home," Harvey Ginsberg said on the left. "You're awful pale."

Miller dabbed his sweaty brow with a handkerchief; his stomach felt queasy. "You need four players. I'd ruin the game for everybody."

"Screw the game," Harvey said.

As usual, Iris pursed her lips in pretended shock at Harvey's vulgar language.

Miller's forehead throbbed. "You won't think I'm a poor sport?"

"What I'll think, Frank, is you're a damned fool if you're sick and you don't go home."

Miller smiled. "Such good friends."

"I'll call you tomorrow and make sure you're feeling better," Harvey said.

3

The instant Miller stepped from the hall, an icy wind stung his face. Shocking snow pelted him as he trudged toward the parking lot across the street, clutching his overcoat. At least he didn't feel ill anymore. The gusts revived him, affirming his suspicion that his headache and nausea had been caused by excessive heat inside the hall. He fondly remembered the winters of his youth. Toboggan rides and ice-skate races. My mind's still spry, he thought. It's this damned body that's let me down.

The street was deserted; the arc lamps in the parking lot were shrouded by falling snow. He reached his car— an Audi, a gift from his son—unlocked the driver's door, and heard a voice behind him.

Frowning, he turned, straining to see through the swirling snow. The voice had been muffled by the shriek of the wind. A *man's* voice, he thought, but when he didn't hear it again, he began to wonder if his ears were playing a trick on him.

He shrugged and gripped the latch on his car door. But again he heard the voice behind him, closer, though still not distinct. It seemed to be saying a single word, a first name, *his* first name.

Once more, he turned. "Is someone there?"

No answer.

He opened the Audi's door.

A hand grasped his shoulder, preventing him from getting in. Another hand slammed the door shut. A third hand spun him with such force that he almost lost his glasses. Three men. The snow obscured their faces.

"Please. I'm old. Take my wallet. But just don't hurt me."

"Wallet?" One of them laughed.

The snow lessened. When he saw their faces and understood what they really wanted, he despaired.

4

Sounds we don't hear can sometimes wake us. So it was that William Miller, unconsciously aware of the silence outside his bedroom windows, began to squirm in his sleep. Like a father whose rest is not complete until his teenage son or daughter comes home from a date that shouldn't have lasted past midnight, he felt uneasy because no car had entered the driveway, no automatic garage door had rattled as it opened and shut. But he wasn't a father who waited for his son. The opposite—a son, who waited for his father. His mental alarm went off. He opened his eyes and blinked at the digital clock beside his bed.

2:38 A.M.

Taking care not to wake his wife, he eased from bed and peered out a window toward the driveway below. A distant streetlight glinted off falling snow. Fir trees were cloaked with white. There weren't any tire tracks in the driveway.

"What's the matter, hon?"

He turned to his wife. "Sorry. I tried to be quiet."

"I couldn't sleep either. What are you looking at?"

"It's what I'm *not* looking at that bothers me."

Miller explained.

"No tire tracks?" She slipped from bed and put on a robe. "Maybe it snowed after he got in."

"Yeah . . . maybe."

He left the bedroom, passed his children's rooms, and reached his father's room at the opposite end of the hallway. When he didn't see a form on the bed, he flicked on the light. The room was empty.

His wife appeared beside him. "Let's think a minute. This might not mean anything. He might be downstairs asleep in front of the television."

"Maybe."

They went downstairs but couldn't find him.

"Car trouble?"

"He'd have phoned," Miller said.

"Unless he's with a friend."

"This late? He hardly ever stays out past midnight."

"I said with a *friend*. He might have decided to spend the night."

"With a *woman*?"

She smiled. "Why not?"

"It doesn't make a difference. He'd still have phoned."

"Unless he felt embarrassed."

"*What?*"

"You know, with your mother dead a year now and . . ."

"Hey, I loved my mother, and I'm sorry she's gone. But if he's still interested in women at his age, more power to him."

"Maybe he doesn't know that's how you feel. Have you ever talked about sex with him?"

"With my seventy-three-year-old father? Give me a break." He studied the kitchen clock. "It's close to three. If he isn't home by three-thirty, I'm calling the cops."

But his father *wasn't* home by three-thirty, and Miller did call the cops. No auto accidents involving an Audi had been reported. No old men had been admitted to the local hospitals after midnight, and none of those admitted earlier had been Miller's father. The Audi, covered with snow, was discovered in a parking lot across the street from the community service hall. The keys had been dropped and somehow kicked beneath the car.

But Miller's father was never found.

5

Mexico City. April. Martin Rosenberg, seventy-two, stepped out of the synagogue, tucked his yarmulka into his suitcoat pocket, and surveyed the cobbled street. From two blocks away, the drone of traffic along the Paseo de la Reforma disturbed his sense of tranquillity. To his right, the lights of the ancient castle on Chapultepec hill gleamed against the darkening sky.

He exchanged shaloms with a group of young people coming out of the synagogue and turned left toward a corner. His son's home was five blocks away, one of the historic Spanish mansions interspersed with high-rise apartments in this affluent section of Mexico City. As usual, his son had offered to have him driven to and from the synagogue, but Rosenberg had insisted that walks were essential to his health, and besides, the scenery throughout this district never failed to give him pleasure.

He rounded the corner, proceeding toward the well-lit broad avenue that connected Chapultepec hill with government buildings.

6

"I don't care how old he is!" Aaron Rosenberg said. "It's never taken him more than an hour to walk back home!" He paced in front of the arched windows that took up one wall of his living room. "But it's been more than *two* hours, not one!"

With his pencil-thin mustache, aquiline nose, and dark burning eyes, Rosenberg looked more Spanish than Jewish. He seldom went to the synagogue anymore, but he donated generously to it and knew the rabbi, whom he'd telephoned forty-five minutes ago, learning that his father had left the synagogue at dusk.

"Perhaps he stopped to visit with someone," his wife said. Her face was deeply tanned. Thirty-eight, lithe from daily tennis workouts, she wore a solid-gold watch, a turquoise necklace, and a bright red designer version of a peasant skirt and blouse.

"Who? And surely not for two hours."

He saw the headlights of a Mercedes sedan pulling up at the curb. "Esteban's come back. Perhaps he found him."

But Esteban reported that he'd driven along every route that the father would have used to return from the synagogue. Then he had widened his search to every street within a twenty-block grid. Other servants, having searched on foot, came back with the same disturbing report.

"Go back out again! Keep looking!"

Rosenberg called every hospital in Mexico City. Nothing. At midnight, when the servants again returned without his father, he sacrificed a cardinal rule of his import-export business—never deal with the police except to bribe them—and phoned a captain whose home on Lake Chalco, eight miles south of the city, had recently been renovated thanks to Rosenberg.

One month later, his father had still not been found.

7

Toronto. May. From the window of his first-class seat in the Air Canada 727, Joseph Kessler peered down at the glinting expanse of Lake Ontario. Even at twenty thousand feet, he could see the distinctive length of a Great Lakes freighter. Ahead, close to shore, he saw the smaller outlines of barges, the gleam of wind-swollen sails. Despite the brilliance of the day, Kessler knew that the water would be numbingly cold. The crews of the sailboats down there had to be fanatical about their sport.

He nodded with approval. Because of his own ability to harness his obsessions, he'd developed a small Providence electronics firm into a thriving corporation that had made him a millionaire by the age of forty. But at the moment, his obsession was not related to business. It was personal, fueled by rage.

He didn't allow himself to show it. Throughout the flight, he'd maintained composure, studying business documents while inwardly he seethed. Patience, he told himself. Success depends on patience. Keep control.

For now.

Below, he saw the sprawl of Toronto, its flat residential subdivisions stretching along the lake shore, its skyscrapers projecting from the heart of the city. He felt a change in pressure as the jet began to descend. Six minutes later, it landed at Toronto's international airport.

He went through customs. "Nothing to declare. I'm here on business." His briefcase and carry-on bag were not inspected. He proceeded through a sliding glass door into the noisy concourse, scanned the crowd, and approached a muscular man who wore the same blue-and-red striped tie that Kessler did.

"How much did you pay for that tie?" Kessler asked.

"How much did *you* pay?"

"Someone gave it to me."

"I found mine." The code completed, the muscular man added, "Have you got any luggage?"

"Just what I'm carrying."

"Then let's get out of here." The man's Canadian accent made "out" sound like "oot."

From the terminal, they entered a parking lot, got into a station wagon, and soon reached a divided four-lane highway, heading west on Highway 401.

Kessler looked behind him toward the receding skyline of Toronto. "How soon till we get there?"

"An hour."

"Everyone showed up?"

"You're the last," the man said.

"Good." Kessler felt his fury blossom. To distract himself, he pointed toward the farm fields and stands of timber at the sides of the highway. "Something's missing."

"What?"

22

"No billboards."

"Right. They're against the law."

"Three cheers for Canada."

Kessler put on his sunglasses and stared straight ahead. The small talk was over.

8

Eighty kilometers farther, they reached the exit ramp for Kitchener. Instead of entering the city, the driver used side roads to head deep into farm country, finally turning up a zigzag gravel driveway toward a mansion on a bluff above a river.

Kessler stepped from the station wagon and studied the estate—surrounding wooded hills, a nine-hole golf course, a tennis court, a television satellite receiver, a swimming pool. He turned toward the five-car garage, then toward the mansion. With its dormer windows, towers, and gables, it looked like it belonged in New England more than in Ontario.

"Mr. Halloway knows how to live well," the driver said. "Of course, he owes it all to—"

One of the double doors at the mansion's entrance came open. A lithe man of medium height, wearing a perfectly fitted exercise suit and expensive jogging shoes, stepped out. He was in his early forties, had thick wavy hair, and beamed with health. "Thank you, John. We won't be needing you for the rest of the day. If you like, you can use that new set of exercise machines in the gym. Have a steam bath. A drink. Relax."

"I appreciate it, Mr. Halloway."

The driver got in the station wagon. Halloway came down the granite front steps and held out his hand. "Joe? Or is it . . . ?"

"Joseph." Kessler shook hands with him.

"We've been a long time meeting. With so much in common, it's a pity we had to wait for misfortune to bring us together."

23

"Misfortune's not exactly what I'd call it."

"What then?"

"Fucking insanity."

"The nature of the world. That's why I prefer to live out here. Away from the madness." Grimacing, Halloway gestured toward the road hidden beyond the wooded hills. "Come. The others feel as distressed as ourselves. They're waiting."

9

The mansion's foyer was shadowy; its slate floor emphasized the click of their footsteps. Still needing to calm himself, Kessler paused to examine a colorful landscape painting. The artist's signature was Halloway.

"My father's," Halloway said. "His acrylic period."

The reference to Halloway's father rekindled Kessler's indignation. Down the hall, he heard angry voices and, preceded by Halloway, entered a large oak-paneled room where eight men interrupted their fierce discussion to look at him.

Kessler studied them in return. They were of different heights, weights, and facial structures, but they shared one physical characteristic: their ages fit within the same narrow range, late thirties, early forties.

"It's about time," one said.

Two others spoke in rapid succession.

"I've been here since yesterday."

"This meeting was supposed to be urgent!"

"My flight got delayed," Kessler told them. "I came as soon as I could."

The three men who'd spoken had accents—Spanish, Swedish, and American midwestern. Coming down the hall, Kessler had heard other accents—French, British, Italian, Egyptian, and American southern.

"Gentlemen, please," Halloway said. "If we start to argue among ourselves, we help the enemy achieve the second half of his purpose."

24

"*Second* half?" The Frenchman frowned.

"And what do you mean 'his'?" the Texan asked. "*One* man couldn't have done this!"

"Of course," Halloway said. "But no matter how many, they're organized, and they share a common goal. That's why I think of them as one and why *we* have to act as one."

"It's true," the Italian said. "We can't allow ourselves to be distracted by our frustrations. We mustn't be divided. Isn't that why we got in touch with each other so many years ago and why we *stayed* in touch? Because as a group we're stronger than each of us is alone. We can better protect ourselves."

"But we're not the ones who need protecting!" the Spaniard said.

"Not physically perhaps," Halloway said. "At least not yet. But in our hearts? And suppose they're not satisfied? Suppose they decide to come for *us* now, our wives, our children?"

The others straightened.

"That's what I meant by the second half of our enemy's purpose. It's to torture us with uncertainty, to make us suffer from constant dread."

"Dear God." The Egyptian paled.

"You understand?"

"It's the Night and Fog all over again."

Kessler couldn't restrain himself. "What's the matter with all of you?"

They stared at him.

"Before you pat yourselves on the back about how smart you were to stay in touch with each other, why don't you admit you've been your own worst enemy?"

"What are you talking about?"

"How do you think they found us? All they had to do was track down just one and follow the trail to the rest."

"We took precautions."

"Obviously not well enough. And look at us now. All together."

The American midwesterner stepped forward, his features twisted with resentment. "My father would never have told."

25

"Under torture? Come on," Kessler said. "How much pain can an old man stand? Or what if chemicals were used? I was late because I almost didn't come at all. The reason I did was to warn you. You're as much to blame as whoever did this. Don't stay in touch with each other. I don't want to know anything more about you, and I don't want you to know anything more about me."

"That won't solve the problem," Halloway said. "We'd still be in danger, and it doesn't bring our fathers back."

"I've already accepted the fact—mine's dead."

"I don't give up as easily as you," Halloway said. "But what if you're right? What if your father and mine and everybody else's are dead? Do you intend to let the matter end?"

"Oh, believe me, I want the bastards to pay."

"In that case, we have plans to discuss."

Kessler stepped quickly forward. "You have something specific?"

"Indeed. It may be you didn't notice. You weren't the only member of the group who had second thoughts about coming. Two of us in fact declined. In many respects, the most important members."

Kessler glanced at the group in confusion and suddenly understood.

"Given what I intend to propose, their participation is crucial," Halloway said.

Kessler nodded.

Seth and Icicle.

10

Sydney, Australia. June. St. Andrew's Cathedral, the foundation of which had been set in 1819, was as impressive as the guidebook maintained. Kessler roamed the shadows of its echoing interior, studied its vaulted ceiling, admired its stained-glass windows, and strolled outside. Squinting in the painfully brilliant sunlight, he descended a wide tier of steps to the sidewalk. Next to the cathedral here on George Street, he reached the town hall, used for concerts and assembly meetings, his guide-book explained. After lingering as long as seemed appropriate, he strolled to the corner, hailed a taxi, and proceeded to one of the many Oriental restaurants that Sydney was famous for. He'd arranged to meet his business connection there, but he arrived deliberately early, went to a phone booth, and dialed the number Halloway had given him.

A male voice answered. "Bondi Beach Surf and Dive Shop."

"Mr. Pendleton, please."

"The son or the father?"

"It doesn't matter."

"I'm the son."

"Mr. Pendleton, do you have icicles in Australia?"

For a moment, the silence was so intense that Kessler thought the phone had gone dead. "Mr. Pendleton?"

"Who *is* this?"

"A friend."

"I've got customers waiting. I rent and sell surf-boards. I sell and fill scuba tanks. Icicles I don't need. Or people with stupid questions."

"Wait. Perhaps if I mentioned a name. Thomas Conrad. Post office box four thirty-eight."

Again the line was silent. When Pendleton finally spoke, his voice sounded muffled, as if he'd cupped a hand to his mouth. "What do you want?"

"A meeting. It's obvious if I meant you harm, I didn't need to call. I wouldn't have put you on guard."

"You're from *them*, aren't you?"

"My name is Kessler."

"Christ, I made it clear. I want nothing to do with—"

"Things have happened. Circumstances have forced me to come here."

"You're in *Sydney*? Mother of God!"

"I'm using a pay phone in a restaurant. I've never been here before. This call can't possibly be overheard or traced."

"But you know my name, where to reach me! If you're picked up . . . !"

"I was careful not to be followed."

"Careful?" Pendleton's voice was contemptuous. "If you're so sure you weren't followed, you wouldn't have called me. You'd have come here."

"I didn't want to risk surprising you in person. If I seemed a threat, I might not have had the chance to explain."

Pendleton swore.

"I've tried to show good faith," Kessler said. "Please, we need to meet. The sooner we talk, the sooner I'm out of the country."

"Not here."

"Not at the shop? Of course. I wouldn't want to put you in danger."

"Don't write this down," Pendleton said. "At four this afternoon . . ."

11

The instructions completed, Pendleton set down the phone. He'd kept his voice low. His assistant, waiting on a customer at the front of the store, could not have heard. Even so, he felt threatened. To be contacted so directly broke one of the most sacred rules he'd ever learned. God save me from amateurs. He stepped from his office, passed a row of scuba tanks, and pretended an interest in his assistant's customer.

"That wetsuit's the top of the line. You shouldn't have trouble keeping warm in it," Pendleton told the customer. "Any problems, if the fit seems wrong, make sure you come back and tell us. We'll make it right." Though he and his father had come to Australia almost ten years ago, Pendleton still retained American patterns of speech. The local beach hogs thought him quaint; he liked it that way. Invisibility was sometimes better achieved by standing out. As a local character, he created the illusion of being ever-present, except for occasional diving expeditions, his absences easily explained.

He waved goodbye to the customer, patted his assistant on the back—"Nice big sale"—and returned to his office, stepping out the back door. Even in the off-season, Bondi Beach was surprisingly crowded. Tourists. A few diehard surfers. Some muscle-bound gays on the make. In his terrycloth pullover, faded jeans, and canvas deck shoes (no belt, no shoelaces, no socks), Pendleton looked like a beach hog himself. Overaged, granted. But even at forty, with his sun-bleached windblown hair, his deeply tanned face, and his iron-hard shoulders and chest, he could give the beach hogs competition if he wanted to. Not that he'd ever show off his full skills.

He scanned the activity on the beach and saw his father waxing a surfboard, talking to teenagers gathered around him, holding court.

Pendleton's eyes crinkled with affection. He stepped from the deck at the back of the dive shop, crossed the sand, and reached his father.

Waves lapped the shore. The cool wind smelled salty. Pendleton waited respectfully while his father described to his audience an astonishing series of waves five years ago. His father—as tall as Pendleton, as muscular, and, even at seventy-two, wrinkled by age and ten years of sun, almost as ruggedly handsome—glanced at him.

"A minor problem's come up, Dad. I need to talk to you."

His father sighed in mock frustration. "If it's really necessary."

"I'm afraid it is."

"I'll be back, lads."

Pendleton walked with his father toward the shop. "A contact from your former friends just phoned me. He's here in town."

His father's sigh was genuine now. "I told those fools to stay away from me. I never approved of maintaining contact. If it weren't for the priest, I should have anticipated the problem and solved it years ago."

"The contact wanted a meeting. It sounded like an emergency."

29

"It must have been for someone to come all this way. The planet isn't big enough to hide in."

"The letter they sent last month . . ."

"Demanding a meeting in Canada." Pendleton's father scoffed. "Do they think I'm a fool?"

"It seems that they're the fools. But I have no choice now. To keep him from coming to the shop, I have to meet with him somewhere else."

"For the first and last time. Make sure he understands that."

"What I wanted to tell you . . . While I'm gone, be careful."

"Icicle's always careful."

"I know." Pendleton smiled and hugged him.

12

Entering Sydney's Botanic Gardens precisely at four as instructed, Kessler felt nervous. He suspected he hadn't been convincing when he'd used sudden illness as his motive for leaving his business meeting in the middle of delicate negotiations. Though business was hardly the reason he'd come to Australia, it was what he believed was called his "cover." Of the group that had met in Canada, he had the best excuse for traveling to Sydney without attracting attention. But now, by interrupting negotiations for a long-sought merger between his electronics firm and one in Sydney, he'd attracted the attention he'd hoped to avoid. In retrospect, he wished that he'd insisted to Pendleton that their meeting take place later, but on the other hand, Pendleton had been so reluctant to meet that Kessler was in no position to make demands.

As he proceeded along a path rimmed by exotic plants, Kessler worried that, despite his precautions in coming here, he'd been followed. Not just to these gardens but all the way from America. I'm a businessman, not an expert in intrigue, he thought. Perhaps my father would know—he almost changed the tense to "would have known" but tried to be hopeful—would know how to conduct himself in this sort of situation, but I was never trained for it.

Still, he didn't think he could go wrong if he used his common sense. Don't look around to see if you're being watched. The recent disappearances had demonstrated that the enemy was remarkably organized and skillful. A "tail"—he allowed himself what he believed was the correct melodramatic expression—surely wouldn't be careless enough to let him know he was being followed. He'd made sure to bring his guidebook along. Though the nape of his neck itched from the strain of resisting the impulse to look back down the path, he forced himself to peer at the guidebook and then at the abundant plants before him. The path led upward. He reached a bench flanked by shrubs and paused, facing west, apparently to survey a building that his book explained was Government House, the home of the governor for New South Wales. His actual motive for pausing, though, was to obey the instructions Pendleton had given him.

Pendleton was another reason Kessler felt nervous. In his prime, Pendleton's father, Icicle, had been one of the most feared men in Europe. Though Icicle would now be in his seventies, there wasn't any reason to assume he wasn't still dangerous. Rumor had it—Halloway was the source—that Icicle's son was equally to be respected, trained by his father. This meeting, exposed, in a public place obviously chosen for its cover and its many escape routes, could pose a danger from Icicle's son as much as from the enemy.

As instructed, Kessler sat on the bench. From the far side of shrubs where the path curved around and continued, he heard the voice of the man he'd spoken to on the phone.

"All right, so you've got your meeting. Make it quick."

Kessler's instinct was to turn toward the bushes, but the voice anticipated him.

"Look straight ahead. Keep staring toward Government House. If anybody comes along, shut up. And this better be important."

Kessler swallowed. He started explaining.

13

On the bench on the opposite side of the bushes, wearing jogging clothes, wiping his sweaty forehead as if exhausted and needing a rest, Pendleton peered north toward the State Conservatorium of Music. Its design dated back to 1819, and Pendleton wished that he lived in that simpler time. No instant satellite communications. No computer files. No jets that made Australia no longer a hard-to-reach outpost. "The planet isn't big enough to hide in," his father had said. Of course, the obverse was that without those modern conveniences of communication and travel, he and his father would not have been able to practice their trade.

His face hardened as Kessler, unseen behind the bushes, explained. *"What? All of them? Disappeared? For God's sake, why didn't the message you sent make that clear?"*

"I didn't draft the message," Kessler said. "It seemed obscure to me as well, but I understood the need for caution. Since my own father had disappeared, the reference to 'recent losses' made me realize the implications."

"Implications?" Pendleton's voice, though low, had the force of a shout. "We thought the message meant that some of my father's old acquaintances had died! We thought we were being invited to a wake! We didn't come all the way to Australia to risk exposing ourselves by going to Canada for toasts and tears!"

"Then your father's all right?"

"No thanks to you! Coming all this way! Maybe letting our hunters follow you!"

"The risk seemed necessary."

"Why?"

32

"Just a moment. Someone's coming."

Pendleton debated whether to stay or disappear.

"Two kids and a dog. They went up a fork in the path. It's fine," Kessler said.

"Answer me. *Why did you come?* We made it clear we want nothing to do with the rest of you."

"Halloway told me that's what you'd say. I'm aware Icicle was never known for being sociable. But the group insisted."

"Despite our wishes? At the risk of endangering . . . ?"

"With a proposition," Kessler said. "If Icicle feels no nostalgia for his former friends, no sense of kinship in mutual adversity, then maybe he—or you—can be swayed by a different motive."

"I can't imagine . . ."

"Money. The group's been financially successful. We have resources. You and your father—we know what you are, what you do. We're willing to pay you handsomely to find out what happened to our fathers. And if"—Kessler's voice became hoarse—"God help me for thinking it let alone saying it, if they're dead, we want you to be our revenge."

"*That's* what this is all about? You came all this way to *hire* me?"

"We don't know what else to do."

"No, it's impossible. I can't."

"The fee . . ."

"You don't understand. You could offer a fortune, it wouldn't matter. It's too risky."

"But under the circumstances . . . old friends . . ."

"And lead the enemy to us, as you maybe have? I'm leaving." Pendleton stood. "Tell them no."

"I'm at the Captain Cook Lodge! Think about it! Change your mind!"

"I won't." Pendleton started to walk away.

"Listen to me!" Kessler said. "There's something else you should know!"

Pendleton hesitated.

"Cardinal Pavelic!" Kessler said.

"What about him?"

"He disappeared as well."

33

14

His chest aching, Pendleton rushed down a sandy slope toward Bondi Beach. It was half past five. His jogging suit clung to him. He'd switched taxis several times to elude possible surveillance. When the final taxi had been caught in a traffic jam near the beach, he'd paid the driver and run ahead.

He had much to fear. Not just the risk that Kessler's arrival had posed. Or the disturbing information that the priest had disappeared. What truly bothered him was that his own father might vanish as the others had. Icicle had to be warned.

But when he'd called from a phone booth near the gardens, he'd received no answer either at the dive shop or at the ocean-bluff home he shared with his father. He told himself that his assistant must have closed the shop early, though that had never happened before. He tried to convince himself that his father had not yet returned home from the beach, though his father never failed to get home in time to watch the five o'clock news. Closer to Bondi Beach, he'd phoned the shop again; this time his call had been interrupted by a recorded announcement telling him the line was out of order. His stomach felt as if it were crammed with jagged glass.

He reached the bottom of the sandy slope and blinked through sweat-blurred vision toward a line of buildings that flanked the ocean. Normally, he'd have had no trouble identifying his dive shop among the quick-food, tank-top, and souvenir stores, but chaotic activity now obscured it. Police cars, a milling crowd, fire engines, swirling smoke.

His pulse roaring behind his ears, he pushed through the crowd toward the charred ruin of his shop. Attendants wheeled a sheet-covered body toward an ambulance. Ducking past a policeman who shouted for him to stop, Pendleton yanked the sheet from the corpse's face. The ravaged features were a grotesque combination of what looked like melted wax and scorched hamburger.

A policeman tried to pull him away, but Pendleton twisted angrily free, groping for the corpse's left hand. Though the fingers had been seared together, it was clear that the corpse was not wearing a ring. Pendleton's assistant had not been married. But Pendleton's father, though a widower, always wore his wedding ring.

He no longer resisted the hands that tugged him from the stretcher. "I thought it was my father."

"You belong here?" a policeman asked.

"I own the place. My *father*. Where's—?"

"We found only one victim. If he's not your father—"

Pendleton broke away, running through the crowd. He had to get to the house! Inhaling acrid smoke, he darted past a police car, veered between buildings, and charged up a sandy slope. The stench of scorched flesh cleared from his nostrils. The taste of copper spurted into his mouth.

The home was on a bluff a quarter-mile away, a modernistic sprawl of glass and redwood. Wind-ravaged trees surrounded it. Only as he raced closer did he realize the danger he himself might be in.

He didn't care. Bursting through the back door, he listened for voices from the television in the kitchen where his father always watched while drinking wine and preparing supper. The kitchen was silent, the stove turned off.

He yelled for his father, received no answer, searched the house, but found no sign of him.

He grabbed the phone book in his father's bedroom, quickly paged to the listing for the Captain Cook Lodge, and hurriedly dialed. "Put me through to Mr. Kessler's room."

"One moment . . . I'm sorry, sir. Mr. Kessler checked out."

"But he couldn't have! *When?*"

"Let me see, sir. Four o'clock this afternoon."

Shuddering, Pendleton set down the phone. His meeting with Kessler had been at four, so how could Kessler have checked out then?

Had Kessler been involved in his father's disappear-

ance? No. It didn't make sense. If Kessler were involved, he wouldn't have announced his presence; he wouldn't have asked for a meeting. Unless . . .

The suspicion grew stronger.

Kessler might have been a decoy, to separate father and son, to make it easier to grab Icicle.

Of course, there was an alternative explanation, but Pendleton didn't feel reassured. Someone else could have checked Kessler out, the checkout permanent. To spread the reign of terror. In that case, Pendleton thought, the next logical victim ought to be . . .

Me.

Professional habits took over. He withdrew his father's pistol from a drawer, made sure it was loaded, then went to his own room and grabbed another pistol. He searched the house again, this time more thoroughly, every alcove, not for his father now but for an intruder.

The phone rang. He swung toward it, apprehensive; hoping it was his father, he picked it up. The caller broke the connection.

His muscles became like concrete. Wrong number? An enemy trying to find out if I'm home?

He had to assume the worst. Quickly he took off his jogging suit and put on warm woolen outdoor clothes. Dusk cast shadows. Creeping from the house, he reached a nearby bluff from which he could watch every approach to the building.

Timer lights flicked on. The phone rang again; he could hear it faintly. After two rings, it stopped. Before he'd left the house, he'd turned on his answering machine, which now would instruct the caller to leave a message. Though desperate to know if the call was from his father, he couldn't risk going back to the house to listen to the tape. He'd anticipated this problem, however, and brought a cordless phone with him, leaving it turned off so that it wouldn't ring and reveal his position on this bluff. But now he switched the phone on. As if he'd picked up an extension within the house, he heard the end of the machine's request for a name and number. But as before, the caller simply hung up.

A police car arrived, presumably because of the fire at the shop, though maybe this wasn't a real police car. An officer knocked on the door and tried to open it, but Pendleton had left it locked. The officer went around to the back door, knocked and tested it as well, then drove away. No one else approached the house.

His father had disappeared! Just like all the other fathers. But unlike the sons of those fathers, Pendleton wasn't typically second-generation, wasn't an amateur. Icicle had trained him well. *One day, the enemy will return*, his father had warned.

Indeed it had. And taken his father.

So now it's my turn! Pendleton inwardly shouted. He'd refused the job the other sons had offered him because he had to avoid attracting attention to his father. But avoiding attention no longer mattered. I'll do it! he thought. But this isn't business! This is personal!

If my father isn't back by tomorrow, after forty years you bastards will finally get what's coming to you!

For Icicle!

For me!

THE RETURN OF THE WARRIOR

1

North of Beersheeba. Israel. Hearing a sudden rattle of gunfire, Saul threw his shovel to the ground, grabbed his rifle, and scrambled down from the irrigation ditch. He'd been working in this field since dawn, sweating beneath the blaze of the sun as he extended the drainage system he'd constructed when he first came to this settlement almost three years ago. His wife, Erika, had been pregnant then, and both of them had been anxious to escape the madness of the world, to find a sanctuary where the futility of their former profession seemed far away. Of course, they'd realized that the world would not let them ever escape, but the illusion of escape was what mattered. In this isolated village where even the conflict between Jews and Arabs was remote, they'd made a home for themselves and the baby—Christopher Eliot Bernstein-Grisman—who'd been born soon after.

The villagers had commented on the boy's unusual name. "Part Christian, part Jewish? And why the hyphen at the end?"

Bernstein was Erika's last name, Grisman Saul's. Christopher had been his foster brother, an Irish-Catholic with whom he'd been raised in an orphanage in Philadelphia. Eliot had been their foster father, the sad-eyed gray-faced man who always wore a black suit with a rose in his lapel, who'd befriended Chris and Saul, been the only person to show them kindness, and recruited them

38

for intelligence work, specifically to be assassins. In the end, their foster father had turned against them. Chris had been killed, and Saul had killed Eliot.

The bitterness Saul still felt over what had happened —the grief, disgust, and regret—had been his main motive for wanting to escape from the world. But love for his foster brother and indeed, despite everything, for Eliot had prompted him to want to name the baby after the two most important men in his life. Erika, understanding, had agreed. Generous, wonderful Erika. As graceful as an Olympic gymnast. As beautiful as a fashion model—tall, trim, and elegant with high strong cheeks and long dark hair. As deadly as himself.

The sound of gunfire scorched his stomach. Racing frantically toward the village, his first thought was that he had to protect his son. His second was that Erika could protect the boy as well as he could. His third was that, if anything happened to either of them, he'd never rest till their killers paid.

Though he hadn't been in action since he'd come to Israel, old instincts revived. Some things apparently could never be forgotten. He leapt a stone wall and neared the stark outline of the village, making sure that dust hadn't clogged the firing mechanism or the barrel of his rifle. Though he always kept it loaded, he inspected the magazine just to be certain. Hearing screams, he chambered a round and dove behind a pile of rocks.

The shots became louder, more frequent. He stared at outlying cinder-block buildings and saw strangers wearing Arab combat gear who fired from protected vantage points toward the homes at the center of the village. Women dragged children down alleys or into doorways. An old man lurched to the ground and rolled from repeated impacts as he tried to reach a young girl frozen with fright in the middle of a street. The girl's head blew apart. An invader tossed a grenade through an open window. The blast spewed smoke and wreckage. A woman shrieked.

Sons of bitches! Saul aimed from behind the pile of rocks. He counted six targets, but the volume of gunfire told him that at least six other invaders were on the opposite side of the village. The shots increased, other rifles joining the fight. But the sound of these weapons was different from the characteristic stutter of the Kalashnikovs that the invaders were using and that he himself used, preferring a weapon whose report would blend with that of the type Israel's enemies favored. No, the rifles that now joined the fight had the distinctive crackle of M-16s, the available weapon that Saul had taught the teenagers of the village to shoot.

An invader fell, blood erupting from his back. The five remaining terrorists on Saul's side of the village directed their aim toward a corrugated-metal shed from which the volley had come. The shed quivered, dozens of holes appearing along its side. The M-16 became silent.

But others, from different buildings, sought vengeance. Another invader spurted blood, falling. Saul eased his finger onto the trigger, smoothly absorbed the recoil, and disintegrated an invader's spine. He switched his aim, hit another target, this time in the skull, and scrambled from the pile of rocks, firing as he ran.

Another enemy fell. Caught in a crossfire, the remaining Arab glanced backward and forward, sprinted toward a low stone wall, and halted in astonishment as Saul's favorite student popped up, firing at point-blank range, blowing his enemy's face apart. A mist of blood hovered over the falling body.

Using the cover of ditches and walls that he and his students had constructed to provide defensive positions, Saul charged toward the opposite side of the village. At the corners of his vision, he noticed his students spreading out and heard the crackle of other M-16s, the answering stutter of more Kalashnikovs. A second grenade exploded within the building already partially destroyed by the first. This time, as a wall erupted, Saul heard no shrieks. With doubled fury, he completed the semicircle that brought him to the other group of invaders. He emptied his magazine, grabbed a Kalashnikov that a retreating Arab had dropped, emptied it, picked up an

M-16 that his second-favorite student had dropped when dying, emptied it, and outraced a terrorist whose hand-to-hand combat skills were no match for the killer-instinct training that Saul had received twenty years ago. Using the palm of one hand, then the other, lunging with all his force, he drove the enemy's rib cage into his heart and lungs.

The gunfire stopped. Saul squinted toward the enemy at his feet. His students, excited by victory, gathered around him.

"No! Don't form a crowd! Split up! Take cover! We don't know if we got them all!"

He followed his own directive and dove toward a ditch. But he cursed himself for being so right. He told himself that his soul was doomed for being professional. He tried to remind himself that the good of the village came first. In a culture barely hanging on, individuals had to come second. Here, sacrifice was the norm. But he desperately wanted to know about Erika and his son.

Forced to set a good example, he divided his students into groups and methodically scoured the village. Cautiously, he approached and checked every enemy corpse. Despising himself for being responsible, he supervised the search of intact buildings, verifying that no invader hid within them. He organized assessment teams—ten villagers dead, fifteen wounded.

"Where's the medic squad? Communications, did you radio an SOS to the base at Beersheeba?"

Only when every emergency procedure had been followed, when every precaution had been taken, did he allow his humanity to assert itself. And knew again that he was doomed. His former life had intruded, controlling him. Responding to the rote with which he'd been trained, he'd behaved correctly. And from another perspective, completely, absolutely, the correctness was wrong. He'd allowed his public duties to overwhelm his private needs.

The building that had received the most gunfire, that had erupted from two grenade blasts, was his own. As villagers and students surrounded him, in awe of his control, deeply respectful, he finally absolved himself of his public function. Tears streaking down his cheeks, he stalked toward the ruined building, the refuge of his wife and child. The right wall had toppled outward. On that side, the roof had collapsed, its angle bizarre.

When the first grenade had exploded, he'd heard a woman shriek. Apprehensive, he peered through what had been the window but was now just a wide jagged hole. The curtains were blackened and tattered. To his left, he saw the remnants of a toy wooden truck he'd made for his son. Next to it lay shattered plates, fallen from a shelf that no longer existed. The ruins of a table almost covered them. He smelled burnt wood, scorched cloth, and melted plastic. The fallen roof obscured his view of the central part of the kitchen.

He reached the door, which came off its hinges as he touched it, and swallowing sickly, stepped inside. He moved slowly, suddenly fearful of what he might step on, afraid of desecrating twisted limbs and—he hated to think about it—dismembered portions of bodies. He shoved away a sheet of metal, lifted a wooden beam, stepped over what used to be a chair, but he saw no blood, and hope made his heart beat faster.

He tugged at a section of roof, throwing it out the open doorway, stooping, hefting more rubble. Still he found no blood. He heaved against the section of roof that leaned down into the kitchen, budged it far enough to expose the only part of the room that he hadn't been able to see, and squinted at shadows.

He saw no bodies. The well-disguised trapdoor broke two of his fingernails as he clawed at it. Fingers bloody, hefting the trapdoor against a wall, he stared into the murky chamber below him.

"Erika!"

The pit absorbed his voice, giving off no echo.

"Erika! It's Saul!"

Too impatient for an answer, he squirmed down, his shoes touching earth four feet below him. "It's over."

He strained his eyes to penetrate the darkness. For a desperate instant, he suspected he was wrong, then suddenly realized he hadn't given the all-clear signal. An enemy might try to mimic his voice. In this darkness, the trick might work. "Baby Ruth and roses."

"Lover, it's about time you said that. You had me worried. I was trying to decide if I should shoot you." Erika's deep sensual voice came reassuringly from the rear of the chamber. "I hope you gave them hell."

He couldn't help it; he laughed. "Jews aren't supposed to believe in hell."

"But under certain conditions, it's a wonderful concept. For attacking this village, *our home*, I hope the bastards roast."

In the dark, his son asked, "Daddy?"

"It's me, son. You don't need to worry. But, Erika, watch your language in front of the boy, huh?"

"You'll hear a lot worse if you don't tell me what took you so long."

He tried to interpret her tone; his best guess was that she was joking.

"The shooting stopped a while ago," she said. "What did you do, stop off for a drink?"

Because Erika knew that Eliot had conditioned him to abstain from alcohol, Saul was sure now that she was joking, and slumping with relief, not only because she and the boy were safe but because she wasn't angry with him for being so inhumanly professional, he couldn't subdue his tears.

Shoes scraped against dirt. Bodies squirmed along the earthen tunnel.

"Saul?" Erika's voice was close and resonant, concerned, against his ear.

"Daddy?"

"Son, I'm fine. I just..." Sorrow cramped his throat, choking his voice.

Erika's strong arm hugged him. "What's wrong, Saul?"

"I..." Wiping his eyes, he struggled to explain. "We killed them all. But if..." He mustered his strength. "If I'd run here right away, if I'd looked out only for us, for you and Chris, then everything I tried to teach those kids

43

in the village...every principle about the group being more important that the individual...would have seemed a lie. The next time we were attacked, they'd have looked out for themselves instead of..."

In the dark, Chris nuzzled against him.

Erika hugged him tighter. "You're a dope."

Surprised, he stifled his tears. "What?"

"We're professionals. Or used to be. We both know what combat means. Personal needs are a luxury. If the group doesn't defend itself, no family has a chance. The minute the shooting started, I grabbed Chris with one hand and this Uzi with the other. I told myself that if you were still alive, you'd do what the rules required—and so would I. Which in my case meant hiding our son and protecting him. And which in *your* case meant doing your best to protect the village. There's no need for tears. I dearly love you. *My* job was to guard the family, *yours* to defend the group. I've got no complaints. If anything, I'm proud of you. We did it right."

Saul had trouble breathing. "I love you."

"After the village calms down, when we organize a sentry schedule and it gets dark and we put Chris to bed, I'd be glad for you to show me how much."

2

Twenty minutes later, an Israeli combat helicopter circled the rocky fields around the village, checking for other invaders. Two trucks filled with soldiers jounced along a potholed road and stopped at the outskirts. Their eyes reminding Saul of hawks, the soldiers scrambled down, scanned the devastation, and snapped to attention while a captain gave them orders. Well-trained, strongly disciplined, they established defensive positions in case of another attack. A squad searched the pockets of the enemy corpses.

A hot wind blew dust.

The captain, his face like a shale slope furrowed with

gullys, came over to Saul. "Your radio team said the attack had been subdued." He gestured toward the bodies. "Isn't 'crushed' more accurate?"

"Well"—Saul shrugged—"they pissed us off."

"Apparently." The captain lit a cigarette. "The way I hear it, the last thing anyone should want to do is piss you off. It's Grisman, right? Saul Grisman? American? Former CIA?"

"That gives you a problem?"

"Not after what just happened. This must be Erika."

Saul turned. He hadn't heart Erika come up behind him.

"Christopher's next door," she said. "He's still afraid, but he promised he'd close his eyes and try to sleep. He's being watched." She faced the captain.

"You were with the Mossad," the captain said to her. "I'm surprised this village isn't boring for you."

"Today it certainly hasn't been."

The captain cocked his head toward the teenagers holding M-16s. "Where are the men?"

"In the military," she said. "Or Jerusalem, or Tel Aviv. This is a village of widows, orphans, and deserted wives. It was barely hanging on when we got here."

"But that's what we wanted," Saul said. "A place on the edge of the world. So we decided to improve the civil defense."

"You're telling me these *kids*, with some help from you, took care of this team?"

"All they needed was a little encouragement." Grinning, Saul hugged the two nearest teenagers.

"My source says that *you*," the captain told Saul, "had a reason for wanting to get away from it all."

"Did he say what my reason was?"

The captain shook his head.

"Allergies."

"Sure. My source also said that *you*," he told Erika, "could have stayed in Israeli intelligence. Your record was clean. So you didn't have to come here."

"Wrong," she said. "I had the best reason possible."

"What?"

45

"To be with him." She gestured toward Saul.

The captain drew on his cigarette. "Fine. What happened here—I have a few problems about it."

"I know," Saul answered. "So do I."

"For starters, this team wasn't just a bunch of amateurs. They're well armed. Soviet weapons. It wasn't impromptu—they'd planned the attack, six approaching this side of the village, the other six the other. That number of men, it isn't easy, it takes a lot of determination, and a damned good reason, to try to sneak past our border defenses. A village in contested territory, I could see them trying for it. A strategic target—let's say an air base, a munitions site—a risky surprise attack would make sense. But a village of widows, orphans, and deserted wives? Fifty miles from the border? *What's going on?*"

"Don't think it hasn't worried me," Saul said.

3

At sunset, a dusty sedan arrived. Outside the ruin of what had been home, facing a small fire fueled by the wreckage he'd carried out, Saul heard the engine as he ate rehydrated chicken noodle soup and watched Erika spoon the broth into Christopher's mouth.

Glancing up, he saw soldiers step from cover and gesture for the driver to stop at the edge of the village. The car was too far away, its windshield too dusty, for Saul to see who sat behind the steering wheel. The soldiers spoke to someone inside, examined the documents they were handed, and turned toward the village, pointing the driver in Saul's direction. The car approached.

Saul stood. "Do you recognize it?"

Erika peered at the car and shook her head. "Do you?"

"The village is getting too crowded."

The car stopped twenty feet away. Villagers watched suspiciously from open doors. The driver shut off the engine. Something wheezed beneath the hood. A man got out.

He was six feet tall, thin, his shoulders bent slightly forward. He wore a rumpled suit, the top button of his shirt open, his tie hanging loose. He had a mustache, a receding hairline. Saul guessed that he was in his late thirties, and sensed that his thinness was due to enormous energy held in check, constantly burning calories even when sitting at a desk, a position suggested by the stoop of his shoulders.

Grinning, the man approached. Saul had never seen him before, but the delight in the stranger's eyes made it clear that the stranger knew *him*.

In a moment, Saul realized his mistake.

It isn't me he knows.

It's Erika.

Her eyes glinted with the same delight as the stranger's. She smiled broadly, ecstatically, her voice an incredulous whisper. "Misha?"

"Erika."

She rushed forward, hugging him. "Misha!" she whooped.

Saul relaxed when he heard the name. If his guess was right, the last name would be Pletz. He'd never met the man, but he remained grateful for favors that Misha —at Erika's request—had done for his foster brother and himself three years ago.

He waited respectfully until Erika stopped hugging Misha. Then stepping forward, holding Christopher in his left arm, he extended his right. "Welcome. Are you hungry? Would you like some soup?"

Misha's grip was strong. "No, thanks. I ate two bagels in the car. They gave me heartburn."

"I often wondered what you look like."

"As I did you. About your brother—I'm sorry."

Saul nodded, retreating from painful emotion.

"Misha, why aren't you in Washington?" Erika asked.

"Two years ago, I was transferred back to Tel Aviv. To be honest, I wanted it. I missed my homeland, my parents. And the transfer involved a promotion. I can't complain."

47

"What's your assignment now?" she asked.

Misha reached for Christopher's hand. "How are you, boy?"

Christopher giggled.

But Misha's avoidance of Erika's question made Saul uneasy.

"He's a fine-looking child." Misha surveyed the ruined building behind the small fire. "Renovations?"

"The interior decorators came today," she said.

"So I heard."

"Their work wasn't to our liking. They had to be fired."

"I heard that as well."

"Is that why you're here?" Saul asked.

Misha studied him. "Maybe I'll have some soup, after all."

They sat around the fire. Now that the sun was almost gone, the desert had cooled. The fire's heat was soothing.

Misha ate only three spoonfuls of soup. "Even while I was in Washington," he told Erika, "I knew that you'd come here. When I went back to Tel Aviv, I kept up with what you were doing."

"So you're the source of the rumors the captain heard," Saul said. He pointed toward the officer who stood at a sentry post on the outskirts of the village, talking to a soldier.

"I thought it was prudent to tell him he could depend on both of you. I said he should leave you alone, but if you got in touch with him, to pay attention to what you said. I wasn't trying to interfere."

Saul watched him steadily.

"After what happened here today," Misha said, "it was natural for him to get back to me, especially since the raid had its troubling aspects. Not just the pointlessness of attacking a village so far from the border, one with no military or geographic value."

Saul anticipated. "You mean their fingernails."

Misha raised his eyebrows. "Then you noticed? Why didn't you mention it to the captain?"

48

"Before I decided how much to depend on him, I wanted to see how good he was."

"Well, he's *very* good," Misha said. "Dependable enough to share his suspicions only with me until I decided how to deal with this."

"We might as well stop talking around it," Saul said. "The men who attacked this village weren't typical guerrillas. Never mind that their rifles still had traces of grease from the packing crate, or that their clothes were tattered but their boots were brand-new. I could explain all that by pretending to believe they'd recently been reequipped. But their fingernails. They'd smeared dirt over their hands. The trouble is, it hadn't gotten under their nails. Stupid pride. Did they figure none of them would be killed? Did they think we wouldn't notice their twenty-dollar manicures? They weren't terrorists. They were assassins. Imported. Chosen because they were Arabs. But their usual territory isn't the desert. It's Athens, Rome, Paris or London."

Misha nodded. "Three years out here, and you haven't lost your skills."

Saul pointed toward the ruined building behind him. "And it's pretty obvious, the attack wasn't directed against the whole village. Our home took most of the damage. The objective was *us*."

Erika stood, walked behind Misha, and put her hands on his shoulders. "Old friend, why are you here?"

Misha peered up sadly.

"What is it? What's wrong?" she asked.

"Erika, your father's disappeared."

4

The stability of the past three years had now been destroyed. The sense of peace seemed irretrievable. The constants of his former life had replaced it—tension, suspicion, guardedness. Escape was apparently impossible. Even here, the world intruded, and attitudes he'd been desperate to smother returned as strong as ever.

In the night, with Christopher asleep at a neighbor's house and Misha asleep in his car, Saul sat with Erika by the fire outside the ruin of their home.

"If we were the target," he said, "and I don't think there's any doubt that we were, we have to assume other teams will come for us."

Erika repeatedly jabbed a stick at the fire.

"It wouldn't be fair to allow our presence to threaten the village," he added.

"So what do we do? Put up a sign—the people you want don't live here anymore?" The blaze of the fire reflected off her eyes.

"They'll find out we've gone the same way they found out we were here."

"But why did they come at all?"

Saul shook his head. "Three years is a long time for the past to catch up to us. And my understanding with the Agency was if I stayed out of sight they'd pretend I didn't exist."

"That's one thing we did, all right," she said bitterly. "We stayed out of sight."

"So I don't think this has anything to do with the past."

"Then whatever the reason for the attack, it's new."

"That still doesn't tell us why."

"You think it's coincidence?"

The reference was vague, but he knew what she meant. "Your father's disappearance?"

"Yesterday."

"And today the attack?"

"Bad news always seems to come in twos and threes," she said, "but . . ."

"I don't believe in coincidence. The obvious shouldn't be ignored. If a pattern stares you in the face, don't turn away from it."

"So let's not turn away," she said.

"You know what it means."

She poked the stick harder at the fire. "It's another reason to abandon our home. What's *left* of our home."

Saul thought about the irrigation ditches he'd worked three years to construct and improve. "It makes me angry."

"Good. This wasn't worth having if we give it up easily."

"And we don't have a chance against whoever we'll be hunting if we go after them indifferently."

"I'm not indifferent about my father. One of the sacrifices of living out here was not seeing him."

The fire crackled. Erika suddenly stood. "We'd better get ready. The men who attacked us did us a backhanded favor. What's left of our possessions we can literally carry."

"To find out what happened to your father."

"And pay back whoever drove us from our home."

"It's been three years." Saul hesitated. "Regardless of Misha's compliments, are we still good enough?"

"Good enough? Hey, for the past three years, I've just been resting. The people who took my father will wish to God they'd never messed with us when they find out exactly how good we are."

THE PENITENT

1

South of Cairo, west of the Nile. The Nitrian Desert. Egypt. It wasn't a mouse this time but a lizard he was watching, and it didn't do tricks as Stuart Little had. It didn't tug Drew out of his self-denying shell. It didn't make him miss the company of others—his friends, or even strangers. All it did was crawl from its hole beneath a rock and bask in the sun for a few hours just after dawn. At dusk, it stretched out on a slab, absorbing radiant heat. Between times, during the full destructive blaze of the day, it hid. A foot-long, squat, wrinkled, yellow, unblinking, tongue-flicking testament to God's perverse creative whims.

Slumping in the dark at the back of the cave, Drew watched the monster assume its regular morning position at the tunnel's entrance. He hated the thing and for that reason tolerated it, because he knew that God was testing him. The lizard was part of his penance. As the sun rose higher, sending rays into the cave, Drew surveyed the rocky contours of his cell, comparing their bleak austerity to the relative luxury he'd known for six peaceful years in his simple quarters in the Carthusian monastery in Vermont. Again he compared the lizard, which he alternately called Lucifer and Quasimodo, to Stuart Little, the mouse that had been his companion for the last two years of his stay at the monastery. But the mouse had been killed, assassins had attacked the monastery to get at Drew, and he'd been forced to leave his haven, a sinner confronting a sinful world. The resulting events—his war with Scalpel, his reunion with Arlene, his encounter with the Fraternity of the Stone—had paradoxically redeemed him and yet damned him again, compelling him to seek out this hole in the rock in the desert where Christian monasticism had first begun, here to strive once more for purity through penance and the worship of God.

He'd done so for a year now. With no change in seasons, each day tediously the same as the one before, time seemed strangely extended and yet compressed. The year could have been an eternity or a month or a week. His only ways of measuring how long he'd been here were checking the growth of his hair and beard and watching his food supply, which gradually dwindled until he had to trek across the desert to the nearest village, a day away, and replenish his simple provisions. The villagers, seeing this tall, lean, sunburned man with haunted eyes, his robe in rags, gave him distance and respect, conferring upon him the status of a holy one, though he refused to consider himself as such.

Apart from that interruption, his routine was constant—exercise, meditation, and prayer. Lately, however, he'd felt too weak to exercise and lay at the back of the cave, intoning responses to imaginary masses. He wondered what the lizard thought of the Latin that sometimes made it cock its ugly unblinking head toward him. Or was its reaction due to nothing more than stimulus-response? If so, what purpose did this monstrous creation serve? A rock, though unthinking, had a beauty to be appreciated. But the lizard could not appreciate the rock, except for the heat its ugly yellow skin absorbed. And no conscious being could appreciate the obscenity of the lizard.

That was the test, Drew thought. If I can appreciate the lizard, I can save myself. I can show that I've opened myself to every aspect of God.

But bodily needs disturbed his meditation. He had to drink. A spring—one reason he'd chosen this spot—was not far away. As usual, he'd postponed slaking his thirst, partly to increase his penance, partly to increase his satisfaction when he did at last drink. This balancing of pain and pleasure caused him great mental stress. He finally resolved it by concluding that the pleasure of drinking had been intended by God as a survival mechanism. If he denied himself that pleasure, if he didn't drink, he would die. But that would be suicide, and suicide was the worst sin of all.

In his weakened state, his thoughts began to free associate. Pleasure, pain. Arlene, and being separated from her. If things had been different, he could imagine nothing more rewarding than to have stayed with Arlene for the rest of his life. But the Fraternity of the Stone had made that impossible. To save Drew's life, Arlene's brother had killed a member of the Fraternity, and to save his savior, Drew had made himself appear to be the guilty one, running and hiding. Craving love, Drew had sacrificed himself for love of a different type.

He tried to move, to get to the spring, but couldn't. His lips were blistered from thirst. His body was ravaged by his failure to eat. His mind began to swirl. The lizard raised itself, repelled by the heat of the day. It scuttled beneath its rock. Time became even more fleeting. A shadow hovered over the entrance to the cave. Was it sundown already?

Or am I hallucinating? Drew wondered. For the shadow became the silhouette of a human being, the first such silhouette Drew had seen here since he'd occupied this cell. It couldn't be.

But the shadow, growing longer, did indeed become the silhouette of a person.

And the person impossibly was—

2

When she saw the lizard scuttle from the mouth of the cave, Arlene muttered, "Shit." More forcibly, she felt a stab of suspicion that she'd been given wrong directions. After all, would the lizard have chosen that vulnerable spot in which to soak up heat if the cave were occupied? The way the squat ugly reptile had jerked its head toward the clatter of the rock she'd dislodged as she climbed the slope, the way it had tensed and fled as her shadow fell over it told her unmistakably that the lizard had been frightened by her alone, not someone in the cave. Did the corollary follow, that the cave was deserted?

She paused, discouraged, but the heat of the sun on her back thrust her forward. Exhausted, so dehydrated that she'd stopped sweating, she needed to get to shelter. She plodded the rest of the way up the slope, her shadow stretching toward the cave, and strained to see within the darkness. The silence from inside reinforced her suspicion that she'd been misdirected.

The question was, had the misdirection been an honest mistake or a deliberate deception? Yesterday morning, two hours after she'd left the nearest village, her rented car had stopped, its engine coughing into silence. An experienced mechanic, she'd lifted the hood and tried to diagnose the problem, but she couldn't find what was wrong. She'd debated returning to the village, but the distance she'd traveled by car was a half day's walk, almost the same amount of time it would take to continue forward and reach her destination. She'd filled her canteen before she left the village. Familiar with desert survival, she knew that if she conserved her body's moisture by resting in shadow during the heat of midday, hiking at dusk and through the night, she'd have enough water to reach this cave in the morning, with enough left over to return. Provided she rationed her intake.

But when she'd made camp just before noon, anchoring a thin canvas sheet across the space between two boulders, crawling under to shield herself from the worst of the sun, she'd heard the faint crunch of footsteps— from behind her and to her right. Their stealthy approach had told her everything. She'd been unwilling to risk using her handgun, the reports from which would have carried for miles across the otherwise silent desert and perhaps have attracted her predators. So she'd pretended to be alarmed and defenseless when the two Arabs, each wearing a sun-bleached cotton headscarf and robe, confronted her with pistols, gesturing for her to take off her clothes. Distracting them with a glimpse of her breasts, she'd pivoted, kicking, disarmed the nearer gunman by breaking his wrist, continued spinning with the blur of a dervish, kicked the second assailant's gunhand, again snapping bone, and killed them in rapid succession with fists to the throat, cracking their windpipes. It happened so quickly that they died still leering. She hid their bodies among rocks where the scavengers of the desert would dispose of them. Proceeding to another campsite, again erecting the thin canvas sheet, she wondered whether the men had found her by accident or whether they'd followed her from the village where she'd asked directions. If the men who'd tried to assault her were indeed from that village, if they'd sabotaged her car, it wasn't surprising that this cave was abandoned—she'd been given false information simply to lead her deeper into the wilderness.

Again she despaired. Having come all the way from New York City, only to find that her search was not yet over, she wanted to raise her fists and curse at the sky. But she needed to escape the sun. The thought of rinsing her dry swollen mouth with tepid water from her canteen compelled her. A tall, limber, green-eyed, auburn-haired, sensuous woman, in her mid-thirties, wearing a wide-brimmed canvas hat, a knapsack, khaki shirt and pants, and hiking boots, she aimed her handgun against unseen dangers and entered the cave.

3

It smelled vinegary, like carbon dioxide. Beneath that odor was another—a musky animal smell that made her conclude that the cave had recently been used for a den.

Standing just inside the entrance, blocking out the sunlight, she stared toward the darkness. Though the cave was by no means cool, it was much less hot than the outside inferno. Handgun ready, she held her breath, straining to listen for sounds.

"Drew?" Her voice was tentative, uneasy. After all, if he were here, he'd have spoken to her by now. Unless, like the lizard, he'd noticed her coming and scuttled to a hiding place. In which case, her quest had been useless, her hope that he'd welcome her a cruel tease.

The echo of her voice died down. Again she held her breath, listening. Something—intuition—told her that the cave was occupied. She heard—or *thought* she heard—a subtle brush of cloth, a slight exhale of air, a faint scrape of flesh against stone. The almost imperceptible sounds came from far in the back. She crouched and shifted to the right, away from the mouth of the cave, simultaneously hiding her silhouette and allowing sunlight to enter the cave.

Now that her eyes were accustomed to the dark, the added illumination was sufficient for her to see the worn sandals on the dusty feet of the scabrous legs of a man sprawled against the rear wall. His tattered robe was tugged above his fleshless knees. The hands stretched out against each thigh looked skeletal.

"Dear God." The echo of the cave amplified her anguished whisper. "Drew," she said louder.

She rushed to him, tugging him toward the sunlight, shocked by his matted waist-long beard and hair, by his gaunt ravaged face. "Oh, Jesus, Drew."

Through eyes that were slits, he studied her. His blistered mouth quivered.

She hurried to unhitch the canteen from her belt, twisting its cap off. "Don't try to talk."

But he persisted, his voice so weak she could barely hear it. The sound reminded her of a footstep on dry crusted mud. "Ar..." He made a desperate effort to try again. "Ar...lene?" The tone communicated surprise, disbelief. And something else. Something akin to the awe one would feel when having a vision.

"It's me. I'm here, Drew. I'm real. But stop trying to talk."

She raised the canteen to his blistered lips, pouring just a few drops of water between them. Like a sponge, his flesh seemed to absorb the water. She gripped his wrist, his pulse so weak she could barely feel it. She ran her hands along his body, startled by how much weight he'd lost.

"You finally got what you wanted," she said. "You fucked yourself up. If you weren't so weak"—she poured a few more drops of water between his parched lips—"I'd be furious instead of sorry for you."

Amazingly his eyes crinkled. They glowed faintly with . . .

What? Amusement? Love? He inhaled as if to . . .

"Laugh," she said, "and I'll hit you over the head with this canteen."

But somehow he did have strength to laugh, just a short stubborn "hah," and of course she did not make good on her threat. She simply poured another few drops of water into his mouth, knowing she wouldn't be able to give him more for a while, lest he become sick to his stomach, but reassured because his attempt at a laugh was a life sign. She'd gotten here in time. His spirit hadn't failed. He was going to be all right.

4

But when she let him have another sip of water, she stiffened with doubt. Despite the heat, apprehension chilled her. There wasn't enough water for both of them to walk out of here.

Her swollen tongue stuck to the roof of her mouth. She had to drink. The tepid water tasted bitter. Even so, she swallowed, felt less lightheaded, took another sip, then poured a few more drops between Drew's lips.

Gradually his pulse strengthened. He breathed easier, deeper.

But his voice remained a croak. "Misjudged..." He grinned with embarrassment, like a child who'd been naughty.

She shook her head, not understanding.

"Should have drunk sooner..." He coughed.

Again she shook her head.

"Should have gone for food sooner... Didn't realize ... how weak I was... Couldn't reach the spring."

"*What* spring?"

His eyes drooped.

"Damn it, Drew, what spring?"

"Outside... down the slope... to the right."

"How far?"

"A hundred yards... around the curve of the hill... a cluster of rocks."

She gave him one more sip of water and stood. "I'll be back."

She took off her knapsack, left the dark of the cave, and at once felt the hammer force of the blinding sun. Wincing from a pain behind her eyes, she clambered down the dusty slope and followed the curve of the hill.

But after what she judged was a hundred yards, she still hadn't found a cluster of rocks at the base of the slope. Panic slithered within her. Had Drew been delirious? Had he only imagined there was a spring?

No, there *had* to be a spring. Otherwise how could he have survived here? If she didn't find it, if Drew didn't become more lucid before the canteen was emptied, there was every chance both of them would die.

She walked twenty-five yards farther, felt her knees weaken, and knew that she couldn't risk continuing. For as far as she could see along the slope of this hill, no mound of rocks provided a goal. Discouragement weighed upon her. Mustering strength, licking her parched lips, she turned to go back to the cave. Instead of swinging to the right toward the contour of the hill, she pivoted left toward the broad expanse of the desert. And tingled when she saw the mound.

She stumbled toward it. As far as they went, Drew's instructions had been accurate. But he'd left out a crucial detail. The cluster of rocks was a hundred yards around the curve of the hill, all right. But *out* from the hill, not against it. And if you looked that way, the cluster was so obvious, so tall and wide, so clear a landmark, that you couldn't fail to notice it.

She made her feet move faster. The rocks became larger. Climbing over them, down to a hollow, she found a stagnant pool protected from wind, skimmed dust to the side, glanced around to make sure no skeletons of animals warned against trusting the water, and dipped her mouth beneath the surface. Hot, the water did not refresh her. Nonetheless, she felt her body absorb it.

Quickly she filled the canteen. Ten minutes later, she stooped to enter the dark of the cave.

Drew was flat on his back. Eyes slitted, he shrugged and tried to grin. "Forgot to tell you..."

"I *know* what you forgot to tell me, friend. I found it just the same."

She raised the canteen to his lips. He swallowed gratefully. She drank as well.

That still left the problem of food. In her knapsack, she'd carried enough provisions for an emergency—peanuts and beef jerky, along with dried fruit. But after she searched the cave and found nothing to eat, she had to conclude that what she'd brought was not sufficient for both of them to cross the desert.

She gave Drew more water, took some herself, and became more hopeful as his energy returned.

"Why are you here?" he asked.

"Isn't it obvious?"

He shook his head.

"Because I love you," she said.

He breathed deeply, overcome with powerful emotion. "Love...Yes." It was hard for him to continue. "But how did you find me?"

"Persistence."

"I don't understand." He gathered strength. "I thought I'd hidden my trail."

She nodded.

"Then how...?"

60

"The Fraternity."

Drew shuddered.

5

"You ran from them," she said, "to save my brother's life. Because he saved yours. You thought you'd eluded them. You haven't."

She reached in her knapsack and pulled out a bag of peanuts. Chewing, she savored their salt.

He reached for one.

"Promise not to swallow it right away."

He nodded.

She pressed one between his lips. "If you weren't so grungy, I'd kiss you."

"Threats'll get you nowhere." He slumped. "The Fraternity?"

"They followed you from the moment you left my brownstone in New York," she said. "The reason you thought you'd gotten away was they never made a move against you. After England, Italy, and Morocco, you felt it was safe to come to Egypt. But they followed you here as well. They've been keeping track of you."

"You know this . . . ?"

"Because two weeks ago, one of them came to see me."

Drew groaned. "Then all of this has been for nothing?"

"No, it saved your life. The way the priest explained it to me," she said, "the Fraternity decided your exile here was worse than any punishment they could have thought of. From the looks of you, they were right."

His pitiful appearance dismayed her—his gaunt torso, his haggard face, his matted waist-long hair and beard. "We have to get some strength back into you. Do you think your stomach could hold down another peanut?"

"It better. I need the salt."

She gave him one and nibbled on a piece of beef jerky.

"The priest told me the Fraternity's decided you've suffered enough for the death of their operative."

Drew stared at her.

"You'd return to me sometime in Lent—that's what you promised." She tenderly kissed his forehead. "Each day before Easter, I waited, hoping. When you didn't come this first year, I worried that you'd never come."

"No matter how hard I tried, I couldn't stop thinking of you," he said.

"I love you."

With a tremble, he touched her arm. "And now my exile's over? They've pardoned me?"

She hesitated.

"What's wrong?"

"Not pardoned," she said. "You're being summoned. 'To pursue your calling' is how the priest described it."

He frowned. "What do you mean?"

"There's something they want you to do for them." Troubled, she glanced away. "It's the only condition under which they'll let you leave. When the priest told me where you were, I grabbed at the chance to see you again, just to be with you. Since you ran away that night, I've never felt so empty. Losing you the first time, and then..." She kissed him again.

He returned her embrace. "Arlene?"

She waited.

"What do they want?"

"That's the problem. The priest wouldn't tell me. He sent me here. To talk to you. To convince you. To bring you to him."

6

At sunset, she helped him squirm from the cave. The evening's lower temperature made the heat that radiated from the rocks feel soothing. In the last light of day, she unsheathed her survival knife and snicked its edge across his hair and beard. When she'd finished, he looked like, in her words, "a sexy ascetic by El Greco."

She stripped off his robe and sloshed water from her canteen all over his body, washing him thoroughly. She dressed him and cautiously fed him. Before the sun completely faded, she went down the slope toward the cluster of rocks around the spring, refilled the canteen, and returned to the cave.

By then, night cloaked them. In his cell, she lay huddled next to him, her pelvis against his hips, spoonlike, giving him warmth.

"Water's not a problem," she said.

"But food is."

"Right. There's enough for me, but not enough for you to regain your strength. How are we going to manage to cross the desert?"

"I've got an idea," he said.

7

At dawn, she waited, poised with her knife. When the lizard crawled from beneath its rock, she stabbed it, skinned it, and cut it into strips. The lizard, after all, did have a purpose. The strips of its flesh, spread out in front of the cave, baked in the sun. She brought them inside to Drew, who bit off a piece and chewed until it was like gruel and would not offend his stomach.

"I used to hate the thing," he said.

"And now?"

"I'm sorry it died for me. It's a part of me. I love it."

8

They left at night. He'd gained sufficient strength to stay on his feet, provided he leaned against Arlene. Taking their direction from stars, they plodded across the desert. He shivered against her. With her arm around his back, she felt him sweating. But as long as he was sweating, she didn't worry. Sweat meant his body fluid had been replenished.

They rested frequently, eating the last of their food, trying not to fall asleep. At dawn, they reached a pass between low hills. She exhaled in distress. The pass was near where her car had failed, halfway between Drew's cave and the village. They hadn't walked far enough. In a couple of hours, the heat would be so intense they'd have to stop and put up the canvas sheet. They wouldn't be able to proceed again until late afternoon. At the earliest, they wouldn't reach the village till tomorrow morning, provided they maintained the pace they'd set throughout the night. But now that their food was gone, Drew's strength would diminish rapidly. Already she could feel him leaning more heavily against her. If they didn't reach the village by the morning, they'd have to stop and rest again throughout the next day, and by then Drew might be so weak that she'd never be able to get him to the village.

I might have to leave him, she thought. To go for help.

But what if he becomes delirious and wanders? What if I can't find him?

A bullet struck a boulder on her right. A splinter of rock sliced the back of her hand. The report from the rifle followed at once, its echo filling the pass. Ignoring the blood that dripped from her hand, she dove with Drew behind the boulder.

In the same motion, she unholstered her pistol. As she squinted from the edge of the boulder, scanning the rocky slope on the right, searching for a target, she flinched from the impact of a second bullet spewing rock shards behind her.

She realized sickly that the second bullet had come from the left, from the opposite side of the pass. She and Drew were trapped in a crossfire.

"Leave me," Drew told her weakly.

"No."

"Listen." He breathed with effort. "You can't fight them and take care of me. I'll get both of us killed."

"I told you no."

Almost simultaneously, two bullets spewed rock shards—from behind them and from in front—so close her ears rang.

"Their argument's better than yours," Drew said.

"I didn't come all this way to get separated again." She scanned one slope, then the other.

"Listen to me."

She was shocked to see the blood streaming from his knees where they'd landed on jagged stones.

"Our friends up there," he said, "they could've killed both of us before we knew it. They're either lousy shots, or they missed on purpose."

"So?"

A bullet from the left sprayed pebbles over Arlene's boots. A bullet from the opposite slope *carammed* off the boulder.

"They've got something else in mind," Drew said. "Don't give them a chance to keep pinning us down." He struggled to a crouch. "Leave. Go after them. Until they get what they want, they won't kill you unless they have to."

"But what about you?"

"I'll take my chances. I'd only hold you back. This way, *you* at least have a chance."

She shook her head, aiming anxiously one way, then the other, toward the rocky slopes.

"Okay," Drew said. "I'll make the choice for you."

As weak as he was, he hefted himself to his feet and staggered from behind the boulder, knees buckling, rolling into a ravine.

"You bullheaded . . . !"

Gunshots echoed.

She charged toward the slope on the right, diving below a mound.

But he'd judged correctly. The bullets that sprayed stones before and behind her seemed calculated to box her in, not kill her.

Okay, then, she thought. Let's dance.

9

Drew winced from the jolt as he tumbled off the rim and down the ravine. He landed hard, losing his breath. The morning sun was still so low its rays didn't penetrate to the bottom. In shadow, he mustered the little strength he had, took care to keep his head down, and wavered along the bottom of the ravine.

To a certain extent, what happened next was predetermined, he knew. The snipers, having seen Arlene support him and realizing how weak he was, would fear him less than they did her. Granted, in Arab culture, women were not held in high regard, but the snipers would still have to give her credit for being brave enough, having knowledge enough, to travel through the desert unprotected, and after all, she was an American, an incalculable factor. When she started shooting at them, they'd definitely give her their respect.

So, for the sake of efficiency, they'd eliminate the easy target first. One sniper would distract Arlene while the other went after Drew. Once he was taken care of, they could devote all their attention to her. But not kill her. No. He remained convinced that the snipers could have hit them both if that had been their intention. The purpose of the shots was to play with the quarry, to restrict, to corner, to trap without killing. At least not kill just yet.

He was too weak to fight, but even if all he did was keep moving, he'd still be helping Arlene. Divide and conquer—that's what the snipers were hoping to do. But that tactic could work the other way around.

10

As Arlene lunged up the rocky slope, dodging from boulder to boulder, the sniper shot at her again. Diving behind cover, she suddenly recognized where she was.

This cluster of jagged stone was where she'd hidden the bodies of the two men who'd attacked her. She glanced around, startled.

But this *couldn't* be the place. There wasn't any sign of the bodies. Even allowing for the efficiency of the desert scavengers, the corpses wouldn't have disappeared completely yet. There ought to be something—bits of flesh, bone, and cloth—crumbs, as it were.

All the same, she was positive that she recognized the spot.

Then how...?

A bullet ricocheted off shale. She peered upward through a chink between boulders, pistol ready, eager for a target. The shot made her wonder if this ambush in the same spot where she'd been attacked earlier was more than coincidence. Had the bodies been found and carried away? Were these snipers avenging friends who'd been killed? If so, the ambush made sense, as did the way the snipers seemed deliberately to have avoided killing her. Before that eventuality, they meant to do to her what their friends had intended to do. Her chest heaving, she stared harder through the gap in the boulders, straining to see the target.

But when she did distinguish a blur of movement—a scarved, robed Arab scurrying down the slope, over boulders, across a ridge, and down the continuation of the slope—she became confused again. Because the Arab took cover and aimed a rifle, but not toward her. Instead he aimed toward the ravine at the bottom of this slope. *The ravine into which Drew had tumbled.*

Swinging her gaze in that direction, she saw the second sniper: another Arab, his scarf flapping behind him as he ran down the opposite slope, converging on the ravine.

A welter of possibilities occurred to her. Perhaps the snipers had not been convinced that Drew was as weak as he appeared. Or else these Arabs felt so superior to women that even an obviously weakened man seemed more of a threat to them than an able armed woman.

But yet another possibility insisted, its implications so

disturbing it had to be considered before the others. Now that she thought about it, it was the most obvious explanation but so outrageous that she must have subconsciously rejected it.

She wasn't the target. Drew was!

11

Drew flinched from a bullet that grazed the right edge of the ravine, continued its downward trajectory, and walloped shale below him to his left. Dizzy, he lunged toward an indentation in the wall to his right, the direction from which the bullet had come.

But in that instant, a bullet from the left cracked against that indentation. Avoiding the crossfire, he toppled backward. Through a swirl of weakness, he fought to reason out his dilemma. He'd been convinced that Arlene was the primary target, that one of the gunmen would grudgingly take the time to kill him, then join his partner to assault Arlene. But both were now attacking him! It didn't make sense!

He rubbed his aching jaw where his teeth had smacked together from the force of his fall. Hearing rifle shots from his right and left, he shielded his eyes from shale spewing off both rims of the ravine. He heard another shot, this one less powerful, from a handgun, not a rifle. Arlene.

But another sound, subtle, like a breeze or a deflating tire, was more obtrusive. Down here in the muffled ravine, it had paradoxically deafening force.

An angry cobra rose to strike at him.

12

Arlene ignored the risk of breaking an ankle and continued to charge down the rocky slope. She cursed herself for letting her judgment be clouded by sexual arrogance. Admit you took for granted that the biological accident of your being female makes you an irresistible target for lust. You were so self-absorbed you didn't understand what was going on. You helped them without knowing it.

Scrambling lower, she shifted her gaze from one Arab to the other as they flanked the ravine below her. Her handgun wasn't accurate at this range. They shot again into the ravine. She stopped and fired, hoping that the bullet would at least distract them.

It didn't.

The Arab on the left dropped into the ravine. The Arab on the right moved parallel to it, glancing warily toward her, making sure she wasn't close enough to be a threat, then darting his eyes toward the depression his partner had entered.

"Look out, Drew!"

The echo of her scream merged with another scream.

The Arab who'd entered the ravine staggered halfway up its steep slope, his face in agony. Raising his eyes toward the sky as if in prayer, he shuddered and fell back out of sight.

The second Arab froze in astonishment. His paralysis lasted just long enough for Drew to crawl to the top of the ravine, aim a rifle, and shoot him in the face.

The rifle's echo subsided. Drew collapsed back into the ravine.

By now, the sun was high enough to scorch her. Despite the brutal strain on her body, she ran even harder. Scrambling into the ravine, she found him.

His voice was guttural. "Be careful. There's a cobra down here."

She whirled.

The snake lay coiled on the sand fifteen feet away from her. Unblinking, it assessed her.

"It's going to strike!" She aimed her pistol.

"Wait," Drew said.

"But . . . !"

"Give it a chance to live."

The cobra poised itself. Just as Arlene decided she couldn't afford to delay, the snake sank its head to the ground again, flicked its tongue, and slithered away. It seemed contemptuous, dismissive.

"I froze when I saw it," Drew said. "The gunman jumped down here. The sudden motion diverted the snake's attention."

"And it bit the gunman instead of you?"

"With a little help."

She shook her head, not understanding.

"The snake was only an arm's length away from me. When it turned toward the gunman, I grabbed it behind the head and threw it. It flopped across his shoulder."

Arlene felt sick.

"It bit his stomach. When he screamed and dropped the rifle to shove the thing off him, I yanked the gun off the ground. He tried to crawl to the top of the ravine. The snake bit him again. By then, I was over here, out of its reach."

"And while the gunman's partner was distracted by the screaming, you shot him." She studied him with admiration.

"I was lucky."

"No, you made your luck. As weak as you are, when you had to, you thought and moved fast. Instinct. Reflex."

"I'm not sure that's a compliment."

He stood with effort. She steadied him and helped him from the ravine. After its shadow, the sun stabbed her eyes.

"The snake reminded me of the lizard," he said. "I hated it. Now I love it."

"As long as we don't have to eat it. There's a sure test to learn if you're a mystic. Can you bring yourself to love the men who tried to kill you?"

"No." Drew stared at the body of the Arab he'd shot in the face. "God help me, I can't."

They searched the corpse. Inside a packet attached to the gunman's waist, they found dates and figs.

"That solves our food problem."

"Extra bullets for the rifle. No papers. No identification." Drew turned to her. "It's clear they were after me, not you. Why?"

Arlene shook her head in puzzlement. "I don't know this. In case they're from the nearest village, we'd better avoid it."

"Sure. But they weren't from the village."

She followed his gaze toward the gunman's mouth and tingled when she realized what he meant.

The bullet's impact had parted the gunman's jaws, exposing his teeth. Even those in back were clearly visible. They glinted from the rays of the sun, amazingly perfect, stunningly white.

"No fillings," Drew said.

"But *everybody* has fillings."

"In America maybe, if you've got the money to go to a dentist. Out here, though?"

"There might not be fillings. But there'd be cavities."

"If you still had teeth. But this guy doesn't just have teeth. He's got *perfect* teeth. It's been a while since I went to a dentist, so I don't know what the going rate is. But my guess is . . . since when do Arabs from outlying villages have a mouthful of three-hundred-dollar crowns?"

She nodded in outrage. "Professionals."

Book Two

COMPULSION

BETWEEN AN
ANTEATER AND A DOG

1

Icicle: that was how Pendleton now thought of himself. Angry, determined, identifying with his lost father, he drove his rented car along the narrow blacktop road that fronted his destination. He saw the gravel lane that led up through trees toward a sloping lawn and a mansion on a bluff above the river. Instead of turning up the lane, however, he continued along the blacktop, rounded a bend, crossed a metal bridge above the river, and five kilometers later turned left at the next intersection. Fields of knee-high corn surrounded him. Turning left twice more, completing a square, he came back to the road along which he'd first driven. This time he stopped two kilometers away from his destination, hid the car on a weed-grown lane among trees off the blacktop, and hiked overland, through woods, toward the mansion on the hill.

He wore brown outdoor clothes and woodsman's boots purchased in a town called Milton that was along Highway 401 halfway between Toronto's airport and this lush farming area near Kitchener. He hadn't risked bringing a handgun through Canadian customs, nor had he attempted to buy even a rifle at a sporting goods store—Canada's laws controlling the sale of every type of firearm were extremely strict. If this had been a country in Europe, Africa, or South America, he could have easily retrieved a weapon from one of his many hiding places or have purchased one from a black-market contact. But he'd worked in southern Ontario only once, seven years ago, within a rigid time limit that had prevented him from establishing caches and contacts.

Still, to find his father, Icicle had to take this present risk. He shifted with greater resolution through the forest. Thick leaves shut out the sun; the pungent loamy ground absorbed his weight, making his cautious footsteps soundless. He reached the edge of the trees and stooped, concealing himself among dense bushes. Ahead, he saw a waist-high wire fence. Beyond, a well-maintained lawn led up to a tennis court and a swimming pool next to the mansion on top of the hill.

The sun was behind the mansion, descending toward the opposite side of the hill. Dusk would thicken in just a few hours. He scanned the top of the hill but saw no one. Earlier, though, when he'd driven past the entrance to the estate, he'd noticed two cars in front of the mansion, so he had to conclude that the house was not deserted. He'd also noticed that the estate was not equipped with an obvious security system. There weren't any closed-circuit television cameras in the trees near the lane, for example, or guards, or roaming attack dogs. For that matter, there wasn't even a decent high solid fence around the property, only a flimsy wire one, and the front gate had been left open.

But despite the apparent innocence of the place, Icicle had no doubt he'd found his target. Before leaving Australia, he'd gone to the safe-deposit box he and his father kept for emergencies. He'd hoped that his father, on the run perhaps, had reached the box not long before him and left a message, explaining his sudden disappearance. He'd found the weapons, money, and documents he and his father had stored there, but heart-sinkingly, there hadn't been a message. Nonetheless, as he'd sorted through the documents, he *had* found the sheet of directions his father had been sent for what they'd assumed was a wake, but what was actually an emergency meeting, here in Canada. The directions had been specific, complete with the name of the exit ramp from 401, the number of a side road, and a note about the silhouette of a greyhound on the mailbox outside the estate. Icicle nodded. This was the place, all right, but as he studied the grounds, he became more puzzled by the lack of obvious security.

He stared at the waist-high wire fence ahead of him. There were no glass insulators on the posts. The wires were rusty. If the fence was electrified, how could the current be conducted? Whatever security there might be, it didn't depend on the fence.

Were there pressure-detecting grids beneath the grass *beyond* the fence? he wondered. He focused on the grass. Faint depressions from tires were evident. Tracks from a power mower, a big one, the kind a groundskeeper rode. But that kind of mower weighed more than a human would. Every time the lawn was trimmed, the alarm would have to be shut off, and that made the system worthless. All an intruder would have to do would be to enter the grounds while the caretaker was on duty. No, he decided, the only place to bury pressure-detecting wires was in a forest, and the forest would have to be within the fence, where hikers and large roaming animals wouldn't press down on the soil with a weight sufficient to activate the system. But there wasn't even a small band of woods within the fence. If there *were* sophisticated detectors, they hadn't been placed down here but instead on top of the hill, around the mansion.

He would soon find out. The sun had now descended behind the hill. Dusk would deepen to night, and the night was his friend.

2

Lights glowed inside the house. Two spotlights came on, at the front and side of the house. Again Icicle felt puzzled. If the house had an adequate security system, there ought to be more outside lights. On the other hand, perhaps the few outside lights were intended to deceive, to make it seem as if the mansion were unprotected.

Six of one, half a dozen of the other. He stood, emerged from the bushes, and prepared to climb the fence. But he froze when headlights blazed on the hill. A car engine droned. The headlights veered down the gravel lane toward the blacktop in front of the estate, disappearing into the night. The noise of the engine dwindled until the only sound was the screech of crickets.

But there'd been *two* cars parked at the top of the hill. He couldn't afford to assume that the estate was now unoccupied. He climbed the fence, dropped onto the lawn, and knelt, not moving, straining to detect a threat.

He waited five minutes before creeping upward, periodically interrupting his cautious ascent to study the night. A hundred yards and thirty minutes later, he reached the edge of a tennis court on top of the hill. Wary of triggering alarms, he snuck toward a swimming pool, its placid water reflecting light from the mansion. A small structure next to the pool seemed to be a changing room. He ducked behind it, peering past a corner toward the five-stalled garage to his right, its doors all closed. He shifted his position and stared left toward the car, a dark Cadillac, in front of the mansion. Then he studied the mansion itself.

It was peaked, with chimneys and gables. On this side, a flagstone patio led to closed French doors; beyond the windows, lamps glowed in a room lined with paintings and books. He tensed as a man walked past the windows. The brief glimpse showed the man was well-built and middle-aged, dressed in a blue exercise suit—he seemed to be alone.

Icicle studied the windows in the other rooms. Most were dark. The few with lights didn't seem occupied. Not seeing any guards, he sprinted from behind the small building near the pool, crossed the driveway, and dove below the cover of a concrete balustrade that flanked the patio, then studied the area before him. At once he realized that the patio, which went all along this side of the mansion and presumably along the other sides as well, held the only alarm system the mansion needed. An intruder couldn't get inside unless he crossed the flagstones, but they weren't joined by concrete. The light from the room beyond the French doors made clear that each flagstone was rimmed by sand. The sand was sloppy, grains of it speckling the patio. But why would the owner of a million-dollar property cut costs on so minor a detail? Why this inconsistency in an otherwise carefully maintained estate? The answer was obvious. Because each stone, independent, rested upon a pressure detector. The moment an intruder stepped upon *any* stone in the patio, an alarm would sound.

He glanced to the right and left, hoping for a tree whose branches would allow him to climb through an upper window. Seeing none, he decided to look for an equipment shed where a ladder might have been stored. By setting one end of the ladder on top of the patio's balustrade and easing the other end of the ladder onto the sill of a window in a darkened room farther along, he'd have what amounted to a bridge he could use to crawl across above the flagstones.

He began to creep backward.

"So you guessed," a voice said.

Icicle spun.

"About the patio." The voice was flat, thin, emotionless. It came from his left, from an open window of the Cadillac parked in front of the mansion. "I'd hoped you would. I wouldn't want your reputation to exceed your ability."

Icicle braced himself to run.

"I'm not your enemy." The Cadillac's passenger door came open. A tall gangly man stepped out. "You see. I willingly show myself. I mean you no harm." The man stepped into the full blaze of the spotlight in front of the mansion. He held his arms out, away from his gray suit. His face was narrow, his nose and lips thin, his eyebrows so sparse they were almost nonexistent. His red hair contrasted with his pallid skin.

The patio doors burst open. "Is he here? Pendleton, is that you?" The man in the exercise suit reached toward

79

the inner wall and flicked what seemed to be a switch, deactivating an alarm, before he stepped out onto the patio. *"Pendleton? Icicle?"*

For an instant, Icicle almost lunged toward the darkness beyond the swimming pool. Already he imagined his rush down the slope toward the fence and the trees and . . .

Instead he straightened. "No. Not Icicle. I'm his son."

"Yes, his son!" the man on the patio said. "And this man"—pointing toward the Cadillac—"is Seth, or rather Seth's son! And I'm known as Halloway, but I'm the *Painter's* son!"

The cryptonym "Painter" had force, but "Seth" made Icicle wince as if he'd been shot. He stared at the lanky, pale, impassive man beside the Cadillac. Seth's gray suit matched his eyes, which even in the spotlit night were vividly unexpressive, bleak.

But Seth didn't matter, nor did Halloway. Only one thing had importance.

Icicle swung toward Halloway on the patio. "Where's my father?"

"Not just *your* father," Halloway said. "Where's *mine?*"

"And mine," Seth said.

"That's why we've been waiting for you."

"What?"

"For you to come here—to help us find *all* our fathers," Halloway said. "We'd almost despaired that you'd ever show up." He gestured toward the mansion. "Come in. We've a great deal to talk about."

3

When they entered the study, Halloway closed the patio doors, pulled the draperies shut, and activated the alarm switch on the wall. Next to the switch, Icicle noticed a landscape painting.

"My father's," Halloway said.

Similar colorful paintings hung on the other walls.

Icicle nodded. "I'd heard he was talented. I've never seen his work."

"Of course not. His early paintings were either stolen or destroyed. For precaution's sake, even though no one saw his later work outside this house, he changed from watercolor to acrylic, and just as important, he altered his style." Halloway's tone changed from reverence to dismay. "What did you plan to do? Attack me?"

"I had to make sure I could trust you," Icicle said.

"Trust me? Right now, Seth and I are the only ones you *can* trust."

"I had to find out about Kessler."

"He went to see you in Australia."

"I *know* that! I met him there!" Icicle said. "But after I saw him, he disappeared. So did my father. Did Kessler set me up? Was Kessler a way to separate my father and me, to make it easier for someone to grab him?"

Halloway spread his hands. "He never returned from Australia. He was reliable. If you'd been here at the meeting, you'd have realized that once he committed himself to a purpose, he wouldn't back out. So when he didn't return . . . when he disappeared . . ."

"You assume he's dead?"

"Yes." Halloway thought about it. "In all probability, yes."

"So either your meeting was bugged or one of the group betrayed you."

"No. I took precautions," Halloway insisted. "Believe me, this house has never been bugged. And I can't imagine why one of us would betray his own best interests. But there are other considerations."

Icicle raised his eyebrows.

"At the time of the meeting, your father and Seth's were the only members of the original group who hadn't yet disappeared," Halloway said. "We sent messengers to each—to emphasize the danger, to convince them . . . and yourselves . . . to join us. Unfortunately, Seth's father disappeared before the messenger could reach him. That left only *your* father."

Icicle stared. "Go on."

"If our enemies were in place to attack your father, if they discovered Kessler in the area, they might have given in to temptation and taken Kessler as well, hoping he hadn't yet warned your father and yourself."

Icicle shook his head. "But Kessler disappeared at almost exactly the same time my father did. If they wanted to stop him from warning my father, they'd have taken Kessler first and only then have set up the trap for my father. No, they must have had another reason for picking up Kessler."

"Several explanations occur to me. They may have wanted to make you suspect—as you did—that Kessler was responsible for your father's disappearance. To turn you against *us*. Or they may have wanted to make you realize that no one, not even the children of the fathers, was safe. To instill fear in *you*. For *yourself*."

"We think they're bringing back the Night and Fog," Seth said.

Barbed wire seemed to bind Icicle's chest.

"Yes, the ultimate terror," Halloway said. "Not only to punish the heads of each family but to imply a threat to us, their children, and to torture our imaginations because we don't know what was done to them and what might be done to ourselves."

"From one generation to the next." Icicle grimaced. "It never ends."

"Oh, but it will," Seth said. "I guarantee it." Despite the anger in his words, his voice remained flat.

The contrast made Icicle tingle. He stared at Seth's red hair, his pale, gaunt, expressionless face, the effect so hypnotic he had to force himself to turn toward Halloway. "What made you sure I'd come, so sure that you waited for me?"

"We felt you had no other choice. When Kessler didn't return, it was obvious his mission had gone terribly wrong. Neither he nor you responded to our further messages. We concluded, reluctantly, that your father too had vanished. Perhaps you'd been taken as well. But if you were free, we knew you wouldn't stop until you found your father. Your logical destination? Here. To the site of the meeting you didn't attend, to the group who sent Kessler to find you. What other lead did you have?"

"I hope," Seth added, his voice dry and inflectionless, "you don't mind working with me."

No explanation was necessary. Icicle knew very well what he meant.

Seth's father and Icicle's father had once been two of the most feared men in Europe. Though linked by a common purpose, they'd nonetheless been rivals, as close to enemies as cohorts could be. What one achieved, the other fought to surpass, for the rewards of success, the advantages of being favored by their leader, were considerable. Both men had loved the same woman, and when Icicle's father had been chosen instead of Seth's, professional differences became personal. Jealousy—at least on Seth's father's part—turned to hate. Their conflict worsened after the failure of the cause to which they'd pledged their lives. As subsequent freelance specialists, they often found themselves on opposite sides, an extra incentive for Seth's father. Eventually retired, they'd put the world between them, one living in Australia, the other in South America. At Bondi Beach in Sydney, Icicle's father had always worn a T-shirt, to hide the two bullet scars on his chest. From his rival.

4

Now Icicle faced the son of his father's lifelong enemy. The sight of the lean, pale, severe-faced man in the gray suit made his stomach swarm with spiders. Even the cryptonym "Seth" implied the unnatural. Seth, the Egyptian god of the desert, of barrenness, drought, and chaos, of darkness and destruction. The red god, red like this man's hair. When depicted in human guise, Seth was always pale, as this man's skin was pale. But most often, the god was a monstrous animal, its body that of a greyhound, its snout an anteater's, its ears square, its tail inexplicably forked.

The god of death.

Seth. The perfect cryptonym for an assassin.

And what about *my* cryptonym? Icicle?

Seth reached out his hand. "My father loved your mother very much."

Icicle nodded. "My father always regretted that he and *your* father couldn't be friends."

"But you and I can be friends. Or if not friends, then allies. Joined by a common purpose."

Icicle sensed that Seth could never be a friend to anyone. It didn't matter. No conflict existed between them directly, and they had the best of reasons to join forces. The combination of their considerable talents couldn't be matched by their opponents. They would triumph, either finding their fathers or gaining revenge.

Icicle shook his dry, cold hand. He turned again to Halloway. "Where do you suggest we start?"

"Go after the common denominator. Our fathers never associated with each other. True, they kept in touch, so they could help each other if they sensed danger, but they carefully separated their past lives from their present ones. They lived thousands of miles away from each other. Yet their enemies found out where they were."

"It's not surprising," Icicle said. "All the enemy had to do was locate *one* of our fathers. Under chemicals, he'd have told how to find the rest. My father always felt uncomfortable about that flaw in the pact."

"But the pact had a limitation," Halloway said. "Precisely to guard against that danger, each member of the group knew the location of only one other member. Your father and Seth's remained ignorant of each other, for example. If the enemy tracked down one father and made him tell what he knew, the enemy would then have to go to the next man, and the next, in sequence, till all of the group had been discovered."

"But it didn't happen like that," Seth said.

Halloway resumed. "Some members of the group disappeared simultaneously. Besides, that still leaves the question, how did the enemy find the *first* man who disappeared? No." Halloway's voice became hoarse. "Our fathers didn't unwillingly betray each other. The information about them came from outside the group."

"*How?*"

"I told you—the common denominator. The one man who knew about all of them. A different kind of father. A priest. Cardinal Pavelic."

Icicle suddenly remembered the last thing Kessler had said to him in Sydney. "Cardinal Pavelic! He disappeared as well."

"Find out what happened to the cardinal, and you'll find out what happened to my father," Halloway said, "and yours and—"

"Mine," Seth said. "And everyone else's."

"THE HORROR, THE HORROR"

1

Vienna. Saul stood respectfully in the background, holding Christopher's hand, as Erika morosely surveyed her father's living room. It occupied the second level of a three-story rowhouse on a quiet tree-lined street three blocks from the Danube. Outside, a heavy rain made the day so drab, the room so glum, that even in early afternoon Misha Pletz had been forced to turn on the lights when they entered.

The room was simply furnished, a rocking chair, a sofa, a coffee table, a plain dark rug, a hutch with photographs of Erika, Christopher, and Saul. No radio or television, Saul noticed, but he did see a crammed bookshelf—mostly histories and biographies—and several reading lamps. From studying the austere room, a stranger would not have guessed that Erika's father, retired from the Mossad, received an adequate pension from Israel. With supplementary dividends from a few modest investments, her father could have surrounded himself with more belongings and better ones. But after disposing of his wife's possessions when she died five years ago, Joseph Bernstein had preferred to live ascetically. The sole luxuries he allowed himself were morning and evening cups of hot chocolate at a small café that bordered the Danube. And pipe tobacco, the fragrance of which permeated the furniture and walls of the apartment. Saul himself had never smoked—another legacy from Eliot. But the sweet lingering odor pleasantly widened his nostrils.

Though he didn't see any photographs of Erika's father, Saul remembered him as a tall stocky man in his late sixties, slightly stooped, with thick white hair that never stayed in place, dense white eyebrows, and a thin inch-long scar along the right ridge of his narrow jaw. On his own initiative, the man had never commented on the scar, and when asked, he'd never explained what had caused it. "The past," was the most he'd ever allowed himself to murmur, and the expression in his gray eyes, behind his glasses, would grow sad.

Occasionally rubbing his son's back to reassure him, Saul watched Erika turn her gaze slowly around the room.

"Tell me again," she said to Misha.

"Four days ago"—Misha sighed—"Joseph didn't come to the café for his morning cup of hot chocolate. The owner didn't think much about it till your father failed to show up that evening as well. Even if your father wasn't feeling well, if he had a cold for example, he *always* went twice daily to that café."

"And my father seldom even had a cold."

"A strong constitution."

"A man of habit," Saul interrupted.

Misha studied him.

"I'm assuming the café owner is one of you," Saul said. "Mossad."

Misha didn't respond.

"Joseph's visits to the café weren't just for hot chocolate, were they?" Saul asked. "Despite his retirement, he still kept a schedule, a customary routine that made it easy for a contact to reach him without attracting attention."

Misha stayed silent.

"Not that his skills would probably ever be needed," Saul said. "But who can tell? Sometimes a knowledgeable old man, no longer officially a member of his network, to all appearances divorced from intelligence work, is exactly what a mission requires. And this way, it made Joseph feel he still had a purpose, was being held in reserve as it were. Even if you didn't have a use for him, you were kind enough to make him feel he hadn't been discarded."

Misha raised his eyebrows slightly, either a question or a shrug.

"Plus . . . and this was probably your network's principal motive . . . his schedule, dropping in twice a day, was a subtle way for you to make sure he was doing all right, wasn't helpless at home, hadn't suffered a stroke or a heart attack, for example. You also made sure he wasn't being victimized by an old enemy. In a way that didn't jeopardize his pride, you protected him."

Erika stepped close to Misha. "Is that true?"

"You married a good man."

"I knew that already," she said. "Is Saul right?"

"What harm was done? We took care of our own and made him feel he had worth."

"No harm at all," she said. "Unless . . ."

"He wasn't working on anything for us, if that's what you mean," Misha said. "Though I'd have welcomed him on an assignment. Nothing violent, of course. But for stakeouts or routine intelligence gathering, he was still a first-rate operative. You have to remember, Erika. Your father's retirement was *his* choice, not ours."

"What?"

"You mean you didn't know?"

She shook her head.

"Despite his age, I could have bent some rules and kept him," Misha said. "We're not so rich with talent we can afford to throw away a seasoned specialist. But he *asked* for retirement. He *demanded* it."

"I don't understand," she said. "His work meant everything to him. He loved it."

"No question. He loved his work and his country."

"But if he loved his country so much," Saul asked, "why did he choose to live here? In Vienna? Why not in Tel Aviv or Jerusalem or . . . ?"

Erika agreed. "That bothered us. Saul's arrangement with his network was if he stayed out of sight they'd leave him alone, and the other networks would leave him alone as well. In exchange for the information he gave them, they agreed to ignore the rules he'd broken. As long as he lived where we did, in a village on the edge of the world. But my father didn't have to live here. Repeatedly we asked him to join us, to add to our family, to watch his grandson grow up. And he repeatedly refused. It didn't make sense to me. The comforts of civilization weren't important to him. As long as he had hot chocolate and tobacco, he'd have been content anywhere."

"Perhaps," Misha said.

Erika watched his eyes. "Is there something you haven't told us?"

"You asked me to explain it again, so I will. After your father missed his morning schedule and didn't complete the evening rendezvous, the café owner—Saul's right, he *is* one of ours—sent an operative who works for him to bring some sandwiches and hot chocolate as if your father had ordered them over the phone. The operative knocked on the door. No answer. He knocked again. He tested the doorknob. The lock had not been secured. When the operative unholstered his weapon and enter-ed, he found the apartment deserted. The sheets"—Misha pointed toward the door to the bedroom —"were tucked in, stretched taut, in military fashion."

"The way my father always makes his bed," Erika said. "He's addicted to order. He tucks in the sheets as soon as he wakes up."

"Correct," Misha said. "Which meant that whatever had happened, your father either didn't go to bed the night before, when he came back from the café, or else he made his bed the morning of his disappearance and for some reason didn't go to the café again as he normally would have."

"So the time frame is twenty-four hours," Saul said.

"And Joseph wasn't sick at home. The operative briefly concluded that something had happened to Joseph while he was coming to or from his apartment. A traffic accident, let's imagine. But the police and the hospitals had no information about him."

"A moment ago, you used the word 'briefly,'" Saul said.

Misha squinted.

"You said, the operative *briefly* suspected Joseph had left the apartment and something happened to him. What made the operative change his mind?"

Misha grimaced, as if in pain. He reached in a jacket pocket and pulled out two objects. "The operative found these on the coffee table."

Erika moaned.

Saul turned, alarmed by her sudden pallor.

"My father's two favorite pipes," Erika said. "He never went anywhere without at least one of them."

"So whatever happened, it happened here," Misha said.

"And he didn't leave willingly."

2

The room became silent. The rain lashed harder against the window.

"Our people are searching for him," Misha said. "We're about to ask friendly networks to help us. It's difficult to focus our efforts. We don't know who'd want to take him or why. If the motive was revenge for something Joseph did while he still worked for us, why didn't the enemy merely kill him?"

"Unless the enemy wanted"—Erika swallowed—"to torture him."

"As a means of revenge? But that would make it personal, not professional," Misha said. "In my twenty years of intelligence work, I've never heard of an operative allowing his emotions to control him so much he violated protocol and used torture to get even with someone. Assassination? Of course—on occasion. But sadism?" Misha shook his head. "If other operatives found out, the violator would be shunned, despised, forever mistrusted, judged undependable. Even you, Saul, with all the reason you had to hate Eliot, you killed him but didn't torture him."

The memory filled Saul with bitterness. "But we all know there's one circumstance in which torture *is* acceptable."

"Yes, for information," Misha said, "though chemicals are more effective. But that brings us back to my earlier questions. What network would want him? What would they want to know? We're searching for him. That's the best I can tell you for now. . . . Of course, as soon as our local people understood how serious the situation was, they contacted our headquarters. Because of my relationship with Joseph and you—remember, he was one of my teachers—I decided to take charge of the assignment rather than delegate it. I also decided to bring you the bad news in person, rather than give it to you coldly in a message. But I would have come to you anyhow, as soon as I heard about the raid on your village. The coincidence can't be ignored. I don't like my premonition."

"That the two events are connected? That *we're* targets as much as my father was? The thought occurred to us," Erika said. "But why would *we* be targets?"

"I don't know any more than I know why your father disappeared. But wouldn't it be wiser if you and your family stayed out of sight while we investigate? If you *are* a target, you won't be able to move as freely as we can."

"You think I'd be satisfied doing nothing, waiting, while my father's in danger?"

Misha exhaled. "In conscience, I had to suggest the prudent course of action. But before you commit yourself, there's one thing I still haven't told you."

Saul waited uneasily.

"What we found in the basement," Misha said.

For an instant, no one moved. At once Saul reached for the doorknob, about to go out to the stairs in the hallway, when Misha's voice stopped him.

"No, through there." Misha pointed toward the bedroom door.

"You said the basement."

"The part I'm talking about can't be reached from downstairs. In the bedroom, in the far right corner, there's a door."

"I remember," Erika said. "The first time I came here to visit, I thought the door led into a closet. I tried to open it and found it locked. I asked my father why. He claimed he'd lost the key. But you know my father never lost anything. So I asked him what was in there. He said, 'Nothing important enough to call a locksmith.'"

"Then why did he lock the door?" Saul asked.

"Exactly my question," she said. "His answer was he didn't remember."

Misha opened the door to the bedroom—the shadows beckoned.

"When our investigators searched the apartment, looking for anything that might explain your father's disappearance, they came to that door, and obviously they had to know what was behind it, so they picked the lock and . . . well, with a little research, they learned that this house has a history. They checked old city directories. They located the architectural firm that built the house. They managed to find a few former neighbors, quite old by now. In the thirties, a doctor owned this building. His name was Bund. Well-to-do. Large family. Seven children. They lived on the second and third stories of the building. Bund had his offices on the first floor. He kept his records and supplies in the basement."

Misha's shoulders sagged as he continued.

"The war started. And in 1942—the Holocaust. From files our investigators found, carefully hidden beneath the basement floor, they learned that many of the doctor's patients were Jewish. Beyond that—and this reaffirms my belief in humanity, a belief sorely tested from time to time—the records made clear that even after the war began, after the *Holocaust* began, he continued to treat his Jewish patients. It's astonishing. He truly believed in his Hippocratic oath. Our good doctor continued to care for his Jewish patients till the day the SS came to take him and his family away to the concentration camp at Mauthausen."

Saul felt a chill.

"But Dr. Bund did more than administer medicine to his Jewish patients," Misha said. "He actually *hid* the sickest ones, those whose weakened condition would have meant automatic execution instead of forced labor. Bund"—Misha glanced toward the ceiling—"the unnameable loves you."

"Hid them?" Erika whispered.

"In the basement. The way the house was set up, Bund had a stairway down from his bedroom to his clinic on the first floor. He never had to pass his patients in the waiting room as he entered his office. He merely admitted them to his sanctum. But as long as he had a stairway through a door in back, from his office to his apartment, why not continue the stairs all the way to the basement? He wouldn't have to go through the waiting room to reach his records and his medications below him. Efficient, direct, simple."

"And"—Erika shook her head—"in the end, it killed him."

"At the height of the pogrom, conscience-torn between his need to survive and his oath to heal, he built a partition across his basement. The front half, reached from an alternate and obvious door at the bottom of the outside stairs, was cluttered with boxes of records and supplies. Bund knew that the SS, prigs at heart, wouldn't dirty their uniforms to wade through the boxes, finally reach the partition, and test it. How could the so-called Elite Guard have strutted in front of the populace with dust stains on their shirts? For a time, that logic saved the doctor's life. Meanwhile, after dinner every evening, the doctor went down to the *back* half of his basement where, hidden by the partition, he took care of his Jewish patients. I don't know what medical horrors faced him, or how the SS learned his secret, but I *do* know he saved at least a dozen Jewish lives, men and women who somehow found ways to leave Europe, before he and his family were arrested. That's the point. Not only Bund. But also his family. His wife and children. They *all* accepted the risk. They chose to reject the obscenity of their nation's politics. They sacrificed themselves for us."

"But how do you know?"

"Because our investigators were able to find two Jews in Israel, now elderly, who in those days were hidden downstairs. To use Christian terminology, the doctor was a saint."

"Then maybe there's hope," Saul said.

"Or maybe not. After all, he was killed," Misha said.

"My point exactly. He died for *us*," Saul said. "So there *is* hope."

His eyes sad, Misha nodded. "We don't know if Joseph chose to live here because of the house's association with the Jewish cause or if he selected this apartment at random. If it *was* at random, there's no way to tell how he learned about that stairway behind his bedroom—because the SS sealed both that entrance and the one from the office down on the first floor. They removed the doors and put in new sections of wall. We asked the landlord about this upper door. He claimed the door wasn't here six years ago when he bought the building. We asked several former tenants about it. The door wasn't here when they rented the apartment."

"So my father must have been the one who unsealed the opening and put the door in," Erika said.

"But then he locked it," Saul said. "I don't understand. What was he protecting?"

"You'll have to find out for yourselves. Experience this the same way I did—with no expectation, no prejudgment. Maybe you'll understand what I still haven't."

"And whatever we find, you think it's connected with my father's disappearance?" Erika asked.

"I haven't made up my mind. If the people who took your father were looking for something, they surely would have been suspicious about the locked door. They'd have investigated. The door shows no sign of having been forced open. So if they did go through it, they must have picked the lock as we did, or possibly they made your father tell them where the key was. When they finished searching, they locked the door again, leaving the apartment exactly as they found it. But I assume if they'd discovered what your father was hiding and it *was* what they wanted, they'd have taken it or else destroyed it. By the way, you might as well leave your son up here with me. He looks like he needs a nap."

"You mean, it's better if he doesn't see what's down there."

"No one should."

4

Saul glanced toward Erika. Apprehensive, they entered the bedroom. It, too, smelled of pipe smoke. The covers on the bed were tucked in neatly. A handkerchief and a comb were on the otherwise bare dresser.

Saul allowed himself only a moment to register these details. The door alone occupied his attention. Already Erika was testing the knob. She pulled, and the door swung open, its hinges silent. Darkness faced them. She groped along the inside wall but didn't find a light switch. Her shoe touched an object on the floor. She picked it up. A flashlight.

When she turned it on, its beam revealed steps descending to the left. The walls were unpainted, stained by mildew. Cobwebs hung from the ceiling; dust covered each side of the steps, the middle section brushed clean by footsteps.

The bitter smell of dust made the inside of Saul's nostrils itchy. He stifled the impulse to sneeze. Peering down, he saw a landing. As Misha had described, the former entrance to the first floor had been sealed by a section of wall. Even the dust and mildew couldn't disguise the contrast between the dark original and the later light wood. In the apartment on the other side, wallpaper or paint would have hidden the renovation. But on this side, no attempt had been made to conceal where a door had been.

Saul went down. The wood of the landing's middle wall was the same type the SS had used to seal the door on the left. Despite its layer of dust, the pallor of pine was evident. Saul shoved at the middle wall—it felt solid. He drew his index finger along it and discovered two barely detectable seams, a shoulder-width apart. Opening a pocketknife, he inserted its blade within one seam, used the knife as a lever, and nudged the handle sideways. A section of the wall creaked loose. He pulled it toward him, setting it to his right. Erika aimed the flashlight through the opening to reveal the continuation of the stairs.

They stepped through, descending. Below, the gleam of the flashlight showed the concrete floor of the basement. A stronger musty smell, accentuated by dampness, attacked Saul's nostrils. Reaching the bottom, he turned left as Erika swung the beam of the flashlight.

He gasped.

The narrow range of the flashlight emphasized the horror. Each object, isolated by the beam, surrounded by darkness, seemed to have greater force alone than it would have had as part of a group. While Erika shifted the light across the room, one terrible image gave way to another, and another, the series becoming more and more unbearable. The blackness toward which the flashlight headed seemed to intensify with the threat of what it hid. Saul's shoulder blades tightened. "Dear God."

Erika stopped pivoting the flashlight. Though she hadn't yet scanned the full length of the basement, she seemed unable to tolerate seeing yet another obscene affront. She lowered the beam and revealed a battered table upon which stood a lamp.

A box of matches lay beside the lamp. Saul approached the table, struck one of the matches, and lit the wick. A flame grew, casting shadows. He set the glass chimney on top of the lamp. The flame became brighter.

He forced himself to look again, only to discover that his initial impression had been wrong. The darkness hadn't made each image worse alone than it would have been if seen in a group.

He was staring at photographs: large and small, black-and-white and color, glossy and grainy, from newspapers and magazines, books and archives. Thumbtacks attached them to the wall, which, unlike the other three walls, wasn't made from concrete but was wooden, the partition Dr. Bund had built across the basement so he could hide his sick Jewish patients in the rear compartment down here. The partition was thirty feet wide and ten feet tall; every inch of it was crammed with photographs.

Of concentration camps. Gaunt-cheeked prisoners. Gas chambers. Corpses. Ovens. Pits filled with ashes. Trucks crammed with clothing, shoes, jewelry, human hair, and teeth. In a snapshot, SS officers, their lightning-bolt and death's-head insignia prominent on pristine black uniforms, stood in a line, their arms around each other, grinning at the camera while in the background bodies formed a disheveled pyramid so large it stunned the mind.

Saul slumped on a rickety chair beside a table. He reached for Erika's hand, squeezing it.

"What was my father *doing* down here?" Erika asked. "He never mentioned ... I never knew he was obsessed by ... This wasn't sudden. All along he had this room down here."

"Madness confronting madness." Saul scanned the rest of the room. It was cluttered with stacks of cardboard boxes. Drawn as if toward a vortex, he approached a stack, pried open the flaps on a box, and found documents.

Some were originals. Others were carbons, photostats, Xeroxes. Brittle yellow pages alternated with smooth white ones. The language varied—English, French, German, Hebrew. Saul's French and German were good, and Erika's Hebrew was perfect. Between them, they managed to translate enough of the documents to understand the common theme.

Concentration camp records kept by German commandants. Lists of SS officers, of Jewish prisoners. Military dossiers. Progress reports on how many inmates were executed at which camp on which day, week, month, and year. Lists of the comparatively few Jews who'd survived the death camps, of the correspondingly few Nazis who'd been punished after the war for their participation in the Holocaust.

Saul's eyes ached from translating faded typescript and cramped handwriting. He turned to Erika. "I met your father only once, when we were married. I never had a chance to get to know him. Was he in one of the camps?"

"My father and mother almost never talked about what had happened to them during the war. When I was young, though, I once overheard them mention it to each other. I didn't understand, so I pestered them with questions. It was the only time they discussed the war in my presence. Other times, they were willing to talk about the pogroms, the persecutions. They wanted me to know about the Holocaust, in detail, as history. But their own experience . . . They were both in the Jewish ghetto in Warsaw when the Nazis laid siege to it."

Saul grimaced, understanding. In 1943, Nazi soldiers had surrounded the Warsaw ghetto. Jews were forced into it, but no one was allowed to leave—except in groups being transported to concentration camps. The 380,000 Jews there were reduced to 70,000. Those that remained revolted against the Nazis. In a massive retaliation that lasted four weeks, the Nazis crushed the rebellion and razed the ghetto. Of the Jewish survivors, 7,000 were executed on the spot. Twenty-seven thousand were sent to labor camps.

"My father and mother were part of the group the Nazis sent to Treblinka."

Saul shuddered. Treblinka hadn't been a labor camp but rather a death camp, the worst of the worst. Arriving prisoners lived less than one hour.

"But how did your mother and father survive?"

"They were young and strong. They agreed to do the work—removing corpses from the gas chambers and burning them—that even the SS couldn't stomach. That's why my parents didn't talk about the war. They survived at the expense of other Jews."

"What other choice did they have? As long as they didn't collaborate with the Nazis, as long as they didn't participate in the killing, they had to do what they could to stay alive."

"The first and last time my father talked to me about it, he said he could justify what he did in his mind—but not in his soul. I always thought that's why he joined the Mossad and dedicated his life to Israel. To try to make amends."

"But even helping to dispose of the bodies would have given your parents just a temporary reprieve. The Nazis fed slave laborers almost nothing. Eventually your parents would have been too weak to work. The SS would have killed them and forced other Jews to dispose of the bodies."

"Treblinka," she said. "Remember where this happened."

He suddenly realized what she meant. The prisoners at Treblinka had revolted against their guards. Using shovels and clubs as weapons, more than fifty had subdued their captors and managed to escape.

"Your parents took part in the revolt?"

"First in Warsaw, then at Treblinka." She smiled wanly. "You've got to give them credit for persistence."

Saul felt her pride and shared it, squeezing her hand again. He scanned the wall. "An obsession. A lifetime's worth. And you never suspected."

"No one else did either. He couldn't have kept his position in the Mossad if they'd known what was festering in his mind. They don't trust fanatics." She seemed startled by a thought.

"What's wrong?"

"My mother died five years ago. That's when he asked to retire from the Mossad, moved from Israel to here, and in secret began setting up this room."

"You're saying, your mother was the controlling influence?"

"Subduing his obsession. And when she died . . ."

"His obsession took over." Saul imagined ghosts around him. "God help him."

"If he's still alive."

"This room . . . Have we found the reason he disappeared?"

"And if we have, was he taken?" Erika asked. "Or did he run?"

"From what?"

"His past."

As Erika's expression became more grim, he spoke before he realized. "You don't mean . . . suicide?"

"An hour ago, if anyone had suggested it, I'd have said my father was too strong to give up, too brave to destroy himself. But now I'm not sure. This room . . . His guilt must have been intolerable."

"Or his hatred for those who'd made him feel guilty."

On the counter, an open book—spread with its pages flat, straining the spine—attracted Saul's attention. He picked it up and read the title. *The Order of the Death's Head: The Story of Hitler's SS.* The author was Heinz Höhne, the text in German, its publication date 1966. Where the pages had been spread open, a passage was underlined in black. Saul mentally translated.

The sensational fact, the really horrifying feature, of the annihilation of the Jews was that thousands of respectable fathers of families made murder their official business and yet, when off duty, still regarded themselves as ordinary law-abiding citizens who were incapable even of thinking of straying from the strict path of virtue. Sadism was only one facet of mass extermination and one disapproved of by SS Headquarters. Himmler's maxim was that mass extermination must be carried out coolly and cleanly; even while obeying the official order to commit murder, the SS man must remain "decent."

"Decent?" Saul murmured with disgust.

In the margin beside the passage, a cramped hand holding a black-inked pen had scribbled several words in Hebrew—two groups of them.

"My father's handwriting," Erika said.

"You're the expert in Hebrew."

"They're quotations. From Conrad's *Heart of Darkness*, I think. The first group says, 'The horror, the horror.'"

"And the second group?"

She hesitated.

"What's the matter?"

She didn't answer.

"You're having trouble translating?"

"No, I can translate."

"Then?"

"They're from *Heart of Darkness* as well.... 'Exterminate the brutes.'"

5

An hour of searching brought them back to the confusion with which they'd started. In that shadowy room, Saul finally couldn't bear it any longer. He had to get away.

Erika closed a box of documents. "How could my father have come back repeatedly to pin those photographs to the wall and go through these records? The persistent exposure *must* have affected him."

"There's still no proof he committed suicide."

"There's no proof he didn't, either," Erika responded grimly.

They extinguished the lamp and started up the stairs. In the darkness, Saul suddenly remembered something. He gripped Erika's shoulder.

"There's one place we didn't look." He guided her back down the stairs, scanning the flashlight along the floor.

101

"What are you . . . ?"

"Misha wouldn't tell us what we'd find down here. He didn't want us to have preconceptions. But inadvertently he did tell us something about this room. During the war, the doctor hid his sickest Jewish patients down here. And also hid their files."

"He said that, yes. But how does . . . ?" Erika's voice dropped. "Oh."

"Yes, 'oh.' The doctor hid the files beneath the floor, Misha said. There must be a trapdoor."

Saul scanned the flashlight across the floor. In a corner, behind a stack of boxes, he found a layer of dust that seemed contrived. He felt a niche where fingers could grab and lifted a small section of concrete.

A narrow compartment. The stark gleam from the flashlight revealed a dusty notebook.

Saul flipped it open. Though the words were written in Hebrew, Saul couldn't fail to recognize a list.

Of names.

Ten of them.

All Jewish.

6

The rain persisted. Christopher slept on the sofa. Beside him, Misha stared toward the open bedroom door.

Saul stepped through, gesturing angrily with the notebook.

"So you found it," Misha said.

Erika entered, even more angry. "We almost didn't. That makes me wonder if you *meant* for us to find it."

"I wasn't sure."

"Whether you *wanted* us to find it, or whether we would?"

"Does it matter? You did."

"For the first time, I'm beginning not to trust you," she said.

"If you hadn't found it and you'd still insisted on

wanting to hunt for your father, I'd have resisted," Misha said.

Christopher squirmed in his sleep.

"Think about it," Misha said. "From my point of view. How do I know how soft you got in the desert?"

"You should try it some time," Erika said.

"I'm allergic to sand."

"And to telling the truth?"

"I didn't lie. I merely tested you."

"Friends don't need to test each other."

"Professionals do. If you don't understand, you did get soft in the desert."

"Fine. So now we've found it." Saul's grip tightened around the notebook. "Tell us the rest. What does the list of names mean?"

"They're not the names of the Jewish patients the doctor hid in the war," Erika said. "This notebook's dusty, yes, but the paper's new. My father's name is included. The handwriting isn't his."

"Correct. The notebook belongs to me."

"What do the names on the list have to do with what happened to my father?"

"I have no idea."

"I don't believe that. You wouldn't have made the list if there isn't a connection among them."

"Did I say there isn't a connection? We know their backgrounds, their addresses, their habits, their former occupations."

"Former?"

"These men are all ex-Mossad, all retired. But you asked how they related to what happened to your father, and that puzzle I haven't been able to solve yet."

"They claim they don't know my father? They won't answer your questions? What's the problem?"

"I haven't been able to ask them *anything*."

"You're doing it again. Evading," Erika said.

"I'm not. These men share two other factors. They survived the Nazi death camps . . ."

"And?"

"They've all disappeared."

CHURCH MILITANT

1

Despite the worsening heat of the desert, excitement overcame exhaustion, making Drew and Arlene stumble quickly toward the tire tracks in the sand at the far end of the pass.

After their encounter with the two Arab assassins, they'd taken the small canvas sheet from Arlene's knapsack and anchored it across a space between two rocks where, protected from the sun, they'd sipped water sparingly, then eaten some of the dates and figs the killers had carried with them. But the killers hadn't brought enough food to sustain them long out here.

"What about their water supply?" Drew had wondered. "We searched the slopes from where they shot at us." He held up two canteens and shook them. Water sloshed hollowly. "Not enough here for them to walk any distance. So how did they hope to get back?"

With a sudden thrill of understanding, they got to their feet, ignoring the hammer force of the sun. Reaching the end of the pass, they veered to the right, followed the indentations in the sand, and came to a clump of boulders behind which a jeep had been hidden.

"Outsiders, for sure," Drew said. "No local villager has a jeep, let alone a new one. It even has air-conditioning. Those killers were used to traveling first-class."

The jeep had a metal top. The angle of the sun cast a shadow over the driver's side. Arlene welcomed the slight relief from the scorching blaze as she peered through the open driver's window. "Small problem."

"What?" he asked.

"No ignition key."

"But we searched both bodies and didn't find it on them."

"So logically they must have left it in the jeep."

But fifteen minutes later, they still hadn't found the key.

"In that case . . ." Drew climbed inside.

"What are you doing?" she asked.

"Waiting."

"For what?"

"You to hotwire the ignition."

She laughed and leaned beneath the dashboard.

But after she started the engine, as they jolted across the bumpy desert, he lapsed into sober silence. He had many questions. Though he didn't want to, he had to talk to the priest.

2

Cairo. The next afternoon. Sitting on the bed in the Western-style hotel room, Arlene listened to the spray of water from the bathroom as Drew took a shower. But her attention was focused on the telephone.

She didn't know what to do. When the priest had contacted her in New York, directing her to go after Drew, he'd given her a Cairo telephone number. "Call me as soon as you bring him out of the desert." At the time, she'd been so grateful to be told where Drew was, to have the chance to be with him again, that she'd readily agreed to the priest's condition. But now that she and Drew were together, she hesitated. Whatever the Fraternity wanted from Drew, it would surely not be a dispensation. No, by definition, a summons from the Fraternity meant trouble. She'd lost Drew once when he entered the monastery. She'd lost him again when he fled to the desert. She didn't intend to lose him a third time.

But what if the Fraternity's punishment for disobedience was...?

To kill Drew, whom they'd spared till now, and instead of killing her as well, leave her to grieve for the rest of her life.

She decided to make the call. But her hand felt so heavy she couldn't raise it toward the phone on the bedside table.

In the bathroom, the water stopped flowing. The door came open, and Drew stepped out, naked, drying himself with a large plush towel. She had to smile. After his six years in the monastery, after his monk's vow of celibacy, he had sexual inhibitions, true. But modesty? He was more comfortable with his body, naked or clothed, than any man she'd ever met.

He grinned as he toweled himself. "Once a year, whether I need it or not."

She touched her still damp hair. "I know. I feel like I lost a ton of sand."

Drew had used her Egyptian money to buy shampoo, scissors, shaving soap, and a razor. His beard was gone now. He'd trimmed his hair. Tucked back behind his ears, it made his gaunt cheeks look even thinner. But the effect was attractive.

He set down the towel. "I've had a lot of time...too much...to think," he said.

"About...?"

"Some laws are God-made, others are human-made."

She laughed. "What are you talking about?"

"My vow of chastity. If Adam and Eve weren't allowed to have sex, God wouldn't have made them man and woman."

"Is this your way of telling me sex is natural? I knew that already."

"But as you've probably noticed, I've been confused."

"Oh, *that* I've definitely noticed."

"So I've decided..."

"Yes?"

106

"If you wouldn't mind . . ."

"Yes?"

"Choosing nature over artificial laws . . ."

"Yes?"

"I'd enjoy making love to you."

"Drew . . ."

It was his turn now to ask, "Yes?"

"Come over here."

3

In the late afternoon, with the draperies closed and the room in cool shadows, they held each other on the bed after making love. Naked, relaxed, enjoying the touch of each other's skin, neither spoke for quite a while. But preoccupations intruded.

"The priest," Drew said.

"I know. I wish we didn't have to."

"But the problem won't go away."

Brooding, he reached for his clothes.

"There's something I'm curious about," Arlene said.

He stopped buttoning his shirt. "Curious?"

"Before, when you had to leave the monastery, you couldn't stop asking questions. About how the culture had changed in the six years you'd been away and who was president and what had happened in the world. But this time, after a year in the desert, you haven't asked me anything."

His cheek muscles rippled. "Yes. Because the last time, I didn't like what I learned."

"Then why call the priest? Why don't we disappear? Retreat. Together."

"Because I no longer believe I *can* retreat. I want this settled. So I don't have to worry about the Fraternity. Or anyone else interfering with us. *Ever again.*"

4

Cairo was heat, noise, crowds, and traffic jams. Automobile exhaust fought to destroy the fragrance of Arabian food and spices sold at bazaars. The complex directions they'd been given over the telephone led Drew and Arlene through a maze of narrow streets. They reached a door to a restaurant whose Egyptian sign Drew translated as "The Needle's Eye." He glanced both ways along the lane, seeing no sudden reaction from anyone, no interruption of the natural rhythm of the crowd. Of course, the absence of unusual activity didn't prove they weren't being followed; a professional tail wasn't likely to give himself away so easily. On the other hand, at least they hadn't proved they *were* being followed, and for the moment, that consolation would have to do.

They entered the restaurant's murky interior. Drew's first impression, apart from shadows, was one of smell. Pungent tobacco smoke. Strong coffee aroma. Next came touch—the gritty feel of the stone floor beneath his shoes. In a moment, his eyes adjusted to the layout of the restaurant—wooden tables and chairs, no tablecloths, but several ornate Arabian rugs on the walls, except in back, where behind a counter colorful bottles and polished brass containers were stacked on shelves below a mirror. Here and there along the walls, intricately carved wooden partitions surrounded the tables. Apart from a white-aproned waiter behind the counter and two men dressed in dark suits and red fezzes sitting at the far left corner table, the place was deserted.

Drew and Arlene chose a table on the right. The table was equidistant between the entrance and what Drew assumed would be a rear exit through the kitchen behind the counter. They sat with their backs to the wall.

"What time did he say he'd meet us?" Drew asked.

"He didn't exactly. All he said was, he'd be here before sundown."

108

Drew tapped his fingers on the table. "You want some coffee?"

"*Egyptian* coffee? That stuff's so strong I might as well put a gun to my head and blow my brains out *that* way."

Drew started to laugh but stopped when he heard a chair scrape behind a wooden partition to his left. A man in a white suit appeared from behind the partition and paused at the table.

The man was solidly built, olive-complexioned, with a thick dark mustache that emphasized his smile. The smile was one of amusement as much as friendliness. "Ms. Hardesty, I spoke to you earlier on the phone."

"You're not the priest who came to me in New York," Arlene said.

Drew braced himself to stand.

"No," the man said agreeably. "You're right, I'm not. The priest you spoke to—Father Victor—was called away on an urgent assignment." The man continued to smile. "My name is Father Sebastian. I hope the shift in personnel is acceptable. But of course, you'll want credentials."

The man held out his left hand, palm down, revealing a ring on his middle finger.

The ring had a large perfect ruby that glinted even in shadow. Its band and setting were thick gleaming gold. On the tip of the ruby, an insignia showed an intersecting sword and cross. Religion and violence. The symbol of the Fraternity of the Stone. Drew shuddered.

"I see you're familiar with it." Father Sebastian kept smiling.

"*Anybody* can wear a ring."

"Not *this* ring."

"Perhaps," Drew said. "May the Lord be with you."

Father Sebastian's smile faded. "Ah."

"That's right." Drew's tone became gruff. "The code. Go on and finish it. The Fraternity's greeting. 'May the Lord be with you.'"

"And with your spirit."

"The rest of it?"

"Deo gratias. Are you satisfied?"

"Just getting started. *Dominus vobiscum.*"

"Et cum spiritu tuo."

"Hoc est enim . . ."

"Corpus meum."

"Pater Noster . . ."

"Qui est in coeli."

Arlene interrupted, "What are you two talking about?"

"We're exchanging the responses of a traditional mass," Drew said. "The Fraternity's conservative. In the mid-sixties, it never shifted Catholic ritual from Latin into the vernacular. And you"—Drew studied the swarthy, Egyptian-looking man with the ring who'd said his name was Father Sebastian—"are younger than I am. Thirty? Unless you belonged to the Fraternity, you wouldn't have seen a *real* mass in so long you couldn't remember the Latin responses. Who founded the Fraternity?"

"Father Jerome."

"When?"

"The Third Crusade. Eleven ninety-two."

"His real name?"

"Hassan ibn al-Sabbah. Coincidentally the same name as the Arab originator of terrorism a hundred years earlier. Though a monk, Father Jerome was recruited as an assassin by the crusaders because he was an Arab and hence could mix freely with the heathen. But in contrast with Arab terror, Father Jerome's was *holy* terror. And since that time, we've"—Father Sebastian shrugged—"done whatever was necessary to protect the Church. Now are you satisfied?"

Drew nodded.

The priest sat at the table. "And *your* credentials?"

"You had plenty of chance to study me through that partition. You must have a photograph."

"Plastic surgery can work wonders."

"Your ring has a poison capsule inside. Your monastery is on the western coast of France, across from England, in the territory contested by France and England

110

during the Third Crusade. Only someone who'd been approached, to be recruited, by the Fraternity would know these things."

"True. Approached. And now we approach you again."

Drew felt suddenly tired. It was all coming back. There was no escape. His voice shook. "What do you want? If you knew where I was hiding, why did you force me to spend a year . . . ?"

"In a cave in the desert? You had to do penance for your sins. For your soul. To purify you. We kept you in reserve. You refused to join us, but we found a way to encourage you to help us if we needed it."

"Help?"

"Find."

"What?"

"A priest."

The room exploded.

5

The concussion struck Drew a millisecond before he heard the actual sound of the blast. The room became bright, then smotheringly dark as he flew back against the wall. The back of his head struck stone. He rebounded toward the table. It collapsed from his weight and the force of the explosion. The impact of his chest against the floor took his breath away. As he squirmed in pain, the room burst into flames.

The counter, now obliterated, must have been where the bomb had been hidden. The waiter behind it and the two men near it never screamed, presumably torn apart by the detonation. But this understanding came much later.

He did hear screaming. Not his own. A woman's. Arlene's. And his urgent loving need to save her brought him back to the flames in the devastated room.

Smoke made him gag convulsively. Crawling toward

Arlene's anguished screams, he felt someone grab him. He struggled and cursed but couldn't stop himself from being lifted and dragged away. Outside in the hot, dusky, narrow street, encircled by a crowd, he couldn't hear Arlene screaming any longer. He made a final frantic effort to free himself from the arms that encircled his chest, to lunge back into the ruined building.

Instead he collapsed. Through swirling vision, he peered up, convinced he was hallucinating, for the face above him ... belonged to Arlene.

6

"I was afraid you were dead."

"The feeling was mutual," Arlene said.

He squeezed her hand.

They sat on metal chairs in a sandy courtyard enclosed by a high stone wall. Beyond the walls, the din of Cairo intruded on the peacefulness of one of the few churches in this Arab city. A Greek Orthodox church, its bulbous spires in contrast with the slender minarets of a mosque.

It was early the following morning. Shadows filled one side of the courtyard. The heat was not yet oppressive.

"When the fire started, I heard you screaming." He continued to squeeze her hand.

"I *was* screaming. Your name."

"But you sounded so far away."

"I sounded far away to me as well. But after the blast, I wasn't hearing *anything* that didn't sound far away. Even my breath seemed to come from outside. All I knew was, I could move better than you could. And both of us had to get out of there."

He laughed. The laugh made his ribs hurt, but he didn't care. It felt too good to know that Arlene was alive. "How did we escape?"

"Father Sebastian had a backup team."

"Professional."

"They got us away from the restaurant before the police arrived," she said. "I don't remember a lot after we reached the street, but I do remember both of us being carried through the crowd and lifted into the back of a truck. After that, things got fuzzy. The next thing I recall is waking up in our room in the rectory of this church."

"Where's Father Sebastian?"

"Very much alive," a voice said.

Drew turned. Father Sebastian, looking more Italian than Egyptian now that he wore a priest's black suit and white collar, stood in the open doorway. He held a handkerchief to his nose. When he stepped from the rectory's shadows into the sunlit courtyard, the handkerchief showed spots of blood, a consequence of the explosion, Drew assumed.

The priest brought over a metal chair and sat down. "I apologize for not joining you earlier, but I was celebrating morning mass."

"I could have served for you and taken communion," Drew said.

"You were still asleep when I looked in on you. At the time, your bodily needs seemed more important than your spiritual ones."

"Right now, my psychological needs are even *more* important."

"And those are?"

"I get miserable as hell when someone tries to blow me up. Under other circumstances, I might believe we simply happened to be where terrorists decided to set off a bomb. In Israel, say. In Paris or Rome. But in Cairo? It's not on their itinerary."

"That isn't true any longer. While you were away in the desert, Cairo too became a target of terrorists."

"But in an unimportant restaurant, in an out-of-the-way part of the city? What political purpose would the explosion have served? That bomb wasn't placed at random. We didn't just happen to be there when the blast went off. We were the targets."

"For the second time in two days," Arlene added.

Father Sebastian straightened in his chair.

"That's right. For the *second* time," Drew said. "While Arlene and I were crossing the desert..."

He told the priest about the two Arab gunmen in the pass. Arlene elaborated.

"You don't think they were simply marauders?" Father Sebastian glanced toward Arlene. "You mentioned an earlier attack by two would-be rapists. In that same pass. Possibly the second pair...They could have been relatives out to avenge..."

"The first two were amateurs," Arlene insisted. "But the second pair..."

"If not for the grace of God and a cobra, we'd have been killed," Drew said. "Those men were fully equipped. They were pros."

"Someone knew I'd been sent to get Drew. But I told no one," Arlene said.

"So the leak could have come only from within your organization," Drew said.

Father Sebastian rubbed his forehead.

"You don't seem surprised. You mean you'd already suspected—?"

"That the order had been compromised, that someone in the Fraternity was using his position to gain his own ends?" Father Sebastian nodded.

"How long have you—?"

"*Merely* suspected? Almost a year. Became virtually certain? Two months. Too many of our missions have ended badly. Twice, members of the order have been killed. If not for our backup teams, the bodies of our fallen brethren would have been found by the authorities."

"And their rings," Drew said.

"Yes. And their rings. Other missions were aborted before such disasters could occur. Our enemies had been warned they were in danger and changed their schedules, increased their security. All of us in the Fraternity fear we're in danger of being exposed."

Arlene's eyes blazed with resentment. "So that's why you sent me to bring back Drew. You wanted an outside

114

operative, someone not associated with you but nonetheless *controlled* by you."

Father Sebastian shrugged. "What's the gambler's expression? An ace in the hole. And indeed," he told Drew, "apart from your skills and reputation, you do seem to have a gambler's luck."

"We all do," Drew said. "For sure, we didn't survive that blast because of skill, but only because the bomb was placed in the only likely hiding spot, away from us, behind the counter in back."

"Two customers and a waiter died in the explosion," Arlene said. "If you hadn't sent us there . . ."

Father Sebastian sighed. "Their deaths were regrettable—but unimportant compared to protecting the Fraternity."

"What's important to me is survival," Drew said, "the chance for Arlene and me to live in peace, some place where you and your colleagues can't get to us."

"Are you certain there *is* such a place? Your cave wasn't it."

"I want the chance to keep looking. I asked you yesterday. What do I have to do to stop being threatened by you? You mentioned a priest. You wanted me to—"

"Find him. His name is Krunoslav Pavelic. He's not just a priest. He's a cardinal. Extremely influential. A member of the Vatican's Curia. Seventy-two years old. On the twenty-third of February, a Sunday evening, after celebrating a private mass in the Papal city, he disappeared. Given his important position within the Curia, we consider his abduction to be a serious assault upon the Church. If Cardinal Pavelic wasn't safe, no other member of the Curia is. We believe it's the start of an ultimate attack. But because the Fraternity seems threatened from within, we need your help. An outsider, an independent but motivated operative."

"What if he can't be found? What if he's dead?" Drew asked.

"Then punish those who took him."

Drew flinched inwardly. He'd vowed to himself—*and to God*—that he'd never kill again. He concealed his abhorrence. Though determined to keep his vow, he negotiated.

"What do I get in exchange?"

"You and Ms. Hardesty are relieved of your obligation to us, your need to atone for your part in the death of one of our members. I consider this condition to be generous."

"That's not the word I'd have used." Drew glanced toward Arlene, who nodded. With a silent crucial qualification, he continued. "But you've got a deal."

Father Sebastian leaned back. "Good."

"There's just one thing. Break your word, and you'd better keep praying an Act of Contrition. Because, believe me, Father, when you least expect it, I'll come for you."

"If I broke my word, you'd have every right. But as far as an Act of Contrition is concerned, my soul is always prepared."

"Then we understand each other." Drew stood. "Arlene and I could use some breakfast. A fresh change of clothes. Travel money."

"You'll both be given an adequate amount to start with. In addition, a numbered bank account will be opened for you in Zurich, along with a safe-deposit box. The Fraternity will have a key for it. We'll use the box as a way to send messages between us."

"What about travel documents? Since the enemy knows we're involved, it isn't smart for us to use our own."

"To leave Egypt, you'll be given Vatican passports, under different names, for a nun and a priest."

"We'll attract attention in an airport filled with Arabs."

"Not if you leave with other nuns and priests who've been in Egypt on a tour. You'll fly to Rome, where a priest and a nun will attract no attention at all. If you choose to switch to lay identities, other passports, American, several, under various names, will be placed in the Zurich safe-deposit box."

"Weapons?"

"Before you leave Egypt, you'll give me the ones you have. When you reach Rome, others will be supplied to you. Weapons will also be left in the Zurich safe-deposit box."

"Fair enough. As an added precaution..."

Father Sebastian waited.

"I don't want to test my luck a third time. Our weapons, our passports—make sure they're supplied by an outside contractor, not someone in your network. Open our Zurich bank account yourself."

"Agreed. The leak in my network makes me as nervous as it does you."

"One thing you haven't told us."

Father Sebastian anticipated. "Where do you start to look? The same place your predecessor narrowed his search and failed."

"Predecessor?"

"The priest who contacted Ms. Hardesty in New York and sent her to find you. Father Victor. I said he'd been called away on an urgent assignment. He was. To his Maker. He was killed in Rome, two days ago. Take up the hunt where he left off. He must have been very close."

7

In the room where they'd slept in the rectory, Drew and Arlene put on the religious costumes the priest had supplied. Except for Drew's black bib and white collar, he looked as natural as if he'd put on a dark business suit. But he'd been concerned that Arlene, with her athletic grace, would seem awkward in a nun's robe. Quite the contrary. The black garment flowed in rhythm with her figure. The white cowl that hid her auburn hair and framed her green eyes turned worldly beauty into innocent loveliness.

"Astonishing," Drew said. "You look like you've found your vocation."

"And *you* could be a confessor."

"Well, let's just hope no one asks us for religious counseling."

"The best advice is 'go in peace and sin no more.'"

"But what about us?" Drew asked. "What *we're* about to do—for the second time I'd hoped I wouldn't have to face the decision—will *we* sin no more?"

She kissed him.

"Just one more assignment," she said. "We'll watch over each other and do our best."

"And if our best is good enough . . ." he said.

"We'll be free."

They held each other.

Book Three

PINCER MOVEMENT

DEATH'S HEAD

1

Halloway stood on the granite steps before his mansion, watching Icicle and Seth get into the Cadillac. The three of them had spent the night and morning making plans. Now at last, in midafternoon, the plans were ready to be, activated. Seth would drive Icicle to the rented car he'd hidden down the road the night before. Icicle would follow Seth to Toronto's international airport. This evening, the two assassins would fly from Canada to Europe. Soon—*yes, soon,* Halloway thought —normality would be reestablished.

But as he squinted from the bright June sunlight, watching Icicle and Seth drive away, Halloway wondered if his life could in fact ever again be normal. His father had disappeared seven weeks ago, abducted while sketching a river gorge at a nearby painters' community called Elora. The assailants had left his father's materials—sketch pad, charcoal, and equipment case—on a picnic table a hundred yards from his father's car. With no word about him since then, Halloway was forced to suspect, with grim reluctance, that his father was dead.

He watched from the steps of his mansion till the Cadillac disappeared among the trees on the road below him. Turning toward the large double doors of the mansion, he reconsidered the thought. His father dead? He paused, exhaled, then continued morosely up the steps. All he could do was hope. At least he'd done what he could to protect his family and himself, to stop the madness. If his father indeed had been killed, this much consoled him—Icicle and Seth were perfect weapons. The enemy would pay.

He entered the mansion, proceeded along the shadowy hallway, and reached the telephone in his study. Though he didn't want to think about it, other decisions, other arrangements had to be made. Four months ago, before the Night and Fog had been reinstituted, he'd made a business commitment that no amount of personal pressure could allow him to ignore. He'd demanded a fortune, guaranteeing delivery of merchandise the deadly nature of which was exceeded only by the homicidal tendencies of his clients. To fail to abide by his agreement would be fatal. With no alternative, Halloway drew on resources ingrained in him by his father and picked up the phone.

2

Mexico City. For the third time since he'd started making love to his wife, Aaron Rosenberg's erection failed him. He attempted to arouse himself, but his wife restrained his hand. At first, he suspected she'd become impatient with his repeated failure and intended to ask him to give up. Instead she kissed his chest, then his stomach, murmured "Let me do the driving," and shifted lower.

Sunlight gleamed through the parted drapes of the bedroom windows. A breeze cooled the sweat on his body. Closing his eyes, feeling his wife's hair dangle over his groin, he barely heard the roar of traffic outside on the Paseo de la Reforma.

His inability to perform had many causes: concern about his missing father, fears for his family and himself. Despite bodyguards, he felt apprehensive every time he went out and as a consequence left the house less often than was good for his business. Ironically, he'd stayed home today precisely *because of* business. Since early this morning, he'd been waiting for a phone call about such sensitive information he didn't dare receive it at his office. For that matter, even the phone in his house and indeed the house itself, both of which were tested daily for eavesdropping devices, couldn't be fully trusted.

As his wife continued, his penis responded. He made a determined effort to ignore yet another reason for his earlier impotence. For the past two months, he was certain, she'd been having an affair with her bodyguard, Esteban. Glances between them couldn't be ignored, nor could her newly expanded catalogue of sexual techniques, one of which was her sudden fondness for "doing the driving." At least he had one thing to be thankful for—the affair was discreet. Otherwise, to maintain respect among the police and his business contacts in this city of Spanish values, Rosenberg would never have been able to pretend to be unaware of his wife's infidelity.

He admitted he was partly to blame for her actions. Since his recent troubles, his sex drive had virtually disappeared, and even before then, his business had kept him away from home so much that she spent more time with Esteban than she did with him. All the same, he thought with a brief flare of anger, if his business required her to be lonely, didn't she have the compensating reward of luxury? Her solid-gold watch, her imported French-designed clothes, her $100,000 Italian sports car.

His penis began to fail once more. She moaned in what seemed genuine disappointment. She'd been the one to suggest making love this afternoon; he wondered if there was still a chance to salvage his marriage.

The phone call, Rosenberg thought. When would that damned call come through? The truth was, if it weren't for his wife's expensive needs, if it weren't for his own need to impress her, he would never have allowed himself to become involved in the terrible risk that the call represented.

But what was the alternative? To confront his wife about her affair? If the scandal became public, honor would require him to divorce her, which he did not want to do. His wife was stunning, a descendant from Indian royalty. Apart from his pride in being married to her, she added to his attempt to look Mexican—his hair dyed black and combed straight back, his skin cosmetically treated to look swarthy, his eyes fitted with non-corrective contact lenses to make them look dark. He needed her to help him be a chameleon. And as for Esteban, the giant was too formidable a bodyguard for Rosenberg to feel safe without him during the present emergency.

His penis began to respond again.

The phone rang. He pulled away from his wife and lunged toward the bedside table. *"Hello?"*

The male voice wasn't Halloway's, but it did have a southern Ontario accent, a vague Scottish burr. Rosenberg realized the sequence he was part of. Halloway had made an untraceable local call to a conduit, who in turn had used a secure phone to relay the message. "Maple trees."

"Chaparral."

"Be ready to talk in forty minutes." A click concluded the call.

Rosenberg shut his eyes with a mixture of relief and nervousness. "I have to leave."

His wife nuzzled him. "Right now?"

"I need to be somewhere in forty minutes."

"How long will it take you to get there?"

"Twenty-five minutes."

"Ten minutes to wash yourself and get dressed. That still leaves . . ."

Five minutes. They were enough.

3

Rosenberg told his three bodyguards to wait outside in the car, entered a dilapidated building, hurried up its creaky stairs, and unlocked a room on the second floor.

The room was little more than a closet with a window.

Except for a phone on the floor and an ashtray on the windowsill, it was empty. He rented it and paid the phone bill under the name of José Fernandez. The arrangement existed for one reason only—to provide a secure location where he could make and receive delicate long-distance phone calls without fear of leaving a trail.

In southern Ontario, he knew, Halloway had a similar safe phone in a similar office. As soon as Halloway had instructed his conduit to warn Rosenberg about the impending call, Halloway would have set out toward that office, just as Rosenberg had set out toward his. Rosenberg knew this because, if Halloway had been in place, he wouldn't have needed a conduit; he'd have made the call directly. So circumstances had now changed sufficiently that Halloway refused to waste time calling Rosenberg from the safe phone, then waiting for Rosenberg to get to his. By using the conduit, Halloway was signaling that even the forty minutes it took him to reach his own safe phone were critical.

He opened his briefcase and removed an electronic device the size of a portable radio. He plugged it into a wall socket, checked its dial, and scanned it around the room. The device emitted a hum. If a microphone had been hidden in the room, the device would not only send but receive the hum that the microphone was relaying. The resultant feedback would register on the dial. But the dial remained constant. No hidden microphones.

Not satisfied, Rosenberg removed a second electronic device from his briefcase and used a clip to attach it to an eighth-inch section of exposed wires on the telephone cord. The device monitored the strength of electrical current in the telephone line. Because a tap would drain power, the strength of the current would automatically increase to compensate for the drain. The dial Rosenberg watched indicated no such increase in power. The phone wasn't tapped.

He hastily lit a cigarette—a Gauloise; he hated Mexican tobacco—then checked his watch, the mate to his wife's. The call should come through in the next two minutes. If it didn't, if he or Halloway had been detained, the agreement was to wait another thirty minutes and, if necessary, another thirty minutes after that.

He inhaled and stared at the telephone. When it finally rang, he grabbed it. "Aztec."

"Eskimo."

"I expected your call this morning. What took you so long to get in touch with me?"

"I had to wait till they left," Halloway said, his acquired Canadian accent convincing. "It's started. They'll get there tomorrow morning."

"Europe?"

"Rome. Everything points to Cardinal Pavelic. If they find out why he disappeared—"

"How long will it take them?" Rosenberg interrupted.

"How long? They're the best. Their fathers were the best. It's impossible to predict. The most I can say is they won't take longer than necessary."

"The *least* I can say is if we fail to honor our business agreement..."

"You don't need to tell me," Halloway said. "As if the Night and Fog isn't bad enough, we have to worry about our clients."

"Who *insist* upon delivery."

"Our guarantees remain valid," Halloway's voice said. "I have confidence in Seth alone. But now that Icicle's joined him, *nothing* can stop them."

"I hope, for everyone's sake, that you're right."

"If I'm wrong, we'll face two different kinds of enemies. Call our contact in Brazil. Tell him to arrange for delivery. Our clients are desperate enough to ignore the delay, provided we can assure them it's safe to accept delivery, and I think we can do that now. If the enemy knew what we were doing, they'd have used that knowledge as a weapon against us weeks ago."

"Or maybe the Night and Fog operatives are waiting for us to trap ourselves."

"Soon the Night and Fog won't exist."

"I want to believe that," Rosenberg said.

"We *have* to believe it. If Icicle and Seth can't stop them, no one can—and in that case, we're as damned if

126

we go ahead with the shipment as if we don't. So do it. Give the order. Send the merchandise."

4

Rome. The bored American, his back sore from slumping too many hours on an unpadded chair, gagged on a mouthful of bread, salami, and cheese when he realized what he'd just seen on the monitor. "Holy . . . !"

He dropped the remnant of his sandwich beside the can of diet Coke on the metal table before him and leaned abruptly ahead to stop the videotape machine.

"Come here! You've gotta see this!"

Two operatives, a man and a woman, turned in his direction, their features haggard from too many hours of watching their own monitors.

"See what?" the man asked. "All I've been doing is seeing—"

"Nothing," the woman said. "These damned faces all blur together till they're just dots on the screen, and then they're—"

"Hey, I'm telling you. Come here and see this."

The man and woman crossed the spartan office and flanked him.

"Show us," the woman said.

The first man rewound thirty seconds of videotape and pressed the play button.

Dots on the screen became images.

"Faces," the woman sighed. "More damned faces."

"Just watch," the first man said. He pointed toward airline passengers coming out of an exit tunnel into Rome's airport. "There." He pressed the pause button.

Minuscule lines furrowed over the face and chest of a man suspended in midstride about to enter the concourse. The man wore a loose-fitting sports coat, an open-collared shirt, but his muscular chest and shoulders were nonetheless evident. His face was square and tanned, his eyes intelligent, his hair bleached by the sun.

"I wouldn't kick him out of my sleeping bag," the woman said.

"But would you still be alive after he'd screwed you?" the first man asked.

"What?"

"Just watch." The first man released the pause button on the tape machine and pushed the play button. Other faces moved past the camera. Italy's intelligence service had installed the system at every exit ramp in Rome's airport, an attempt to improve security, specifically to guard against terrorists. After Italian specialists had watched, the tapes were released to other networks of various sorts, civilian, military, and political.

"Okay, who else should I notice?" the second male operative asked.

"Him. *Right here*," the first man said and again pressed the pause button.

Another exiting male passenger froze in place, lines across his face and chest. Tall, thin, pale, red-haired, bleak eyes.

"Holy . . . !" the woman said.

"What a coincidence. Exactly what I said." The first man straightened, his pulse speeding. "If you'll check the mug shots of—"

"That guy's—!"

"Cryptonym Seth," the first man said. "As assassins go, they don't get more scary. Except for..." He stopped the tape, rewound, and expertly stopped it again. "Take another look at . . ." Excited, he pressed play.

Again the blond muscular man stepped out of the passenger tunnel toward the camera.

"Yes . . . !" the second man breathed.

"It's Icicle," the first man said. "Fans, what we've got here is—"

"A reminder to pay attention," the second man admitted. "Those bastards do show up, even if we get too bored to expect them."

"And not just that," the woman said. "We watch for days and days. Now suddenly we get *two* of them, *to-*

128

gether, trying to appear as if they're traveling separately."

"Or maybe each didn't know the other was on the plane," the second man said.

"Give me a break," the woman said. "These guys are state of the art."

"Okay, all right, I grant the point."

"Which raises the question," the first man said. "Did they know beforehand, or did they find out after the plane took off?"

"What's the city of origin for their flight?" the woman said.

"Toronto," the first man said. "So what went down in Toronto?"

"Nothing recently, so far as we know. Not even a rumor," the woman said.

"So if they weren't on a job there—"

"They must have met there, been sent from there."

"Unless they both just happened to catch the same flight," the second man said.

"With these guys, nothing's accidental."

"Maybe they're working for opposite sides," the second man said. "No, that's no good. They didn't look nervous getting off the plane."

"Of course not. They're professionals," the woman said. "Unlike some of us." She glanced at the second man, then turned to the first. "But the feeling I get—"

"Is they're traveling together," the first man said. "They're being discreet, but they didn't try to disguise themselves; they don't care if we notice. Something big's going down, and they're giving us a signal. It isn't business."

"Personal?" the woman asked.

"My guess is, *extremely* personal. They're telling us, 'we're here, we're playing it open, we're cool, so *you* be cool, this doesn't concern you.'"

"Maybe," the woman said. "But if you're right, God help the target they're after."

St. Paul, Minnesota. William Miller stomped the accelerator of the Audi that had been left behind when his father disappeared four months ago. Despite his polarized glasses, the afternoon sun stabbed his eyes. His head throbbed, but not from the sun. He skidded around a corner, raced along his tree-lined street, and veered up his driveway, stopping so abruptly he jolted against his seat belt.

As he scrambled out, his wife ran frantically from the house and across the lawn.

"I had to meet with the city engineer," he said. "When I checked in with my secretary..." Anger strained his voice. "Where is the damned thing?"

"The swimming pool."

"What?"

"I didn't see it when I had coffee on the patio this morning. Whoever did this must have waited till I left to play tennis this afternoon."

She followed as Miller hurried past the flower beds at the side of the house. He reached the back and stood at the edge of the swimming pool, staring apprehensively down.

The swimming pool was empty. He'd been planning to have one of his construction crews come over this weekend and reline it before he filled it for the summer.

At the bottom, someone had used black paint, drawing a grotesque symbol whose borders stretched from end to end, from side to side of the pool.

His throat felt sandy. He swallowed before he could talk. "They wanted to give us time to think they'd gone away, to make us believe they were satisfied just to have taken my father."

He made a choking sound as he stared at the symbol —large, black, obscene.

A death's head.

"What the hell do they want?" his wife said.

He answered with a more insistent question. *"And what the hell are we going to do?"*

SHADOW GAME

1

Vienna. Again it was raining, though compared to yesterday's storm this was only a drizzle. Saul had to remind himself that this was June and not March as he put his hands in his overcoat pockets and continued along a concrete walkway next to the Danube.

But then, he admitted, it wasn't hard to feel chilled after having been used to the heat of Israel's desert. He remembered the irrigation ditches he'd worked so hard to complete. These two days of Austrian rain would have turned his meager cropland into an oasis. Imagining that wondrous possibility, he ached to go back home but wondered if he'd have the chance to do so.

Barges chugged along the river, hazy in the drizzle. He passed beneath dripping trees, entered a wooded park, and reached a gloomy covered bandstand. Its wooden floor rumbled hollowly as he crossed it.

A man sat with one hip on the railing, angled sideways, smoking a cigarette, peering out toward the rain. He wore a pale brown nylon slicker, its metal fasteners open, a darker brown suit beneath it. In profile, his chin protruded. His cheeks showed sporadic pockmarks. As he exhaled smoke from his cigarette, he seemed unaware of Saul's footsteps coming toward him.

For his part, Saul was aware of another man in an identical brown nylon slicker who waited beneath a nearby chestnut tree and looked with unusual interest at birds huddling in the branches above him.

Saul stopped at a careful distance from the man on the railing. The drizzle on the bandstand's roof seeped through a few cracks and pattered next to him.

"So, Romulus," the pockmarked man said, then turned, "how are you?"

"Obviously out of bounds."

"No kidding. You were spotted as soon as you showed up at the airport. We've been watching you ever since."

"I didn't try to sneak in. The first thing I did was go to a phone and contact the bakery. This meeting was my idea, remember?"

"And *that*, my friend, is the only reason you're walking around." The pockmarked man threw his cigarette into the rain. "You've got a bad habit of breaking rules."

"My foster brother's the one who broke the rules."

"Sure. But you helped him escape instead of turning him in."

"I guess you don't have any brothers."

"Three of them."

"In my place, would you have helped them or sided against them?"

The man with the pockmarks didn't reply.

"Besides, my foster brother was eventually killed." Saul's voice became thick. After almost three years, his grief for Chris still hurt him terribly.

"We're here to talk about you, not him."

"I admit I made a bargain with Langley. Exile. To stay in the desert. But things have happened."

"What things?"

"The settlement where I live was attacked. My wife and son were nearly killed."

"In Israel"—the man shrugged—"attacks can happen."

"But this was personal! My son, my wife, and I were the targets!"

The man's eyes narrowed.

"A day before that, my wife's father disappeared!

132

Here in Vienna! That's why I left Israel—to find out what was—!"

"Okay, I get your point. Take it easy." The man with the pockmarks gave a reassuring gesture to his partner beneath the nearby chestnut tree, who'd started approaching when he heard Saul shout.

"What you're saying"—the pockmarked man studied Saul—"is you're not back in business? You haven't signed on with another firm?"

"Business? You think that's why I'm here? *Business?* It makes me want to throw up."

"Graphic, Romulus, but evasive. When I give my report, my superiors will want direct statements."

"You're giving your report right now. I assume you're wired. That blue van at the entrance to the park is recording every word we say. Am I right?"

The man with the pockmarks didn't bother turning toward the van.

"All right, for the record," Saul said, "I'm not on anybody's payroll. This is a family matter. I'm asking for a dispensation from the bargain I made. Temporary. Till I settle my problem. The minute I do, I'll be on a plane back to Israel."

The pockmarked man's gaze became calculating. "My superiors will want to know why they should make the dispensation."

"As a favor."

"Oh?"

"In exchange, I'll do *them* a favor."

The man slowly stood from the railing. "Let's be clear. A favor? You want to put it on that formal a basis? You're invoking professional courtesy?"

"A favor for a favor. I don't have any other choice."

"You'll do anything they ask?"

"With reservations."

"Ah, then your offer isn't serious."

"Wrong. It's *very* serious. But I'd need to know the assignment. The risk factor's not as important as the ultimate objective. It can't be suicidal. But it *mustn't* be morally repugnant."

"Morals? Don't tell me you've acquired morals, Romulus."

"The desert can do that to you. In case your superiors haven't thought of this, I remind them that an operative publicly exiled from the network but secretly affiliated with it can have great value. I wouldn't be linked with it."

The pockmarked man's gaze became more calculating. "You're that determined to find out what happened to your father-in-law?"

"And protect my family from another attack. *I told you this isn't business—it's personal.*"

The pockmarked man shrugged. "My superiors will have to assess the tape of our conversation."

"Of course."

"We'll get back to you." The man crossed the bandstand, his footsteps echoing.

"I'm staying at my father-in-law's apartment. I'd give you the address and phone number, but I assume you already know them."

The man turned, studied Saul, and nodded. His nod was ambiguous, either in farewell or out of respect.

2

In a bookstore across the street from the park, Erika watched the van pull away. She waited until it disappeared around a corner, then turned her attention back toward the park. In the rain, the bandstand was barely visible. She and Saul had assumed that his contact would have a backup. As a consequence, she had come here earlier, prepared to act as backup for Saul.

She stepped from the bookstore, pulled up the hood on her nylon jacket, and hurried through the downpour.

Saul was waiting for her at the bandstand.

"Do you think they'll agree?" she asked.

"If they feel there's something in it for them. I had to promise a favor for a favor."

Her voice sank in despair. "I'm sorry. I know how much you'd hate going back to work for them."

"But what's the alternative? Do nothing to find your father and protect ourselves? I'd hate that even more. Only one thing matters. Doing what's necessary to keep our family safe."

"The more I know you, the more I love you."

"Step closer when you say that." He pulled down the hood on her jacket, joined his hands at the back of her neck beneath her long dark hair, and gently drew her toward him, kissing raindrops off her cheeks.

But she sensed his nervousness. "What if they don't give permission?"

"I'll have to go ahead anyhow."

"No," she said. "*We* will." She hugged him. "And God help whoever tries to stand in our way."

3

"I'm staying at my father-in-law's apartment. I'd give you the address and phone number, but I assume you already know them."

Exhaling cigarette smoke, the pockmarked man leaned forward from a leather-covered chair and shut off the tape machine positioned on the conference table. He turned to the CIA's chief of station for Austria. "You want to hear it again?"

Fluorescent lights hummed. Three other men in the oak-paneled room sat motionless, showing no reaction as the station chief tapped his fingers on the table.

His name was Gallagher. A short wiry man in a blue pinstriped suit, he stopped drumming his fingers and splayed them firmly across the edge of the table. "No, the third time was sufficient. I'm clear about what he told you. But you were there. I wasn't. You saw the expression in his eyes. Did Romulus *mean* what he told you?"

135

"A gut reaction?" The pockmarked man stubbed out his cigarette. "Yes."

"Provided Romulus feels the mission isn't suicidal, provided he doesn't object to the mission's objective, he'll do *anything* for us?"

"Again a gut reaction? Yes."

"My, my."

A balding man decided to risk a comment. "It's a major shift in his position. The original agreement was— he promised to remain in exile, but *we* had to promise to leave him alone."

"A man of his talents," Gallagher said, "he could be useful if he rejoined the game and no one knew he was working for us. A master operative. A world-class assassin. And he's throwing himself on our mercy."

"But only once," the pockmarked man reminded him.

Gallagher lifted his callused fingers, the product of his black-belt karate training, and massaged his temples. "Well, then, if he wants to pursue a personal vendetta, let him do it. Something bothers me, though."

The men in the room waited to hear what it was.

"This personal vendetta might have professional consequences. We don't know who's responsible for the attack on Romulus and his family, after all. Or who's responsible for the disappearance of his wife's father. We have to make sure he remains independent, unaffiliated."

"I don't understand," the pockmarked man said.

"You will. Romulus must be impatient to hear from us. It's time I got clearance from Langley."

4

The rain had stopped. Streetlights reflected off wet grass and puddles. The night air smelled sweet. Scanning the shadows of the park, Saul left the walkway beside the Danube and once again approached the bandstand.

Again the pockmarked man sat on the railing, waiting for him.

"Romulus"—grinning, the man spread his arms in welcome—"it's your lucky day. I've been authorized by Control to agree to your proposal."

Saul breathed out. "All right." He steadied himself. "When I've settled my family concerns, I'll wait to be contacted—so the network can have its half of the bargain."

"Oh, believe me, you'll be contacted."

Saul turned to leave.

"There's just one problem, Romulus."

"Problem?" Saul tensed, looking back.

"Well, maybe not exactly a problem. Let's call it a condition. A stipulation."

"What are you talking about?"

"You can't have any help from your Israeli friends."

"What?"

"The way my superiors look at it, you're valuable to them only if you're perceived to remain a freelance."

"Perceived to . . . ? Damn it, say what you mean!"

"What you're about to do has to stay on a personal basis. If you accept help from Israeli intelligence, it'll look as if you're cooperating with them, working for them."

"My father-in-law used to be in their network, for God's sake! Of course I'm cooperating with them! *They* want to find out what happened as much as I do!"

"Then I'll say it again. You can't accept Israeli help. Or any other network's help, for that matter. Our plans for you require an absolute detachment from every organization. You have to be totally disaffected. Otherwise, if the mission we send you on is compromised, if *you're* compromised, the enemy could blame the Israelis, and then the Israelis would blame *us*, and we'd be in the same shit as if you were still on our payroll. You said this matter was personal. Keep it that way. No outside help. If you don't agree to this condition, we'll be forced to punish you for breaking your original bargain with us."

"Bastards. I should have known better than to—"

"Negotiate with us? Romulus, for what it's worth, you had no other option. Otherwise you'd be dead."

"And how am I supposed to—?"

"Use the talents you're famous for. I'm sure Israeli intelligence has already compiled information that gives you leads. By all means, take advantage of it. The professional community wouldn't be surprised if Mossad got in touch with you about your wife's father, one of their former operatives. But from here on, reject them. You're on your own."

"And who's supposed to believe this?"

"I don't know what you mean."

"This park. This bandstand. We meet here twice in one day. No attempt at concealment. Other networks *must* be watching us by now."

"That would be my assumption. I certainly hope so."

Furious, Saul raised his hands.

"Excellent, Romulus. It's time to put on a show."

Bewilderment made Saul lower his fists.

"You're supposed to try to attack me," the pockmarked man said. "My backup's supposed to try to shoot you. To demonstrate your disaffection. To prove to the other networks you're still divorced from us. Here, let me make it easy for you."

The pockmarked man stood from the railing and punched Saul—hard—in the stomach.

Unprepared, Saul doubled over, gasping.

The pockmarked man braced himself, drawing back a fist to punch Saul's face.

Instinct overcame surprise and pain. In a blur, pivoting angrily to avoid the blow, Saul thrust the palm of his hand against his assailant's shoulder. Cartilage cracked.

The man fell, groaning, his shoulder dislocated.

"You stupid son of a bitch!" Saul said. "I could have killed you!"

A gunshot shattered the silence of the park. A bullet slammed against a post that supported the roof of the bandstand. Saul dove to the floor.

The pockmarked man lay near him, holding his

shoulder, in agony. Through gritted teeth, he murmured, "Welcome back to the shadow game, Romulus. Get out of here."

"That sniper's one of you?" Saul demanded in disgust.

"I said get out of here!"

A bullet splintered the bandstand's railing. Saul scrambled across the floor. A third shot walloped the bannister on the steps leading down from the bandstand. He lunged toward the railing on the opposite side of the bandstand and vaulted it, landing on rain-softened grass. With the bandstand between him and the supposedly serious sniper, he raced through darkness toward a carousel. The way he'd been manipulated enraged him. His contact's readiness to suffer if his network ordered him to suffer was sickening. "Welcome back to the shadow game," the pockmarked man had said. *Exactly.* *Shadows.* *Illusions,* Saul thought with revulsion. In the night, the sniper—no matter how skilled—could easily have made a mistake and not have missed.

A shot roared behind him, blowing off the nose of a spotted horse on the carousel. That's enough! Saul mentally shouted. You've made your point!

A murky figure appeared ahead of him, from behind the carousel. For an instant, Saul thought it was Erika, who, not understanding the show the network had choreographed, was coming to help him. The figure raised a handgun.

It's not Erika! I'm the target!

Misha Pletz had given him a Beretta. He yanked it from his dark windbreaker, but instead of firing toward the enemy ahead of him, he darted toward the right, hoping to blend with trees and bushes. A gunshot, much closer, made his ears ring. A bullet slashed the leaves of a bush beside him. He dove behind a concrete bench and spun to fire at the figure near the carousel.

But the figure was gone. Behind him, urgent footsteps ran along a sidewalk, from the direction of the bandstand. Ahead, he saw a shadow step from behind a tree and aim. Saul fired.

But the figure ducked behind the tree.

A bullet cracked against the bench, chunks of concrete making Saul flinch. The bullet had come from a *third* sniper in the park! Not from behind him or ahead! But to his right! He charged past a fountain. Someone shouted. Sirens wailed. His lungs burning, he surged from the park. The trees ended. The walkway beside the Danube appeared before him. He spun to the right. Fifty yards away, a figure raced out of bushes. He spun to the left. Another figure! Gripping the metal guardrail, his lungs protesting, he heaved himself over.

Cold water enveloped him. He couldn't be sure, but swimming under the surface, resisting the weight of his sodden clothes, struggling toward the middle of the river, he thought he heard a bullet strike the water.

5

Erika hid among shadows on the street side of the park, watching the murky bandstand. She stiffened when she saw Saul's contact punch him in the stomach. Rushing forward, handgun drawn, determined to protect her husband, she noticed Saul pivot to avoid another blow and knock the man to the bandstand's floor. A shot. Saul scrambled off the bandstand. Chaos. First one, then two, then *three* gunmen raced through the shadowy park. More shots. Sirens wailed in the distance. Erika's only thought was to get to Saul, to help him. But the chaos intensified as Saul charged through the darkness, burst through bushes at the edge of the park, and vaulted the guardrail next to the Danube. A gunman shot at the water, turned, and saw other figures racing toward him. Firing repeatedly toward the shadows, not aiming so much as providing distraction, the gunman hurried along the walkway, vanishing into the night. The sirens wailed louder. Figures darted in separate directions out of the park.

She was one of them. She couldn't guess where Saul would surface along the river. Knowing he'd do everything possible to save himself, she had her own obligation. Indeed she took for granted that Saul would *expect* her to do what she now intended. Retreating from the park in the direction from which she'd arrived, she raced across the street and into an alley, reaching its far end just as police cars stopped at the park. She sprinted across another street and into a farther alley, her mind repeating the same frantic thought. Yes, Saul would understand she couldn't find him; he had to try to save himself on his own. *She* had to save . . .

A restaurant glowed before her. Lunging into its lobby, barely registering the smell of sauerkraut, she shoved coins into a pay phone.

She dialed her father's apartment. One buzz. Two. But nobody answered. Three.

She shuddered with relief when she heard a familiar, reassuring voice say, "Hello."

"Misha, it's Erika! I don't have time to explain!" She struggled to catch her breath. "It's bad! Wake Christopher! Don't even bother dressing him! Get out of there!"

No response.

"Misha!"

"Where shall I meet you?"

"Where my father was supposed to go but didn't!" she said. "You understand? Every morning and evening."

"Yes," Misha said. "I'll wake the boy at once. He'll be safe."

"I pray to God."

"Just make sure *you* remain safe."

"Get moving!"

She hung up the phone and turned to see startled patrons of the restaurant staring at her in the lobby. She rushed past them, leaving the restaurant.

But what about Saul? she worried as she ran along the street. Would *he* remain alive to reach the rendezvous they'd agreed upon?

Gallagher's voice had the force of a shout. *"Were they ours?"*

The pockmarked man winced, adjusting the sling on his dislocated arm. "Not unless you assigned another team to cover this. They sure as hell weren't on *my* team."

"Jesus." Gallagher sat rigidly at the head of the conference table. Two other men waited in nervous silence. Gallagher drummed his fingers. *"Three* of them?"

"In addition to our own man, yes," the pockmarked man said. "We played it exactly as you wanted. I punched him. He defended himself. Our marksman opened fire, pretending to want to kill him."

"I want to know about the others," Gallagher said.

"The first was hidden behind a carousel. The other two seemed to come out of nowhere. They tried to catch Romulus in a pincer movement."

"And they weren't pretending? You're certain they meant to kill him?"

"Romulus surely believed it—he returned their fire. Before the police could arrive, the intruders fled. Of course, so did we."

Gallagher's lips tightened. "If only Romulus had managed to kill one. Then at least we'd have a body. We'd be able to find out who else was in the game. Damn it, your team should have kept closer watch on the park!"

"We couldn't. You said you wanted witnesses from other networks. The point of the demonstration was to convince every organization that Romulus was still an outcast. We had to back off, to let our audience take position."

"Great. The operation worked so well it failed."

"Maybe it didn't fail," the pockmarked man said.

Gallagher raised his eyebrows in question.

"If anything, since Romulus almost *was* executed, the other networks will be even more convinced he's not involved with us," the pockmarked man said. "Nothing's changed. He can still pursue his vendetta. He still has to give us the favor he promised."

"Does he? *Will* he? What if Romulus believes the intruders belonged to us? Suppose he decides the mission went out of control and your men did try to kill him? He won't repay any favor. What he might do is turn against us. What a mess! To keep him on our side, to use him later, we might be forced to help him."

"On the other hand," the pockmarked man said, "we don't even know if he survived."

7

Chilled and exhausted, Saul waded from the murky Danube. It had taken him fifteen minutes to swim out of range down current and then across the river. The lights along this opposite shore glinted coldly. He plodded from mud to a concrete ramp, passed a boathouse, and finally reached a narrow street beyond a warehouse. No one had pursued him across the river. For the moment, he felt safe. But questions tortured his mind. Who'd tried to kill him? Had his former network decided to punish him after all? He shook his head, not believing it. The pockmarked man wouldn't have put himself in the line of fire. Then had the mock-assassination become too realistic? Or had his as-yet-unknown enemies been waiting for an opportunity to make another attempt against him? If he'd been killed back there in the park, his former employers would have seemed responsible. They'd never convince other networks of their innocence. And the actual assailants would go undetected.

Shivering, Saul mustered strength for an even more distressing concern. Erika and Christopher. His wife, having seen the attack against him, realizing she was powerless to help, would have gone to protect their son. He *counted* on her doing so, that reassuring thought his only consolation. Erika's mandatory first step would have been to contact Misha Pletz and warn him to rush

Christopher to safety. He trudged ahead with greater determination. For the moment, a single goal obsessed him —the fall-back site he and Erika had agreed upon. He had to get there.

8

Christopher's eyes still ached from his abrupt awakening. His blue pajamas were covered by a sweater that the stoop-shouldered man named Misha Pletz had made him put on. His nostrils felt pinched by thick clouds of tobacco smoke, but his mouth watered from the sweet cocoa smell in this room of many tables and red-cheeked, laughing men. He recalled the urgency with which Misha had carried him down the stairs. The rush of the taxi ride. The scurry into this "coffee house," as Misha called it. His mother suddenly appearing, her eyes red with tears as she hugged him. All bewildering.

He sat on a bench against a wall, his mother on one side, Misha on the other. Their conversation confused him.

"If he isn't here in fifteen minutes," his mother said, "we can't risk staying any longer."

A hefty man wearing a white apron leaned his head down toward his mother. "Come into the kitchen. We've just received a rare form of coffee."

More confusion. His mother carrying him through a swinging door, Misha leading them. Glinting metal counters. Steaming pots. His father, clothes wet, stepping out of a room. Misha laughing. His mother sobbing, embracing his father. "Thank God."

9

"Quickly. We have to go," Misha said.

"Where?" Saul asked.

"Back to Israel."

"No," Erika said. "Not us."

"I don't understand."

"Just you and Christopher. Take him with you. Protect him."

"But what about *you*?" Misha asked.

"Christopher won't be safe till Saul and I are. If something happens to us, put Christopher in a kibbutz. Give him a new identity."

"I don't believe the Agency tried to kill me," Saul said. "It was someone else. The people we're after."

"Even so, can you trust your former network?"

"I have to. But I had to make a deal with them. In exchange for their letting me come back from exile, I promised I wouldn't take your help. We have to do this on our own."

"But..."

"No. We have the information you gave us. We've got to accept the risk. But if we fail, take over for us. Don't let the bastards win."

"You're sure there's no other way?"

"For us to survive?" Saul shook his head. "To get back to Christopher? No."

10

His father kissed him. Why was his father crying?

"Goodbye, son. Misha, take care of him."

"Always remember, Christopher..."

Why was his *mother* crying too? More kisses. Her tears wet on his cheek.

"We love you."

Shouts from beyond the swinging doors. "You can't go back there!"

"They've found you! Hurry!" Misha said.

A rush toward another door, this time into darkness, an alley, neverending, into the night. But when he looked in terror behind him, he saw that he and Misha had gone one way, his parents another. Eyes brimming with tears, he couldn't see them any longer.

ETERNAL CITY

1

Dressed as a priest and a nun among many actual priests and nuns, Drew and Arlene walked along Rome's crowded Via della Conciliazione. Though the street wasn't narrow, it seemed constricted when compared with the vista ahead of them. The eastern edge of Vatican City... St. Peter's Piazza... Like the head of a funnel, the street opened out to the right and left, melding with the four curved rows of Doric columns that flanked the piazza's right and left side.

"I've heard this called St. Peter's Square," Arlene said. "But it isn't square. It's oval."

They reached the piazza's center. An Egyptian obelisk stood between two widely spaced fountains. Though impressive in themselves, the obelisk, fountains, and surrounding columns seemed dwarfed by the majesty of St. Peter's Basilica, which rose beyond the piazza, its massive dome haloed with radiance from the midafternoon sun. Renaissance buildings stretched to the right and left of the basilica and the huge tiers of steps leading up to it.

"I didn't realize how big this place is," Arlene said.

"It all depends on your perspective," Drew said. "The piazza, the basilica, and everything else in Vatican City would fill less than a seventh of New York's Central Park."

She turned to him in disbelief.

"It's true," he said. "The whole thing's only a fifth of a square mile."

"Now I know why they call this the world's smallest city-state."

"And it hasn't even been a city-state very long," Drew said. "It wasn't until 1929—believe it or not, thanks to Mussolini, who wanted the Church to give him political support—that Vatican City was established and granted independence as a state."

"I thought you told me you hadn't been here before."

"I haven't."

"Then how come you know so much about it?"

"While you were asleep on the plane from Cairo, I read a guidebook."

"Devious," she said as he grinned. "Since you're such an expert, how do we get to the rendezvous?"

"Just follow me, Sister."

He guided her to the left, along a walkway next to the steps leading toward the basilica. Showing Vatican passports, they walked by Swiss guards, the Pope's traditional bodyguards, whose long-handled battle-axes and striped uniforms with billowy sleeves looked more theatrical than threatening, and proceeded beneath the Arch of the Bells, finally within the capital of the Catholic Church. Though the Vatican's permanent population was only slightly more than one thousand, the crowd of clergy and tourists was considerable. Guides surpervised the laity.

They crossed a small rectangular open area, the Piazza of the First Roman Martyrs. On its right, the basilica loomed. But on the left, at the end of a narrow street, cypresses canopied a tiny cemetery.

"Important sponsors of the Church used to have the honor of being buried here," Drew said. "To add to the honor, the Vatican brought in dirt from the hill in Jerusalem where Christ was crucified."

They passed beneath two further arches, reached the Vatican courthouse, rounded the back of St. Peter's Basilica, and followed a maze of wooded lanes till they came to their destination, the Vatican gardens. Fountains and hedges, ponds and flowers surrounded them, creating a sense of peace. One of the fountains was shaped like a Spanish galleon. Cannons on each side spouted water, as did the horn in the mouth of a child on the bow.

"I thought you'd appreciate these gardens," a voice said behind them. "They make Rome—and indeed the world—seem far away."

Though sudden, the voice wasn't startling. Drew had been expecting contact soon. He turned toward Father Sebastian. "Is this where he died?"

"Father Victor?" The priest wore a white collar, black bib, and suit. His eyes were bleak. "At two o'clock in the morning. Over there, by that lily pond. Beside that marble angel. Shot twice in the head."

Drew frowned. "What was he doing here so late?"

"Meeting someone. Father Victor was thorough. He kept an appointment book, which he submitted to us before his daily activities. The record indicates he didn't know whom he'd be meeting here at such an hour. But his notation makes clear, the meeting concerned Cardinal Pavelic's disappearance."

Drew peered past the trees of the gardens toward the towering basilica and the other buildings within the Vatican. "Do we assume that whoever met him lived in one of the Vatican's apartments? That would explain why the gardens were chosen as the meeting place." Drew shook his head. "On the other hand, maybe that's what we're supposed to think. Maybe someone from outside chose the gardens just to make it seem as if he lived in the Vatican."

"Or maybe the person who was scheduled to meet Father Victor didn't show up, or someone else came along after the meeting," Arlene said. "An unidentified contact, a meeting place that might be intended to mislead us. We don't know anything."

"Except for the nature of Father Victor's wounds," Father Sebastian said.

Drew's interest quickened. "What about them?"

"Both were full in the face. The powder burns indicate extremely close range. You understand?"

149

"Yes. Anything's possible in the night. But from what you've said about Father Victor, he was a professional. Even granting that a professional is capable of being fooled, the powder burns suggest the killer was probably someone he knew, someone he trusted enough to come up close to him."

Father Sebastian's dark eyes blazed. "Conceivably a member of my order."

Drew glanced toward the ring on Father Sebastian's left hand, middle finger. Gold setting. Magnificent ruby. Its insignia an intersecting cross and sword. Again he felt chilled by the symbol of religion and violence, by his enforced involvement with the Fraternity of the Stone.

"Perhaps the same member of my order who twice tried to stop you from cooperating with us," Father Sebastian continued. "To keep you from finding out why Cardinal Pavelic disappeared. Be careful, Brother Mac-Lane. Coming to this rendezvous, I made triply sure I wasn't followed. But after this, it isn't wise for us to meet again. Use the safe-deposit box in Zurich to pass on messages."

"We don't have the key for it, or the number of the bank account, or—"

"The records Father Victor kept that led him to be summoned to these Vatican gardens at two A.M. You'll also want the weapons I promised."

"Those in particular."

"After I leave, stroll over to the marble angel beside that lily pond. The site of Father Victor's death. Behind the angel, a metal plate covers a niche in the marble. Raise the metal plate. Beside the tap that controls the flow of water for the fountain, you'll find a package. It contains everything you need."

2

The package—ten inches long and wide, four inches thick, wrapped in coarse brown paper, addressed to an

150

illegible name and stamped as if it had gone through the Vatican's postal system—was heavy out of proportion to its shape. Drew held it with deceptive casualness while he and Arlene left the Vatican, crossing St. Peter's Square. So far, their cover as a priest and nun had allowed them to seem invisible, but now he anticipated what they'd have to do next, and the disadvantage of their disguise quickly became apparent.

Arlene said what he was thinking. "If we keep hanging around together dressed like this, we *will* attract attention. We'll cause a damned scandal."

"Sister, such language. I'm shocked."

She made a face at him. "Where are we going to study the documents? Not in public. And a nun and a priest can't rent a room together. I can't even visit you if we rent rooms separately. What about tonight? It isn't safe to sleep apart."

"Safe? Your sense of romance touches me deeply."

She grinned. "Not to disillusion you, but . . ."

"Yes?"

"Your body isn't high on my list of priorities right now."

"Commendable, Sister. Subdue carnal thoughts." Drew glanced at the shops along the Via della Conciliazione. "But a change of wardrobe might not be a bad idea."

"Where do we put on the clothes? We'll raise a lot of eyebrows if we do it in the stores."

"We'll find a place. How hard can it be?"

3

How hard? Drew mentally repeated after fifteen minutes of washing his hands in the train station's men's room, waiting for it to be empty. *How hard?* It seemed an unwritten law that every patron of this rest room had to pass the time of day with the padre with whom they shared such intimate facilities. "Yes, my son. Very good, my son," Drew answered in Italian, continuing to wash his hands.

At last the men's room was empty. Ducking into a stall, he quickly changed from his priest's black suit and white collar into gray slacks, a blue shirt, and a navy blazer. He stuffed the priest's suit into the paper bag from which he'd taken his purchases, then carried both the bag and the small heavy package of weapons and documents from the stall just as a security guard walked into the rest room. Drew restrained himself from saying "Good day, my son," and went out into the train station.

The noise of the crowd was awesome, reverberating within the cathedral-like structure. From habit, he scanned the surge of bodies, looking for anyone who didn't fit the pattern of hurried travelers. Satisfied, he made his way to a pillar, behind which Arlene—wearing beige slacks, a matching jacket, and an emerald blouse that emphasized the green of her eyes—was waiting.

"What took you so long?" she asked. "I was starting to think I'd have to come in after you."

"Talking to my flock. See these hands. The cleanest in the city."

4

The draperies were closed. Beyond them, the roar of evening traffic intensified. The husk of the opened package lay on the hotel bed, next to a safe-deposit box key, Italian money, two Mausers, and the sheaf of documents.

Drew divided the documents between Arlene and himself. All were photocopies. Of newspaper clippings, Father Victor's appointment book, transcripted telephone conversations, reports from informants, files compiled by the lay investigators assigned to the case.

Arlene looked up, impressed. "Father Victor's sources were excellent. He had access to everything Interpol and the local police knew."

"And a lot they *didn't* know, thanks to his contacts within the Church. Look at this. He even had sources in all the major intelligence networks, including the KGB."

It took them three hours before they felt they'd studied the documents sufficiently. Drew slumped on the sofa. "Looks like the Fraternity went through a lot of wasted trouble bringing us into this. I don't see anything that gives us a lead."

Arlene rubbed her tired eyes. "Father Victor did everything I'd have done. He covered every angle—religious, political, criminal."

"And apparently came up with nothing. Yet someone killed him. Why?"

"It could have been an unrelated matter. Nothing to do with the cardinal's disappearance," she said.

"Could be. But his appointment book suggests the meeting at the Vatican gardens involved this case. And something else bothers me. The Fraternity's one of the best networks I've ever seen. With all its resources, what are *we* supposed to do that it can't?"

"Just what Father Sebastian explained," she said. "A member of the Fraternity wants to sabotage the order. Two motivated outsiders have a better chance of learning why Cardinal Pavelic disappeared."

"Because the traitor within the network won't know what we're doing and can't interfere." Drew stood and paced. "Does that make sense? Why doesn't Father Sebastian detach himself from his order and rely on his own devices to do what he expects *us* to do? What's the difference? Why *me*? Why *us*?"

"You think we're being set up?"

"Sure looks that way. The ambush in the desert. The bomb in Cairo. The traitor obviously knows you were sent to bring me to Father Sebastian. Maybe Father Sebastian chose us because as outsiders we're expendable. Instead of risking his life or someone else's in the Fraternity, he lets us take the risk and hopes the traitor will make a mistake when he comes after us."

"But wouldn't *any* outsider have served his purpose?" Arlene asked. "For sufficient money, Father Sebastian could have had his pick among any number of independent contractors." She hesitated. Her green eyes flared. "Except no amount of money would have kept an independent contractor on the job after two attempts against him. *We* were chosen because we had a better motivation. If we don't cooperate, the Fraternity will kill us."

"Life does seem very sweet right now." Drew smiled and squeezed her hand. "We've got the greatest reason in the world to want to keep living." His voice became hoarse. "So we weigh a certain death against a less certain death. And here we are. We know we're being manipulated, but we have to permit it."

"Then let's get the job done."

"And get on with our lives." He picked up a photostat of a newspaper story.

CARDINAL'S DISAPPEARANCE REMAINS A MYSTERY

ROME, ITALY, February 28 (AP)—Vatican officials and Rome police remain baffled five days after the disappearance of Cardinal Krunoslav Pavelic, influential member of the Roman Catholic Church's central administration group, the Curia.

Pavelic, seventy-two, was last seen by close associates after celebrating a private mass in the chapel of his Vatican living quarters Sunday evening. On Monday, he had been scheduled to give the keynote address to a widely publicized conference of Catholic bishops on the subject of the Church's political relations with Eastern European communist regimes.

Authorities at first suspected right-wing terrorists of abducting Cardinal Pavelic to protest a rumored softening of the Vatican's attitude toward any communist regime willing to ease restrictions on Church activities. However, no extremist group has so far claimed responsibility for Pavelic's disappearance.

Drew finished reading. He turned to Arlene, who'd leaned forward to read past his shoulder.

"What can a newspaper story tell you that isn't better substantiated in the primary documents Father Victor had?" she asked.

"Right now, I'm interested in what *isn't* in those other documents." Drew's hand tightened on the photostat of the newspaper story. "You said Father Victor had covered every angle—religious, political, criminal? But one angle's missing."

"Missing?"

"It might be the reason Father Sebastian wanted us. Wanted *me*." He had trouble speaking. "It used to be my specialty." Again, unbearably, he suffered through the memory of the explosion that had dismembered his parents before his eyes, the rage that had turned him into an instrument of vengeance and had ultimately driven him to the penance of the monastery.

"Terrorists." The word made bile rise to his mouth. "The newspaper story mentions the possibility that Cardinal Pavelic was abducted by them. But where in these other documents has that possibility been investigated and dismissed? Is *that* our direction?"

5

The morning sun fought through a veil of smog. Escaping the blare of traffic, Drew entered a pay phone near the Colosseum and dialed a number he hadn't used in almost eight years. He felt an unnerving sense of déjà vu.

A man, whose raspy voice Drew didn't recognize, answered in Italian. "Forum Dry Cleaners."

Drew replied in Italian, "Mr. Carelli, please."

"No Carelli here."

"But can you relay a message to him?"

"I told you no Carelli. I never heard of him." The man hung up.

Drew replaced the phone on its hook and leaned against the glass wall of the booth.

Arlene stood just outside. "From the look on your face, I gather you didn't make contact."

"Apparently some changes have been made."

"Eight years. It isn't surprising. Relays are changed as often as every week."

"I guess I'd hoped we could do this easily."

"Who *is* Carelli?"

"A pseudonym for a man called Gatto. In the old days, when I was an operative, he was a middleman. Sometimes we used him as a backup, in case a mission went sour. More often, we bought information from him."

The look in her eyes made clear she understood. Terrorists usually operated in small groups independent of one another. This tactic gave them the advantage of secrecy, but it also meant they had no network to depend upon for weapons, information, and safety routes. After all, an assassination required careful planning. Unless a terrorist group was engaged in a suicidal mission, they needed "clean" weapons, never before used, untraceable to them. As soon as a mission was completed, these weapons would be disassembled and either destroyed or discarded in widely separated areas, preferably at sea. Such virgin weapons were expensive. But even before an operation, the victims had to be located, their daily schedules determined, their moments of exposure discovered. This information was costly to acquire. After the mission, of course, the terrorists would need to go to ground. Alibis, escape procedures, safe houses—these too were expensive. A first-class mission, one which by definition meant that the terrorists would survive unapprehended and be able to kill again, had a minimum price tag of $150,000. The money was supplied to terrorists by various governments committed to causing chaos, and the terrorists in turn paid the money to middlemen, sometimes called brokers, who provided the weapons, information, and safe houses, no questions asked. As far as the middleman was concerned, what his clients did with the services he made available was none of his business. Carelli, a.k.a. Gatto, had been one of these middlemen.

"He had professional ethics," Drew said.

"You mean he was careful."

"Exactly. The information he gave us never exposed his clients," Drew continued. "But he had no qualms about accepting money in exchange for what he knew about terrorists imprudent enough not to have hired him."

"Sounds like a charming fellow."

"To tell the truth, if you could forget what he did for a living, he was."

"And of course you hated him."

"Him and the hate he fed off. But if anyone might know if terrorists abducted Cardinal Pavelic, it's Gatto."

"Or it would have been Gatto eight years ago. Either he's changed his conduit system since then, or he's left the business," Arlene said. "Of course, there's a third possibility. Maybe he knew too much and became a liability to his clients. Do business with the Devil . . ."

"And the Devil destroys you. In this case—I never thought I'd say it—I hope the Devil held off."

"It looks like you'll never know."

Drew shook his head. "There were alternate methods to get in touch with him. Different phone numbers, different intermediaries."

He stepped back into the booth. His next three attempts resulted in similar "no Carelli" answers. Glancing with discouragement toward Arlene, he made his final call.

A nasal female voice said, "Pontine Medical Supplies."

"Can you get a message to Mr. Carelli?" Drew asked.

The woman didn't answer.

"Carelli," Drew repeated. "Can you . . . ?"

"I haven't heard that name in almost six months."

"It's been even longer since I spoke with him," Drew said.

"If I *can* get in touch with him, who . . . ?"

157

"Mr. Haverford," Drew told her, supplying the pseudonym he'd always used when dealing with Gatto.

"I'll ask around. Please call again in thirty minutes."

Drew walked with Arlene toward the Colosseum, back toward the phone booth, back toward the Colosseum. Precisely thirty minutes later, he redialed the number.

"I phoned earlier about Mr. Carelli."

"Write down these directions."

6

Filled with misgivings, Drew urged the rented Fiat up a zigzag wooded road. Never, in his many discussions with Gatto, had they met at a residence. The rule was to use a one-time-only public meeting place, a restaurant or a park, a location that could never be traced to Gatto's organization. You didn't do business at anyone's home. For Gatto to jeopardize the safety of whoever lived here, he must have had an extremely good reason.

The moment Drew entered the lavish drawing room in the heavily guarded villa, he knew the reason—Gatto was too sick to leave the premises. The villa was ten miles north of the outskirts of Rome, situated on a bluff with a view for miles around. Every luxury surrounded him. But the once-robust man, formerly engorged on the fees he earned from terrorist killings, was now a shell, his facial skin hanging loose, his complexion liver-spotted, his loss of hair disguised by a wide-brimmed hat. He slumped on a sofa.

"Ah, Haverford." Gatto wheezed. "It's been too long. And such an attractive companion you bring with you."

"Mr. Carelli." Smiling, Arlene grasped the bony fingers he extended. Her smile didn't waver when he pressed his shrunken lips to the back of her hand.

Two bodyguards stood at the narrow ends of the room.

"Yes, it's been a while," Drew said. "I had a change

of heart . . . I might say a change of soul . . . I retreated from the profession."

Gatto coughed. "As did I. Refreshment? Wine?"

"You know I never indulged."

"I remember. But with your permission . . ."

"Of course."

Gatto poured purple liquid into a glass. He had trouble swallowing it. The room smelled of medication. "Now that we've honored the amenities, Haverford, how may I help you?" His grin was a rictus.

"In former times, you used to provide me with information about those foolish enough not to be your clients."

Gatto's sagging clothes shook as he laughed. "Those foolish enough." He chortled. "Haverford, have you seen my new Matisse?" He gestured toward one wall.

Drew turned, assessing it. "Impressive."

"A million dollars, Haverford. What I sometimes earned on one assignment. How many people died, do you suppose, for Matisse to paint that picture?"

"None . . . except a part of Matisse."

Gatto coughed again. "And even if I sold it for the magnificent profit due to me, it wouldn't save my life. Come closer, my dear. Sit next to me."

With a smile, Arlene complied.

"So tell me, Haverford, in my place what would *you* do?"

"In your place?"

"If you were dying."

"I see. In *that* case, I'd confess."

"Oh?"

"To a priest."

"Oh?"

"And do my best to save my soul."

"You've got religion, Haverford?"

"Late. But finally."

"And is it comforting?"

Drew thought about it. "No. In fact, it's quite a burden. But it's powerful."

"Power, I understand."

"And it helps me to adjust to thoughts of death."

"*That*, my friend, is priceless," Gatto said.

"So let me make an offer. A minister of God has disappeared. Can you help me find out why?"

"A minister?"

"Actually a cardinal. Krunoslav Pavelic."

Gatto nodded, recognizing the name.

"We think some of your former associates might be responsible for his disappearance. If you help me find him, I'd consider it a favor. No doubt, the Lord too would consider it a favor. And of course I would pay you."

"Pay me? In this regard, Haverford, I don't *care* to be paid."

"Then . . . ?"

"I want revenge!"

"Against?"

"Those who abandoned me in my infirmity!"

Drew spread his hands. "You know what they're like. You can't blame them. They're survivors."

"Survivors? Not if I can help it!" The effort of his outburst made Gatto close his eyes in pain. "The bastards dispense death readily enough, but they can't bear to do business with someone on the *verge* of death."

"You're that offended because they won't do business with you?"

"Business gave my life meaning."

"Then maybe it's time to find another meaning."

"Religion?" Gatto's spasm of pain subsided. He opened his eyes into slits. "Very good, Haverford. Help you find the cardinal, and in the process save my soul?"

"*Try* to save it anyhow."

"If it isn't too late."

"The greatest sin is despair."

"I meant if it isn't too late to find the cardinal. He disappeared months ago. From rumors I've heard, I gather the fullest efforts were made to find out what happened to him. Now that the trail has gone cold . . ."

"I'm interested in other kinds of rumors," Drew said.

"About my former clients?" Gatto's eyelids trembled

as he fought back his pain. "If they were responsible for taking the cardinal, don't you think they'd have bragged about it? Letters to newspapers, phone calls to Interpol?"

"Since they didn't, I'm wondering if they bragged among themselves."

"The truth?"

"It's always refreshing."

"You won't like it. The truth is, I don't know. My disease was diagnosed in January. Word traveled fast. I haven't heard insider news since February. I always enjoyed discussing world events with you, Haverford, so for old times' sake, I agreed to see you. But your trip here, I'm afraid, has been wasted. I'm not the man to ask." Gatto winced and held his breath. When he exhaled, it sounded like a tire deflating.

Drew stood. "I'm sorry. We've stayed too long. We've exhausted you."

"But I do know who you *should* ask."

Drew kept himself perfectly still. "Who?"

"The maggot who replaced me. The vermin who took my clients, who *would* have insider news. His name in Bonato."

"His pseudonym?"

"Medici."

"Political intrigue. Chaos. Appropriate. Can you arrange an introduction with him?"

"From me? Impossible, Haverford. When he gained the favor of my clients, I became dispensable. I exist by his sufferance, because I'm close to death already. If I told him I was sending you to meet with him, such an introduction would cost you your life. I'll tell you how to get in touch with him. The rest is up to you. Be cautious. Ask him questions at your peril."

"Believe me, I intend to be careful. Tell me about him. Everything."

"Perhaps you're right, Haverford. Perhaps God will look with favor upon me if I show concern for His cardinal."

Dressed in black, Drew stood with Arlene in the shadows of an alley, watching the cars in a parking lot next to a restaurant across the street. The time was shortly after 8 P.M. They'd waited here for fifteen minutes, and if Gatto's information was correct, the broker with the pseudonym of Medici would arrive at the restaurant within the next five minutes. *The restaurant is considered off-limits*, Gatto had said. *Neutral ground. No business is ever conducted there. Medici favors its menu and its wine list. He always arrives at five minutes after eight, eats heartily, tips generously, and at precisely ten o'clock returns to his mansion, where a whore —different each night—attends to his pleasure. His home, of course, is superbly guarded. But his weak spot is that restaurant. Mind you, under usual circumstances, his routine presents no risks. Terrorist groups have no reason to harm him. And the authorities realize that, if they moved against him, all terrorist groups who'd commissioned services from him would automatically revise their plans.*

Then if we move against him, Drew had said, *won't that alert whatever terrorist group might have taken Cardinal Pavelic?*

The cardinal is ancient history. Who'd suspect that the motive for grabbing Medici was to learn about an operation from several months ago? Haverford, you needn't worry.

Drew did, however—about whether what he and Arlene planned was possible. This kind of mission normally required a well-rehearsed team of at least ten people. Two could do the essentials, yes, but what about contingencies? What if the unpredictable happened and backup was needed, for defense and for distractions to implement escape?

In the shadowy alley, Drew put his hand on Arlene's shoulder, pressing it gently, providing reassurance.

She raised a hand, lovingly touching his in return; she

spoke as if she knew what he'd been thinking. "We don't go in unless it looks good. Only two of us, there's a good chance we won't attract attention as even the best of teams can. And Medici certainly won't be expecting us."

Drew agreed. The alternative was to give up this potential source of information. And then what? With no other leads, they'd be forced to hide and bide their time until the Fraternity found them and punished them for their failure. As he and Arlene had decided the previous night, an uncertain death was better than a certain one. To gain his freedom to be with her, he would face—eagerly—the calculated risk awaiting him.

To his left, a limousine swung into the nearest intersection, coming his way. He took his hand off Arlene's shoulder. They stepped back farther into the alley. As the limousine came closer, Drew saw a chauffeur. A shadowy partition separated the driver from whoever was in back. Drew studied the passenger window on his side, but its smoke-colored, reflective, and presumably bulletproof glass concealed the rear seat. Not that Drew needed to see inside. The license plate was identical to the one Gatto had mentioned. The limousine belonged to Medici.

It pulled into the restaurant's driveway and stopped. The chauffeur got out, a handgun in a shoulder holster bulging his jacket. He opened a rear door, allowing another man to step out. This second man wore a suit instead of a uniform, but his jacket too bulged from a handgun. Next came a short weasely-faced man in a tuxedo; he matched Gatto's description of Medici.

The plan was to subdue the chauffeur while he waited for Medici to eat dinner. When Medici came out at ten, Drew and Arlene would cancel the bodyguard in the suit and escape with Medici in the limousine. The plan had the merits of simplicity and practicality. From the information Drew had been given, he gathered that Medici would be too difficult to grab from his home. But here? Regardless of his armed escorts, Medici clearly felt unassailable.

The death merchant walked ahead of his bodyguard

toward the restaurant. The chauffeur turned toward the limousine. Drew took a deep breath, preparing himself to attack the chauffeur as soon as he parked the car in the lot beside the restaurant.

But Arlene suddenly murmured, "Something's *happening*."

It didn't take long. Twenty seconds at most. But the length of time was difficult to determine. Too much occurred. The driver of a small red car stopped behind the limousine and got out, shouting obscenities at the chauffeur. The man wore a peaked cap that almost concealed his red hair. His face, though contorted with fury, was extremely pale. He was taller than the chauffeur but thin, almost emaciated. He shook his fists at the chauffeur, screaming insults at him for having blocked the driveway. The chauffeur strode indignantly to meet him.

At once another man appeared from the shadows of the parking lot. He wore a black knitted cap that didn't completely conceal his blond hair. He was square-faced, tanned, and muscular. He pulled a cannister from his windbreaker and sprayed its contents at the face of the bodyguard, who fell, unmoving, as if he'd been clubbed. Bracing himself like a boxer, the blond man punched Medici's chin and, even as the death merchant toppled, shoved him into the limousine.

The red-haired man confronting the chauffeur easily dodged the punch directed at him and chopped the chauffeur's larynx with a force great enough to break it. The chauffeur fell. The red-haired man jumped into the limousine with the blond-haired man and Medici. The red-haired man backed the limousine onto the street, ran over the chauffeur, and sped away.

It had happened so swiftly, so smoothly that only when the limousine disappeared down the street did a crowd gather, staring down at the bodies. Almost as an afterthought, someone screamed.

Drew pressed his foot harder on the rented Fiat's accelerator. Tires squealed up the winding road.

"'Professional' doesn't begin to describe it. Those guys were *artists*," he said.

Arlene gripped the dashboard, bracing herself against the car's sudden swerves. "They had the same plan as we did. But instead of waiting for Medici to come outside after dinner, they moved in as soon as he arrived. Who *are* they? And why did they want Medici?"

"Let's hope we soon find out." Drew braked. His headlights gleamed toward Gatto's estate. For the second time today, they were coming here for information.

The gate to Gatto's villa was disturbingly open. Two guards lay dead beyond them, chests dark with blood. Drew sped up the lane to the Romanesque house. He rejected caution, suspecting that whoever had killed the guards had departed quite a while ago. The absence of lights in the villa confirmed his suspicion. The attack had occurred during daylight.

He stopped before the huge front door of the villa and raced from the Fiat, Arlene running beside him. Three guards lay dead on the steps. He charged through the open door, found a light switch and flicked it, staring in momentary paralysis at yet more bodies, then scurried from room to room. *Death. Everywhere death.*

Gatto lay on a lounge beside his swimming pool, his throat slit, his cotton robe soaked with his blood.

"The two men at the restaurant. The blond and the redhead," Arlene said. "They must have come here."

Drew nodded.

"It's the only explanation I can think of," Arlene continued. "They made Gatto talk. About Medici. They realized the perfect time to grab him, the same as we did."

Dismay made Drew's throat ache. "Coincidence? I don't believe in it. What happened here and what happened at the restaurant are related." He stared at Gatto's corpse. "I wonder. What do you do to a man who's dying from cancer? How do you add to his misery so much that his cancer can't compare to the pain you inflict upon him? How do you convince him to reveal what he doesn't want to when death is a foregone conclusion?"

Drew tugged open Gatto's robe, revealing the obscene mutilation inflicted upon him.

His mouth soured. "Yeah, those guys are geniuses, all right."

"But Gatto didn't tell them about us," Arlene said. "Otherwise they'd have tried to take us out before they moved against Medici."

Again Drew nodded. "I hope the Lord did look with mercy upon you, Gatto. In the end, you did damned fine."

"The blond and the redhead," Arlene said. "What did they want with Medici?"

"Maybe their motive was the same as ours."

"To find the cardinal?"

"I wish to God I knew. Are those two guys moving parallel to us? Or are they behind us?"

"Drew, they're just skilled enough, they might be *ahead* of us."

Book Four

COLLISION
COURSE

GRAVE IMAGES

1

Mexico City. Using the phone in the backseat of his Mercedes sedan, Aaron Rosenberg called ahead to warn his bodyguards to double-check for suspicious strangers outside his home. Nothing had happened to persuade him an attack was imminent, but now that he and Halloway had decided to honor their business commitment, he'd become increasingly uneasy. The abduction of his father had filled him with foreboding. His wife's affair with her bodyguard had further destroyed his peace of mind. Now, in spite of Halloway's assurances that Seth and Icicle would root out the source of the Night and Fog, no reports of success had arrived. Yet Halloway's prediction of their success had been the major reason Rosenberg had agreed to the danger of going ahead with delivery of the Devil's merchandise. If the Night and Fog learned about the shipment, or if the Devil learned that the Night and Fog might be able to expose the nature of the shipment and who had ordered it, we'd face two enemies, Rosenberg thought. And both would attack, for different reasons.

The Mercedes was trapped in a line of stalled traffic. At the head of the line, steam gushed from beneath the hood of an open truck filled with crates of chickens. Bystanders gesticulated around it. What the hell am I doing in this country? Rosenberg thought. For a nostalgic instant, he had a vision of mountains, streams, and forests.

He jerked his head toward the bodyguard on his left, then with equal abruptness toward the bodyguard next to the driver. Madness, he thought. Before he realized what he was doing, he slid open the hatch on the bar built into the seat ahead of him, took out a bottle of tequila, filled a tumbler, and swallowed its oily contents in one gulp. As it jolted into his stomach, the Mercedes moved ahead, the stalled truck having been pushed to the side of the street.

But the air-conditioning in the Mercedes had been strained. Tepid, recycled air drifted over him. Combined with the tequila in his stomach, it made him want to gag. He raised his fist to his mouth as if to stifle a cough and kept his dignity, anxious to reach the sanctuary of his home.

Perhaps Maria would be in the mood to do more "driving," he fantasized. Anything to distract him from his troubles. She owed it to him, he concluded. Didn't he heap upon her the bounty of his labor? Hadn't he held off confronting her about her infidelity?

His driver managed to turn onto the spacious Paseo de la Reforma, gaining speed along the avenue, reaching the Spanish mansion squeezed between high-rise apartment buildings. Rosenberg's bodyguards scrambled from the Mercedes, assessing potential dangers.

Nonexistent ones apparently. One of the bodyguards nodded to Rosenberg. The mansion's security force stepped from the entrance. Rosenberg darted from the car, up the stone steps, and into the vestibule of his home, where he slumped against a wall. Admittedly his arrival hadn't been dignified, but death wasn't dignified either, no matter what form it took. His security force might joke among themselves about his fear, but he paid them well, and they could joke all they wanted as long as they did their job.

He straightened from the wall when he noticed his maid standing beside the curved staircase, surveying him in confusion.

"It's quite all right," he said in Spanish. "The heat overcame me briefly. Is your mistress upstairs?"

"No, Señor Rosenberg," the servant said. "Your wife has gone out for the afternoon."

"Gone out?" Rosenberg scowled. "Where?"

"She did not tell me, Señor."

"With Esteban?"

"But of course, with her bodyguard."

Her bodyguard? Rosenberg thought. Her body *violator* would be more accurate!

He charged up the stairs. Damn it, they fuck all day while I take the risks!

At the top of the stairs, he stopped abruptly, hearing voices from Esteban's room at the end of the hallway. The voices were too muted for Rosenberg to identify them, but they belonged to a man and a woman, and Rosenberg had the keen suspicion that the maid had been either mistaken or instructed to lie. He was powerless to solve his other problems, but by God, he could settle *this* one right now.

He stormed toward Esteban's room, and even when he'd gone sufficiently far along the hall to realize that the voices in fact came from the maid's room—a television soap opera she'd forgotten to turn off—even then he was too committed to stop himself. He rammed Esteban's door open, bursting in, fully expecting to find his wife and her bodyguard embracing on the bed.

They weren't. The room was deserted, but what he saw on the bed was so much more shocking than the tryst he'd imagined that his knees wavered. He gripped Esteban's bureau to steady himself and, as soon as the spasms in his legs subsided, lunged for the bedspread, clutching it to his chest. An iron band seemed to tighten around his rib cage. He spun, staring furtively behind him, apprehensive lest the maid might have followed him upstairs and seen what was on the bedspread. She still might come up and wonder about his actions. He had to get the bedspread out of sight.

He compacted the bedspread and shifted it from his chest to his right side where the maid might not notice it as he hurried along the hallway, past the upstairs landing, and along the opposite hallway toward the master bedroom. He'd already entered the bedroom, closed the door, and rushed toward the dresser to hide the spread when he saw the reflection of his own bed in the dresser's mirror—and what was *on* the bedspread.

It was identical to what he'd found on the spread in Esteban's room. Huge, black, grotesque, so unnerving that after Rosenberg crumpled this spread too and shoved it into a drawer with the other, he didn't consider driving to the secret office he maintained. He quite simply, absolutely panicked and lurched toward the bedside phone.

2

Halloway was appalled by Rosenberg's stupidity in using an unsecured phone. That lapse in procedure, combined with Rosenberg's babbling, made clear that the man had obviously lost all control. "Slow down, for Christ's sake," Halloway urged. "What are you talking about? You found *what*?"

"A skull! A fucking death's head! Painted in black on my bedspread! My wife's bodyguard had one on *his* bed too!"

"Take it easy. This might not mean what you think. It might be just a death threat. There's no reason to assume—"

"If we're dealing with the Night and Fog, I *have* to assume! It's more than just a death threat! You know what else the symbol means! Whoever painted those skulls wants to remind us they know all about us!"

Halloway kept his voice low, not wanting to attract the attention of his bodyguards outside in the corridor. "All right, suppose they *are* reminding us, what difference does it make? It doesn't change things. We already *knew* they'd found us out."

"It changes everything!" Rosenberg's voice verged on hysteria. "It proves they weren't content to take our fathers! Now they want *us*! The sins of the fathers! The

172

next generation has to suffer! And they can do it! They managed to sneak inside my home despite every possible security precaution!"

"We can't keep talking about this on an unprotected phone," Halloway warned. "Hang up. Call me an hour from now at . . ."

Rosenberg rushed on. "And that's not all! Why *two* skulls? Why on my *bed*? Why on the bed of my *wife's bodyguard*?"

"I assume to double the effect. To . . ."

"Damn it, you don't understand! My wife and her bodyguard are having an affair! I thought no one knew! I've been trying to pretend I don't suspect! But the Night and Fog know! That's why they painted the skulls on both beds! They're telling me they know everything about me, including who's screwing my wife! They're bragging they know all my secrets! All *our* secrets, Halloway! The merchandise! The shipment! If they've learned about . . . !"

"You're jumping to conclusions."

"Jumping to conclusions?" Rosenberg moaned. "Dear God, why did I ever go into business with you? You're so damned self-confident you won't admit . . . !"

"Seth and Icicle will take care of—"

"*Will* take care of? *Will*? But they haven't done it yet, have they? And that's all I care about! While those two chase shadows, I've got a situation here! I'm cancelling our arrangement right now!"

"What are you—?"

"Either that, or you let me stop the shipment! I don't need *two* enemies, Halloway! If our clients find out we went ahead without warning them the Night and Fog might know about the shipment, they'll come for us! They'll make the Night and Fog seem a minor nuisance!"

"But I'm telling you . . ."

"No, I'm telling *you*! The moment I hang up, I'm calling Rio! I'll do what I should have done in the first place! I'll tell him 'no'! And then I'll hope to God your two maniacs find a way to stop the Night and Fog!"

Halloway's mouth felt parched. He had no doubt that

173

Rosenberg meant what he said. A balance had tipped. Events were now out of control.

He tried to moisten his dry mouth. "All right," he murmured. "If that's what you think is best."

3

Halloway set down the phone. The truth was—and he would never have dared tell Rosenberg—he'd received three other calls from members of their group, all about death's heads. Miller in St. Paul, Minnesota, had found one painted on the bottom of his drained swimming pool. Culloden in Bristol, England, had found one painted on a billiard table in his game room. Svenson in Göteborg, Sweden, had found one painted on the floor of his kitchen.

The parallels had disturbing implications. In each case, the symbol had been left at the victim's home, as if to say "We can get close to you anyplace, even where you feel most protected. But if we'd wanted, we could have painted the death's head where others could see it, at your workplace perhaps or in full view of your neighbors. We want you to realize—we can expose you at any time, humiliate your wife and children, embarrass your business contacts. And after that? Do you hope we'll be satisfied? Or will we come after you as we did your father? Will you have to pay the ultimate penalty? As our own loved ones had to pay. As *we* had to pay."

Halloway shuddered, disturbed by one other parallel. After Miller, Culloden, Svenson, and now Rosenberg had discovered the death's head, they all had ignored safe procedure and phoned him directly instead of through intermediaries. The Night and Fog was achieving its purpose, eroding discipline, promoting panic. How many others of the group would soon call him? When would *he* discover a death's head? He'd instructed his guards to double security on the safe house in Kitchener where his family was being sequestered. He'd also hired as many extra guards as he needed to protect this estate. But perhaps the time had come to abandon the estate, to give up the exquisite surroundings his father had provided for him.

He shook his head. No! As long as Seth and Icicle were on the hunt, there was every reason to believe in eventual victory. The Night and Fog would be destroyed.

And in the meantime? Determination was everything.

I won't be defeated! Halloway thought. The vermin won't control me!

But again he wondered, When will it be my turn to find a death's head?

He struggled against his misgivings. He'd asked the wrong question, he realized. The proper question was, When will Seth and Icicle be victorious for us all?

4

Rio de Janeiro. From his glass-walled penthouse, the businessman had a perfect view of the throngs of bathers on the sensuous curve of Copacabana Beach. If he'd cared to, he could have walked to the opposite glass wall and peered up toward the far-off massive statue of Christ the Redeemer on top of Corcovado mountain, but he seldom chose that option. Situated between the Spirit and the Flesh, he almost always found himself drawn toward the telescope on his beach-side window and its view of the most arousing women in the world. His wealth guaranteed a temptation few of them could resist.

But at the moment, all he felt was anger. He pressed a portable phone against his ear. "Rosenberg, you think I've got nothing better to do than make deals and then tell the clients it was all a mistake? Never mind that this is a hundred-million-dollar deal and I get fifteen percent of it. Never mind that I accepted a twenty percent downpayment from them, and the money's gaining interest in a Zurich bank. Let's forget all that for a second. Friend to friend, a deal's a deal. In the first place, my clients become severely unpleasant if a contract's cancelled. In the second place, the contracts *can't* be cancelled because the shipment's on its way, and I always take care not to have any connection with it. I don't even know what ship it's on. I use so many intermediaries I wouldn't know how to stop it. You should have thought of this earlier."

Rosenberg started to babble.

The businessman interrupted. "If you've got cold feet, you shouldn't step into the water. Or is it *more* than cold feet? Do you know a security reason that I don't know for not delivering the merchandise? If you do, my friend, and you didn't warn us, you'll find out how truly unpleasant the clients can be. So what's with the second thoughts? What problem's on your mind?"

"Nothing . . ." Rosenberg whispered.

"What? I can barely hear you."

"It's all right. No problem."

"Then why the hell did you call me?"

"Nerves . . . I . . ."

"Nerves?" The businessman frowned. "Friend, this conversation's starting to bore me."

"There's so much money at stake . . ."

"You bet there is, and fifteen percent of it is mine."

"So many risks. The merchandise scares me. The *clients* scare me. My stomach's been giving me problems."

"Try Maalox. You're right about the clients. Any bunch who wants a hundred million dollars worth of black-market weapons is *definitely* scary. Incidentally, don't call me again. I won't do business with you anymore. You're interfering with my peace of mind."

5

Rosenberg set down the phone and stared at his trembling hands. He'd never believed in fate, but he was quickly beginning to wonder if something very like it was taking charge of him. He couldn't recall when he'd felt this helpless, and he found himself mentally grasping for the only chance of salvation now afforded him—Icicle and Seth, their pursuit of the Night and Fog.

His spirit felt buoyed for less than five seconds. About to go downstairs from his secret office, he suddenly stopped, his palm pressed so hard against the doorknob that he felt its cut-glass pattern indent his flesh. If the Night and Fog knew enough about his past to use a death's head symbol to terrorize him, if they knew enough about his present to paint the symbol not only on his bed but on the bed of the bodyguard who was screwing his wife, wasn't it also possible that they knew about *other* secrets in his life?

Such as this office?

With a tremor, he realized that he'd been in such a hurry he hadn't checked for a tap on the phone before he called his contact in Rio. Trying to prevent the Night and Fog from learning about the shipment, had he inadvertently let them find out? Furious at himself, he slammed the door and locked it, hurrying down the stairs.

6

A windowpane absorbs vibrations from a voice in a room.

Across the street from Rosenberg's office, a fan stood in the open window of a second-story hotel room. The fan was actually a microwave transmitter, which bounced waves off Rosenberg's window and received, along with them, the vibrations from Rosenberg's conversation. A decoder translated the waves into words and relayed them to a tape recorder. The tape was picked up every evening.

Rosenberg's home was also under microwave surveillance, as was Halloway's and that of every other member of the group. It didn't matter if they checked for bugs and phone taps. Everything they said was overheard. *They had no secrets.*

7

William Miller stared at the large manila envelope his secretary brought into his office.

"It came special delivery," she said. "I started to open it with the other mail, but you see it's marked 'personal,' underlined, with an exclamation mark, so I thought I'd better let you open it yourself."

Miller studied the envelope. It was eight-by-twelve, crammed till it seemed that not one more sheet of paper could be squeezed inside. A hot pressure made him squirm. "Thanks, Marge. It's probably just a new advertising scheme. Or maybe some young architect who wants to join the firm, trying to overwhelm me with his designs."

"Sure, it could be anything," Marge said, eyes mischievous. "But for a second there, I wondered if you'd subscribed to some pornographic magazine you didn't want your wife to know about."

He forced a laugh. "Whatever's in the package, I didn't send for it."

"Aren't you going to open it?"

"In a while. Right now, I've got this proposal to finish. The city council needs convincing on this low-rent renewal project."

He lowered his gaze to the cold print before him and pretended to concentrate on the cost-projection figures.

"Anything I can do to help, Mr. Miller, just buzz me on the intercom." She left, closing the door behind her.

The envelope—bold black ink emphasizing its PERSONAL! caution—lay on his desk. The postage cost, including the special delivery fee, had been nine dollars and fifteen cents. No return address.

So why am I nervous? he thought. It's just an envelope.

He glanced back down at the cost-projection figures but found himself compelled to glance again at the envelope. Couldn't turn his eyes away.

Well, maybe if I didn't open it at all. Maybe if I threw it in the trash.

No, Marge might find it there and open it.

Then I could take it with me when I left the office and get rid of it on the way home. And anyway, so what if Marge saw what was in it? What difference would that make?

Because it's marked PERSONAL!, and after what you found at the bottom of your swimming pool, you'd better pay attention when your psychic alarm bells start going off. You might not want to open it, but you'd damned well better.

Even so, he sat motionless, staring at the envelope.

At last, he exhaled and inched his fingers across the desk. The envelope felt heavy, dense. He started to tear open its flap and froze, tasting something sour.

This might be a letter bomb, he thought. His impulse was to drop it back on the desk and hurry from the office, but he hesitated, compelled by a stronger impulse to pinch it gently and trace a finger along its edges. The contents felt solid—no give in the middle where cardboard might cover a hollow filled with explosives. Cautiously, he tore open the flap and peered inside.

At a thick stack of photographs. He stared at the image on top. It was black-and-white, a reproduction of what evidently had been a picture taken years ago.

The horror of it made him gasp. Filled with disgust, he leafed through the stack, finding other horrors, each more revolting than the one before, obscenity heaped upon obscenity. His lungs didn't want to draw in air.

Corpses. The top photograph—and the countless

others beneath it—showed corpses, stacks and stacks of corpses, thrown together on top of each other, arms and legs protruding in grotesque angles, rib cages clearly outlined beneath starved flesh. Gaunt cheeks, sunken eyes, some of which were open, accusing even in death. Scalps shaved bare. Lips drawn inward over toothless gums. Features contorted with permanent grimaces of fright and pain. Old men. Women. Children.

So many. He almost screamed.

8

"It's true! You have to believe me! I don't know!" Medici insisted. "Please!"

Again Seth slapped him across the mouth. The slap, though it produced less pain than a punch, resulted in paradoxically greater terror, as if assaulting Medici's dignity was the key to breaking him.

"The priest!" Seth demanded. "Cardinal Pavelic! I'm losing my patience! Who abducted the priest?"

"If I knew, I'd tell you!"

This time Seth used the back of his hand, slapping Medici's head to the side, leaving angry red welts on Medici's cheek. Seth's own cheeks were as red as his hair, his usually nonexpressive eyes bright with what might have been pleasure.

Icicle stood in a corner of the kitchen in the isolated farmhouse they'd rented, watching with interest.

His interest had two causes: Seth's interrogation technique and Medici's response to it. Seth had tied Medici to a chair, bound the prisoner's wrists behind the back of the chair, and looped a noose around the prisoner's neck, the tail of the noose attached to the rope that bound his wrists. Every time Medici's head jerked from a slap, the noose tugged into his throat and the resultant pressure yanked Medici's wrists up toward his shoulder blades.

Ingenious, Icicle decided. A minimum force produces a maximum effect. The prisoner realizes he's inflicting most of the agony upon himself. He struggles to resist the impact of the slap, but the way he's been tied, he *can't* resist. His body becomes his enemy. His self-confidence, his *dignity*, becomes offended. You'll crack any time now, Medici, he decided. The tears streaming down Medici's face confirmed his conclusion.

"One more time," Seth demanded. "Who abducted the cardinal?"

Medici squinted, calculating his answer. Pain had unclouded his mind. He understood his situation now. None of his men realized where he was. No one was going to rescue him. Pain wasn't his problem so much as how to survive. "Listen first. *Why don't you listen before you slap me again?*"

Seth shrugged. "The problem is, I need something to listen to."

Medici tried to swallow, but the tight noose constricted his throat. "I'm just a middleman. Clients come to me. They want weapons, information, surveillance teams, safe houses. I supply these services. They don't tell me *why* they want these services. I don't ask."

Seth turned to Icicle, pretending a yawn. "I ask him about the cardinal, he gives me the story of his life."

"You're not letting me explain!" Medici said.

"I will when you *say* something!"

Medici hurried on. "My clients don't tell me their plans, but I do keep my ears to the ground."

"Now he gives me grotesque images," Seth told Icicle.

"I have to keep up with the ins and outs of the profession, don't I? To keep on top of things?"

"He has a problem with prepositions," Seth told Icicle.

"But I haven't heard any rumors, *not a whisper*, about terrorists going after the cardinal. Believe me, I would have heard." Medici squirmed, causing the noose to bind his neck tighter. He made a gagging sound. "Whoever took the cardinal, they weren't radicals, they weren't . . ."

"Terrorists. Scum," Seth said. "Your clients have no style. They're indiscriminate and clumsy. Bombs on buses." Seth pursed his lips in disgust. "Dismembered children."

For an instant, Icicle wondered if Seth had dimensions of character he hadn't recognized. But then he realized that Seth's objections were aesthetic, not moral. If Seth were paid enough, and if the plan required children to be killed as a distraction from the central purpose of executing a diplomat, this man would do it.

On the other hand, Icicle thought and firmly believed, I'd never agree to killing children. Not under any circumstances. *Never*.

Medici continued. "Terrorists might attack the Church as an institution they believed was corrupt, abduct a cardinal whose politics disagreed with their own. They went after the Pope a few years ago, didn't they? But what I'm telling you is I haven't heard about anyone going after the cardinal. I don't believe you're on the right trail."

"In that case," Seth said and spread his hands magnanimously, "as one professional to another"—his words implied respect, but his tone was mocking—"what course do you suggest we follow?"

Medici's eyes became furtive. "Have you thought about the Church itself? Someone *in* the Church?"

Seth turned to Icicle.

"A possibility." Icicle shrugged.

"I'm not convinced," Seth said.

"That the cardinal might be a victim of the Church?"

"That this predator is telling the truth."

"I *am*!" Medici insisted.

"We'll soon find out." Seth turned to Icicle. "We'll do it your way now."

"Thanks for the belated confidence."

"It's a matter of using every method. Force by itself can lead to convincing lies. Chemicals can elicit programmed responses. But the two together make up for each other's liabilities."

"In that case, I'll fill a hypodermic with Sodium Amytal. Stand back. As you say, it's *my* turn now."

9

With the noose removed from his neck but his body still tied to the chair, Medici slumped, semiconscious. In theory, the Sodium Amytal had eliminated his mental censors, making it possible to elicit information that Medici otherwise, even in pain, might not reveal. The trick was not to inject so much Amytal that Medici's responses became incoherent or that he sank fully into unconsciousness.

Now it was Icicle's turn to stand before the prisoner. Holding the almost empty hypodermic in one hand, he asked the key question that had brought him from Australia to Canada and finally to Italy. "Does the expression Night and Fog mean anything to you?"

Medici responded slowly. His tongue seemed stuck in his mouth. "Yes . . . from the war."

"That's right. The Second World War. The Nazis used it as a terrorist tactic. Anyone disloyal to the Third Reich risked vanishing without a trace, disappearing into the Night and Fog." Icicle spoke slowly, distinctly, letting the words sink in. "Has the Night and Fog come back? Have you heard rumors about its being reactivated?"

Medici shook his head. "No rumors. No Night and Fog."

"Try to remember. Did terrorists or a group pretending to be terrorists approach you? Did anyone ask for information about Cardinal Pavelic? Did anyone hire you to put surveillance on the cardinal?"

"No surveillance on the cardinal," Medici whispered. "No one asked me about him."

"Who do you think abducted the cardinal?"

"Don't know."

"*Why* would he have been abducted?"

"Don't know."

"Could someone within the Church be responsible?"

"Don't know."

Seth stepped forward. "That last answer's interesting. He doesn't know whether someone in the Church was responsible."

Icicle understood what Seth meant. Forty minutes ago, Medici had insisted that they direct their attention toward the Church. "Before, he was grasping for any way he could imagine to distract us. He doesn't know anything."

"But the more I think about it, his suggestion is worth exploring."

"The Church? Why not? We have to eliminate the possibilities. It's conceivable that someone within the Church discovered what the cardinal knew and passed it on to the Night and Fog."

"Or that someone in the Church *is* the Night and Fog."

"Pavelic." Icicle's voice was fraught with hate. "For forty years, the bastard kept his hooks in our fathers. The records he kept. God knows how much money he demanded in exchange for keeping those records a secret. Pavelic was the only outsider who had the information that linked all our fathers. The Night and Fog couldn't have organized its terror against them without knowing what was in the cardinal's files."

"Logical," Seth said, "but not necessarily the case. There could be an explanation we've overlooked."

"Such as?"

"That's the problem. We don't know enough," Seth said. "But this man doesn't either. I suggest we investigate the cardinal's private life."

"'Private'?" Icicle laughed. "I didn't know priests were allowed to have 'private' lives." He hesitated. "And what about . . . ?" He gestured toward Medici.

"Kill him, of course. He's useless to us, even a danger. Another injection of Amytal should be sufficient. Painless." Seth raised his shoulders. "Perhaps even pleasureful."

184

"That still leaves the man and the woman in the alley across from where we grabbed him. You noticed them as I did. They weren't hiding there by coincidence. They had the same interest in Medici that *we* did."

"If we see them again, we'll kill them." The blaze in Seth's eyes suggested that too would be a pleasure.

NIGHTMARES THEN AND NOW

1

As the mountain road curved higher, the rented Volkswagen's engine began to sputter. The car refused to gain speed to compensate for the incline. A half-kilometer later, Saul smelled gasoline and veered toward an observation point at a bend in the road. He shut the ignition off.

Beside him, Erika squirmed and wakened. When she peered toward the valley below them, the bright morning sun made her squint. The sky was turquoise, the farm fields emerald. Yawning, she glanced at her watch. "Ten forty-six?" Concern made her fully alert. "You've been driving since dawn. You must be exhausted. I'll change places with you."

"I can manage. We've only got fifteen kilometers to go."

"Fifteen kilometers? If that's all, why did you stop?"

"We almost had a fire."

Her nostrils widened. "I smell it now. Gasoline."

"I think it's the carburetor." He opened the driver's door, approached the front of the car, and lifted the hood. A film of liquid covered the engine. Vapor rose. Erika appeared beside him and studied the engine.

"Hand me your pocketknife," she said.

She opened its blade and adjusted a screw on the carburetor's stem. Saul knew what she was doing. The car,

186

which they'd rented in Vienna, must have been tuned for lowland city driving. Now after struggling against the thin air of the mountains, the carburetor hadn't been able to mix sufficient oxygen with gasoline to allow the fuel to be detonated by the spark plugs. The engine had flooded. The excess fuel had backed up into the carburetor, which had overflowed. The simple adjustment to the carburetor would remedy the problem.

"Another five minutes, and we'd have been walking," Saul said.

"Running's more like it." She laughed self-critically. "Before the gas tank blew up. We've been living in the desert too long. We forgot the problems altitude can cause." Her long dark hair glinted in the morning sun. Her beige jacket emphasized the deep brown of her eyes.

Saul had never loved her more. "I hope that's all we forgot. I'd hate to think we've just been lucky so far, and now, out of practice for years, we're making mistakes."

"Keep thinking that way. It'll stop us from being overconfident."

"That's one thing I'm not."

Eager to get moving, they subdued their frustration and waited for the gasoline to evaporate from the engine. The surrounding slopes, above and below, were lush with evergreens. The thin air of six thousand feet made breathing difficult. Snow-capped mountains towered in the distance. Under other circumstances, these dramatic conditions—the Swiss Alps, south of Zurich—would have been mesmerizing.

Saul shut the car's hood. "It's probably safe to drive now. According to the map, the road'll take us down to the neighboring valley. But Misha investigated the names on the list he made. His agents must have already been where we're going. If they'd learned anything important, we'd have been told about it. Let's be prepared for disappointment."

"We have to start *somewhere*."

Saul's voice thickened. "Right. And if the answer isn't here, it's somewhere else. . . . We'll keep searching till we finish this."

2

The village was Weissendorf: a cluster of perhaps a hundred buildings perched upon a small plateau with a gently sloping pasture above and below. A road ran through it. The buildings were narrow, often four stories tall, the upper levels projecting an arm's-length out from the bottom one so that they seemed like awnings designed to keep pedestrians dry when it rained. With their peaked roofs that curved slightly up at the eaves, the buildings reminded Saul of fir trees. At the same time, elaborately carved designs on railings, windowsills, and doors reminded him of gingerbread houses.

He parked the Volkswagen outside an inn. An oversized ale tankard with a handle and hinged lid hung above the entrance. He turned to Erika. "Which one of us should ask directions to where Ephraim Avidan lives?"

She realized the problem. Switzerland had no language of its own. Its citizens spoke the language of the nearest bordering country. "Your German's better than mine," she said. "But this is *southern* Switzerland. Our French is about the same, but my Italian's—"

"Better. Besides—excuse a sexist remark—they might be more receptive to a female stranger. You want to give it a try?"

With a grin that didn't disguise her troubled mood, she opened the passenger door and entered the inn.

Saul waited uneasily. Before promising his former network that he wouldn't accept help from any intelligence agency, he'd already received a great deal of help from Misha Pletz and the Mossad. He didn't think he could be accused of reneging on his agreement if he took advantage of that prepromise help. For one thing, Misha had supplied them with Israeli passports using cover names and fictitious backgrounds that, if questioned by the authorities, would be endorsed by Israeli civilians and businesses secretly affiliated with the Mossad. For another, Misha had given them sufficient money to conduct their search. He'd also provided them with weapons, though Saul and Erika had hidden these before leaving Austria, not wanting to risk crossing the border with them.

But at the moment, the most important of Misha's contributions was a photocopy of his notebook—the list of names he'd made and the information about them. The first name on the list was Ephraim Avidan.

"What do the names on the list have to do with what happened to my father?" Erika had asked.

"I have no idea," Misha had answered.

"I don't believe that. You wouldn't have made the list if there isn't a connection among them."

"Did I say there isn't a connection? We know their backgrounds, their addresses, their habits, their former occupations."

"Former?"

"These men are all ex-Mossad, all retired. But you asked how they related to what happened to your father, and that puzzle I haven't been able to solve yet."

"They claim they don't know my father? They won't answer your questions? What's the problem?"

"I haven't been able to ask them anything."

"You're doing it again. Evading."

"I'm not. These men share two other factors. They survived the Nazi death camps . . ."

"And?"

"They've all disappeared."

As Erika's father had disappeared.

The inn door swung open. Saul couldn't interpret the expression on Erika's face when she got in the car.

"Anything?" he asked.

"They didn't exactly gush with information. I gather we're not the only strangers who've asked about Avidan, and these people don't take well to strangers, male *or* female, who aren't here just to spend money as tourists."

Saul thought about it. "Whoever came before us must have belonged to Misha."

"Maybe. Let's find out. I managed to get directions."

Saul started the car and drove along the narrow street. "Tell me when to turn."

"It's outside town. The third farmhouse on the left."

He increased speed.

The house was old, with white stucco walls, on a level section of the upper grassy slope. Though wider than the buildings in town, it did have a high peaked roof, its silhouette conforming with a mountain beyond it. Saul turned and drove up a rutted dirt lane, hearing cowbells from the pasture as he stopped outside the house. The sun made the valley even more brilliant. He didn't pay attention to the scenery, his thoughts completely preoccupied with the list they'd discovered.

And the first name on the list.

They stepped from the car.

A woman with handsome, almost mannish features came out of the house. She was in her early thirties, with short sunbleached hair and ruddy cheeks. Muscular, she wore sturdy ankle-high shoes, woolen kneesocks, leather shorts, and a blue-checked shirt with its sleeves rolled up. Her shoes thunked on a wooden porch, then on stairs leading down to the car. When she stopped, her eyes flashed with suspicion.

Saul took for granted that Erika would do most of the talking, just as he would have if this had been a man. Erika used Italian. "We're sorry to bother you, but we're told that Ephraim Avidan used to live here."

The woman spoke in English. "Your accent. American?"

Erika replied in kind. "No, I'm Israeli, but I lived in the United States for many years. In fact, I'm more comfortable with English than I am with my native language. Would you prefer...?"

"To speak in English?" The woman shook her head and switched to Italian. "I could use the practice, but not when discussing Ephraim Avidan. He used to live here, but he's gone." She seemed sullen. "Are you with the others who came to ask about him?"

"Others?"

"Two men. Five days ago. They claimed to be old friends of Avidan. But they were thirty years younger. Like Avidan and yourself, they said they were Israeli.

They claimed they owed Avidan money. Such conscientious debtors, don't you think? They wanted to know where he'd gone."

"And what did you tell them?"

"The same thing I tell you. I don't know where. He left abruptly. In February. One evening he was here, the next morning he wasn't. As far as I could tell, he took nothing with him. After several days, I notified our policeman in town. A search was organized, but we didn't find a body." She gestured toward the mountains. "We didn't expect to. No one goes hiking in the woods at night during winter. Suicide was a possibility. He'd been moody. But without a body...Our policeman notified the authorities in Bern. The matter passed out of our hands. But we treated him fairly, the same as if he'd been one of us. And he treated *me* fairly. Before he disappeared, he paid his rent. I never had trouble with him."

"Of course."

The woman tightened her arms across her chest. "And what about yourselves? Are you also 'old' friends who owe him money?" She directed her question toward Saul.

"We didn't know him at all."

The woman smiled, apparently not having expected a candid response.

Saul nodded toward Erika. "My wife's father was a friend of Ephraim Avidan, though." He paused for effect. "And her father has also disappeared."

The woman seemed caught between surprise and skepticism. "On the other hand, your explanation might merely be more inventive than that of old friends owing money to someone."

"Why are you so suspicious?" Erika asked. "All we want is information."

"Suspicious? If your husband had left you...If you had the responsibility of managing..." Her voice trailed off. She stared toward swollen-uddered cattle in the pasture. "I probably wouldn't be suspicious if not for the priest."

191

Saul's pulse quickened. "Priest?"

"Not that he said he was a priest. He was rugged, handsome. A hiker, so he claimed. He arrived two weeks before the Israelis did. He had blue eyes and straw-colored hair. He chopped wood for his supper. He was muscular. His chest was strong. But what I noticed most were his hands."

"What about them?"

"He took extreme care of them. I didn't think it unusual when he wore gloves to chop wood. A precaution against slivers and blisters. But later, after he'd taken off the gloves and washed his hands, when I ate supper with him, I couldn't help noticing how soft and smooth his hands were in comparison with his muscles. He was tanned, but on his left hand... here at the base of his middle finger... he had a white rim of skin where he'd recently taken off a ring. I still don't understand why he'd have done that. Who knows? Perhaps he'd merely lost it. But his right hand... here... the thumb, the first and second fingers... those he was especially self-conscious about. He didn't want food to touch those fingers, and later, when he helped me wash dishes, he kept a towel around his right hand, using his left to pick up the plates. Do you see the significance?"

"I'm sorry," Erika said. "I'm afraid I don't."

"As an Israeli, you wouldn't, I suppose. I myself am a Lutheran, but I know that for a Roman Catholic priest the thumb, first, and second fingers of his right hand are the most important parts of his body. They're blessed. They're what he uses to hold the wafer of bread that he consecrates and changes into what Catholics believe is the spiritual presence of Jesus Christ. If a priest's right thumb and first two fingers were amputated, he couldn't be a priest any longer, not totally. He couldn't say mass. He couldn't perform the ritual of consecrating the host and giving out Communion. And because those fingers have been blessed, he has to protect them not only from physical harm but also from indignities."

Erika was puzzled. "But couldn't he merely have been left-handed, and that's why he seemed to favor his right?"

"After supper, he put his gloves back on and offered to go to the barn, to do a few more chores. I needed help, so I promised him breakfast and agreed." She pointed toward the barn, a corner of which projected from behind the house. "He worked longer than I expected. When I went in to see if anything was wrong, I caught him by surprise. He shoved a small black book into his knapsack. Then I knew for certain."

"I don't follow you," Erika said.

But Saul did. He remembered what his foster brother, Chris, an Irish-Catholic, had taught him about the Church. "The small black book was probably a breviary," he explained. "The collection of prayers a priest has to read every day." He faced the woman. "But you said you knew 'for certain.' Forgive me, it still seems like supposition."

"No," the woman said. "In the night, I went to his room in the barn and searched through his knapsack. The small black book *was* a breviary."

"Searched through his . . . ?"

"You think I was bold? How could he rebuke me when he was as bold as I was, when he'd snuck from his room and gone up the hill to search *Avidan's* room?" Her face flushed with indignation. "I'd left the cabin as Avidan had left it. There was always the chance Avidan would return, and since no one else had asked to rent it, I didn't care to waste my time by moving his possessions. Where would I have put them anyhow? When I crept up the hill, I heard the priest in the cabin. I heard drawers being opened and shut. I saw the waver of a flashlight beam through cracks in the window shades."

"What did you do about it?"

"What would you expect? A woman alone? An apparently innocent guest who turns out to be a prowler? I returned to the house and did nothing. In the morning, I pretended not to know he'd gone to Avidan's cabin, and he—if he'd guessed I'd searched his knapsack—pretended not to have noticed. He ate the breakfast I prepared, asked if there were other chores he could do, and, when I declined, continued the hiking vacation he claimed to be on. For the next few nights, I kept a close

193

watch on the cabin. So far as I know, the priest never came back."

"And what would be the significance of the ring he took off?" Erika asked.

"It could have been the insignia of his order," Saul said. "A few religious groups wear them."

"I didn't find a ring in his knapsack," the woman said.

"Maybe he considered it so valuable he kept it in a pocket."

"Perhaps. Then, two weeks later, the Israeli pair arrived. They asked if they could see Avidan's cabin in case something in it might tell them where he'd gone—you understand, so they could repay the fabulous debt they said they owed him."

"Did you let them?"

"Yes. I had the sense that, if I refused, they'd return in the night and search it anyhow. Or search the cabin right then, despite my objections. I didn't want trouble. I hoped that, if I agreed, I'd see the end of it. Besides, what did I have to hide?"

"Or what did Avidan have to hide?" Saul said.

"Now *you* arrive, and you ask why I'm suspicious. Who *was* this Avidan? Why are you and those others interested in him?"

"I can't speak for the priest," Saul said. "He's as puzzling to me as he is to you. But the two Israelis were probably intelligence operatives. Mossad. Avidan used to belong to their organization. When one of them—even one who's retired from them—disappears, they want to know why, especially if his disappearance seems linked to the disappearance of yet another ex-Mossad operative. My wife's father."

The woman inhaled sharply. "Politics? I don't want anything to do with politics."

"We're not sure it's politics. It could be a personal matter from years ago. Honestly, we don't know. For us, it's definitely personal, though."

"Are *you* Mossad?"

Erika hesitated. "I used to be."

"Politics."

"I said I *used* to be. Look, please, we've told you a lot more than we should have. How can we make you trust us?"

"How? Tell me a way to keep strangers from coming around here asking about Avidan."

"If you help us, maybe we'll be able to find out what happened to him. Then the strangers will stop coming around."

The woman studied them.

"May we see Avidan's cabin?" Saul asked.

The woman remained motionless. Saul held his breath.

The woman nodded.

3

The cabin was past the house and the barn, up the continuation of the sloping pasture. Behind it, dense forest rose to rocky bluffs. The Alpine air smelled pure and sweet, tinged with the fragrance of evergreens.

The cabin was small, single-story, made from logs whose bark had long ago disintegrated. A rusty stovepipe projected from a roof that needed reshingling. Saul turned to survey the view: the lush lower part of the valley, a far-off small lake, the towers of the town, partly obscured by intervening fir trees, a kilometer to his right.

Why would Avidan choose such primitive, secluded lodgings? Saul wondered.

"How long did Avidan live here?" he asked the woman.

"He came last fall. In October."

"He planned to spend all winter here?"

"He said he was a writer. He needed solitude and privacy to finish a novel."

A retired Mossad operative a novelist? Saul thought. It was possible. Anything was possible. But probable? Once the winter storms started blowing . . . Solitude and privacy? Avidan had certainly gone to an extreme for those conditions. What had made him choose this place?

They entered the cabin. It was divided into a bedroom and a kitchen. In the absence of a fireplace, a large black woodburning stove served for heating the cabin as well as preparing food. The rooms were spartan. Plain pine boards covered the walls. A slab of wood on trestles was the kitchen table, a bench beside it. There were austere cupboards, a rocking chair, another bench along one wall. The bed was a top-and-bottom bunk, its mattresses packed with straw. A cracked mirror hung above a battered bureau, the drawers of which were lined with yellowed newspapers from 1975. The drawers contained a few items of clothing. Books, mostly histories related to Israel, filled a shelf beside the bureau. Photographs of Israel's desert, along with images of crowded downtown Tel Aviv, were tacked here and there on the walls. In the kitchen, Erika found plastic cups and plates in a cupboard, along with cans of food. Dish detergent was in a compartment beneath the sink.

A man could go crazy spending a winter up here, Saul thought.

He turned to the woman. "You said you didn't remove Avidan's possessions because you thought he might come back. It doesn't look like he had all that much to pack up."

"And if he was working on a novel," Erika said, "he must have taken it with him. I don't see a typewriter. I can't find a manuscript."

The woman stood silhouetted by sunlight at the open doorway. "From October to February, I almost never saw him. From my house, sometimes I couldn't see the cabin for the gusting snow. Sometimes I thought the snow would *smother* the cabin. But on clear days, as long as I saw smoke from the stovepipe, I didn't worry. And the first of every month, he waded down through drifts to pay his rent."

Saul remembered that the woman had said she'd been deserted by her husband. Avidan's monthly rent must have been sufficient comfort for her to ignore her tenant's eccentricities.

"Something was wrong," the woman said. "I knew that. And when he disappeared, in case the police reopened the investigation, I was determined not to touch *anything*."

"But so far as you know, you don't think the priest and the two Israeli men learned anything from their search," Saul said. "We could sort through the pages of these books. We could sift through the packages of food. We could test for loose floorboards. My guess is we'd be wasting our time. Avidan was a professional."

"The priest and the two Israeli men assumed they could take advantage of me, trick me, dominate me," the woman said angrily. "They never offered money."

Saul's skin tingled. "But if *we* offered money...?"

"It's difficult to manage this farm alone."

"Of course," Erika said. "We want to help you. Our resources are limited. We recently had to leave our home in Israel. But we're willing to make a contribution."

The woman moved her head from side to side, calculating, and named an amount. It was high, almost half of what Misha Pletz had given to Saul and Erika. But it was insignificant if the woman's information was as important as her rigid features suggested.

"Done," Saul said. "Provided you don't merely show us an out-of-date address book or..."

"A diary," the woman said. "The dates are from October of last year until he disappeared. It's about this cabin. It's about *him*. There are photographs. They made me sick."

Saul's chest contracted.

Erika stepped forward. "How did you get them?"

"I found where they were hidden."

"Yes, but *how*?"

"After the priest searched this cabin, I wondered what he was looking for. When I felt he was really gone, I came up here and searched as well. I tested the floor. The walls. The ceiling. I even budged the stove and pried up the firebricks beneath it."

"And?"

"I found nothing. But the priest wasn't thorough," the woman said. "He didn't identify with Avidan's routine.

197

He didn't put himself in Avidan's mind. There's another building."

Saul knew. "The outhouse."

"I found the diary and the photographs attached beneath the platform of the hole above the pit. Each day when he came and went along the path he dug through the snow, he must have taken them with him, possibly even concealed them beneath his clothes."

"And they're worth the sum you asked?"

"The worth is your concern. The sum you know."

Erika reached into a pocket. "The money's Austrian."

"It could be Japanese for all I care. This is Switzerland. Every currency is welcome here." The woman counted the bills.

"Where's what we paid for?"

"Come down to the house."

4

They sat at a table in a rustic kitchen. As the woman made coffee, Saul opened the plastic-wrapped packet she'd given them. He winced when he saw the photographs. Erika's hands shook sorting through them.

Nazi concentration camps. SS soldiers aiming submachine guns at refugees being shoved from trucks and railway cattle cars. Gaunt-faced prisoners staring with haunted eyes through barbed-wire fences. Endless trenches, quicklime-covered corpses, bulldozers poised to fill in dirt. Gas chambers, naked people—mostly children, old men and women—so squeezed together they'd died standing up. Open doors of massive ovens. Unimaginable quantities of ashes and bones.

Saul studied them all, every obscene one, and when he'd finished, he'd learned what he already knew—that the human ability to invent new methods of brutality was boundless.

He stacked the photographs and turned them facedown on the table. "The examined life isn't worth living," he said, his voice trailing off. He stared at the diary. "God knows what else is in . . ."

"The night I looked through that packet, no matter how many logs I put on the fire, I was still cold," the woman said. "I paced until dawn. I knew about such atrocities, but to see them, to read about them . . ."

"Read about . . . ?" Erika looked at the diary, reached for it, hesitated, and drew her hands back as if from vomit.

"Yes, the diary," the woman said. "Avidan, his parents, his sister, and two brothers lived in Munich. In 1942, when the Holocaust was set into motion, the SS arrested them and trucked them to the concentration camp at Dachau. It was only twenty kilometers away from their home. A work camp, not a death camp, though the way he describes it, there wasn't much difference. With the other prisoners, he and his family were used as slave labor at an ammunition factory. They received a minimum of food. They were given little time to rest or sleep. Sanitary facilities were inadequate. Toilets were nothing more than open trenches. Drinking water was contaminated. Their barracks leaked. There were rats. For two years, Avidan and his family slaved for Hitler's war. And one by one, they died. Avidan's mother went first—she collapsed in the factory and died from exhaustion. When Avidan's father couldn't get off the barracks' floor one morning, the SS dragged him outside and shot him in front of the other prisoners. His corpse was left in the assembly area for three days before prisoners were ordered to put the body on a cart and push it to a burial pit outside the camp. Next, Avidan's ten-year-old sister coughed herself to death. His older brother didn't move fast enough to suit a guard and had his head split open with a club. His remaining brother went insane and gashed his wrists with a splinter of wood. Avidan himself became determined to survive. In small unnoticeable ways, he rested while he worked, conserving his strength. He devoured spiders, flies, worms, anything he could find in camp. And he *succeeded*. In 1944, in September, he was part of a work force trucked from the camp to pick up liquor and food from town for an SS party that night. The truck blew a tire. In the confusion, prisoners fled. The SS soldiers recovered quickly and shot three of the four escaping prisoners. The fourth was Avidan. The thrill of freedom was so overwhelming he pushed himself to limits he didn't know he had. He stole food from storage bins. He slept in haystacks. He kept moving. Dachau is a hundred kilometers from Switzerland. In his diary, he doesn't say how he passed the Bodensee, but he arrived at neutral territory, and still he kept going, still not sure he'd reached sanctuary, till he finally came to rest here. My former husband and I bought this farm in 1978. I have no idea who owned it during the war. But whoever lived here found Avidan cowering in the barn one night. They understood his circumstance, took pity, and let him stay in the cabin. They supplied him with food. He remained from October of 'forty-four till the end of the war the following May, when he went to Palestine."

The woman stopped. The room became eerily silent. Saul had listened so raptly that it took a moment before a reference at the end of her words tugged at his memory.

"He reached the cabin in October of 'forty-four?" Heat rushed into Saul's stomach. "But didn't you say he came back last year . . . ?"

"In October," the woman said. "Given what he wrote in his diary, about his ordeal in the war, I doubt the parallel of the months was coincidental. The past was on his mind. Something must have driven him to return. His diary's so vivid it's as if he did more than recall his terrors—he *relived* them."

"To be that obsessed . . ." Erika shuddered.

"As obsessed as your father was," Saul said. In the presence of their hostess, he didn't mention the photographs in the basement of the Vienna apartment building.

"But you said that in 1945 Avidan left here in May, at the end of the war," Erika said. "*This* year, though, he left in February. The pattern isn't exact."

"Unless he intended to leave in May," the woman

said, "and something forced him to leave early, just as something had forced him to come back here. He left without warning. He took almost nothing with him. His decision must have been abrupt."

"Or someone abruptly made the decision for him," Erika said, "just as I suspect someone did for my father."

· "Abducted him?" the woman asked.

"It's possible." Erika exhaled. "We still don't know enough."

Through open windows, Saul heard the drone of a car coming along the road. The drone became louder. All at once it stopped.

His shoulder blades contracted. He left the kitchen and, careful to stand to the side of the big front window, peered out past the porch. A black Renault stood in the open gate of the rutted lane that led from the road toward the house. He saw the silhouettes of three men inside.

Erika came into the living room. "What's the matter?" The woman followed her.

Saul turned to the woman. "Do you recognize that car?"

The woman stepped toward the window.

"Don't show yourself," Saul warned.

The woman obeyed, moving to the side of the window as Saul had. "I've never seen it before."

The three men got out of the car. They were tall and well-built, in their mid-thirties. Each wore thick-soled casual shoes, dark slacks, and a zipped-up windbreaker. The jackets were slightly too large.

In June? Saul thought. On a warm day like this? Why zipped-up windbreakers?

As the men walked up the lane, each pulled down the zipper on his jacket.

Saul felt Erika close behind him.

"They could have driven all the way up to the house," she said.

"But instead they blocked the gate. Until they move their car, we can't drive out."

201

The men walked abreast of each other. Though their expressions were blank, their eyes kept shifting, scanning the Volkswagen, the house, the pasture on either side, the woods and mountains beyond. Each had his left hand raised toward his belt. They were halfway up the lane now, close enough for Saul to notice the bright red ring each wore on the middle finger of his raised left hand.

He spun toward the woman. "Have you got a gun in the house?"

The woman stepped back, repelled by the force of his question. But her voice was steady. "Of course. This is Switzerland."

She didn't need to explain. Switzerland, though a neutral country, believed in military preparedness. Every male from the age of twenty to fifty was obligated to undergo military training. Every family had to keep a weapon in the house.

"Get it. Quickly," Saul said. "Make sure it's loaded. We have to leave here *now*."

"But why would . . . ?"

"Now!"

Eyes widening, the woman rushed to a closet, removing a Swiss-made *Sturmgewehr*, or storm rifle. Saul knew it well. The length of a carbine, it was chambered for NATO's 7.62-mm caliber bullets. It had a fold-down tripod beneath the barrel and a rubber-coated stock that helped to lessen the force of the recoil.

The woman groped for two magazines on the shelf above her. Erika took them, checking to make sure they were full to their twenty-round capacity. She inserted one into the rifle, switched off the safety, set the weapon for semiautomatic firing, and pulled back the arming bolt to chamber a round. She shoved the remaining magazine under her belt.

The woman blinked in dismay. "Those men surely wouldn't . . ."

"We don't have time to talk about it! Get out of here!" Saul lunged for the diary and the photographs on the kitchen table and crammed them into their cardboard packet. With the rifle in one hand, Erika yanked open the rear door to the kitchen. Saul grabbed the woman's arm, tugging her with him, and charged out after Erika.

They raced across a small grassy area, through the barn, and up the slope toward Avidan's cabin.

Saul heard a shout behind him. Legs pounding, he pressed the cardboard packet against his chest and risked stumbling to glance backward. Two of the men darted around the left side of the barn while the other man appeared at the right, pointing upward. The third man yelled in French. *"Ici!"*

Each pulled a pistol from beneath his windbreaker.

"Erika!" Saul shouted.

She looked back, saw the three men aiming, and spun. In a fluid motion, she dropped to one knee, propped an elbow on her upraised other knee, and sighted along the rifle. Before the three men could fire, she pulled the trigger, then shot again. And again. The range was fifty meters. She was a skilled sharpshooter, but with no time to steady her muscles, the barrel wavered. She grazed one man's shoulder, the other bullets slamming against the barn.

The injured man grabbed his arm and darted back behind the barn. His companions ducked out of sight inside it. If she hadn't killed them, at least she'd distracted them, and she rose, sprinting after Saul and the woman, who'd already reached the top of the slope. A bullet tore splinters off a log on Avidan's cabin as she took cover behind the building.

Saul and the woman waited for her, breathing deeply. Erika took a chance and showed herself to shoot twice more down the slope at the men scrambling after them.

The men sprawled flat.

"You know these woods," Saul told the woman. "Take us into the mountains."

"But where will we ...?"

"Hurry. *Move.*"

5

The woman squeezed through a line of bushes and came to a narrow path that veered up a wooded slope, her muscular bare legs taking long forceful strides toward the summit. Saul and Erika followed, struggling to adjust to the unaccustomed altitude. At the top, the path changed direction, angling to the left, then descending between two chest-high boulders. Dense trees shut out the sun. Saul sensed their pine resin fragrance, their fallen needles soft beneath the impact of his shoes, but what occupied his attention was the crack of branches behind him, the muffled echo of angry voices.

The woman led them down the path to a shallow stream. Saul splashed across it, ignoring the cold wetness of his pants clinging to his legs, and forced himself into the shadowy continuation of the forest. He heard Erika's feet plunge through the stream behind him.

The woman led them up another slope, but this slope was steeper, the trail almost indiscernible. Saul zigzagged past deadfalls, thickets, and clumps of boulders. Finally at the top, his lungs on fire, he pivoted to stare past Erika down toward the hollow. The men weren't in sight, but he could hear footsteps splashing through the stream.

The woman had brought them to a grassy plateau. A hundred meters away, another stretch of dense forest angled up, it seemed forever. They raced ahead. High grass tugged at Saul's shoes. His back itched as he imagined the three men suddenly appearing at the top of the slope behind him, but no bullet punched through his spine. He threw himself to the ground behind bushes at the opposite edge of the clearing. Erika dropped beside him, aiming the rifle. The woman rushed farther, stopped when she realized her protectors weren't racing to follow, then sank to her knees behind a tree.

In contrast with her obvious terror, Saul felt almost joyous. We made it! he thought. We crossed before they saw us! They didn't catch us in the open! Now it's our turn!

Beside him, Erika calmed her breathing, pulled down the tripod attached to the rifle's barrel, steadied her aim, and became rock-still.

Not long now, Saul thought. Not long. He wiped sweat from his eyes and concentrated on the opposite edge of the clearing. Any moment, the bushes over there would part. The men would show themselves.

Five seconds became ten. Fifteen. Thirty. After what seemed two minutes, Erika scrambled backward, and Saul knew exactly why. The situation was wrong. The men should have reached the top of the slope by now. *They should have shown themselves.*

He followed Erika, scurrying toward the woman. When the woman opened her mouth to speak, he clamped a hand across her lips and gestured forcibly toward the continuation of the forest. She reacted to the desperation in his eyes and ran, leading them upward through the trees.

He could think of only one reason the men hadn't shown themselves. They'd approached the clearing, sensed the trap, and separated, following the rim of trees on either side, trying to get ahead of their quarry. It was possible they'd already done so.

The crack of a gunshot parallel to Saul, on his left, spurred him faster up the wooded slope. The bullet shredded leaves beside him. He heard it—*felt* it—zip past him.

But was the shot meant to force them toward a sniper waiting at the top of this slope? Or was it intended to make them stop and take cover while the three men encircled them?

Instincts assumed control. Motion—*escape*—was everything. Saul understood why Erika didn't bother returning fire. She didn't have a target, and even if she did, the trees would interfere with her aim. He knew they couldn't even hope that the gunshots would attract help from the village. In Switzerland, mandatory military training required farmers to practice their marksmanship on a regular basis. Gunshots in the Alps were as ordinary as the tinkle of cowbells. No one would pay attention.

The air had cooled. Clouds had covered the sky. Drops of moisture pelted his shirtsleeves. He pressed the cardboard packet of photographs and Avidan's diary harder against his chest, grateful for its plastic wrapping. The rain increased, drenching him. He shivered. Black clouds scudded over the mountains, making him realize how dangerous the weather had become. The strain of racing ever higher in unaccustomed altitude could lead to delirium from oxygen privation. Add to that a cold extended rain, and conditions were perfect for hypothermia, a rapid drain of strength and body heat, death from exposure.

Three hours, Saul thought. That's the maximum time hypothermia takes to kill. That's how long we've got now. His only consolation was to imagine the similar apprehension of his hunters.

Trembling from cold, he reached the top of this farther hill, only to wince when he saw yet another wooded ridge above, obscured by darker clouds and worsening rain. The downpour muffled a shot from his right. The bullet slammed against a tree behind him.

Propelled by fear, the woman raced ahead. Saul had trouble keeping up with her. She guided them through a maze of obstacles. Higher. Steeper. We must be at eight thousand feet by now, Saul thought. The thin air threw him off-balance. No matter how quickly and deeply he breathed, he couldn't satisfy his lungs. His thoughts began to swirl. Movement became automatic, a reflexive struggle. Twice he fell, helped up by Erika. Then Erika fell, and he helped *her* up. His head throbbed. But the woman, as agile as a mountain goat, scrambled ever higher.

He wasn't sure when the trees became less dense, when pine needle–covered ground gave way to more and more rocks and open space, but suddenly his thoughts and vision cleared sufficiently for him to realize that he'd passed the treeline, that only granite and snow-covered peaks rose above him.

We're trapped, he thought. We can't go much higher. We'll faint.

Or freeze to death. The rain, which had chilled him to his core, had changed to snow. Above the timberline, a June blizzard wasn't unusual; experienced mountaineers took that danger into account and carried woolen clothes in their knapsacks. But Saul hadn't expected to be up here; he was dressed for summer conditions. Far below him, in the untouched village, this sudden far-off storm would have been merely picturesque, but up here, it was life-threatening. Already the snow had accumulated on his scalp. His shoulders were covered, his hands numb.

We're going to die up here, he thought. We've gone so far, even if we turned around and tried to get back to the woman's farm, we wouldn't make it there before we fainted from exposure and froze to death. And somewhere along the way we'd be ambushed by our hunters.

The snow obscured the gray of the granite slopes above. But despite the freezing wind, the woman persisted, climbing higher. She's crazy, Saul thought. She's so afraid of those men she'll scramble up till she collapses, and in the meantime, the men'll realize the danger we're heading into. They'll hang back. They'll stay below the treeline, take shelter beneath a deadfall, and stalk us when the storm is over. They'll find us frozen where we fell and simply leave us there. In July, after the snow melts, hikers will come upon us and report another mountain accident.

The thought made Saul angry enough to keep following the woman. The flakes cleared sporadically, allowing him to see that the three of them had reached another plateau, this one completely barren. The woman pushed onward.

But not toward the next even steeper slope, instead toward a wooden door set into a granite wall.

The door had been placed here precisely for conditions such as this—a common Swiss precaution against unexpected storms. The snow gained such volume that he couldn't any longer see the door, let alone the granite slopes beyond it. There wasn't a choice. He and Erika had to follow.

But when the woman opened the door, revealing a murky cave beyond, he balked.

"The door's two inches thick!" the woman insisted. "Bullets can't go through it! Those men will die if they try to wait us out!"

Saul understood her logic. From years of living next to the mountains, she was conditioned to think of this cave as a refuge. But his own years of training rebelled against enclosing himself. A refuge could also be a trap. What if the storm let up? What if the men decided not to linger beneath a deadfall at the treeline and instead followed their tracks through the snow and besieged the cave? What if the men had carried more than pistols beneath their slightly too large windbreakers?

Explosives, for instance.

No! He had to fight the enemy on open ground, free to maneuver. But he couldn't leave Erika unable to defend herself. Tempted to reach for the rifle she carried, he forced his arms to remain by his sides. "I'll be back. If you don't recognize my voice, shoot anyone who tries to open the door."

Snow clung to Erika's face. The falling temperature had blanched her skin. She squeezed his arm. "I love you."

The snow fell harder.

"If I knew another way..." he said. "But there isn't."

She opened her mouth to say something else.

He echoed her "I love you" and, knowing she'd understand, shoved her toward the cave. She acquiesced, darting inside after the woman. Darkness cloaked her. The door slammed shut with a thud that was almost inaudible in the wind.

6

He spun toward the slope below him. With his back turned toward the gusts, he saw more clearly now. Boulders that had been invisible loomed murkily in the storm. Going down, he'd have a slight advantage against his hunters. They'd be blinded by the snow squalling at their eyes, just as he'd been blinded when he came up. Perhaps that advantage would compensate for his lack of a weapon. *They* had the advantage of three against one. The equalizer was the numbing cold.

He didn't dare analyze—he had to act. Snow stung him harder. It covered the ground, preventing him from judging where he could safely place his feet. He knew that a sprained ankle would be disastrous, but he couldn't worry about it. He had to keep scrambling down the slope, to reach cover before his hunters arrived.

He stayed well away from the trail that he, Erika, and the woman had made in the snow. Though the storm was quickly filling in the tracks, they were still apparent enough to provide a direction for his hunters. Of course, the men wouldn't stay in a group. Down in the forest, shots had come from the left and right as the men spread out, trying to outflank their quarry. Obstacles might force them to converge, but wherever possible, they'd keep far away from one another. Saul would have to maintain a considerable distance from the tracks he'd made coming up. His plan was to descend well away from his hunters, get below them, turn, and stalk them from behind, taking them out, widely separated, one at a time.

If he could control his shivering. His shirt and pants were shockingly cold, the wind excruciating. His hands stiffened, his fingers losing sensation. He slipped on a snow-slick slab and tumbled, bumping his arms, his legs, and his back over rocks, jolting to a halt against the trunk of a pine tree at the bottom of the slope. Branches drooped over him, protecting him from the streaking snow. He lay on his back, exhausted, struggling to catch his breath. His vision grew fuzzy. With agonizing effort, he forced his eyes to focus, his body to respond. He sat painfully up, pushing at the pine limbs, about to stand . . .

And halted when he saw motion, a dark figure creeping upward past scattered storm-obscured trees.

The figure—a man, his dark windbreaker and trousers evident now—stopped often, aiming his handgun from side to side before him, then glancing right, toward what must have been another member of his team, though Saul couldn't see the other man. The cold metal of the handgun must be painful in his grip, Saul thought. His fingers might not respond if he tries to shoot.

But with an inward groan, Saul changed his mind. The snowgusts lessened briefly, just long enough for him to see that the man wore gloves. He remembered the woman's description of the hiker-priest. That man's left hand had shown a pale circle on the middle finger where a ring had recently been removed. Saul began to wonder if that ring would have matched the bright red ring he'd seen on the left hand, middle finger, of each of these men as they'd stalked up the lane toward the farmhouse.

He remembered something else the woman had said —that the hiker had shown unusual caution about his hands, wearing gloves whenever possible. Just as *these* men had taken care, even in summer, to carry gloves in their windbreakers. Were these men associated with that hiker? Were they *priests*, just as the woman suspected the hiker had been?

Priests who carried guns? Who stalked him like professionals? Who were obviously prepared to kill? It didn't seem possible! The woman must have been mistaken! What would priests have to do with the disappearance of Erika's father and of Avidan? Religion and violence? They were incompatible.

The wind changed direction, lancing through the pine boughs, stinging his eyes. He shivered, envying his hunters for the jackets and gloves they wore. The repeated impacts of his tumble down the slope had numbed his joints. He felt caked with ice. No time. Don't analyze! Just do!

His hunter crept closer. Saul eased behind the tree trunk. Pressed against the ground, he saw his hunter's shoes and trouser legs pass next to the tree. He imagined the man scanning right and left, then up the slope.

But the shoes paused. They turned as if the man were looking at this tree. Saul clenched his teeth in dread, expecting to see the man peer beneath these boughs and fire.

Instead the shoes shifted forward again, the man proceeding upward. Saul wriggled after him. The gusts increased with such intensity that the man became obscured.

It had to be now! Saul rose to a crouch and lunged. The force of his attack jolted the man to the rocky slope. Saul landed with a knee on his target's spine, grabbed the man's head, and jerked up with all his might. His hunter's spine snapped just before his larynx gave. Despite the shrieking wind, Saul heard the sickening double cracks. His hunter trembled, whistled through his teeth, and suddenly stilled.

In a rush, desperate not to be seen, Saul dragged the body down beneath the cover of the pine boughs. He fumbled to peel off the corpse's leather gloves. His own fingers—swollen and numb—didn't seem to belong to him. Putting the gloves on his hands was even more difficult. He had to cram his fingers beneath his armpits, trying to warm them into flexibility. But his armpits too were achingly cold, and he knew he was close to the danger point. If his temperature dropped any lower, he'd lose consciousness.

For a disorienting instant, he fantasized about the heat of Israel's desert. He reveled beneath an imaginary blazing sun. Abruptly he became aware again of the terrible wind, of the snow-shrouded slope. Appalled by the symptoms of altitude sickness and hypothermia, he compelled himself to strip the corpse of its windbreaker and put it on. The jacket's protection was minimal, but compared to his thin shirt, the added layer was luxurious.

He scurried to the edge of the pine boughs, glanced to his right, toward where the remaining two men would probably be creeping upward, and darted forward, reaching the spot where he'd attacked. He pawed through the snow and gripped the pistol his victim had dropped. But his first finger refused to obey his mind's command, wouldn't squeeze into the trigger guard. He slapped one gloved hand against the other, trying to make them pliant, his efforts useless. From the wrist down, he had no sensation.

He shoved the pistol beneath his belt and retreated down the slope, stopping when he reached a dense line of trees. Using them for cover, he stalked toward his right, toward the other men, trying to get behind them. Soon they'd notice that the man on their left flank was missing. They'd investigate. In his weakened condition, without the advantage of surprise, he'd have little chance of subduing both of them together. He had to confront them singly, before they realized they were being hunted.

Flakes streaked harder. After what he judged was fifty meters, he came to fresh footprints in the snow. They led upward. He followed, emerging from the trees, suddenly unprotected. Above, amid a squall, he saw the back of another dark figure. Mustering strength, he lunged. By now, the gloves had returned some warmth to his hands, making them flexible enough that he could grip the pistol, though his fingers still weren't agile enough to fire it. He slammed its barrel savagely against the crown of the figure's head. The tip gouged deeply into bone. Hot blood pelted his face. The figure moaned. Saul struck again, with greater force. The figure toppled, shuddering. Saul struck again. And again! He couldn't stop himself. He struck, pulping bone until in a crimson drift the man lay quiet.

Saul pivoted toward his right, straining to see the third man. He rushed along the slope, squinting through gusts, desperate for a glimpse of dark slacks and a windbreaker. But fifty meters farther, he still hadn't found his quarry.

Has he already gone up the slope? Did I pass below him?

Saul glanced toward the crest, unable to see it in the storm. If he's above me, I'd have passed his tracks! No, he has to be farther along this hill!

But twenty meters farther, still failing to glimpse the man or his tracks, he came to a sudden stop. A terrible suspicion filled him with panic.

They wouldn't have stayed this far apart. I made a mistake. The first man I killed—he wasn't on their left flank! *He was in the middle!* Somewhere behind me along this slope, the third man, the one who was really on the left flank, must have noticed he's alone! He'll find the marks in the snow where I killed his partner! He'll find the body! He'll search for me!

Saul whirled to stare behind him, appalled by the unavoidable trail he'd left in the snow. All the third man had to do was follow the footprints till they led him to...! A handgun cracked, a bullet nipping Saul's sleeve. He dove to the snow and rolled down the slope, ignoring the impact of rocks beneath him. The handgun cracked again, its bullet kicking up snow. Saul reached the bottom of the slope and scrambled to his feet, hearing a third crack from the handgun. He didn't dare stop, didn't dare let the man pin him down. With his frozen hands, he wouldn't be able to return fire. The man would merely circle till he had a clear aim and shoot Saul from a safe distance.

Saul raced on. Exertion in this unaccustomed altitude made him afraid he'd vomit. The trees became more frequent, less far apart. He charged down a farther slope. The man wouldn't follow directly along Saul's tracks but instead would stay to the side, to avoid a trap. Counting on that strategy, Saul veered away from the man, scrambling through a gap between boulders. He saw a dead branch projecting from a drift and yanked it free. He ran back up the slope, in the direction from which he'd come, hoping a line of bushes would conceal him. At the top of the slope, he angled back toward the man. His intention was to make a wide circle, get behind the man, find his tracks, and stalk him. In a moment, he crossed his own tracks and entered the enemy's territory. The falling snow transformed afternoon into dusk. Objects as near as ten meters were indistinct. He crept from tree to tree and suddenly found his pursuer's tracks.

He calculated his next moves. By now, the man would have reached Saul's own trail, would have seen where Saul stopped descending and doubled back. The man would realize the likelihood that Saul intended to circle behind him. The man would hurry back this way to intercept him.

Clutching the jagged branch he'd picked up, Saul glanced along his pursuer's downward trail. He saw a clump of boulders the man had passed and approached them, staying within the tracks his enemy had made. When he came to the boulders, he leapt as far as he could, hoping the new imprints would be sufficiently spaced from the trail he'd just left that his hunter wouldn't see them in time to realize that Saul was hiding among the boulders.

Braced in a cleft, he imagined the sequence he willed to occur. His hunter, coming back this way, would ignore his own tracks and keep staring ahead in search of Saul's. By the time he came abreast of these boulders, he'd be able to see where Saul's tracks intersected with his own farther up the slope. Briefly distracted, the man wouldn't be prepared for an immediate attack.

So Saul hoped. There were many variables he couldn't control. Suppose the man didn't retrace his tracks exactly but instead moved *beside* them, passing these boulders on the left instead of the right. It was difficult enough for Saul to concentrate in one direction, let alone both. Or suppose the man followed Saul's tracks where they circled back up the slope. In that case, the man would approach these boulders from ahead, not behind, and Saul would be in full view.

I should have kept running, Saul thought.

But to where? The farmhouse is too far away. In the storm, I'll lose my way. And what about Erika and the woman? I can't abandon them.

But I wouldn't be abandoning them. They've got shelter, a rifle. All I've got is handgun my stiffened fingers can't shoot.

And a branch.

The weapon seemed ludicrous now. He shivered, fearful he'd freeze to death before his hunter ever searched in this direction. He felt weak, dizzy, nauseous.

I can't believe I've done this.

At once it occurred to him that the man must be shivering too. *His* judgment has to be weakened, the same as mine. It could be we're even.

Tense seconds passed, accumulating into minutes. Snow gathered around him. *On* him. His joints felt immobilized. He wasn't sure he'd be able to move now, even if his hunter did creep into the trap.

The forest darkened. Soon he'd be completely disoriented, unable to fight his adversary or find his way back to the cave. Not that he'd ever have to contend with either problem. If he stayed immobile like this, the cold seeping deeper into his core, he'd be dead long before nightfall.

Snow half-filled his enemy's tracks. If the man couldn't see them, there'd be little chance of his passing these boulders. Already so much time had elapsed that Saul suspected the man must have chosen another direction. Or perhaps he couldn't bear the cold anymore and retreated, trying to get back to the farmhouse.

I have to move, make my muscles work, get my circulation flowing!

His patience snapped. He stepped from the cleft between two boulders, turned to the right . . .

And found himself face-to-face with his hunter. The man had just come abreast of the boulders, looking carefully up the slope. Shock paralyzed them; cold retarded their reflexes. Saul swung the branch as the man pivoted, aiming his pistol. The branch had a finger-long projecting barb. It impaled the hunter's right eye. Gel spurted, followed at once by blood. The man screamed, a soul-rending wail of outrage and violation. The force of Saul's blow had thrust the barb all the way through the

215

eye socket, cracking the crust of bone behind the orb, lancing the brain. The man's arms flapped as if he tried to fly. His scream, now only a motor reflex, persisted, then stopped. His mouth remained open. He dropped his pistol and gripped the branch. In quick succession, he stood on tiptoes, dropped his hands to his sides, peered at Saul with his remaining eye, and fell.

The branch projected sideways, obscenely, from his face. Horror, fear, exhaustion, cold, and the altitude all had their effect. Saul vomited. It seemed impossible that the contents of his frigid stomach would steam so. He staggered back against the boulders he'd hidden among. He clutched his midsection, doubled over, and heaved yet again, collapsing to his knees. The snowy forest floor tilted one way, then the other.

I'm going to die, he thought. I've won, but I'm going to die.

His disgust at what he'd just been forced to do shifted suddenly into anger: at himself, the circumstance, the weather, his weakness! He raised his face and roared in rebellion.

No! If I'm going to die, it won't be because I gave up!

He staggered to his feet, pushed himself away from the boulders, and lurched through snowdrifts up the slope. A mental vision of Erika's face swirled before him. It changed to that of his son. He wanted desperately to live. But not for himself.

For his family.

His shoulders felt like blocks of wood, his legs like posts, but he persisted, reached the top of this slope, and staggered up another. Snow struck his eyes. He lost his balance and fell, squirmed upright, fell again . . .

And crawled.

Higher.

Farther.

Though his consciousness was clouded, he sensed that the stronger bite of the wind meant he'd left the shelter of the treeline, had reached the rocky slope up to the open plateau.

But the plateau seemed to go on forever. The harder

216

he worked, the less ground he seemed to cover. On his hands and knees, he struck his head against a rock, struggled to crawl over it, couldn't, and realized that the rock was a wall.

The wall on the far side of the plateau.

The door. If his memory wasn't tricking him, the door had to be against this wall. *But which way? Right or left?* His survival depended upon an instantaneous decision. Completely disoriented, he chose left.

And almost passed the door before he understood what it was. Exhaustion negated excitement. Stupefied, he pawed at the door, scraping his fingernails against it. "Erika, it's Saul. For God's sake, Erika."

The snow became a warm blanket. It covered him. He sank, toppling forward as the door swung open.

He landed hard on a rocky floor.

And heard Erika scream.

7

His first impression was that Erika's horrified face swirling above him was but another vision of her face that had acted as a beacon, drawing him onward through the storm. A dim part of his remaining consciousness jabbed him, however, rousing him into the realization that he'd reached the door and been granted admission into the cave.

His second impression was of a far-off hissing light. A naphtha-fueled lantern. Its almost mystical glow revealed shelves of canned food and bottled water, a white plastic box with a red cross stenciled on it, coats, shirts, socks, and pants, a two-way radio.

His third impression, and the most important, was of warmth. It pained him. He squirmed, groaning as Erika dragged him toward the lantern. He realized that a kerosene-fueled heater stood next to the lamp, that a tube in the ceiling was venting the heater's gases. The tingle of warmth upon his skin made him cringe. Erika's urgent embrace was excruciating. He tried to protest but was powerless.

The Swiss woman slammed the cave door shut, blocking out the wind and snow. She ran to touch Saul's forehead. "His temperature's too low. His body can't warm itself."

Saul understood. The core of heat in his body was like a furnace. If the furnace stopped working, outside heat wouldn't help him. The heat had to come from within. The furnace had to be made to start generating again.

"He'll die if . . ."

"Blankets," Erika said.

"They won't be enough."

"We'll heat up some cocoa."

The woman shook her head. "Hot cocoa won't be enough either. Besides, he doesn't have the strength to swallow it."

"What then? How can I save my husband?"

"Your body heat."

"What? I don't understand."

"Use your body heat! Save him!"

Erika understood. She tugged off Saul's wet clothes. He shivered, clutching his arms across his chest. She grabbed a sleeping bag from a shelf, unrolled it beside him, and opened its zipper. She laid him onto it and tugged it shut.

The sleeping bag was thick and soft.

But cold. "So cold," he murmured.

In the glow from the lamp, he saw Erika take off her own clothes. She threw everything—jacket, blouse, slacks, shoes, socks, bra, panties—into a corner and scurried into the sleeping bag with him.

She squeezed down beside him, put her arms around him, and pressed her breasts, stomach, and thighs against him. The sleeping bag was almost too small for both their bodies. Though her embrace was painful, he felt the down of the sleeping bag trap her warmth. Heat radiated from her onto him. She wedged a knee between his legs, her thigh between his own. She kissed his cheeks, his neck, his shoulders. She breathed deeply, re-

218

peatedly against his chest, anything to smother him with warmth.

The embrace was the most intimate he'd ever experienced. Her urgent attempt to enfold his skin with her own, to thrust her heat into him, to meld her body with his, was a more complete union than he'd ever imagined was possible. Their bodies became the most sensitive organs each possessed, a totality of their separate senses. Saul didn't know how long she pressed herself fully against him, skin to skin, soul to soul, but he gradually felt heat seeping into him, sinking toward his core. His stomach warmed first, then his lungs, his heart. When the nerves in his spine tingled with heat, he realized that his power to generate his own warmth had been revitalized.

Breathing became easier. His chest expanded. He stopped shivering, smiled at Erika, touched her beautiful face, saw it blur before him, and drifted into unconsciousness.

8

When he woke, he was still in the sleeping bag, but he was fully dressed now in dry garments. He felt weak and yet amazingly rested. He stretched his legs against the soft interior of the bag, drew his hands out, rubbed his eyes, and in the glow from the lamp saw Erika and the woman leaning against the cave wall, studying him. Erika too was dressed now.

"How long have I—?"

"It's ten A.M.," she said. "Rise and shine." She opened the cave door.

He jerked a hand to his eyes and turned away. Outside, the sun was searing. "Rise and shine?" He groaned. "That isn't the sun. It's a laser beam."

"You can't sleep your life away."

He groaned again. Water dripped in front of the cave door. Sunlight reflected blindingly off the snow. He

219

pulled a corner of the sleeping bag over his face.

"If you insist," she said.

When he peered up from beneath the corner of the sleeping bag, he saw the gleam of humor in her eyes. She eased the door almost shut. A few inches of daylight intruded, adding to the glow of the lantern.

"You sure know how to put a guy to sleep," he said.

"My pleasure."

Saul shuddered, this time not from cold but emotion. "I love you."

The Swiss woman looked embarrassed by their intimacy and coughed. "Are you hungry? We made some freeze-dried soup."

"I'm starved."

He was strong enough to spoon the liquid to his mouth.

"What happened out there?" Erika finally asked.

"I killed them."

The Swiss woman paled. Erika merely nodded.

He left out the details. "There's a lot to be done." He crawled from the sleeping bag, felt an ache in his back, and waited until his equilibrium became balanced and steady.

Erika collected Saul's wet clothes and gave him the packet that contained Avidan's diary and the photographs. She picked up the rifle. After making sure that the heater, lantern, and stove were shut off, they stepped outside.

The woman closed the door. "I'll have to replace what we used."

"We'll pay," Saul said.

"No. You've paid me well enough. Not just with money. You saved my life."

"But you wouldn't have needed to be saved if we hadn't come to your house. We're still in your debt."

They stepped through melting drifts down the slope, sunlight stinging their eyes. Distressed, Saul sensed they were near the first man he'd been forced to kill.

I don't want to do this, he thought.

But it has to be done.

"You'd better wait here."

He continued downward toward a fir tree while Erika stayed behind to distract the woman. He reached the drooping pine boughs and stooped reluctantly beneath them to study the man whose spine he'd broken. Breath held, with difficulty he removed the ring on the middle finger of the corpse's stiff left hand.

The ring had a brilliant gold band, capped by a large gleaming ruby. An insignia upon the stone showed an intersecting sword and cross.

He searched the corpse thoroughly, finding only a passport and a wallet. The passport was French, made out for Jean Lapierre, a neutral name that was probably a pseudonym. He checked the passport's inside page, finding immigration stamps for Austria and Switzerland. *The same route we've been following,* Saul thought. *Are these the men who attacked me in the park in Vienna?*

He examined the wallet, finding the equivalent of a thousand American dollars in various European currencies. Two credit cards and a French driver's license had the same signature that was on the passport. The address was in Paris. A photograph of an attractive woman and a bright-eyed young daughter provided the proper personal touch to what Saul assumed was an expertly forged set of documents.

It took him forty minutes, but he finally found the other bodies, removed the ring from each, and examined their wallets and passports. Neutral names. A Marseilles address. A Lyon address. Family photographs. The documents looked perfectly in order and, like the first set, were no doubt perfectly forged.

He returned to Erika and the woman where they sat on a sun-dried rock. "The question is, do we hide the bodies or leave them where they are?"

The woman reacted with alarm. "Hide them? But why would—?"

"For *your* sake," Saul answered. "To keep you from being implicated. In good weather, how far are we from your farm? An hour? The cave we stayed in suggests hikers like to come up this way. They'll find the bodies.

221

The authorities will question you. Can you convince them you don't know anything about what happened here?"

"If I have to . . . I can do anything."

"You've proven that. But think about what I've said. Make sure before we leave these bodies."

The woman trembled. "There's a ravine above us. Hikers avoid it. Most of the year, it's filled with snow. Hide them."

"You don't have to help."

The woman didn't make even a token effort to object. She merely stared toward the valley.

Saul glanced toward Erika, who stood. After ninety minutes and three unnerving trips to the ravine, they returned to the woman.

Saul's voice was taut. "It's done."

The woman hadn't changed her position. She continued to stare toward the valley. As if coming out of a trance, she blinked at them. "My husband and I used to come up here. It once was my favorite spot."

They went down toward the valley.

9

At the sun-bathed farmhouse, cows bellowed in pain, needing to be milked. The woman ran to them. Saul sensed that her eagerness to get away was based only partly on her concern for her animals. We're pariahs, he thought. He peered toward the mountains from which they'd descended. The snow-covered peaks were massive gravestones. He walked with Erika toward the Volkswagen they'd driven here.

He showed her an ignition key he'd taken from one of the corpses. "Follow me. I'll drive this Renault. We'll go to Zurich. That's far enough that no one will link the bodies—if they're discovered—to the car. Give me a couple of minutes, though. I assume it's a rented car, but I still haven't found the receipt from the agency. It's probably in the glove compartment. I want to check the trunk, then copy the license number and the serial number that's on the motor block. No matter how many buffers they used, someone had to pay for using that car, and I want to find out who."

"But we don't have access to a network for that kind of information. Remember your bargain."

"To do this on our own? Sure. But I think I've found a way to make the Agency cooperate, to make them agree I've done them a favor. At the same time, I'll get their help."

"I don't see how."

"*This* is how." Saul pulled one of the ruby rings from his pocket. "I wanted to be away from the woman before I showed you. It would only have confused her."

Erika examined the ring. "I've never seen anything like it. A gold band. A perfect ruby with an inset sword and cross. The design's medieval, right?"

"But the surfaces are smooth. The manufacture's recent."

"Sword and cross."

"Religion and violence. All three of the men had rings like this. It's obviously a symbol for a group. A recognition device for those who understand. It's probably the ring the hiker took off before he came to this farm."

Saul tugged at the gleaming ruby on the ring. With a snick, the ruby swung up on a hidden swivel, revealing a compartment.

In the compartment, Erika saw a capsule. It was yellow. She raised it to her nostrils.

"Cyanide."

"Or something even quicker." Saul pressed the ruby cap down on the poison. "My guess is, if those men had lived they'd have swallowed the poison before I could question them. I think we're dealing with a death cult. Very old, and very skilled. Between us, you and I have almost thirty years of experience in the profession. But neither of us has seen this ring or this insignia. Another network exists, one we don't know about and I'm betting no one else does either."

"But how could that be possible?"

"I don't know how they stayed secret so long or why they'd risk exposing themselves. But clearly they exist. And clearly they're expert. So wouldn't you think, if I offered this information to the Agency, they'd cancel my obligation to do them a favor?"

"As long as I find out what happened to my father and see my son again."

"*Our* son." Saul's voice rose; he thought of bloody snow. "And if they accept my offer, maybe I won't ever have to kill again."

UNNATURAL CONJUNCTION

1

Zurich. In his former profession, Drew had often sought refuge here; it was one of his favorite cities. But on this warm clear morning, as he walked with Arlene along the river that divided the city, he barely noticed the quays and pleasure boats or the gardens and guildhouses on the opposite shore. Instead, in his memory, he saw the dead security men at the villa outside Rome and Gatto's tortured corpse sprawled on a lounge beside his swimming pool. After discovering the massacre site the night before, Drew and Arlene had at once made arrangements to leave Rome, flying to Zurich as soon as possible. Now they left the sidewalk beside the river and, without a word, proceeded along a street of imposing buildings, approaching the Swiss Zurichsee Bank. It was here that Father Sebastian had said he'd open a safe-deposit box for them. In a trouser pocket, Drew had the key—in his memory, the code words "Mother of God"—that would give them access to the box.

As they reached the entrance to the bank, Arlene's green eyes flashed with apprehension. "Suppose the code words don't work. Or the key. Suppose Father Sebastian didn't plan to back us up as he said he would."

"So far he's kept his word. He met us at the Vatican gardens. He supplied us with weapons, passports, money, and Father Victor's research about Cardinal Pavelic's disappearance. There's something terribly wrong

225

for sure, but I don't think Father Sebastian's to blame."

"We'll know soon enough."

They entered the bank. Its marble floor, massive pillars, and high curved ceiling reminded Drew of a church. Echoing voices had the awe of parishioners responding at mass. They passed guards and clerks, desks and counters, found a sign in German, French, Italian, and English that directed them toward safe-deposit boxes in the basement, and descended as if to a crypt.

"Mother of God," Drew said in German to a severe-faced woman, the guardian of the sanctum, and showed her the number on his key.

She examined a list of box numbers and code words, then directed her narrow gaze toward Drew. "Very good, sir."

Drew suppressed his tension while the woman escorted him into a vault of safe-deposit boxes and used Drew's key, along with her own, to open a metal slot. She pulled out an enclosed tray and, with the reverence of a priestess conferring a sacrament, handed it to him.

Three minutes later, he and Arlene were alone behind the closed door of a cubicle. Drew opened the lid, finding two pistols, two passports, and an envelope that, as Father Sebastian had promised, contained money.

"He kept his bargain," Drew said. "It's good to know a priest who belongs to the Fraternity can be trusted."

"So far," Arlene said.

They concealed the weapons behind their jackets. Before they'd passed through the metal detectors in Rome's airport, they'd rented a locker and hidden the handguns Father Sebastian had earlier given to them. Oppressed by the weight of the pistol against his spine, Drew pocketed the money and passports, then pulled out a pen and a piece of paper, printing boldly IMPERATIVE WE MEET WITH YOU SOONEST POSSIBLE. LEAVE INSTRUCTIONS FOR TIME AND PLACE. THE PENITENT.

He set the note in the tray, closed the lid, and opened the cubicle door. The guardian came to attention as if about to receive a holy relic. The tray safely locked away, the key in his pocket, Drew followed Arlene from the temple of the money changers. He scanned the busy street, found no indication that he and Arlene were under surveillance, and walked back toward the river.

"So now we wait," Drew said. "We'll come back this afternoon and tomorrow morning and however many other mornings and afternoons it takes. Maybe a miracle will happen, and we'll *never* be contacted. This isn't our fight. We were forced into it. We've done our part for now. After this, it's up to Father Sebastian, and if he doesn't get in touch, we can't be blamed. I could gladly wait here forever with you."

"But you know it won't happen that way," she said.

In despair, Drew nodded. "The Fraternity never lets up. Until we accomplish what they want, we won't be free of them. I hate the things I was trained to do, but I'll use those skills to finish this. So we can start our lives together."

Arlene held his hand. "We already *have* started our lives together. All we can count on is now."

2

At four o'clock that afternoon, Drew opened the safe-deposit box for the second time that day. Instead of the note he'd left, he found a different one, its printing more forceful than his own. The instructions were clear, professional, precise. Below them, in a melted drop of wax, an insignia had been indented, a sword intersecting with a cross.

This time, he'd entered the bank alone. He left, walked in the opposite direction from the river, and reached the Bahnhofstrasse, Zurich's main business district, where he paused to peer at flowers in a window. A moment later, Arlene stood beside him. He saw her reflection in the window. She'd been following him since he'd left the bank.

"No one showed any interest," she said.

That didn't prove they weren't being watched. None-

227

theless, they'd have been foolish not to take the precaution. They joined the stream of shoppers along the street.

"We got a message," Drew said. He didn't show it to her. Couldn't. In the cubicle at the bank, he'd torn the note into minuscule pieces and kept them in a pocket of his trousers. While he'd walked to the Bahnhofstrasse, he'd surreptitiously dropped the bits here and there along the sidewalk.

"Assuming the message was actually from Father Sebastian," Drew said, "he gave us a time and place for a meeting tonight. He also gave us two fallback times and places for tomorrow in case we didn't get his message today."

"Thorough."

"No more than I'd expect from a member of the Fraternity."

Again her eyes flashed with apprehension. "Where do we meet him?"

3

At 1 A.M., they emerged from the darkness of an alley, crossed the narrow stone expanse of the Rathausbrucke, and reached an ornate fountain. Mist from the river drifted toward them.

"I can think of better places for a meeting," Arlene said.

"One less exposed?" Drew asked. "On the other hand, anyone following us would have to cross the bridge. This late at night, hardly anyone else around, we'd be sure to notice him."

The instructions had been to reach the fountain at five minutes after one, but they knew that the rendezvous might not occur until as long as a half-hour later. Father Sebastian would want to satisfy himself that they hadn't been followed before he showed himself.

But a half-hour later, the priest had still not arrived.

228

"I don't like what I'm feeling. We'll try the fallback time and place tomorrow morning," Drew said. "We'd better get out of here."

Arlene didn't need encouragement. She walked from the fountain, but not back toward the bridge, instead toward the street along this side of the river. Drew followed.

The mist thinned. Reaching a murky side street, they passed a restaurant, its windows dark. Ahead, a young man drove a motorcycle through an intersection, the noise so loud that for a moment Drew didn't hear the car behind him. He spun toward its headlights. The car raced toward them. Drew pressed Arlene back toward a doorway and reached for his pistol. The car was already stopping.

Through an open window, Father Sebastian said, "Get in. Quickly."

They did. Drew barely had a chance to close the door before Father Sebastian stepped on the throttle and urged the car down the street.

"What took you so long?" Drew said. "Why didn't you meet us?"

Father Sebastian sped around a corner. "I've been watching you from a block away. In case you'd been followed, I wanted to make it seem the meeting had been aborted and you'd given up. I waited till contact was least expected, with little chance of anyone catching up to us."

The priest wore dark slacks, a dark zipped-up windbreaker, and dark driving gloves. The ring on the middle finger of his left hand made a bulge in the glove.

"I'm surprised you got our message as soon as you did. We left it at the bank only this morning," Drew said. "Are you staying here in Zurich?"

"No. In Rome."

"Then how . . . ?"

"From the moment I gave you the safe-deposit box key and the code words, my most-trusted assistant has been assigned to a cloister here in Zurich. He checks the box daily. When he found your message, he phoned me

229

in Rome. I told him to arrange for several possible meetings and left at once for Zurich. My flight arrived this evening."

"But if your assistant knew about your plans . . ."

"Exactly. As much as I trust him, prudence required me to add my own variation. By such precautions, the Fraternity has kept itself secret all these centuries. And we mustn't forget—I recruited you, an outsider who had no choice except to help me, precisely because I have reason to believe there is an enemy within the order." The priest sped around another corner and checked his rearview mirror. "No one behind us. It seems we've accomplished our purpose. Would you care to do some late-night sightseeing?"

The priest sped north, toward the wooded hills outside the city.

4

"Your request for a meeting was unexpected. Indeed, from a security point of view, most distressing." Father Sebastian continued driving. "What do you want?"

"Information," Drew said.

"You couldn't have put your questions in writing and left them at the bank?"

"So your assistant could learn what I needed before *you* did? What precautions could you have taken after that?"

"I grant your point."

"Besides, a great deal's happened since we met you at the Vatican."

"I hope that means you've made progress."

"It means there are other players in the game."

Father Sebastian turned sharply toward him. *"Who?"*

"If I knew, I wouldn't have had to risk asking for this meeting. I need your resources, your network, to help me find out."

The priest concentrated on the road. "Explain."

Drew began with his decision to investigate the possibility that terrorists were responsible for Cardinal Pavelic's disappearance. "Terrorists used to be my specialty, after all," he said bitterly. "But Father Victor's research seemed to indicate he hadn't explored that possibility."

"Cardinal Pavelic's disappearance might have been the first stage of a terrorist attack against the Church? My compliments. It hadn't occurred to me."

"I'm not sure I'm right. But two other men had the same suspicion." Drew explained about his conversation with Gatto and how the arms merchant, no longer privy to confidential information, had directed him to Medici. "But when Arlene and I were set to grab Medici, two men took him first. And when we returned to Gatto to ask what he knew about these men, we found his villa had been attacked. His bodyguards were dead. He'd been tortured. His throat had been slit."

Father Sebastian gripped the steering wheel. "Then you assume the two men forced Gatto to reveal what he'd already told you?"

"Yes. I believe those two men tortured Gatto to learn if terrorists were involved in the cardinal's disappearance. I think they have the same purpose I do. And I want to know who they are."

"Describe them."

Drew remembered his view from the alley as the two men subdued Medici's bodyguard and chauffeur, then shoved Medici into his limousine. The confrontation and abduction had been amazingly quick—no longer than twenty seconds—but Drew's expert memory envisioned it again as if he were watching a filmstrip.

"They were in their early forties," he said. "They both wore caps. Even so, I could see hair at the back of their necks and along their ears. One man was a blond, the other a redhead. The blond was six feet tall, tanned, well-built, as if he lifted weights, big shoulders and chest, wide forehead and jaw. The redhead was taller, maybe six foot two, extremely thin and pale. His cheeks were gaunt. His face seemed squeezed together."

"A charming couple," Father Sebastian said. "But

without more information, I don't see how my sources can identify them. A muscular blond and a pasty redhead. Did you get any sense of their nationality?"

"Only in a negative sense. I had the impression they weren't French, Spanish, or Italian. Still, we do have other information."

"Oh?"

"Those men were professionals. I don't mean just that they knew what they were doing. I mean world-class. I've seen few men better, and in my former life, I dealt with a lot of experts. They can't be that good and not have a reputation. My guess is the color of their hair is part of their trademark. Ask your sources about top-of-the-line assassins. Find out if two of them are a blond and a redhead. And something else—assuming they're not Italian, they had to come through immigration. Check with your Opus Dei people in Italian security, Interpol, the CIA. Maybe our two friends entered Italy recently. Maybe somebody spotted them."

"It still isn't much of a lead."

"It's all we've got," Drew said. "All *you've* got. I'm handing the case over to you for now."

"For now? Or is this your attempt to bow out completely? You haven't forgotten your bargain, I hope. If you cooperate, we'll pardon your sins against us."

"I haven't forgotten. All I want is the chance to be with Arlene. I know if I betray you I'll never get that chance. *But how can I cooperate if I don't get the information I've asked for?*"

Father Sebastian debated. "As you say, it's in my hands for now. Check the safe-deposit box every morning at ten, every afternoon at three."

Exhausted by the discussion, Drew leaned back. Next to him, in the rear of the shadowy car, he felt Arlene gazing at him searingly.

"I'll try to have an answer for you soon," the priest said.

5

The Langenberg Wildlife Park, off a scenic road southwest of Zurich, allowed its visitors an intimate glimpse of chamois, marmot, deer, and boar. Drew and Arlene drove from the park's two acres of rocky forested hills and proceeded farther south along a series of rising switchbacks until they stopped at the top of Albis Pass. From its 2,600 feet, they had a view of rolling countryside. More important, their position gave Father Sebastian a chance to see if they'd been followed from the park.

Ten minutes later, Father Sebastian pulled up beside them. After Drew and Arlene got in, the priest sped down the road from the pass. He soon turned onto a wooded side road and checked his rearview mirror. It was the afternoon after their late-night meeting. The sky was cloudy, with a threat of rain.

"Icicle and Seth."

Drew didn't understand. "Icicle and . . . ?"

"Seth," the priest repeated. "Those are their cryptonyms. I confess I didn't think I'd learn anything about them. But as soon as I mentioned a blond and a redhead, I got an immediate reaction from my Opus Dei contacts in Interpol. I'm embarrassed I hadn't heard about these two men before. The only excuse I can think of for my ignorance is they haven't made a move against anything that involves the Church. They're not terrorists; you wouldn't have known about them either."

"What about them?" Drew asked.

"They're extremely expensive, extremely skilled, extremely deadly. They don't work often, but when they do, it's a major job. They're experts at hiding. No one knows where they live."

"By definition," Drew said. "Otherwise there'd have been reprisals against them."

"One Interpol theory is that they use a major proportion of their income to buy protection. But even so, they've made a few mistakes. Along the line some security cameras took photographs of them. Only a couple. The images are blurred. But these days, computers can do wonders to add high-resolution to murky photographs. And those enhanced photographs were used to identify two men who came through Rome's airport two days ago from Canada. Each man alone might not have triggered interest. But both of them on one plane . . ."

"Sure. They attracted attention to each other. The watcher was bound to notice."

"That's part of the reason they were spotted," Father Sebastian said. "But there's a stronger reason for both of them on one plane to be unusual. I told you their code names are Icicle and Seth. Both are appropriate to killing."

"Death is an iceman. Seth is the red-haired Egyptian god of the underworld."

"And forty years ago, the men with those code names were mortal enemies," Father Sebastian said.

"That's impossible! Forty years ago, the men I saw would have been infants!"

"I'm talking about the fathers whose code names the sons inherited. In the Second World War, Icicle and Seth were Hitler's personal principal assassins. Each tried to outdo the other's body count—to gain approval from the Führer. And after the Third Reich collapsed, the favored assassins continued to challenge each other. On several occasions, they tried to kill each other. Because of a woman, some sources say. Do the sons of old enemies consort with each other? Travel on the same plane? Cooperate to kidnap an informant? *That's* what attracted Interpol's attention. Whatever's happening is more disturbing than I feared. Icicle and Seth—the conjunction's unnatural."

6

The sky became grayer. A light rain started falling as Father Sebastian let them off at the top of Albis Pass. "And now the case is yours again," the priest said. "I don't know how you can use the information I've given you. But I recruited you precisely because I didn't want to risk involving the Fraternity in the investigation. If you need me to do your work for you, why should I have bargained with you? I'm becoming impatient." With an angry glare, the priest sped away.

Drew watched him disappear down the pass. The rain was like a heavy mist. It drifted across his face. Despondent, he and Arlene got into their car.

"What now?" Arlene asked. "Even with what he told us, I feel helpless. Where do we go?"

"I think back to Rome." He tried to sound confident. "Where Cardinal Pavelic disappeared, where Father Victor was shot, where Seth and Icicle went after Gatto and Medici."

Her gaze became hopeful. "But what's the connection?"

"Between the sons of Hitler's private assassins and the disappearance of Cardinal Pavelic? I'm not sure there *is* a connection, not a direct one anyhow. Seth and Icicle didn't abduct the cardinal—otherwise they wouldn't be looking for him. They want answers the same as we do. Why, though? Why are they so interested? What would make the sons of Nazi executioners —and remember their fathers were enemies—want to join forces to find a missing cardinal? From the start, we overlooked the obvious. The cardinal's the key to this. But we are thinking of him only as a figurehead, a Church luminary, not as a man. Who *was* he? We hardly know anything about him."

Drew turned the ignition key and steered toward the road. At once he saw a Renault go by, driven by a man speeding down the pass toward Zurich. Behind the Renault, another car, a Volkswagen Golf, followed closely.

In it, a woman stared at the car ahead with intensity, as if the worst thing that could happen would be for her to lose sight of the Renault. Drew was positive he'd never seen them before, yet he felt a puzzling kinship. He pulled onto the road and drove behind them down the pass, but wherever they were headed, he and Arlene were going toward Zurich's airport and the next flight back to Rome.

7

Saul found a space in a crowded parking lot near Zurich's railway station. The skin on his face felt taut from exhaustion. I tried to do too much, he thought. I should have rested longer at the cave. Mustering strength, he stepped from the Renault and locked it. The drizzle persisted. He glanced at the Renault's closed trunk, which he'd discovered contained automatic weapons and plastic explosives as well as three sets of passports, credit cards, and driver's licenses providing alternate identities for the men who'd used this car.

They wouldn't have risked bringing that stuff through Swiss customs, Saul thought. They got everything after they entered the country. Which means they weren't alone; they had contacts, an organization to back them up. They must have thought we wouldn't be suspicious and run. Otherwise they'd have come after us sooner.

Their mistake.

Erika pulled up in the Volkswagen. He got in beside her.

"A couple of times, you wavered on the road," she said. "Your eyes look dull. Your skin's pale. Are you sick?"

His raw throat made him cough. "Let's not worry about it till I make a phone call."

"After that, this Jewish lady's going to pamper you."

"I'll hold you to that promise," Saul smiled. "Drive toward the lake."

236

He could have used a telephone in the train station, but by habit, he avoided all phones in public transport terminals—security agencies frequently tapped them. Halfway along the Bahnhofstrasse, he pointed toward a phone booth. "It's as safe as any, I suppose."

Erika stopped at the curb.

"Keep circling the block," he said, then darted from the Volkswagen. He picked up the receiver, inserting Swiss coins.

A gruff voice answered in German. "Zurich Flower Shop."

"This is a priority order. Put me through to your international dispatcher."

"Have you dealt with us before? To expedite delivery, I'll need an account number."

"My account was listed under a name."

"What is it?"

"Romulus."

The German voice hesitated only briefly. "I'll check your invoice file and see if the dispatcher's available."

"Tell him I've found a flower shop I don't think he knows about."

"I'm sure he'll be interested—if I can reach him."

"I'm sure you can."

Saul studied his watch. Forty seconds later, another voice—speaking English—came on the line.

"What kind of flowers did you wish to send?"

"Roses. I'm calling from a Zurich phone booth. I want to send the order to the Black Bread Bakery in Vienna. My friend there was nicknamed Pockmark. This is the number in the booth." Saul dictated it. "I don't have an alternate phone. Tell Pockmark to call as soon as possible. Tell him I want to discuss the favor he wanted."

"This might take a while."

Saul knew they would use the number he'd given them to locate this phone and verify by sight that he was who he claimed to be. "I understand. Just make sure Pockmark calls me."

Saul hung up and glanced out the rain-streaked window of the booth. He saw Erika drive the Volkswagen

237

past him and gestured reassuringly to her.

He waited. Through the phone booth's window, now misted by his breath, he saw Erika drive past several more times.

Ten minutes later, the phone rang. He grabbed for it.

A German voice again, but this one sounded as if its accent had been learned in New England. "I'm calling about some flowers you want to send to me."

"Your accent's terrible, Pockmark."

"And you're as discourteous as ever. You agreed not to get in touch with us."

"I want to discuss my near-accident in Vienna."

Pockmark spoke quickly. "We had nothing to do with that."

"I know. I found out who was involved. You'll be surprised. Do we talk about it now or switch to another phone?"

The line became silent.

"Romulus?"

"I'm listening."

"You're sure I'll be surprised?"

"Utterly fascinated."

"How would you like to rent a hotel room? Our treat."

"Which hotel?"

"By now, the flower shop should have found the booth you're using."

"A man's been standing outside for the past five minutes. He looks cold in the rain."

"I'll try to get back to you by tonight."

The phone went dead. Saul stepped from the booth. A gray-haired man stood close to a building, trying to avoid the rain.

"You like flowers?" Saul asked.

"Roses."

"Know any good hotels?"

"Oh, indeed!" the man said.

Erika drove around the corner.

8

"Ouch! It's too hot!"

"We have to sweat the cold out of you."

"I liked it better the way you got me warm last night."

"How'd you guess my backup plan? Now take off the rest of your clothes and get in the tub."

He stripped and sank slowly into the steaming water. She scrubbed his back. He couldn't help smiling when she toweled him dry. "Now about that backup plan of yours."

She shook her head. "We'll have company soon."

He made a face.

"Besides, you need your strength," she said. "You have to eat."

It was evening. They'd already called for room service. By the time Saul dressed—there'd been clothes in various sizes in the hotel room's closet—they heard a knock on the door. Saul confirmed that the knock was from room service. He opened the door. The waiter who wheeled a cart into the room had a pockmarked face.

"I hope you don't mind," Pockmark said and closed the door. "I ordered for three. I haven't had anything since breakfast."

"It's all on the company's tab," Saul said.

"Exactly. And all of us hope what you're offering is worth our hospitality."

"I wouldn't have called if I didn't think it was worth more than that." Five minutes earlier, Saul had been hungry. Now he barely glanced at the dishes on the cart.

"And this must be Erika," Pockmark said. "I've never had the pleasure." He shook hands with her and poured three cups of coffee. Neither Saul nor Erika picked theirs up.

Pockmark tasted his. "So. Let's review the situation. Rules were established. We ignored your violation of the exile we agreed upon. In exchange, you promised us a favor. But to get the maximum effect from your favor, we wanted you to keep a distance from us . . . and from every other network. You had to appear to be disaffiliated. Would you say that your call this afternoon was in keeping with that promise? We constantly monitor our communication system, on guard against eavesdroppers. But no safeguards are foolproof. It's possible other networks know about your call. You identified yourself by your cryptonym. There's a chance...slim but of concern...that unfriendly ears overheard. You've jeopardized the nature of the favor we wanted from you."

"I think I've already *done* you the favor."

Pockmark sipped again. "That's hard to imagine."

"By gaining information you don't have."

"So you said on the phone. Be specific. What *kind* of information?"

"Are you wired?"

"Our conversation is completely one-to-one."

"Of course. *But are you wired?*"

Pockmark shrugged. "I suppose the next thing you'll search me." He pulled a small tape recorder from a pocket of his white jacket and set it on a bedside table. Even from a distance, Saul could see the tiny reels turning.

"That's the whole of it?" Saul asked. "No radio transmitter?" He stepped toward the cart.

"All right," Pockmark said. "Just leave it alone. You'll screw up the transmission." He gently lifted the white linen on the cart, revealing a microphone and a power unit on a shelf underneath. "Happy now?"

"I want this official. I want your directors to know. I want to avoid misunderstandings."

"More than anything, believe me, we want to understand."

"Three men tried to kill me."

"Yes. In Vienna. I was there, remember."

"Not just in Vienna."

Pockmark lowered his cup in surprise.

"Here in Switzerland," Saul said. "In the mountains. South of Zurich. I assume the same three men. This time I discouraged them."

"Too bad for them."

"I've got their rings."

"Say that again?"

"Rings. You can have them if we reach an agreement. They're my favor to the network. In exchange for fulfillment of our bargain."

Pockmark blinked. "Wait just a second. Let me understand this. You're saying you'll show us some rings, and that fulfills your obligation?"

"Along with automatic weapons, plastic explosives, and bogus IDs. You're going to love it. There's a network no one knows about."

Pockmark laughed. "Don't be absurd."

"Fine. Then shut off your tape recorder, wheel your cart out, and give us five minutes to get away."

"Five minutes? You'd never make it. But just because I said 'absurd' doesn't mean I won't listen."

"More than that, you have to agree. I give you the rings. I tell you where to find the car the men drove. *But our agreement has to be fulfilled. I don't want shadows behind me.*"

Pockmark hesitated. "I'll need to discuss this with..."

The phone rang.

Saul had expected the call, but Pockmark jerked in surprise.

"That'll be our faithful listeners," Saul said. "Let's find out what our ratings are."

Pockmark picked up the phone. He listened, nodding as if eager to please. "Yes, sir. Of course. If that's what you want, sir." He set down the phone. "All right then, Romulus, damn you. Tell us what you have. If it checks out, if it's as new as you claim, you've done your favor. I emphasize the *if*. Don't try to jerk us around. And remember, we could have used chemicals to get the same information."

"But chemicals only get answers from questions, and you don't know what questions to ask." Saul was aware of Erika sitting on the bed, one of the gunmen's pistols beneath a blanket on her lap. "Besides, I've got too much to lose."

"The rings." Pockmark thrust out his hand.

Saul took them from his pocket and dropped them into Pockmark's hand.

"A sword and a cross?"

"Religion and violence," Saul said. "There's a clasp on the side of each ring. Tilt the ruby up."

Pockmark lifted the stone. His eyes narrowed when he saw the yellow capsule. "Poison?"

"Ever seen a ring like that?"

"Sure, every day."

"Like hell. The men who wore those rings were extremely well trained killers."

Pockmark shook his head. "But that's not enough to fulfill your obligation. It still doesn't prove they belonged to a new network."

"Did I say it was new? Look at the design on those rings. Medieval. I think the network's very old."

"But nobody's ever heard of it? Ridiculous."

"I'll give you the chance to find out." Saul wrote down the license number he'd memorized and handed the note to Pockmark. "Their car's a black Renault. Last year's model. It's at the parking lot near the railway station. You'll find the automatic weapons, plastic explosives, and bogus IDs. And maybe fingerprints, though I doubt it. These men were fond of gloves. But to rent a car, they had to leave a paper trail."

"With bogus IDs, the paper trail won't take us far."

Saul hadn't expected to lose control. "Quit being deliberately stupid. To rent a car, they had to use a credit card. Even if the card's made out to an alias, somebody has to pay the bill. The money has to come from somewhere."

"Take it easy."

"I didn't promise answers! I told you what I said I would! Do we have a deal or not? Is our bargain finished? Tell your bosses to make a decision! Put it on the record! Abide by it! *I want to find Erika's father and see my son again!*"

One floor down, in a room directly under Saul's, Gallagher sat at a long narrow table, watching the reels turn on a tape recorder connected to a radio receiver. The Agency station chief for Austria, he glanced down the table toward his counterpart, a short man with soft pale manicured hands, the station chief for Switzerland.

Gallagher's suit was rumpled from his hurried flight with Pockmark from Vienna. Strictly speaking, he didn't have authority here. But Romulus had insisted on dealing with the Vienna bakery, not the Zurich flower shop, and the bargain for a favor from Romulus had been made in Vienna, so that involved Gallagher regardless of whether his counterpart objected to his being here, though Zurich in fact didn't seem to mind at all.

"What do you think?" Gallagher asked, pretending deference to his host.

Zurich assumed a look of grave deliberation. "It's out of our power really. Langley will have to make the decision."

"Based partly on our recommendation," Gallagher said. *"What do you think?"*

"I'd like to see those rings and look at the car."

"That's not the deal Romulus offered. He wants a decision *before* you check out the car."

"He hardly has much say in the matter, does he? What recourse does he have if his information leads us nowhere and we tell him he still owes us the favor?"

Gallagher grimaced, appalled by Zurich's attitude. "You've never worked with Romulus, have you?"

"No. But so what? I know all I have to about him. He's a troublemaker."

"He's a man of character. In Vienna, he made his bargain with us in good faith. I fully expect he'd have done us the favor."

"Would have? Past tense?" Zurich looked puzzled.

"Because now he expects good faith from us, and if we jerk him around, he'll refuse to cooperate."

Zurich spread his hands. "Then we punish him and use him as an example of what happens to troublemakers. Honestly, I don't see the problem."

Gallagher wanted to slam his hands on the table. Instead he managed to keep his voice calm. "Let me explain. I *have* worked with Romulus, and I know how he thinks. He's shrewd. I take for granted he hasn't told us everything. He'll have kept some important detail in reserve, as a further negotiation tactic."

"So we pretend to agree until he tells us everything."

"And what happens when word gets out that we didn't show good faith? The repercussions would be disastrous. Freelance operatives wouldn't deal with us. We have to say yes or no to Romulus. Maybe isn't good enough. Besides, we need him."

"To gain the extra information you think he hasn't told us?" Zurich asked. "Unlike you, I doubt that information exists."

Again Gallagher mustered patience. "Listen. Romulus got into this because his wife's father is missing. They want to find out what happened to him. Now they claim they found a network no one's heard of. Assuming the network does exist, it's related to what happened to the missing father. Everything Romulus knows about the one is pertinent to what we want to know about the other. We have to encourage him, not fight with him. As long as he keeps searching for his wife's father, he'll be doing the favor we wanted from him."

Zurich surprised Gallagher. He agreed. "Yes, the search for the father is by extension a search for the unknown network. I see that now, and it does make sense to encourage Romulus. But there's a further implication. We want him to do a favor for us. But if we investigate the possibility of this other network, if this other network has something to do with the missing father, we'll be helping Romulus in his search. We'll be doing a favor for *him*." Zurich's eyes twinkled. "He's as shrewd as you said he was. He's found a way to turn the situation around, to manipulate us into backing him up."

As Zurich started to make his phone call to Langley,

Gallagher picked up another phone and dialed the number in the room directly above.

"Put Romulus on. . . . This is Gallagher. I'm in the hotel. I've been listening with interest. We're asking Langley to accept the bargain you're offering. Understand, all we can do is recommend. Langley has the final say."

"Of course."

"But this is a good-faith gesture," Gallagher said. "I promise I'll do everything I can to back you up. I need something more from you, though. You haven't told us everything. I'm sure of it. Give me something extra, something to help tilt the balance with Langley."

"Good faith?"

"You have my word. I might have manipulated you, Romulus. But I never lied to you. Tell me something more."

"The three men who wore the rings." Romulus hesitated. "The men I killed."

"What about them?"

"I think they were priests."

Book Five

IMPACT

MEDUSA

1

Washington, D.C. Though it was only 9:16 A.M. and the kosher restaurant had not yet opened its doors to the public, eight elderly men sat at a banquet table in a private room in the rear. The room was usually rented for Bar Mitzvah parties and wedding feasts, but the present occasion was not a celebration. Memories of death, and despair pinched each face, though solemnity did not preclude grim satisfaction as each man raised a glass of wine and drank ceremoniously. To retribution. To vindication.

Their first names were Abraham, Daniel, Ephraim, Joseph, Jacob, Moshe, Nathan, and Simon. Each man was in his late sixties or early seventies, and each had a number tattooed on a forearm.

"Has everything been arranged?" Ephraim asked.

He studied his comrades. They nodded.

"The mechanisms are in place," Nathan said. "All that remains is to set the final process into motion. A week from today will see the end of it."

"Thank the Lord," Abraham said.

"Yes, that justice will finally be achieved," Jacob said.

"No, that our part in achieving justice will have been concluded," Abraham answered. "What we've done is distressing enough. But now we go farther."

"What we do is necessary," Moshe objected.

"After all these years, what good is served?"

"It doesn't matter how much time has gone by. If justice had value back then, it must have value now," Simon insisted. "Or do you question the value of justice itself?"

"Do you urge passivity and forgiveness?" Joseph asked.

Abraham answered with force. "Passivity? Of course not. To be passive is to risk extinction." He paused. "But forgiveness is a virtue. And justice is sometimes merely a word used to hide the ugliness of revenge. God's chosen people must defend themselves, but do we remain His chosen people if we become obsessed by ignoble motives?"

"If you don't approve of what we're doing, why don't you leave?" Jacob asked.

"No," Joseph said. "Abraham is right to raise these issues. If we act without moral certainty, we do become ignoble."

"I confess to hatred, yes," Ephraim said. "Even now, I can see the corpses of my parents, of my brothers and sisters. What I want—what I crave—is to punish."

"I have as much reason as you to hate," Abraham said. "But I resist the emotion. Only feelings that nourish have worth."

"And we respect your opinion," Ephraim said. "But it's possible for each of us to do the same thing for different reasons. Let me ask you two simple questions."

Abraham waited.

"Do you believe that those who profited from our suffering should be allowed to retain those profits, to enjoy them?"

"No. That isn't justice."

"So I believe as well. Do you believe that the sins of the fathers should be allowed to be repeated by the children?"

"No, evil must not be permitted to thrive. Weeds must be destroyed before they can reproduce."

"But in this case, they *have* reproduced, and once again our people are threatened. We must act, don't you see that? Whether some of us do so for revenge doesn't matter. The end is what matters, and this end is good."

The room became silent.

"Are we all agreed?" Joseph asked.

They nodded, Abraham reluctantly.

"Then let us eat together," Ephraim said. "To symbolize our united resolve, the beginning of a too-long-postponed end."

2

Mexico City. Aaron Rosenberg sat between two bodyguards in the backseat of his bulletproof Mercedes sedan, staring past the driver and the bodyguard in the front seat toward the Oldsmobile filled with more security personnel ahead of him. He turned to peer through the rear window toward the Chrysler van behind him filled with yet another team of guards. His imagination was tortured by images of what his wife and her bodyguard were probably doing with each other now that he'd left the house. At the same time, he dreaded whatever other threats the Night and Fog might leave at his home while he was gone. He'd tripled his security precautions, both at home and while away. He now refused to go anywhere unless his Mercedes was flanked front and back by protective vehicles. Nonetheless, he would never have left the house today if it hadn't been absolutely necessary, if he hadn't been summoned by one of the growing number of men he couldn't refuse. There's no question about it, Rosenberg thought. My life's out of my control.

The caravan proceeded along the Paseo de la Reforma, maintaining a constant moderate speed, keeping a close formation. Soon the group drove south, leaving the sweltering city, heading toward the cool air of the estates at Lake Chalco. The compound through which his Mercedes passed was familiar to him. The red tiled roof on the sprawling main house had been reconstructed at Rosenberg's expense. The large swimming pool in back, with its stunning view of the lake, had been Rosenberg's gift to the occupant. The many gardeners and servants no doubt received their salaries through the special bank account into which Rosenberg deposited a considerable sum the first of every month.

The cost of doing business, Rosenberg thought, again reminded him of how much his life was out of control. Depressed, he stepped from the car and approached the house.

A high-ranking member of Mexico City's police force stepped outside to greet him. His last name was Chavez. He wore sandals, shorts, and a bright red shirt open to his pudgy stomach. When he smiled, his pencil-thin mustache somehow maintained its straight horizontal line.

"Señor Rosenberg, how good of you to come."

"It's always a pleasure, Captain."

Rosenberg followed the captain from the shadow of the house into the glaring sunshine beside the pool. He considered it significant that he hadn't been offered a drink and began to feel apprehensive.

"Wait here, please," the captain said. He went through a sliding glass door at the back of the house and returned with a slender packet. "I've received information of importance to you."

"A problem of some sort?"

"You tell me." The captain opened the packet and withdrew a large black-and-white photograph. He handed it to Rosenberg.

Fear squeezed Rosenberg's heart. "I don't understand." He raised his eyes toward Chavez. "Why would you show me a photograph of a German soldier from World War Two?"

"Not just a soldier, an officer. I'm told the rank... excuse my poor German accent... was *Oberführer*, or senior colonel. He belonged to the *Totenkopfverbande*, the so-called Death's Head formation. You can see the silver medallion of a death's head on his military cap. You can also see the twin lightning bolts on the sleeve of his jacket—the symbol for the SS. The photograph is so

252

detailed you can even see the unit's personal pledge to the Führer on his belt buckle—'My loyalty is my honor.' Note carefully in the background—the mounds of corpses. The Death's Head division was in charge of exterminating the Jews."

"You don't need to tell me about the Holocaust." Rosenberg bristled. "Why are you showing me this photograph?"

"You don't recognize the officer?"

"Of course not. Why should I?"

"Because he bears a striking resemblance to your father, whose photograph you gave me when you asked me to investigate his disappearance a few months ago."

"That man is not my father."

"Don't lie to me!" Chavez snapped. "I've compared the photographs in detail! Add facial wrinkles! Take away some hair! Add gray to the rest! Allow for minor reconstructive surgery! That man *is* your father!"

"How could a Jew be an SS officer?"

"Your father wasn't a Jew, and you're not either! Your real family name is Rodenback! Your father's first name was Otto! Yours is Karl!" Chavez took documents from the packet. "That officer's picture appeared on SS identification records and on immigration forms when he came to Mexico. The face is the same, though the name is different. Government authorities will soon be told who he really is! The United States authorities will also be told, and as both of us know, the United States bolsters its relations with Israel by pretending indignation toward Nazi war criminals."

Rosenberg couldn't move. "Who told you these things?"

"You don't expect me to reveal my sources," Chavez spread his arms in a gesture of goodwill. "But I wonder, how much are you willing to pay for me to neutralize my information, to assure the authorities there's been a mistake?"

Rosenberg wanted to vomit. Blackmail never ended. It only bought time. But time was in limited supply. It would last only as long as his money did. He thought of

253

the cargo in the ship headed toward the Mediterranean and what he assumed now was certain disaster.

"How much do you want?" he asked.

The glint in the captain's coal-black eyes didn't reassure him.

3

St. Paul, Minnesota. William Miller feigned a polite smile of greeting as he crossed the cocktail lounge and approached the man in the left rear booth.

On the phone, the man had said his name was Sloane. He was with the Associated Press, he claimed, and wanted to talk about Miller's father.

Now Sloane imitated Miller's smile of greeting, stood, and extended his hand.

They surveyed each other.

"Somebody sent you what?" Sloane asked. "On the phone, you said something about filth."

"You're really a reporter?"

"Cross my heart."

"Shit." Miller swallowed, disgusted at himself. "I'm sorry I lost my temper when you called. I thought for sure . . ."

"That's why we're here. To talk about it." Sloane gestured toward the booth.

They sat across from each other. Sloane was in his mid-thirties, short, heavy-chested, with dark thin hair and intelligent eyes. "What do you mean by filth?" he asked.

"Photographs."

"Of?"

"Nazi concentration camps. Corpses. Ashes." Miller massaged his forehead. "God. My father disappeared. Then somebody painted a death's head on the bottom of my swimming pool."

"Death's head?"

"Now you show up . . ."

"And you assumed . . ."

"Well, wouldn't *you* assume? My wife doesn't know about the photographs."

"Slow down," Sloane said. "What you're telling me connects with what I came for. I'll give you my side, and we'll see what we come up with."

"Credentials."

"What?"

"You're an AP reporter. Prove it."

Sloane sighed and pulled out his press card.

"Anybody can have a card printed up," Miller said.

"There's a phone number. The AP central office."

"And anybody can hire a voice to claim he's in the AP office."

"Right. And I bet you've got all kinds of fascinating theories about the JFK assassination. The UN's controlled by drug dealers. Satan's responsible for heavy-metal rock."

Reluctantly, Miller laughed.

"Good," Sloane said. "As long as you can laugh at yourself, you're in control."

"Sometimes I wonder. You said you wanted to talk about my father. Why?"

"I have contacts in the Justice Department. It's what you might call a symbiotic relationship. I do them a favor, write stories that bolster their public image. They do me a favor, let me know when they're working on something I can use."

"I still don't understand. What does the Justice Department have to do with my father?"

"Someone sent them documents that made them decide to investigate him."

Miller clutched his drink so hard he feared the glass would break. "This gets more and more insane."

"And since your father disappeared—"

"You already knew that?"

"I figured the only other person to talk to was you."

"Okay," Miller said wearily. "Give it to me all at once. Worst case. Bottom line."

"Your father's name is Frank Miller. The theory is,

255

he's really Franz Müller, a German officer in World War Two. He's supposed to have been an *Obersturmbannführer."* Sloane spoke the German haltingly. "In English, that means lieutenant-colonel. During World War Two, Franz Müller commanded a unit in an SS formation known as *Einsatzgruppen.* They were a special military task force that followed regular Nazi soldiers into newly invaded German territory—Czechoslovakia, Poland, and Russia, for example—where they executed every Jew they could find, shot them where they stood or herded them into pits to make it easy to bury them after the firing squad was finished. Their body count in Russia alone was a half million."

"And you're telling me the Justice Department suspects my father was part of that insanity? *A Nazi mass murderer?"*

"They more than suspect. They're convinced of it. They claim they've got proof. And they think your father disappeared because he'd been warned about their investigation. As far as they're concerned, your father *ran* from them. Are you all right? You just turned pale."

"My whole fucking world's falling apart, and you ask me if I'm all right? Jesus, I . . . Look, somebody has to stop this craziness. Just because my father's name is similar to Franz Müller . . ."

"No, there's more than that. The Justice Department wouldn't base an investigation on something that tenuous. Your father emigrated here from Germany. You knew that?"

"Sure. After the war. A lot of Germans did. There wasn't anything illegal about it."

"But did you also know he changed his name?"

A muscle twitched in Miller's cheek.

"My God, you *did* know," Sloane realized.

"Let me explain. I knew. But not the specifics. All he told me was he'd Americanized his name to avoid anti-German feelings here after the war."

"Did he tell you he'd been a German soldier?"

"I don't have to listen to this crap." Miller stood.

Sloane reached out, careful not to touch him. "For

sure you'll have to listen when an investigator from the Justice Department comes around. If I were you, I'd think of this as a dress rehearsal, and while I was at it, I'd think about *this*. It would do your family a lot of good to be treated sympathetically by the press."

Miller hesitated. "Sympathetically?"

"The past comes back to haunt a family that didn't even know about the past. I can build an effective human interest story out of that. A story in your favor. Assuming, of course, that you're telling the truth about your father."

"I meant what I said." Miller sat down. "I can't believe anybody would accuse my father of—"

"Accusing him's one thing. Whether you knew anything about his past is another. You truly believe he's innocent?"

"Damn it, yes!"

"Then answer my questions. Did he tell you he'd been a German soldier?"

Miller thought about it. "Sometimes, as he got older, he talked about the war. He said, toward the end every male he knew, even kids, had been conscripted. Despite his inexperience, he was made a sergeant and ordered to defend a bridge. When the Allies invaded, he hid till the worst was over and then surrendered."

"You didn't think it strange that a German soldier was allowed to come to America? That was hardly standard procedure."

"He explained about that too. German soldiers were placed in POW camps. The Allies didn't exactly take kindly to them, and none of the German soldiers knew how long the imprisonment would last. So the trick was, before the Allies picked you up, you had to find a civilian corpse and exchange clothes and identity papers with it. My father managed to get himself placed in a refugee camp, not a POW camp. He lived there for more than a year before some administrator paid attention to his repeated applications and allowed him to emigrate to America. If what you've told me is true, it sounds like it was my father's bad luck that the dead civilian whose

257

papers he exchanged with his own was named Franz Müller. I mean, Franz Müller's a common German name. There must have been hundreds, maybe thousands of Franz Müllers. But only one of them was this SS hit-squad leader."

Sloane drew his finger through a circle of moisture his glass had made. "The Justice Department has photographs of the SS officer we're talking about. It also has a photograph from your father's immigration file. The face is the same. Why did he disappear?"

"I don't know! Christ, he's seventy-three years old. Where would he run? The Justice Department's absolutely wrong about him!"

"Good. You stick with that attitude, and when the Justice Department decides to go public, you can count on a story that makes you look sympathetic. Even if the Justice Department proves its case, you'll still be presented as an innocent bystander, a loving but misinformed son. On the other hand—I warn you—if you've held back, if you're lying, I'll turn the story around. You and your family will be part of the conspiracy."

"I haven't lied."

"Keep it that way. This isn't just another story to me. I'm supposed to be objective. What I am is furious. Nazi war criminals are all over this fucking country. I could give you dozens of names and addresses right now. There's no mystery about them. The Justice Department knows about them. Most are in their late sixties or early seventies. They keep their lawns mowed. They tip the paperboy. They have the neighbors over for barbecues. I could accuse them in front of their friends. It wouldn't matter. No one would care. Because they don't make trouble. How could that nice man down the street have done all those terrible things? And anyway all of that was a long time ago. Why dredge up unpleasant memories?"

"You're exaggerating."

"If anything, the reverse." Sloane pulled a sheet of paper from his jacket pocket. "Here's a list from my contacts in the Justice Department. Twenty mass murderers. Jack the Ripper, Son of Sam, and John Wayne Gacy are bush-league compared to this bunch."

"And every one of them's a war criminal?"

"There are plenty of others. This is just the tip of the slime heap."

"But if the Justice Department knows who these Nazis are . . . ?"

"Why haven't they been prosecuted? Because after the war American intelligence made a bargain with them. Help us take over your Nazi spy networks and use them against the Russians. In exchange, we'll give you immunity. Or if you don't have a bargain of immunity, we still won't prosecute because your crimes were committed in Europe. To save a lot of diplomatic hassle, we'd just as soon deport you. On the other hand, if we revoke your citizenship, no other country will accept you, so we're stuck with you. Let's forget the whole mess. These Nazis will die soon anyhow. At least that was the theory until a few years ago. A group of idealistic lawyers in the Justice Department decided to do something about the government's lassitude. In 1979, the Office of Special Investigations was formed."

"Then something *is* being done about the men on that list."

"Yes, but not enough. There's no way to be certain about the numbers, but an educated guess is that as many as *ten thousand* Nazi war criminals came to this country. So far the Justice Department has prosecuted *forty* of them. Punishment takes the form of denaturalization and deportation."

"Against mass murderers?"

"The murders didn't take place in the United States. In effect, the only crime they're charged with is lying about their true identity on their immigration forms."

"If the public knew, they'd be outraged."

"Would they? In the cases that have gone to trial, the friends and neighbors of the men who were charged wanted to leave the past alone."

"Is that the point of your story?"

"I want to help the Justice Department. If I can rouse

the public, maybe the Office of Special Investigations will get more government funding. These bastards—I don't care how old they are—should all be made to feel the same terror their victims felt."

"Including my father?"

"If he's guilty," Sloane said, "yes."

Miller matched Sloane's angry gaze. "I've trusted and respected my father all my life. If impossibly the Justice Department is right about him . . . If he's what this so-called proof says he is . . ."

"You agree he ought to be punished?"

"Even my father . . ." Miller felt sick. "Provided he's guilty, even my father can't be absolved."

4

Despite five o'clock traffic, Miller managed to reduce a twenty-minute drive to slightly more than ten. The elevator to the fifth floor seemed to take forever. When he opened the door to MILLER AND ASSOCIATES, ARCHITECTS, he saw that his secretary had not yet gone home.

"How was your meeting, Mr. Miller? Did you get the assignment?"

"It's too soon to tell. I want to make some notes, Marge. If anybody calls, I'm not here. No interruptions."

"Will you be needing me for dictation?"

"No, thanks. Go home when you finish what you're typing."

"Whatever you say."

He went into his office, shut the door, and leaned against it. *How is it possible to know if someone you love is a monster?*

Sweat trickled past his eyes. An eternal five minutes later, the tapping on the keyboard mercifully stopped. He heard the click of switches on the computer, the indistinct rustle of a dustcloth being positioned over the monitor.

"Good night, Mr. Miller."

"Good night," he said through the door.

The tap of high-heeled footsteps. The click of a latch. The snap of the outside door.

Silence.

Miller exhaled, relieving the pressure in his lungs, and stared at the combination safe in the corner to his right, where he stored his plans-in-progress. Two days ago, when he'd received the hideous photographs of corpses and ashes, he'd wanted to destroy them. But an intuition had warned him to move cautiously. The photographs were obviously not just a prank. If he destroyed them, he might lose information he'd need later, clues about why he'd been sent the photographs at all.

Now he wished he hadn't saved them—for fear of the truth he might find. He knelt, dialed the combination on the safe, and removed the packet of photographs. One by one, he studied the black-and-white sheets.

Death. Terrible death.

He'd lied to Sloane, but only in response to one question—and only a part of that response had been a lie. But the lie, even partial, had been out of proportion to all the rest of the truth.

Yes, he'd answered honestly, I knew that my father came from Germany. I knew he'd changed his name. I knew he'd been a German soldier.

Yes, a soldier. But Miller was aware that his father hadn't been an innocent participant in the war, an inexperienced young draftee promoted absurdly to the rank of sergeant. Not at all. His father had been a colonel in the SS.

As Miller's father had aged, he'd been drawn increasingly back to the past. On a handful of days that had unexplained personal significance for him—January 30, April 20, November 8—he'd become more and more sentimental. On those occasions, his father had made and received mysterious phone calls. Then late one night, his father had confessed to his son what he did in the war.

"Yes, I was SS. I followed the Führer's orders. I believed in the master race. And yes, I believed in *lebensraum*, the space we needed to expand and flourish. But I didn't believe in racial extermination. Since we were superior, why couldn't we exist in tolerant harmony with inferior races? Why couldn't we allow them to serve us? I wasn't Death's Head. I wasn't one of the exterminators. Instead I was *Waffen-SS*, the legitimate military branch of the *Schutzstaffel*. I was a decent soldier. I served my country with dignity. That country lost. So be it. History decides morality. Now I live in America. Its citizens call it the greatest nation in the world. So be it. My conscience is clear, and if I had to, I would fight to defend America with the same determination I gave to Germany."

Miller had been convinced. War by its nature blurred judgments and clouded values. Yet surely *some* values remained constant, he hoped.

His father and other *Waffens-SS* commanders had managed to escape the aftermath of Germany's defeat. They'd exchanged identity papers with dead civilians and fled to Bolivia, Mexico, America, Canada, England, Sweden. But they'd remained in touch, phoning each other to remember their heritage, to assure themselves that no matter how severely history had proved them wrong, they were still a part of their country's elite.

Just as the *sons* of the elite had kept in contact. Miller had eventually been drawn into his father's circle of former friends. He and the sons of those other fathers had pledged to help one another in case their fathers came under attack. On the first of each year, there'd been dues to be paid, twenty thousand dollars per family, a bribe to the one outsider who knew their secret, an insurance premium of sorts, blackmail that guaranteed his silence.

Now those bribes had proved useless. The pledge among the sons—to stand as one and defend the group —had turned out to be ineffectual. Despite precautions, their fathers *had* been attacked. They themselves, the sons of their fathers, were also under attack.

Insanity.

Let the past rest, Miller thought. The present and the future are what matter. Our fathers aren't what you think they were. Bring them back. Leave us all alone. You've made a mistake. The Night and Fog has to end.

Yet the handsome young SS officer who gazed proudly from a photograph that Miller couldn't set down reminded him uncannily of his father. No! My father wouldn't have lied to me!

But would he have dared reveal this sanity-threatening truth?

I have to be wrong, Miller thought. I looked at this same SS officer two days ago. It never occurred to me he might be my father.

Or maybe I didn't *want* the thought to occur to me.

But the thought insisted now. Miller's vision focused more narrowly onto the photograph, more intensely toward the SS officer's forehead, just below the peak of the ornate military cap.

He tried to believe that what he saw on that forehead was an imperfection in the photograph itself, a scratch on the negative, but he couldn't convince himself. The scar was identical to the one on his father's forehead, the consequence of a near fatal car accident when he'd been ten.

How is it possible to love a monster?

But how is it possible to know if someone you love *is* a monster?

Before he realized what he was doing, Miller had picked up the phone.

5

"The U.S. Justice Department? Who told you this?" Halloway pressed the phone harder against his ear.

"An Associated Press reporter."

"Jesus Christ."

"He said my father was a Nazi war criminal," Miller

said. "The commander of a goddamned SS extermination team."

"But that's absurd!"

"Is it? I'm beginning to wonder. Some of the things he told me—"

"You mean you actually believed him? He's a *reporter*! He'll tell you anything!"

"But I took another look at those photographs and—"

"You were supposed to destroy the damned things!"

"One shows my father in a Death's Head SS uniform! In front of civilian corpses!"

"A photograph from World War Two? How do you know what your father even looked like back then? That photograph proves nothing!"

"My father had a scar on the top right corner of his forehead! So does this SS officer!"

"Coincidence!"

"That's not a good enough explanation!" Miller's voice rose. "I have to know! *Was* my father in charge of a Nazi extermination squad? What about all the other fathers? Were *they* mass murderers too?"

"If you're suggesting *my* father . . . ? That's ridiculous! It's insulting! I don't have to listen to—!"

"Stop evading the question, Halloway! Answer it!"

"I won't dignify—!"

"Were they Nazi war criminals?"

"Of course not! They were SS, yes! *Waffen-SS!* Legitimate soldiers! Not the Death's Head–SS who killed the Jews! But outsiders don't understand that distinction! Civilians think *all* SS were war criminals! So our fathers had to lie. The Night and Fog made the same mistake we feared the immigration authorities would make, the same mistake the U.S. Justice Department and the Associated Press reporter are making."

"You're trying to tell me the Justice Department can't tell the difference between *Waffen-SS* and Death's Head–SS? Bullshit!"

"Then how did they make this mistake?"

"My father, your father, and the other members of the group used to phone each other on days that were special to them. April twentieth. November eighth. January thirtieth. Do those dates mean anything to you?"

"Of course," Halloway said. "They were birthdays for some of the members of the group."

"You bastard," Miller screamed, "if only you hadn't lied!"

"Lied? About what?"

"April twentieth was someone's birthday, all right. In 1889. *Hitler's* birthday. November eighth is the anniversary of the so-called beer-hall rebellion, Hitler's first attempt to take over the German government. That was in 1923. The rebellion failed. But ten years later he did gain control. On January thirtieth. Those are the three most sacred dates in Nazi tradition. And the three dates on which our fathers, despite the risk, couldn't resist getting in touch with each other."

"All right," Halloway said, "so I didn't realize the significance of those dates."

"I don't believe you. You know what those dates mean. I can hear it in your voice."

"Obviously you're determined to believe what you want. But I assure you—"

"I've got another question," Miller interrupted. "Our fathers were all senior officers. That means they didn't serve together. They commanded separate units. When the war ended, they'd have been widely divided. What's the basis of their bond? What makes them a group?"

"My father said they trained together," Halloway answered.

"But the Nazi army was spread all over. The eastern front, the western front, the North African front. Russia, France, Italy, Egypt. If our fathers trained together, they probably never saw each other again throughout the war. You bastard, you lied again. The bond had nothing to do with their having trained together. Why, out of all the German soldiers who tried to conceal their war records, did this group get in touch with each other? They hid all over the world. But they stayed in touch. Goddamn it, *why?*"

Halloway didn't answer.

"Who were they paying blackmail to?" Miller demanded. "Why?"

Silence on the other end of the line.

"I think the reporter was right," Miller said. "I think there's a hell of a lot my father didn't tell me and you didn't tell me either. But you will. I'm coming up there, Halloway. I'm coming to Canada to choke the answers out of you."

"No! That's crazy! You can't come here! If the Justice Department is watching you, you'll draw their attention to me and—!"

Halloway didn't finish his sentence. Miller had slammed down the phone.

6

Halloway slowly set down his own phone. For several seconds he wasn't able to move. With effort, he turned toward his father's acrylic landscapes, which he'd been nostalgically studying when the phone rang. The row of paintings was broken periodically by patio windows through which he saw his guards patrolling the grounds.

As a rule, he would never have accepted Miller's call at this number; instead, he would have gone to the secure phone in the nearby city, Kitchener. But he didn't feel it was wise to risk leaving the estate, not even to visit his family at the safe house in the city. Achingly, longingly, he missed his wife and children, but he didn't dare endanger them by bringing them back here.

Earlier, Rosenberg—dangerously out of control—had called from Mexico City, babbling that the authorities there had discovered the truth about his father. Similar frightened calls had reached him from the sons of the other fathers in the group. The past was being peeled away. The Night and Fog had managed its reprisal well, twisting its vengeance ever tighter and deeper.

But Halloway had a foreboding that the screw had not yet been fully turned, that another more forceful twist was yet to come. The ship, he kept thinking. By now, it would have passed through the Strait of Gibraltar and entered the Mediterranean Sea. Halloway wished he'd paid attention to Rosenberg's second thoughts about that ship. He wished he'd acquiesced to Rosenberg's fears and ordered the ship to return. Too late now. Even if Halloway tried, he wouldn't be able to get through the complex system of contacts to warn the ship in time.

Whatever would happen now was out of his control. But if the Night and Fog knew about the ship just as they knew about everything else, if the truth about that ship were revealed, we'll face two enemies, the Night and Fog and our clients, Halloway thought, and I'm not sure which is worse.

7

The cargo ship *Medusa* had a registry as tangled as the snarl of snakes associated with her legendary namesake. Her ostensible owner was Transoceanic Enterprises, a Bolivian corporation. But a close examination of Transoceanic Enterprises' incorporation papers would have revealed that the company, whose office address was a post office, was owned by Atlantis Shipping, a Liberian corporation, and in Liberia the company's office was as difficult to find as the mythical continent after which Atlantis Shipping was named.

This company was in turn owned by Mediterranean Transport, a Swiss concern owned by a Mexican concern owned by a Canadian concern. Many of the officers did not exist. Those who did were paid to provide no other service than that of allowing their signatures to be used on legal documents. Of the handful of actual directors, one was Aaron Rosenberg of Mexico City Imports; another was Richard Halloway of Ontario Shipping.

Medusa regularly crisscrossed the Atlantic, carrying textiles, machinery, and food to and from Greece, Italy, France, Spain, England, Canada, Mexico, and Brazil.

But the profit from these shipments was minimal, and if not for another cargo that was often hidden among the textiles, machinery, and food, neither Aaron Rosenberg nor Richard Halloway would have been able to maintain his luxurious life-style.

That cargo was aboard the *Medusa* as she proceeded toward her rendezvous with a freighter whose registration was equally tangled and whose owner had an opulent estate on the Libyan coast. Tomorrow night, off the coast of northern Africa, crates would be transferred. *Medusa* would continue toward Naples to deliver Brazilian coffee, her waterline higher now that she no longer carried plastic explosives, fragmentation grenades, antipersonnel mines, automatic pistols, assault rifles, machine guns, portable rocket launchers, and heat-seeking missiles.

Under usual circumstances, these weapons would have been smuggled out of Belgium, the principal European supplier of black-market arms, and transported under various disguises to Marseilles. There, *Medusa* would have picked up "medical supplies" and distributed them to various terrorist groups along the southern European coast.

But recent antiterrorist surveillance, the result of increased terrorist bombings, made Marseilles and other European ports too dangerous for arms smuggling. The alternative was to bring the arms from South America, where various civil wars had resulted in ample stockpiles of Soviet and American munitions, most of which were readily for sale. Thus *Medusa* had brought Brazilian coffee piled on top of Contra weapons supplied by the CIA across the Atlantic to meet a Libyan freighter in the Mediterranean thirty-six hours from now. Whatever Libya chose to do with the arms was not Transoceanic's concern. The hundred-million-dollar fee was all Rosenberg and Halloway cared about.

Tel Aviv, Israel. The instant the helicopter touched down, Misha Pletz scrambled out. He ran toward the smallest of several corrugated-metal buildings at the south corner of the airport. A burly man in a short-sleeved white shirt waited for him.

"Did you bring it with you?" Misha shouted.

The burly man gestured toward a briefcase in his hand. "Do you want to read it in the car or—?"

"No. Right here," Misha said.

They entered the air-conditioned building.

"We received the message forty minutes ago," the man said, pulling a document from his briefcase. "When I saw the code name, I contacted you at once."

Misha took the paper. He'd been at a kibbutz twenty miles outside the city, fulfilling his promise to Erika and Saul to ensure that their son was protected. Leaving Christopher with Mossad-affiliated guardians had been one of the most difficult things he'd ever been required to do. "Your parents love you, and they'll be back soon," Misha had said. "I love you, too." He'd kissed the boy, and unsure if Erika and Saul were even alive, afraid his emotion would distress their son, he'd hurried toward the waiting helicopter.

Flying back toward Tel Aviv, the pilot had told Misha to put on his earphones—headquarters wanted him. Though the helicopter's radio was equipped with a scrambler, Misha's assistant had refused to reveal the nature of the urgent message they'd received, but he *had* revealed its source. The Coat of Many Colors.

The code name had the force of a blow. It belonged to Erika's missing father, Joseph Bernstein.

His eyes accustomed to the shadows of the building, Misha studied the document. "How did this come in? Which station, which country?"

"Our embassy in Washington," the assistant said. "One of our people there was trained by Joseph ten years ago. So our man's in a coffee shop this morning.

He looks next to him at the counter and guess who's sitting there?"

Misha tingled. "Is our man positive? There's no possibility of doubt?"

"None. It was Joseph for sure. That's probably why Joseph chose him for a relay—because they knew each other well. Apparently Joseph wanted to guarantee that the source of the message wasn't suspicious to us. Contact lasted no longer than a minute. Joseph told our man we weren't to worry about him. He was taking care of unfinished business, he said. The end was near."

"And what was *that* supposed to mean?"

"Our man asked. Joseph refused to elaborate. Instead he passed a note to our man. It was solid information, he said. He wanted you to know about it. He expected you to act upon it. The next thing, he was gone."

"Just like that? Didn't our man try to follow him?"

"'Try' is the word. Joseph knows every trick there is. He lost our man within two blocks."

"Did he say how Joseph looked?"

"Terrible. Pale. Thin. Shaky hands. The eyes were the worst," he said.

"What about them?"

"They seemed—and I quote—our man lapsed into subjectivity here—tormented."

"By what?"

The assistant shrugged.

Misha shook his head. "We've been searching for Joseph everywhere, and all of a sudden he shows up in a coffee shop in Washington."

"At least we know he's still alive."

"For that I'm grateful, believe me. But what's he been doing all this time? Why was he in Washington?" He tapped on the document. "How did he get this information?"

"You always said he was one of the best. I emphasize he told our man in Washington it was solid information."

Misha reread the message. "A cargo ship, the *Medusa*, will rendezvous tomorrow night with a Libyan freighter for the transfer of munitions intended for terror-

270

ist attacks against Israel." The message provided the scheduled time of delivery, the coordinates for the rendezvous in the Mediterranean Sea, and the codes each ship would use to identify itself to the other.

"How did he get this information?" Misha asked again.

"The more important question is, what do you intend to do about it?"

Misha felt paralyzed. Despite Joseph's assurances about the validity of the message, there was still a chance he'd made a mistake. Standard procedure required other sources to corroborate the information before countermeasures could be considered. But there wasn't sufficient time to confirm what Joseph claimed. If the weapons existed and if something wasn't done by tomorrow night, the transfer would occur. The munitions would be distributed. The attacks against Israel would take place. On the other hand, if the weapons did *not* exist and Israeli planes destroyed the ship . . .

Misha didn't want to imagine the international consequences.

"What do you want to do?" his assistant asked.

"Drive me back to headquarters."

"And?"

"I'll tell you when we get there."

The truth was, Misha still didn't know. As they left the building, he distracted himself with the wish that he could contact Erika and Saul.

Erika, your father's alive, Misha wanted to tell her. *He was seen in Washington. I'm not sure what he's up to, but from what I've learned, it's important and I can't decide what to do about it. Find him. Help me. I need to know what's going on.*

Saul, you're not in this alone now. Your former network can't stop you from getting our help. We insist on helping. We're invoking professional protocol. Our national security's at stake. Your search is our search in a way we never imagined. We'll back you up.

Misha got into his assistant's car. He registered almost nothing of the drive toward Mossad headquarters

271

in Tel Aviv. But just before they arrived, he made his decision.

Do you trust Joseph?

Yes.

Do you believe his message is true?

On balance? Yes.

Are you going to order an air strike?

No. Not an air strike. I've got a better idea. It solves a lot of problems. It avoids an international incident. Besides, what's the point of blowing up those weapons? We've got better uses for them than the Libyans do.

He must have been speaking out loud. His assistant turned to him, frowning. "What did you say?"

"I always wanted to be a pirate."

9

With growing dislike for the son of his father's enemy, Icicle sat in a Rome hotel room, watching Seth read what he called his reviews.

The red-haired assassin had bought a copy of every major European, English, and American newspaper he could find. His versatility in languages was considerable, and for the few in which he wasn't fluent he'd asked Icicle's help.

"I knew we'd make the Italian papers," Seth said. "Paris and London, I expected. Athens and West Berlin. But Madrid even picked it up. So did New York and Washington."

Icicle didn't bother hiding his mixture of boredom and disgust.

"I admit it isn't front page," Seth said. "I didn't expect it to be."

The newspaper stories were basically similar. The body of an Italian underworld figure known as Medici had been discovered outside Rome, floating in the Tiber River. Medici, who reputedly had ties to international terrorist organizations, had been killed with what authorities suspected was a lethal drug overdose. The results of an autopsy were not yet available. Rome police theorized that Medici's criminal associates had turned against him for reasons still to be determined.

As such, the story would not have had sufficient scope to merit being reported on an international scale. But investigators had raised the question of whether the discovery of Medici's corpse was related to the much more sensational discovery of nine bodies in a villa outside Rome. Eight of the victims, all shot to death, had been identified as security personnel. The ninth victim, an Italian underworld figure known as Gatto, had been tortured prior to having his throat slit. Gatto, reputed to have ties with international terrorism, had recently retired from criminal activities for reasons of poor health. Reliable but unnamed sources alleged that Medici had taken Gatto's place as a black-market arms dealer. The murders of both men caused authorities to speculate that a gang war was in progress, with obvious international implications.

"As far as the police are concerned, we did them a favor," Seth said. "Better than that, they suspect the wrong people. We can't complain."

"But what happens when the blood tests on Medici show he died from an overdose of Sodium Amytal?" Icicle asked. "The police will compare that to the knife marks on Gatto and decide both men were interrogated."

"So what? They'll never guess it was us or what kind of information we wanted."

Icicle was amazed at how much color his companion's face now had. It was almost as if Seth gained life by administering death, and that made Icicle nervous. For him assassination was a profession, while for Seth it seemed a need. Icicle had never killed anyone he didn't feel morally certain deserved to be eliminated—dictators, drug lords, communist double agents. Seth, on the other hand, gave the impression of not caring who it was he killed as long as the fee was sufficient. If Seth's father had been anything like his son, Icicle didn't wonder why his own father had hated the man.

Granted, both fathers had been Hitler's primary assassins. But Seth's father had specialized in stalking leaders of underground organizations that protected Jews, while Icicle's father had gone after Allied intelligence infiltrators and on more than one occasion had begged for the chance to try for Churchill. The difference was important. Racial extermination was heinous under any circumstances. Political assassination was justifiable if your country's survival depended upon it.

But what if your country was wrong? Icicle asked himself. What if your nation's policy was based on racial hatred? Did patriotism require you to defend an immoral country? Or was national defense merely understandable *self*-defense?

Was my father self-deluded?

Icicle continued to watch the man he loathed. His eyes, Icicle thought. The more Seth killed, the brighter they became.

"Something troubles you?" Seth asked.

"We've got a great body count. Otherwise we haven't accomplished a thing."

"Not true." Seth lowered a newspaper. "We've narrowed possibilities. We've determined that terrorism and the cardinal's disappearance aren't related."

"I never believed they were."

"But the possibility had to be considered. Given Halloway's involvement in black-market arms to terrorists—"

"For Christ's sake, *what*?"

"You didn't know? That's how Halloway makes his living. Munitions."

"You're telling me this is all about illegal weapons?"

"And the cardinal's insistence on a yearly blackmail payment. Surely you knew about *that*."

"I didn't object. I thought of it less as blackmail, more as an extended payment for services rendered."

"Well, some of us thought about killing the priest. Account paid in full."

"He did our fathers a favor."

"Yes, one that was in his own best interest. Or his *Church's* best interest. After more than forty years, the payments amount to a fortune. Eight million dollars."

"If you want my opinion," Icicle said, "the price was

cheap, given the atrocities they committed."

"Including your father?" Seth asked.

Icicle stood. "Not my father! He divorced himself from the others!"

"Really? Sorry to disillusion you, but your father killed as many Jew-savers as my own father did. Their argument wasn't about Jews but about a woman, about your mother! She chose your father over mine! I could have been you! And *you* would not have existed!"

Icicle realized how deep their hatred was. He raised his hands in surrender. "It's a stupid argument. There are too many problems we have to face."

Seth's eyes dulled. "Of course. And we still haven't found our fathers." With effort, he reverted to professional control. "In that case"—he breathed—"in my opinion"—he breathed again—"the situation is as follows."

Icicle waited.

"We've eliminated the theory that what Halloway calls the Night and Fog is a terrorist group that discovered what the cardinal knew, abducted him, and wants to take over Halloway's munitions network."

"I agree," Icicle said. "The theory isn't valid."

"But the cardinal's disappearance is related to the disappearance of our fathers," Seth continued. "The Night and Fog couldn't have found our fathers if not for the cardinal."

"Again I agree."

"So if the purpose of abducting them wasn't to hold them hostage for money, that leaves the possibility that the Night and Fog are doing this for *personal* reasons. That the Night and Fog are Israelis. But to suspect the cardinal, to have discovered what he knew, the Jews would have had to infiltrate the security system of the Catholic Church."

"I doubt that."

"I do as well. And it makes me wonder."

"Wonder what?"

"Eliminate the possibilities. Could someone . . . or some group . . . *within* the Church be the Night and Fog?"

BLACK JESUITS

1

Eight blocks to the east of Zurich's Limmat River, Saul and Erika passed an Agency guard in an alley, opened a door, and entered a garage.

The room was large, its overhead lights brighter than the morning sunlight they'd just left, its concrete floor immaculate. There was only one car, the Renault the three assassins had used. An Agency team had picked it up where Saul told them he'd left it—at the parking lot near Zurich's train station. Overnight, a crew had been working on it, checking for fingerprints, dismantling and searching it. It was now a mechanical skeleton.

"These guys were ready for World War Three," a gravelly voice said.

It belonged to Gallagher. Saul turned as the burly station chief came over, holding an RPG-7 rocket launcher. He nodded toward the munitions laid out on the floor. Plastic explosives, grenades, Uzis, AK-47s.

"Did you find any fingerprints?"

"All kinds," Gallagher said. "But this is a rental car— we can't tell which belong to your friends and which belong to whoever used the car before them."

"You know where we hid the bodies. You could send a team to get their prints."

"I already have. My men should be back by tonight. Aside from the weapons, we didn't find anything unusual in the car. But it was rented in Austria. They wouldn't have risked bringing a trunkful of weapons through Swiss customs. They had to get the stuff in Switzerland."

"Right. And since they were following us, they wouldn't have had much time to pick up the weapons without losing us," Saul said. "Their contacts must be excellent."

"A network we don't know about?" Gallagher said. "Maybe. I can buy that a lot more than I do your suspicion these men were priests. Just because of the rings they wore."

"An intersecting cross and sword."

"That still doesn't make them priests." Gallagher set the rocket launcher down beside the AK-47s. "Religion and violence aren't exactly compatible with the meek inheriting the earth. When I spoke to Langley, I didn't tell them about the religious angle. I'm waiting on that till I'm sure. Right now, our people are checking on the French IDs you took from the men. The passports and driver's licenses are probably fake. Our contacts in French intelligence will let us know soon enough."

"But the credit cards," Saul said. "They're the key."

"No question. My guess is we'll find the cards have a perfect rating. And I'm damned curious about who pays the bills."

A phone rang. Saul glanced at Erika as Gallagher went over to answer it. They couldn't hear what he said. Mostly Gallagher listened, and when he came back, he looked excited.

"The men whose names are on those passports died years ago. The addresses are rooming houses for transients. But the credit cards are three months old, and the bills were paid as quickly as they were received."

"Who paid them?"

"Each man had a different card. Each bill was paid through a different bank. But each bank has photocopies of the checks paid through each account, and the signature on the checks wasn't the bogus name of each man you killed. No, the man who wrote the checks was an accountant. Unusual—don't you think?—for someone

whose address is a transient's rooming house to have a
need for an accountant. Even more unusual for *three*
transients with *separate* addresses to have the *same* accountant. But it gets better. The accountant doesn't exist
either. His checks are good. But he's in a graveyard in
Marseilles. And he has a post office box instead of an
office. So we go past the bogus accountant, and what do
we find? You were right, Romulus. I'm sorry I ever
doubted you."

"Tell me."

"The Catholic Church. The bills were paid through
Rome. Through the Vatican office of a cardinal whose
name is Krunoslav Pavelic. And here's the kicker. The
cardinal disappeared several months ago. So what does a
missing cardinal have to do with three assassins who
might be priests and the disappearance of—?"

"My father," Erika said. "A Jew, not a Catholic."

"But if the cardinal disappeared, who paid the bills?"
Saul asked.

"The cardinal's assistant," Gallagher said. "Father
Jean Dusseault."

2

Hunched over a wooden table in the muffled silence
of a reading room in Rome's Vallicelliana Library, Drew
and Arlene examined the books a librarian had given to
them. The half-dozen titles, all in Italian, were dictio-
naries of religious biographies, the equivalent of *Who's
Who* in the Vatican, the Curia, the Roman Catholic
Church. They found the information they wanted and
glanced at each other with dissatisfaction, returned the
books, and stepped from the library's vestibule to face
the brilliance and noise of Rome.

"Well, at least it was worth a try," Drew said.

Arlene's response surprised him. "As far as I'm concerned, we learned a lot."

"I don't see what. The biographical references in

those books were little more than public relations for the cardinal."

"He doesn't lack ego, that's for sure," Arlene said. "Most *Who's Who*s base their citations on information supplied by the people listed in them. The cardinal apparently views himself as a saint on earth. He has medals and testimonials from dozens of religious groups. He even has a papal decoration. But a list of honors isn't a biography. The cardinal didn't supply many details about his life. Either he thinks his biography is boring, which I doubt given his willingness to let everybody know his various titles and honors, or else—"

"He's got something to hide?"

"Let's put it this way," Arlene said. "We know he was born in 1914 and raised in Yugoslavia. We know he felt an early calling to the Faith and entered the Church when he was eighteen. We know he received his religious training here in Rome. For a time, he served as the Church's liaison with the Red Cross. He moved rapidly up through the ranks of the Church. At thirty-five, he was one of the youngest men to be admitted into the Curia. As a controller of the Church's finances, he holds one of the most powerful positions in the Vatican."

"He must have had talent, all right," Drew said. "The question is, at what? There's nothing in his biography to indicate why he was promoted so rapidly. If you're right, if he's hiding something, it won't be in any official biography. I doubt we'd find it even if we checked the Vatican archives. A member of the Curia has the power to make sure his past is sanitized."

"How do we get the *un*official version of Pavelic's life?" Arlene asked.

"I think it's time to have an intimate conversation with the cardinal's close associates," Drew said. "In the newspaper accounts of his disappearance, I remember a reference to Pavelic's personal assistant. Father Jean Dusseault, I believe the name was."

"French."

"We can narrow the range of our discussion with him. What I'm interested in—"

"Is World War Two," Arlene said, "and why the assassin sons of *Nazi* assassins would be determined to find our missing cardinal. Let's go back to the Vatican."

3

Father Jean Dusseault had an apartment in one of the many Renaissance palaces within the Vatican. The simplest way to contact him, of course, would have been to phone him and schedule an appointment at his office. But the subsequent conversation was unlikely to prove productive. Saul imagined the stony response to the questions he wanted to ask. "Do you know anything about a connection between Cardinal Pavelic and checks written out of your office to assassins who might be priests? Have you ever heard about a secret intelligence network within the Catholic Church? Absurd? Of course. I'm sorry I troubled you." No, Saul thought as he waited in an alcove across from Father Dusseault's apartment building. An interview in his office wouldn't do. A private approach, an intimate—if necessary, forced—conversation: those were the only practical options.

Saul had agreed with Gallagher that, despite the Agency's new willingness to help, it was best for Saul and Erika to go in alone. They had no present affiliations with any network. If they were caught, the worst accusation would be that a man and woman who happened to be Jews had too energetically questioned a Catholic priest about the woman's missing father.

Besides, Saul thought, this really is still a personal matter. Erika's father is all I care about. Gallagher gave me information I didn't have—about the Vatican connection with the men who stalked me. In return, *he* learned about the possibility of a network, the existence of which no one suspected. It's a fair exchange.

Lights flicked off in several apartments. The night became blacker. The Vatican was closed to tourists after 7 P.M., but Saul and Erika had hidden in a basement of one of the office buildings, creeping out after sunset. From his vantage point, Saul glanced down the narrow street toward where Erika waited in a similar alcove. They had flanked the entrance to Father Dusseault's apartment building. As soon as the light went off in his apartment, they'd go up. Or if he came out, they were ready to follow.

As it was, he came out. Saul recognized the robust young Frenchman with his thick dark hair and his slightly weak chin from a late-afternoon visit he'd made to Father Dusseault's office, pretending to be a journalist inquiring if there were developments in the search for the cardinal. The priest had been aloof, abrupt, dismissive. Saul wasn't going to regret demanding answers from him.

The priest paused beneath a light above the entrance to the palace, then headed toward Saul's right, in Erika's direction. His dark suit blended with the shadows; his white collar remained visible, however.

Saul shifted from his hiding place, having given Erika a chance to go after the priest before he himself did. He concentrated on a dim light at the end of the street, waiting to see which direction Father Dusseault would take.

The priest went straight ahead. His apartment building was to the right of St. Peter's Square, near the so-called downtown area of the Vatican, where its supermarket, pharmacy, and post office were located. His route led Saul and Erika between the Sistine Chapel and St. Peter's Basilica, past the Pontifical Academy of Science, and deep within the Vatican woods and gardens, the darkness of which was only partially dispelled by periodic lamps. Twice Saul had to stop and hide— once when two priests walked past him from one building to another, again while a Swiss guard patrolled a street. As soon as he entered the cover of shrubs and trees, he felt less uneasy. But he was troubled by two gestures the priest made. One was to remove his white collar and tuck it into his suitcoat pocket. The other was to push his right hand along the middle finger of his left hand as if he put on a ring.

With an intersecting cross and sword?

Is Father Dusseault connected with the three men who tried to kill me? Is that why their bills were paid through the cardinal's office?

The priest's movements, formerly casual, now became wary. A man of the cloth on a late-night stroll became an operative on guard against danger. He skirted the pale glow of a garden lamp. Without the white collar, his black suit blended perfectly with the darkness of shrubs.

He disappeared.

Somewhere ahead, among trees and bushes, Erika would be watching, Saul knew. Perhaps she was close enough to see where the priest went. But as she stalked him, would the priest be stalking her as well? Had Father Dusseault suspected he was being followed?

Saul was sure of *this*. He and Erika thought so much alike, the same suspicion would have occurred to her. She'd take extra care. Silently he crept forward, past fountains, hedges, and statues. Marble angels had always reminded him of death. The scent of the plants was cloying, as in an undertaker's parlor. He sank to the ground, squirming forward through a gap between shrubs, pausing when he saw a clearing before him. A large fountain in the shape of a Spanish galleon loomed ahead.

At first he thought the priest with his back to the fountain was Father Dusseault. Then the emergence of a quarter moon made him realize that *this* priest wore a white collar. The man was taller than Father Dusseault. His strong-chinned profile made Saul tingle. In these gardens that reminded him of a cemetery, he had the eerie sensation he was seeing a ghost. For an instant, he would have sworn he was looking at his dead foster brother, Chris.

Saul stared in shock. Had Chris somehow survived? Saul had never seen Chris's body; he'd only been told about the knife attack that had killed him. But despite the longing in Saul's heart, he knew in his soul that his hope was groundless. This priest, no matter the resemblance, was not in fact Chris.

A subtle movement at the side of the fountain attracted Saul's attention. Was it Erika trying to gain a better vantage point on this unexpected second priest?

No, he decided. She was too professional to let curiosity force her into the risk of revealing herself.

The movement beside the fountain became more evident. A shadow detached itself from darker shadows. A man stepped forward. In a priest's black suit but without the white collar. A man with a ring on the middle finger of his left hand.

Father Dusseault.

The other priest had apparently been aware of Father Dusseault's approach. Calmly, he turned to his visitor and raised his hands in a gesture of peace. Or so it seemed. The gesture was identical to an operative's invitation to search him, a signal that he wasn't armed.

4

To protect his night vision, Drew had taken care not to glance up at the moon or toward a lamp down a nearby path. Instead he'd concentrated on the darkest group of shrubs before him, keeping his back protected against the fountain. Though Father Dusseault should have arrived by now, he assumed that the priest was being cautious, approaching slowly, on guard against a trap. When he heard soft movement behind the fountain and turned with exaggerated calm, raising his arms in a gesture of nonaggression, he was grateful that Father Dusseault had chosen the darkest approach to this clearing, inadvertently helping Drew to preserve his sight.

Of course, this priest might not be Father Dusseault at all. Drew had never met the man. That afternoon, he'd phoned the priest at his Vatican office and asked for an appointment.

283

"What did you wish to speak with me about?" a smooth voice with a slight French accent had asked.

"Cardinal Pavelic," Drew had said.

"You'll have to be more specific. If this is about the cardinal's disappearance, I've already had one reporter here today, and I told him what I'm telling you. We have no information. Talk to the police."

"I'm not a reporter," Drew had said. "And I don't think you should tell me to see the police. It might make trouble for you."

"I haven't the faintest idea what you're—"

"You asked for something specific. Try this. Two assassins are looking for the cardinal. The sons of Nazi SS men from World War Two. Their fathers reported directly to Hitler. Does that spark your interest?"

The line had been silent for a moment. "Ridiculous," Father Dusseault had said. "What would make you imagine—?"

"Not on the phone. I told you I want an appointment. In private. As soon as possible. Tonight."

"Who *is* this?"

"Sorry," Drew had answered.

"You expect me to trust an anonymous voice on the phone? To meet you in secret and talk about assassins?"

Father Dusseault's outburst had seemed more calculated than spontaneous. Drew had decided to test him. "If you want a character reference, I can direct you to a Fraternity."

Again the line had been silent.

Encouraged, Drew had tested him further, beginning the Fraternity's recognition code. *"Dominus vobiscum."*

"I don't understand why you told me that."

"Surely, Father, you recognize a quotation from the Latin mass."

"Of course. 'The Lord be with you.'"

"Et cum spiritu tuo."

"That's right. 'And with your spirit.' *Deo gratias.*" Drew had held his breath, waiting for the last part of the Fraternity's recognition code.

"'Thanks be to God.' Amen."

Drew had exhaled silently. The code had been completed. "There's a Spanish-galleon fountain in the Vatican gardens."

The reference to the fountain was also a test. Several days ago, when Drew and Arlene had disguised themselves as a priest and a nun to meet Father Sebastian at the Vatican gardens, that fountain had been their rendezvous. It was where Father Victor, the member of the Fraternity who'd sent Arlene to find Drew in Egypt, had been shot.

Any citizen of the Vatican would immediately link the meeting place Drew suggested with the recent murder there. Any indignant but innocent Vatican bureaucrat would call attention to the morbid choice of site. But Father Dusseault, pausing briefly, had merely said, "I'll meet you there at one A.M."

5

Now, fifteen minutes late for the appointment, Father Dusseault stepped from the darkness behind the fountain. He didn't seem surprised that Drew was dressed as a priest. It was understandable, Drew thought. After all, a voice who gave the Fraternity's recognition code would logically, in the Vatican, be expected to wear the appropriate uniform. Where else could a Catholic chameleon safely show his true colors?

Drew couldn't help noticing that Father Dusseault wasn't showing all of *his* colors, though—the priest had taken off his white collar to help him blend with the night. The tactic reinforced Drew's suspicion that the priest's training had not been entirely religious.

But Father Dusseault apparently hadn't discovered Arlene, who like Drew had once again entered the Vatican wearing the costume of a religious order. She'd arrived in the gardens well before the 1 A.M. meeting time, had taken off the white trim from her nun's habit, and had spread herself flat on the ground, merging her black clothing with the darkest group of bushes in the area, the same dark bushes Drew had been looking at when Father Dusseault arrived.

In the glow from the moon, Drew studied the ring on the middle finger of Father Dusseault's left hand: a ruby ring with the insignia of an intersecting cross and sword. It was obvious that Father Dusseault had worn the ring to verify his membership in the Fraternity—and equally obvious that the absence of an identical ring on Drew's finger put him under suspicion.

Indeed Father Dusseault pointed at Drew's naked finger. "I assumed you were one of us."

Drew recognized the resonant voice he'd heard on the phone. "No."

"How do you know our recognition code?"

"A member of the Fraternity once told me . . . when he tried to recruit me," Drew said.

"If he tried to recruit you, you must have special skills."

Drew didn't reply.

"Why did you refuse to join us?"

"I hate everything the Fraternity stands for," Drew said.

"Hate?" Father Dusseault smiled. "A destructive emotion. You ought to confess it and seek absolution for it. But then confession is why we're here." He raised his right hand, blessing Drew. "The Lord forgives you. Now tell me why you're so interested in the cardinal's disappearance."

Drew shook his head.

"Whom do you work for?"

Drew shook his head again. "I'd rather discuss the assassins I mentioned, the two men looking for the cardinal."

"Ah, yes, the ones you claim are the sons of executioners who worked for Hitler. By all means, if that's what you prefer to talk about. For now. How did you learn about them?"

"Let's say we crossed paths. Their code names are Icicle and Seth."

286

Though Father Dusseault's face showed no reaction, his eyes betrayed him.

"You've heard of them?" Drew asked.

"No," the priest lied. "I'm sure I'd remember such vivid names."

"The sons of Nazi assassins," Drew said. "It made me wonder. Why would they want to find the cardinal? I turned the question around. What would the cardinal have to do with *them*? I started thinking about the cardinal's past. What had he done to rise so quickly through the ranks of the Church?"

"There's no mystery about it," Father Dusseault said. "The cardinal was a never-tiring laborer for the Faith. His remarkable energy was repeatedly rewarded."

"Well, the labor I was interested in took place in 1945, just before his first promotion. What's the cardinal's connection with the Nazis?"

6

Saul watched from his hidden vantage point on the dew-wet ground beneath shrubs. The two priests were talking—their voices too low for Saul to hear what they said—when Father Dusseault stepped suddenly forward, lunging with his left hand. Moonlight glinted off...

7

...a knife that must have been in a spring-loaded sheath under Father Dusseault's coat sleeve. Drew leaped back, feeling the blade snick across his lapel. Heat rushed through his body. His nerve ends quickened in response to a scalding spurt of adrenaline. He dodged another thrust of the knife, trying to maneuver so the moon was to his back, its glow on Father Dusseault, hoping to impair the priest's night vision.

But Father Dusseault understood Drew's intention and began to circle Drew, trying to put his own back to the moon.

When the knife flashed toward him again, Drew blocked the thrust and struck the heel of his palm against Father Dusseault's chest, aiming toward the ribs above the heart. But the priest anticipated the blow, twisting to his left, absorbing the impact on his side. At the same time, using the torque of his body, the priest kicked his right foot high toward Drew's jaw.

Drew snapped his head back, avoiding the kick, and grabbed for the foot that sped past him. Father Dusseault spun evasively. In a blur, he slashed again.

Drew slammed the knife arm away and plowed the heel of his palm against Father Dusseault's nostrils, feeling cartilage crunch. Though the blow wasn't fatal, it would be excruciating, so stunning that for the next few seconds the priest wouldn't be able to defend himself. Drew took the advantage, delivering a rapid sequence of forceful punches—to the diaphragm, under the jaw, across the bridge of the nose.

Father Dusseault went down.

8

Saul continued to watch in amazement. The speed of the second priest's reflexes was astonishing, again reminding him of Chris. The priest had struck with the heel of his palm. Just as Chris and I were trained to do. The priest's agility, his rhythm, his accuracy, his *style*—they all made Saul think of Chris.

Or is it just that Chris died in a knife fight and I so wish he'd survived that I'm imposing my fantasy on to the priest who *did*?

No, Saul thought. I'm not imagining the resemblance.

The priest isn't Chris. I know that. But he looks so much like him it's eerie.

Saul's thoughts were interrupted. Someone else was in the gardens. At first Saul suspected the shadowy figure that appeared from bushes to his right was Erika.

But it *wasn't* Erika, he quickly realized. The figure was a woman, yes, but dressed as a nun. She rushed into the clearing. The victorious priest turned to her. They spoke urgently, crouching beside Father Dusseault.

Saul made a sudden dangerous choice. His years of professional conditioning objected. His protective instincts rebelled. They didn't matter. He stood from his murky cover—if his intuition had betrayed him, he could always charge backward into greater darkness—and stepped into the clearing.

9

Alarmed, the priest and the nun swung toward him.

"This is the biggest risk I've ever taken," Saul said. He raised his hands. "I'm not alone, so stay as you are. I trust you. Please don't make a move against me."

The priest seemed paralyzed between conflicting motives, whether to run or to attack. The nun pulled a pistol from beneath her robe.

Saul raised his hands even higher, stepping closer. "You didn't know I was out there watching, so assume I could have killed you if I'd wanted to. Assume we've got mutual concerns."

"Mutual concerns?" the priest asked.

Saul felt another eerie tingle. The voice was Chris's. It couldn't be. But it was.

Or am I going crazy?

"What you did is what *we* wanted to do," Saul said.

"Which is?" The nun continued to aim the pistol.

"Get our hands on Father Dusseault and make him tell us what he knows about..."

The priest cocked his head. "About?"

289

Saul hesitated, unsure how much to reveal, and abruptly committed himself. "About my wife's missing father and why three men—I think they were priests—tried to kill my wife and myself."

"You say you think they were *priests*?"

"Yes, like the man who just attacked you. He wears the same kind of ring they wore. A ruby with the insignia of an intersecting sword and cross."

10

Drew stared in surprise. "You know about the Fraternity?"

The stranger was in his late thirties, tall and muscular, dark-haired, square-jawed, swarthy.

Drew felt a momentary déjà vu, thinking he'd seen him before, though he couldn't imagine where. He disregarded the unnerving sensation and waited for the man to answer.

"The Fraternity?" The stranger frowned. "Is that what they call themselves? No, I don't know about them, but I'd sure like to learn." The man stepped closer. "I do know this—the ring has a poison capsule hidden under the stone."

"Yes, the stone," Drew said. "The Fraternity of the Stone. They're supposed to swallow the poison if there's a danger they'll be captured and forced to reveal the secrets of their order."

"*Order?*" The stranger spoke quickly. "Then I was right? They're all priests?"

Drew nodded. Reminded of the poison, he crouched beside Father Dusseault and took the precaution of slipping the ring off the priest's finger.

"You didn't kill him, I hope," the stranger said.

"I tried my best not to. He'll wake up sore."

"As long as he wakes up. I've got questions to ask him. On the other hand, since you seem to know about the Fraternity, maybe you can save me the effort. You don't wear one of their rings. I assume you're not a member. Something tells me you're not a priest either, any more than your friend's a nun."

"I *have* seen you before," Drew said.

11

Saul felt as if he'd been jolted.

"Yesterday. In Switzerland," the priest said. "At the crest of the Albis Pass."

"I drove over it yesterday. Heading toward Zurich."

"In a Renault."

"How the hell—?"

"A woman was in a car behind you," the priest said. "She drove a Volkswagen Golf."

"She's my wife. But how did you—?"

"She looked so intense, so tired, and yet so determined to concentrate on you driving ahead of her. I can't explain why, but when both of you drove past, I identified with you."

Saul felt a second jolt. He wanted to tell the priest about Chris, about his own eerie sense of identification.

But his attention was drawn toward Father Dusseault.

"We have to get him out of here," the priest said.

"Before a guard comes along," Saul agreed and glanced behind him toward the darkness. "My wife'll be wondering what we're talking about. I'd better let her know it's safe to show herself." He turned toward a clump of bushes and waved for her to come out. "You didn't tell me your names. Unless you're still suspicious of me."

The man and the woman looked uncertainly at each other.

"Drew."

"Arlene."

"Saul. My wife's name is Erika. You'll like her." He waved his arm again for Erika to come out.

Waited.

Waved a third time.

And suddenly realized that she wouldn't be emerging from cover, that the world had gone terribly wrong, that his life was on the verge of destruction.

12

Saul raced toward the edge of the murky gardens and stared toward the massive dome of St. Peter's haloed by the night lights of Rome. He'd searched one half of the grounds while the man who called himself Drew checked the other half. Now, seeing a guard near a palace across from him, he knew he had reached the point where he didn't dare go any farther. If Erika wasn't in the gardens, he certainly couldn't hope to find her in the maze of Vatican buildings. Again he wondered what had happened to her. He struggled to analyze the possibilities and concluded that only two made sense. She'd been forced to run, or else she'd been caught. But forced to run or caught by whom? Guards? Someone else in the Fraternity?

More than the agreed-upon twenty minutes had elapsed since he'd begun to search. By now, Drew would have returned to the fountain. *Maybe Drew had found Erika.*

Saul rushed through the night, charging into the clearing next to the fountain, stunned to see it deserted.

He clenched his fists in outrage but heard a footstep to his right and recognized Drew coming from cover.

"We hid in case a guard came along," Drew said. "You're late."

"Did you find her?"

"No . . . I'm sorry."

Saul felt as if razor blades slashed his heart.

"I'm afraid we have to leave," Drew said.

"I understand."

"Will you be coming with us, or do you plan to go on searching?"

Saul turned toward the dark expanse of the gardens. He felt grievously tempted. "No." He had trouble speaking. "If she were here, she'd have shown herself or we'd have found her. I'll keep looking. Somewhere else." His voice broke. "But I can't imagine where."

"We've still got the problem of where to go with the priest."

Saul studied the gardens one last time. It took all his discipline to rouse himself. If he were discovered here, he told himself, it wouldn't help Erika. On the other hand, Father Dusseault might know why she'd disappeared.

He struggled to concentrate. "You'd better follow me."

They had limited options, he realized. They could try to take Father Dusseault back to his apartment, but the odds were too great that a guard would notice and raise an alarm. And if they did somehow manage to reach the apartment, what would they do after that? Question him there? In the morning, someone on his staff might be puzzled by his absence and come to look for him. No, they had to get Father Dusseault out of the Vatican. But how? They'd certainly be stopped if they attempted to carry him through the Vatican's guarded gates at 2 A.M. They might be able to find a hiding place and stay there till morning, but what then? Walk the priest through the checkpoints while the guards were distracted by the usual throng of tourists? But how would they prevent Father Dusseault's battered face from being noticed, and what if the priest caused a commotion at the gate? Only one solution seemed practical. To leave the Vatican now, but not past the guardposts.

Before coming here yesterday, Saul and Erika had scouted the Vatican's perimeter. The city-state was enclosed by a high stone wall. An invader couldn't climb over it unassisted, and anyone trying to scale it with a rope or a ladder would surely attract police intervention.

But invasion was not the intention now. Escape was, and climbing over the Vatican wall from the inside wasn't as difficult as doing so from the outside. Yesterday, Saul had noticed several places where the trees on the inside grew close to the wall.

While Drew and Arlene carried the unconscious priest, Saul preceded them, hoping he'd find Erika. They reached the rear wall of the Vatican and searched along it till they came to a sturdy tree whose branches they could climb to the top of the wall.

Hoisting the priest up through the branches wouldn't be difficult. Getting the priest down the other side would be less easy, requiring two people to stand at the bottom while someone on top held the priest's hands and lowered him as far as possible before letting him drop into waiting arms. As soon as they had him down, they had to assume they'd attract police attention. It was imperative that they leave the area at once.

"I'll go over first," Saul said. "Erika and I left a rented car nearby. Give me twenty minutes to get back here with it. Then start climbing. Lift the priest to the top of the wall. Who knows? Maybe Erika'll be at the car."

"What happens if it isn't where you left it?" Drew asked.

"I'll steal one. No matter what, I'll be back."

13

Drew sank to the ground, his back to the wall, shivering from the dampness. Arlene slid down beside him. He worried that Father Dusseault might waken, feign unconsciousness, and attack when least expected. He tested the injured priest's pulse. It was steady but weak, definitely not the heartbeat of an assassin mustering his reflexes.

Arlene leaned close to his ear. "Do you trust him?"

"Saul? Yes. I have no idea why, but I do."

Reassured, she eased against his shoulder. "What did you say to Father Dusseault to make him attack you?"

294

"I'm not certain." He had conflicting theories about the attack and needed time to think.

Perhaps Father Dusseault had come to the late-night rendezvous with the same intention as Drew, to force answers.

Or else the priest had reacted impulsively, suddenly threatened by Drew's questions about the cardinal and the Nazis.

But as Drew recalled the incident, he realized that Father Dusseault's seemingly spontaneous attack had actually been quite calculated. The priest hadn't thrust his knife toward vital organs, the throat for example, where the kill would be quick and sure, but instead had concentrated on wounding the chest and stomach, where death would take longer and in fact might not occur at all. *He wanted to question me,* Drew thought. *To find out who I was and why I was so curious about the cardinal. After that, he'd have finished me off.*

I think I've found the man who killed Father Victor beside that fountain.

But why would one member of the Fraternity want to kill another? Are Father Sebastian's suspicions correct about someone in the Fraternity trying to destroy it? Is Father Dusseault the traitor?

The answers would come soon enough, he thought. After Saul got back with the car.

But what had Saul said? His wife's father was missing? The disappearance had something to do with three priests, members of the Fraternity, who tried to kill Saul's wife and himself?

And now Saul's wife too was missing. Drew began to suspect that Saul's quest and his own were somehow related, that the answers to Saul's questions would help to answer his own.

He glanced at his watch. Twenty minutes had elapsed.

Arlene anticipated him. "It's time."

She went up the tree, bracing herself among branches, reaching down while Drew lifted Father Dusseault to her.

295

14

A Peugeot pulled up below them, its headlights gleaming. For a tense moment, Drew wondered if the car might belong to the police or the Fraternity. But Saul stepped out, and Drew relaxed. Arlene edged over the wall, landing smoothly. Drew lowered the priest to them, then went down as well. Seconds later, they were in the car.

To Saul's dismay, Erika had not been waiting at the car. "My wife and I rented a hotel room," he said as he drove. "If she's all right, if she had to run from somebody, the hotel's where she'll know she can get in touch with me." He glanced toward Drew and Arlene in the back, the priest out of sight on the floor. "I suggest we take him there."

Saul exhaled with relief when he heard Drew answer, "Under the circumstances, it's the only choice."

The layout of the hotel had been the reason for choosing it, Saul explained. Both the elevator and the fire stairs were down a corridor invisible from the lobby. A rear entrance, near the hotel's parking garage, led into that corridor.

At 3 A.M., no one paid attention to a priest helping another priest into the building, or to a nun who entered a few minutes later, or to the tall swarthy man who'd gone in ahead of them, carrying a suitcase.

The suitcase contained the street clothes Drew and Arlene had worn before they dressed as a priest and nun. On the way to the hotel, Drew had retrieved it from a locker at the train station. They encountered no one in the elevator or along the corridor that led to Saul's hotel room. Once inside, Drew and Arlene took turns using the bathroom to change back into their street clothes while Saul examined the unconscious priest where he lay on the bed.

"His nose is broken."

"That was my intention," Drew said. "The way he

came at me, I tried my damnedest to discourage him. What about his jaw?"

"The bones seem secure. He'll be able to talk."

"But he's awfully slow waking up," Arlene said.

"Yes, that worries me," Saul said. "I checked his eyes. They respond to light. His reflexes work. We might want to put some ice on his nose."

"I'd prefer he stay in pain. He'll answer questions more readily," Drew said.

"You don't have chemicals to make him talk?"

"No," Drew said. "We were given IDs, weapons, and money. That's all."

"What do you mean 'given'? By whom?"

"Someone in the Fraternity forced us to help him."

Saul's eyes widened.

"It's a debt we're paying off," Drew said.

"Believe us," Arlene said, "we don't feel loyal to them."

Saul studied them, reluctantly committing himself further. "All right. I've trusted you so far. Since you're being honest, I'll do the same. There's a group I owe a favor as well."

"Who?"

"I used to work for them. I don't want anything more to do with them, but they manipulated me into cooperating."

"I asked you—"

"The CIA."

"Dear God!"

"I'd like to call them now," Saul said. "We can kid ourselves about the priest's condition, but the fact is he needs medical attention or he won't be alert enough to respond to questions. You put him down good. For all we know, he's got a concussion. We need a team with the proper facilities to bring him back up."

The room became silent.

Arlene turned to Drew. "He's got a point. By the time Father Dusseault's fully conscious, we'll have lost too much time."

"But the *CIA*," Drew said. "You know how I feel about—"

297

"The way you handle yourself," Saul said, "I would have figured you were with them."

"Not with the Agency. With the State Department's version of it. I want nothing to do with either."

"But you agreed to cooperate with the Fraternity," Saul said.

"There wasn't a choice."

"Listen carefully. *My wife is missing.* That's all I care about right now. But I think if I get some answers from this priest, I stand a good chance of finding out where she is. I can get an expert team over here to help. I can do my best to guarantee the Agency doesn't know about you. I'm asking you to let me make the call."

Drew stared at the floor.

Arlene said, "If it helps to end this, Drew, tell him it's okay."

Drew raised his eyes. "We're getting in deeper."

"Tell him."

"All right"—Drew sighed—"make the call."

Saul grabbed the phone and dialed.

A husky voice answered, repeating the number Drew had used.

"This is Romulus. Tell Gallagher I have a reluctant source of information. I need a medical interrogation team. Now."

"What address?" the voice asked.

"He knows where I'm staying."

Saul set the phone back onto its cradle.

"Where the fuck is my wife?"

15

A half hour later, Saul heard a knock on the door. He glanced through its peephole, expecting the man with the pockmarked face, surprised to see Gallagher himself out there. He made a warning gesture to Drew and Arlene, who took their suitcase and shut themselves into the bathroom. Then he opened the hallway door.

Gallagher stepped in, his eyes puffy from lack of sleep. "'A reluctant source of information'?"

Saul shut the door and locked it.

Gallagher kept talking. "Strictly speaking, I belong back in Austria. Our Zurich people didn't object to my entering their jurisdiction. But our Rome people like to run their show themselves. If you'd just agree to let another station chief be your control..."

"You wanted this relationship. Now you're stuck with it," Saul said. "I won't risk trusting anyone else."

"It's so nice to be popular. What have you got?"

Saul led him down a short hallway into the bedroom.

Gallagher blanched when he saw who was on the bed. "Good God, I don't believe it! You kidnapped a priest! How the hell can I put this into a report? And look at his face! What did you do, run over him with a truck?"

"He's not just a priest. He's a personal assistant to a cardinal in the Vatican's Curia."

Gallagher's mouth hung open. "I'll get even with you for this! You've just made my life—!"

"Before you start worrying about your job, take a look at this." Saul showed him the ring Drew had taken from Father Dusseault.

Gallagher studied it in surprise.

"The details are starting to fit together. You already proved that the men who tried to kill me were funded through an office in the Vatican." Saul pointed toward Father Dusseault. "Through *his* office. His boss is the cardinal who's missing." Saul raised the priest's right arm and rolled up the coat sleeve, revealing the spring-loaded sheath. He handed Gallagher the knife Father Dusseault had used. "Just your basic standard equipment for a priest. Believe me, he knew how to use it."

"Keep going. You're convincing me."

"Not only is there a network we never heard of, but I was right—it's composed of priests," Saul said. "They call themselves after the ruby on their ring. The Fraternity of the Stone."

Gallagher chuckled. "Romulus, you're as good as you ever were. You've learned a lot."

"But not enough. I told your man on the phone. I want a medical interrogation team."

"They won't know all the right questions to ask."

"But I do. As soon as he's ready, I want to be alerted. I'll do the questioning. I intend to squeeze this priest for everything he knows."

"What's wrong? Has something happened to you? Your voice sounds—"

"My wife's disappeared."

"*What?*"

"She was with me when we staked out the priest's apartment. He left the building. We followed him separately, to avoid attracting attention." Conscious of Drew and Arlene in the bathroom, Saul omitted their part in the night's events. "After I got my hands on him, I looked for Erika." His throat squeezed shut; he had difficulty continuing. "She vanished. I searched *everywhere*. She's gone. If this priest knows anything about why she disappeared, by God he's going to tell me. If anything's happened to her, whoever did it is going to die."

Gallagher stepped backward.

The phone rang. Saul lunged for it. "Erika?"

But a man's voice said, "Put Gallagher on."

Saul closed his eyes, trying to control his disappointment. He handed the phone to Gallagher.

"Yes, come up," Gallagher said into the phone and set it back on its cradle. He turned to Saul. "That was the team. They're down the block. I didn't want to send them here till I understood what was happening."

"And now you're satisfied?"

"Take it easy. Remember, I'm on your side."

"Are you? Fair warning, Gallagher. Just tell your team to prep the priest. Then he's mine."

"Under other circumstances"—Gallagher squinted— "I wouldn't put up with your tone." His glance diminished. "But I guess you're entitled. Get some sleep. You'd better eat something. You look awful."

"Sleep? Eat? How the hell, when Erika's—?"

"Do it, Romulus. You're not good to her or anyone else if you fuck yourself up."

300

Saul suddenly realized how close to the edge he was. He took a deep breath. "You're right . . . I'm sorry."

"For what? In your place, I'd be climbing the walls. Count on me. I'll do everything I can to help."

Saul smiled in gratitude.

Five minutes later, three men arrived. One was slight and wore glasses. He pursed his lips when he saw the priest's battered face. He checked the priest's vital signs, then turned to Gallagher. "It's safe to move him."

Gallagher nodded.

The two other men stepped forward. Both were well built. "Where do we take him? Back to the shop or—?"

"Can you do it here?" Gallagher asked. "In another room in the hotel?"

"Sooner or later we'll have to take a skull X-ray, but I didn't see any swelling behind his eyes, so I'm probably being overcautious. His blood pressure checks out. Yes, I guess I can do it here in the hotel."

"I already phoned down for a reservation. They had a room at the end of this floor." Gallagher motioned to one of the well-built men. "Go down and check in. Bring the key."

Ten minutes later, the team was ready to leave with the priest.

"I'll need some equipment from the van," the man who wore glasses said.

"Whatever you want," Gallagher said, "you get."

They checked the hallway outside. It was empty. The well-built men braced the priest between them. Holding his arms around their necks, they walked him down the hall. The man who wore glasses followed. No one saw them.

Gallagher turned from where he'd been watching at Saul's open doorway. "Remember, get some rest. I'll phone when he's ready."

Saul leaned against a wall, his knees weak from exhaustion. "I'll be waiting." He locked the door.

16

The bathroom door came open.

"You," Arlene told Saul, "are going to take Gallagher's advice. I'm calling for room service."

"She thinks she's Florence Nightingale. She gets mean when her patients don't let her help," Drew said.

Saul smiled. Fatigue made him slump toward a chair.

Arlene picked up the phone. "My friend here seldom eats meat," she told Saul. "How about scrambled eggs, rolls, and coffee?"

"I'm too tense already," Saul said. "No coffee."

"Milk," Drew said, "and fruit. Lots of fruit."

Arlene made the call to room service. Saul watched her. She was tall and lithe, reminding him of Erika. But there the similarity ended. Arlene's hair wasn't as dark and long. Her face, though beautiful, was more oval. Her skin, though tanned, wasn't naturally swarthy as Erika's was. The big difference was in the eyes. Arlene's were green while Erika's were brown.

Erika.

To distract himself, he shifted his attention toward Drew and again was reminded of Chris. "You still haven't told me whether you're really a priest."

"No." Drew sounded wistful. "I was once a brother, though."

The reference caught Saul by surprise. "Brother? You mean like—?"

"I'm a Roman Catholic. I used to be a monk."

Saul strained to sound casual. "I had an extremely close friend, a foster brother you might say, who was Roman Catholic. Irish."

"I'm Scottish."

"My friend joined a Cistercian monastery and stayed there for six years," Saul said.

"Really? That's quite a coincidence."

"Oh?" Saul's nerves quivered. "How's that?"

"I was in the monastery almost as long. But I was a Carthusian."

"Yes, my friend told me about the Carthusians. He said his own order, the Cistercians, were tough. They didn't speak. They believed in hard physical labor. But the Carthusians—they each lived alone in a cell, hermits for life, totally solitary—he said the Carthusians were the toughest."

"I enjoyed the peace. What was your friend's name?"

"Chris."

"Why did he leave the order?"

"He had nightmares about things he'd been forced to do before he joined the order. In fact, those things were what made him join the order in the first place."

"Things?"

"He was manipulated into being an assassin."

Drew flinched. His shock was palpable.

"You can't understand unless you know that Chris and I were orphans. The institution where we lived was modeled after the military. From when we were kids, we were taught to be warriors. A man unofficially adopted us. His name was Eliot. He took us on trips. He gave us candy. He made us love him."

Saul had difficulty continuing. "It turned out he worked for the government, and his motive for becoming our foster father was to recruit us into intelligence work. After we went through extensive training, he sent us out on missions. The U.S. doesn't officially condone assassination, of course, but that's what we did just the same. We thought our missions were government-sanctioned, supposedly for a just cause. As it happened, we weren't working for the government but for Eliot himself. We loved him so much we'd do anything for him. So he told us to kill. For his own reasons. Chris broke down from the stress of what we were doing. To atone for the things he'd done, he entered the monastery. But his nightmares kept haunting him, and he retreated even more from the world. He lapsed into trances. The condition's called catatonic schizophrenia. Meditative paralysis. The Cistercians insisted on each monk contributing equally to the labor of the monastery, but Chris's trances kept him from working. The order had to ask him to leave."

"He must have felt torn apart."

"Oh, believe me, he did. But he's at peace now."

"How?"

"He was killed," Saul said.

Drew's eyes narrowed.

"Stabbed to death—because Eliot eventually turned against us. To protect his secrets, he betrayed us. I evened the score for Chris, though."

"How?"

"I killed Eliot . . . And you?"

"I'm not sure what you mean," Drew said.

"Why did you leave the Carthusians?"

"A hit team took out the monastery."

Saul blinked in amazement.

17

Beside him, Drew felt Arlene tense in astonishment at his candor.

"Took out the monastery?" Saul asked.

"I'm an orphan, too. My parents were killed when I was ten," Drew said. "In Tokyo. My father worked for the U.S. State Department there. In 1960, he and my mother were blown up by terrorists. The authorities never found whoever was responsible. I was only ten, but I made a vow that one day I'd track them down or, if I couldn't find them, I'd punish whoever was *like* the people who'd murdered my parents. I was sent to America to live with my uncle." Bitterness distorted his voice. "That didn't work out too well. So my father's best friend adopted me. His name was Ray. He worked for the State Department, the same as my father had, and he took me all over the world on his assignments. Wherever we went, I still intended to keep the vow I'd made—to revenge my parents—so Ray recruited me into a secret State Department antiterrorist group called Scalpel. I was trained to be an assassin. For ten years I killed."

"Ten years? What made you stop? Why did you enter the monastery?"

"The same reason as your friend. I had nightmares. In 1979, I was sent on a mission that ended with the death of an innocent man and woman. I blew them up, just as *my* parents had been blown up. Their son saw it happen just as *I'd* seen it happen to mine."

"This man and woman, you say they were innocent? You made a mistake?"

"No. Scalpel *wanted* them killed for political reasons. But I couldn't justify what I'd done. I'd become a version of the people who'd murdered my parents. I'd turned into the scum I was hunting. I was my enemy. I had a . . . breakdown, I guess you'd call it. I was so desperate to redeem myself, to punish myself for my sins, that I became a Carthusian. For almost six years, through penance and prayer, I achieved a measure of peace."

"And that's when the hit team took out the monastery?"

"Nineteen monks were poisoned. Two others were shot. I was the primary target, but I escaped. I vowed to find out who'd killed my fellow monks and threatened my chance for redemption. In the end, I discovered that the man who'd ordered the hit was Ray. He feared that one day, because of my breakdown, I'd reveal secrets about him. He'd been searching for me all those years, and when he finally learned where I'd gone to ground . . . Well, as you said about the man who ordered your foster brother's death, I found Ray, and I killed him."

18

Saul listened, deeply moved. The parallels between his story and Drew's were unnerving.

But Chris had been killed.

And Drew had survived, resembling Chris, with his fair hair, fiery eyes, hint of freckles, and strong-boned rectangular face. Saul had the sense that a niche had been filled in his life, that a ghost had come back.

"You didn't say if you had any brothers," Saul said.

"No brothers. I'm an only child."

Saul smiled. "If you want a brother, you've got one now. You wouldn't have told me your background if you didn't recognize the similarities between... It's uncanny."

"I noticed the parallels," Drew said, "and I can't explain them either."

"Running into each other. How could—? I can't believe it's just a coincidence."

"The question is," Arlene interrupted, "how many other similarities are there?"

19

The two men turned to her.

Arlene had listened with growing distress as Saul and Drew talked to each other. It was startling enough that two men who'd never met before should quickly become so open with each other. Even more startling were the parallels between Drew and Saul's dead foster brother. What Saul had said just now was true—it was uncanny. And the most disturbing part was that she didn't think the surprises were over.

"Other similarities?" Saul asked.

"You showed up in the Vatican gardens at the same time we did—to force information from Father Dusseault," she said. "Doesn't that make you wonder? You've got to be curious what we were doing there. I'm sure curious to know what *you* were doing there. In different ways, did we come there for the same reason?"

"Your wife's father was missing—isn't that what you said?" Drew asked. "And three men tried to kill you? Men who wore a ring identical to Father Dusseault's?"

Saul didn't answer for a moment. Then he shuddered, and it seemed to Arlene that he did so to force his atten-

306

tion back to this conversation. Because, if she guessed correctly, the disappearance of his wife was related to everything they were discussing.

"Right," Saul said. "And we traced those three men to Father Dusseault. To what you called the Fraternity of the Stone. All priests. What *is* the Fraternity?"

"Soldiers for God," Drew said. "Church militants."

"Explain."

"The order dates back to the twelfth century, the Third Crusade," Drew said. "They follow a tradition established by an Arab who converted to Catholicism, became a priest, and used his knowledge of Arab ways to help the crusaders try to liberate the Holy Land from the Muslims."

"Help the crusaders? How?"

"As an assassin. Since he was an Arab, he could easily infiltrate the enemy. His mandate was to execute Muslim leaders in the same brutal way that *their* assassins had executed leaders of the Crusade. Specifically, he came upon his targets while they slept and cut off their heads."

"Graphic," Saul said dryly. "And no doubt dramatically effective."

"The theory was to fight terror with terror. Of course, the crusaders felt that *their* terror was holy."

"And the Church condoned this?"

"At the time," Drew said. "You have to remember the religious fervor that motivated the Third Crusade. The Pope gave a dispensation for any sins committed during what was supposed to be a divinely inspired war against the heathens."

"Times change, though."

"Yes, but the order founded by that assassin-priest didn't. Unknown to the Church, the Fraternity of the Stone continued to practice holy terror throughout the centuries—whenever they considered it necessary to defend the Faith."

"And the ring?"

"A way for them to identify each other. It's a replica of the ring King Richard wore during the Third Crusade.

A ruby that signifies the blood of Christ."

"But why would they want to stop me and Erika from finding her father?" Saul asked. "Are they involved in *Erika's* disappearance?"

"Maybe Father Dusseault will tell us when we question him," Arlene said. "The reason *we* came to the gardens to meet him involved a disappearance as well. A cardinal named Krunoslav Pavelic. Father Dusseault is his assistant."

"I've heard about the disappearance. But why are you looking for him?"

"To pay off a debt," Drew said. "A priest who belonged to the Fraternity tried to recruit me into the order. When I refused, he tried to kill me to protect the order's secrets. Arlene's brother shot him to save my life."

"The Fraternity thought *Drew* had killed the priest," Arlene said. "To protect my brother, to thank him for saving his life, Drew fled as if he were guilty. For the past year, he's been living in Egypt. Three weeks ago, a member of the Fraternity came to me in New York. He said the order had learned where Drew was hiding. He asked me to go to Drew and convince him to provide a service to the Fraternity. In exchange, the order would consider the debt paid in full for the death of the priest."

"What was the service they wanted?"

"Drew had to find the missing cardinal."

"Why couldn't they handle the job themselves?"

"That's what we wondered, too," Drew said. "A Fraternity priest we met in Cairo told us that someone in the order was trying to destroy it, that the key to finding whoever was responsible had something to do with Pavelic's disappearance. If Arlene and I wanted to live in peace, we had to find the cardinal and in so doing find whoever was trying to sabotage the Fraternity. I have a suspicion that Father Dusseault is involved in the betrayal, so some things are starting to come together. But what puzzles me is that two *other* people are looking for the cardinal. Two assassins, the sons of Nazi assassins."

"The sons of Nazi assassins?"

"Their code names are Icicle and Seth."

Saul stood in distress. "A blond and a redhead?"

"You *know* about them?"

"When I was in the Agency, I heard rumors. About Seth in particular. He's supposed to be crazy. *What the hell is going on?*"

"And is there a connection? Among what you want, we want, and *they* want?" Arlene asked.

"Disappearances—my wife and her father," Saul said. "And priest-assassins."

"A cardinal's disappearance," Drew said. "And the sons of Nazi assassins."

20

In darkness, Icicle sat on a damp concrete floor in the basement of a palace near the Sistine Chapel. He couldn't see the unconscious woman sprawled beside him, but he could feel her body heat and, if he leaned close, hear her faint breathing. Of course, he couldn't see Seth on the other side of her either, but it bothered him that he could *hear* Seth—the faint brush of Seth's hand along her body. Icicle tried to hold his disgust in check.

Yesterday afternoon, determined to force information from the missing cardinal's assistant, Father Dusseault, they'd entered the Vatican among a group of tourists. A guide had escorted the group through St. Peter's Basilica; Icicle and Seth had hung back, looking for a place where they could hide until nightfall. The door to this murky basement had been unlocked. At midnight, they'd left the palace basement and walked toward Father Dusseault's apartment. Experts at becoming one with the night, they were never noticed.

Their plan was to enter the priest's apartment while he slept, to subdue him, and to question him throughout the night. When they reached the corner of the street

309

that ran along the entrance to the priest's apartment building, they paused to study the approach before moving in. But just as Seth stepped forward, Icicle tugged him back behind cover and pointed toward an alcove a third of the way down the street, on the opposite side. That recess, deep and dark, had been one of Icicle's intended hiding places.

But someone else had the same idea. A shadow moved within the alcove. A man leaned forward, gazed up toward a window of the apartment building across from him, then stepped back into the dark. He showed himself for only a moment, but it was enough for Icicle to see that the man did not wear the black suit of a priest —he was an outsider, the same as Icicle and Seth.

They watched the man watch the building. In a while, the man peered down the street, then moved back in. He didn't do so conspicuously. He was obviously experienced. The way he peered down the street suggested that he wasn't alone, that he was waiting to give or receive a signal.

A priest stepped out of the apartment building, glanced both ways along the street and headed to his left, away from Icicle and Seth, away from the man who watched the building. The man remained in place, but farther down the street, after the priest had passed a doorway, a *woman* eased into view and followed. Icicle's muscles tightened. A man and a woman? He and Seth had crossed paths with a man and a woman before. During the abduction of Medici.

But the man shifted out to follow the priest as well, and when Icicle got a good look at him, he decided that this couple was definitely not the couple he'd seen before. The man was more husky, the woman had longer hair.

Despite the differences, the fact that again a man and woman were staking out sites where Icicle and Seth were engaged in a mission made Icicle nervous. Were they, too, after Father Dusseault? Indeed, was the priest he'd just seen Father Dusseault? He'd never met the man or seen a photograph of him. The best thing to do, Icicle decided, was to follow. Icicle motioned to Seth and stepped out into the street.

Their wary pursuit led them deep within the Vatican gardens where, staying carefully back from the man and woman, they had a distant view of a Spanish-galleon fountain in a clearing. Moonlight revealed a priest standing before the fountain. Icicle sank to his stomach. With Seth beside him, he crawled nearer, wanting a better view of the priest, anxious to see if he was the same priest who'd left the apartment building.

No. He wasn't. But with a shock, Icicle realized that this *was* the same man he'd seen in the alley during Medici's abduction. Baffled, he glanced at Seth, who had also recognized the man and shook his head in confusion. A second priest—the one who'd left the apartment building, whom Icicle suspected was Father Dusseault— stepped into the clearing. They spoke to one another. Surprisingly, Father Dusseault lunged with a knife. Just as amazingly, the other priest defended himself superbly. Though Father Dusseault was good, the other priest was better, taking the advantage, striking Father Dusseault repeatedly, knocking him senseless to the ground.

Icicle watched in awe. He'd never heard of priests who handled themselves like warriors. A nun rushed into the clearing—the same woman Icicle had seen the other night in the alley with this man. Icicle wanted more desperately to know what was going on. He and Seth could have used their silenced handguns to disable them and make them explain. But he was aware that he and Seth weren't alone out here. The other couple, the strangers, were hidden somewhere, watching. The man they'd followed stepped into the clearing, his hands raised. Icicle was tempted to risk crawling even closer in the hopes of hearing what they said to one another.

But Seth distracted him. The assassin pulled a flat leather case from a jacket pocket, removed a hypodermic, and crawled not forward but toward the right, as if he meant to circle the clearing. Puzzled, Icicle went after him, and as Seth stopped, scanned dark bushes, and crawled farther, Icicle realized that Seth was stalking the woman they'd noticed outside the apartment building. She hadn't yet shown herself in the gardens; she must have decided to wait to see what would happen in the clearing.

Her shadow rose behind a tree twenty yards to Icicle's left. From the clearing, she could not have been seen, but from Icicle's vantage point behind her, she was distinct. Seth inched toward her, poised himself, and lunged to sweep a hand across her mouth at the same time that he plunged the needle into her arm. She struggled for less than five seconds.

Seth eased her silently backward, away from the clearing. Icicle joined him, reaching to help him carry her, but Seth shoved his arm away. The red-haired man's eyes gleamed fiercely, signaling *she's mine*. Icicle shuddered, realizing that Seth was sicker than he'd imagined. Seth shuddered also, with sexual pleasure, lifting the woman so her stomach was over his shoulder, her breasts pressed against his back.

They returned to this dark palace basement . . . where, the unconscious woman next to him and Seth on the other side of her, Icicle struggled to contain his revulsion, hearing Seth's hand brush along her body. The night had been long. He pressed a button on his digital watch: 7:23. He imagined the daylight outside. He didn't know how he'd be able to bear sitting in this dark musty room, waiting for nine o'clock, when tourists would be allowed to enter the Vatican and they could leave, pretending the woman had suddenly fainted.

21

"Too much wine, too little sleep," Icicle said in Italian to a solicitous desk clerk when he and Seth reached their hotel. They stood with the woman held up between them while they waited for the elevator doors to open. "Jet lag and all-night partying don't go together, I'm sorry to say." He tipped the clerk in appreciation for his concern. "Tonight, she'll probably want to go dancing."

The clerk smiled knowingly and told them if they needed anything...

"We'll phone the front desk and ask specifically for you," Icicle said.

The elevator opened. They stepped inside and went up to their room.

While Icicle locked the door, Seth carried the woman to the bed.

"Is she all right?"

Seth checked her eyes. "She's coming around. We'll soon be able to question her." He took off her shoes and massaged her feet.

Icicle tasted bile. It took all his effort to keep from telling Seth to stop touching her. "Did you recognize the man and woman dressed as a priest and nun?"

"From when we grabbed Medici. They wore street clothes then. It makes me wonder if tonight they were in disguise. And now *another* man and woman are involved. The one couple didn't seem to know the other." Seth brooded. "What was their interest in Father Dusseault? Did each couple have a different motive or the same? Are their motives *ours*?"

"To learn what the priest knows about the disappearance of our fathers?" Sickened, Icicle averted his gaze from where Seth now touched the woman. "No. They're not part of our group. They don't have a reason to look for our fathers."

"But they might have a reason to look for the missing cardinal," Seth said. To Icicle's relief, he took his hands away from the woman. "And there might be a connection between this woman and our missing fathers. She's almost certainly Jewish."

"That could be coincidental."

"Possibly," Seth said, "but not probably."

"We'll soon find out." Seth undid her belt, opened the button on the waist of her slacks, and tugged her zipper down, revealing a glimpse of peach-colored panties.

Icicle couldn't restrain his disgust any longer. "No."

Seth glanced at him, frowning. His voice was hard. "I beg your pardon?"

"What you've got in mind to do to her before she wakes up, forget it."

"Do to her?" Seth smiled coldly. "My indignant friend, what exactly do you think I intend to do to her?"

"I'm telling you to forget it."

"What I intend to do is remove her slacks—to make her more comfortable during the interrogation. As well, her bodily functions are overdue. She'll need to use the bathroom." Seth pulled off the woman's slacks, exposing her legs.

The woman murmured, drawing her knees toward her stomach as if she were cold.

"Come along now." Seth raised her to a sitting position, put her arm around his neck, and helped her to stand. With a challenging look toward Icicle, he started into the bathroom with her.

"I'll go with you," Icicle said.

"No need. I can manage her myself."

"The two of us can manage her better."

Seth squinted. "One moment you're afraid I'll assault her—the next you want to watch her go to the bathroom. Your values are confused."

Refusing to be taunted, Icicle took the woman's other arm and escorted her and Seth into the bathroom. Embarrassed, he watched Seth take off her panties and sit her on the toilet. Her head flopped one way, then the other.

"Try to relieve yourself," Seth said. "We don't want any accidents, do we?"

Icicle almost slapped Seth's hand away when he pressed her abdomen.

No! My father! I have to find my father! Nothing must interfere! I can deal with Seth later, but right now ...!

To Icicle's relief, the woman urinated.

They carried her back to the bed. Again she drew her knees toward her stomach.

"What are you doing?" Seth barked at Icicle.

"Putting her underwear back on."

"She doesn't need them!"

They stared at each other. The room compacted with tension.

Icicle reached for a corner of the bedspread, about to drape it over her.

"No." Seth's eyes blazed in warning. "The drug works better if she's chilly."

Icicle realized they were at the danger point. If he didn't back off, in all probability there'd be a fight. His father had to take priority. "Whatever you say."

"That's exactly correct. Whatever I say. I wouldn't want our friendship to be strained." Seth's tone was mocking. *"Get on with it. Question her."*

While you concentrate on her nakedness, Icicle thought angrily.

He stepped to the bureau, opened a drawer, and removed a vial of Sodium-Amytal powder. In a larger vial, he mixed five hundred milligrams of the powder with twenty milliliters of distilled water. He filled a hypodermic.

22

"Can you hear me?"

The woman didn't answer.

Icicle leaned close and repeated the question.

The woman nodded, her voice weak. "Hear you . . ."

"Good. You mustn't worry. You're safe. You have nothing to fear. You're with friends."

"Friends . . ."

"That's right. Now tell us your name."

"Erika . . ."

"And your last name?"

"Bernstein-Grisman."

The last name left no doubt, Icicle thought. The woman was Jewish, as Seth had suspected.

Icicle's tone was gentle. "Why did you follow Father Dusseault to the Vatican gardens?"

315

"Three men tried to kill us . . ."

The nonsequitur made Icicle close his eyes in frustration. But he persisted with his gentle tone. "You can tell us about the three men later, Erika. What about Father Dusseault?"

Another nonsequitur. "My father disappeared."

The problem, Icicle decided, was whether to keep her talking about Father Dusseault or whether to follow her random associations. What Erika knew might be so complicated that he'd fail to learn vital information if he kept his questions within too narrow a range. Certainly her statement about her father, though seemingly irrelevant, was disturbing enough to merit inquiry. "Disappeared? When?"

"Two weeks ago."

"Where?"

"Vienna."

"Why did he disappear?"

"Don't know . . ."

Even in a stupor, the woman became so agitated that Icicle chose nonthreatening questions—to make her feel at ease, to accustom her to talking freely. "Tell us about your father."

She didn't answer.

Icicle made his questions more specific. "How old is he?"

"Seventy . . ."

"Does he still have a job?"

"Retired . . ."

"From what?" Already Icicle felt bored by the unimportant questions with which he attempted to calm her. "How did he earn his living?"

"Mossad . . ."

The unexpected response cramped Icicle's heart. He pivoted toward Seth, who jerked his surprised gaze up from the woman's legs.

Icicle turned again to the woman. "Your father was once an operative for the Mossad?"

"Yes."

"Do *you* work for the Mossad?"

"No."

The pressure around Icicle's heart eased.

"Resigned . . ."

"Why?"

"Wanted to be with my husband . . ."

"The man who was with you in the Vatican gardens? Does *he* work for the Mossad?"

"No."

"Did he ever?"

"No."

"What's your husband's profession?"

"Farmer."

"Where?"

"In Israel."

"Why did the two of you leave there?"

"To look for my father." Her voice increased in strength. Her eyelids fluttered.

Icicle walked to the bureau, filled a second syringe with the Sodium-Amytal solution he'd prepared earlier, and injected a small amount into her femoral artery. The drug worked almost instantaneously. Her body relaxed.

"When you and your husband left Israel to search for your father, where did you go?"

"Vienna."

"Where he disappeared. Of course. And where did you go after that?"

"Switzerland."

The answer surprised him. "What?"

"The Alps south of Zurich."

Icicle hesitated. "Why did you go there?"

"To look for a friend of my father."

"Did you find him?"

"No . . . Disappeared."

For a second time, an unexpected answer.

"A diary . . ."

"I don't understand."

"Found a diary . . ."

"What was in it?"

"Nazi concentration camp . . ."

Oh, Jesus, Icicle thought.

"Your father's friend wrote a diary about the camp?"

"Yes."

"Was your father ever in a camp?"

"Yes."

Icicle had the terrible sense that a pattern was forming.

But she suddenly shifted topics. "Three men tried to kill us."

Icicle let her lead him. "Yes, you mentioned them earlier. Where did this happen?"

"The Alps."

"Who were they?"

"Think they were priests . . ."

She was talking nonsense. Had the drug distorted her memory?

She began to tremble, agitated by the semiconscious memory of the . . .

"Priests?" Icicle asked. "Why would priests want to kill you?"

Her trembling increased. "Father Dusseault."

Icicle's pulse sped. They were back to the question with which he'd started.

"What about Father Dusseault? Why did you follow him? Is he connected with the priests who tried to kill you?"

"Paid through the cardinal's office."

"Cardinal *Pavelic's* office? The one who disappeared? *Do you know where the cardinal is?*"

"No."

"Are you looking for him?"

"No."

Icicle's excitement changed to frustration. She had led him in a meaningless circle.

23

It took two hours. Icicle guided her back through what she'd told him, prompting her for more details. As before, she became agitated when she talked about her missing father, about the three priests who'd tried to kill her husband and herself. At last, he turned from the woman and paced toward the far end of the room. He'd asked every question he could think of and learned too little. What bothered him were the questions he *hadn't* been able to think of, the unimaginable information she might have volunteered if only he knew what to ask for.

Seth continued to stare at the woman's nakedness.

"What do you make of the rings she described?" Icicle asked.

"Assassin-priests?" Seth turned from her. "I've practiced my trade for twenty years, and I've never heard of such a group."

"Nor have I. That doesn't mean she's mistaken. The group might be extremely cautious. And what about her father's disappearance? Is it related to the disappearance of our own fathers? To the disappearance of the cardinal?"

"The common element seems to be Father Dusseault," Seth said. "For different reasons, our search and this woman's led us to him."

"Let's not forget the other man and woman we saw in the gardens, the ones dressed as a priest and a nun. What reason did *they* have to go after Father Dusseault? Why were they interested in Medici, just as we were? I'm sure it's all connected. Father Dusseault had the answers, but we've lost the chance to question him."

"Perhaps," Seth said.

Icicle frowned. "What are you thinking of?"

"The notion isn't fully formed yet. I'll tell you when I'm sure it'll work." Staring at the woman, Seth took off his sportcoat and began to unbutton his shirt.

Icicle stepped protectively toward her. "Why are you undressing?"

"Relax. For the moment, this woman's body no longer interests me. I need to shave and shower. I'm going out. You'll have to stay here and keep her sedated." Seth walked toward the bathroom.

"Going out?" Icicle's stomach squirmed with suspicion. "Why?" He quickly followed Seth into the bathroom. "What do you—? Of course," he realized. "It's time we reported to Halloway. You'll want to use a safe phone to call him."

"Report to Halloway?" Seth said with contempt. "Not at all. We don't have anything conclusive to tell him. I make a habit of announcing success, not failure." Seth turned on the shower. "But with luck, if my errand proves successful, we will have positive news for him. Very soon."

24

Saul awoke from a nightmare in which, surrounded by darkness, he heard Erika scream. He bolted up, heard his wife scream again, and scrambled from bed to get to her before he realized that the screams were really the ringing of the telephone. Fully clothed, he found himself in the middle of the Rome hotel room. He had slept on a couch, Drew and Arlene on the double bed. Sunlight glowed beyond closed draperies.

Saul picked up the phone, praying he'd hear Erika's voice. Instead he heard Gallagher's raspy, tired.

"Romulus, the priest is ready for you to hear his confession. Come down to the room."

"I'm on my way." Saul looked at his watch. The time was shortly after 10 A.M. He'd gotten six hours' sleep, but his nightmares had tortured him. He felt as exhausted as when he'd lain down.

Drew and Arlene had awoken.

"Who was that?" Drew asked.

"Gallagher. It's quiz time." Saul went into the bathroom, splashed cold water on his face, then returned to Drew and Arlene. "Are you still determined not to get involved with the Agency?"

"I've got trouble enough with the Fraternity. I don't want to complicate my troubles by dealing with another network. After Scalpel, I've had my fill of networks," Drew said. "The Agency would want to know everything about me. They'd try to recruit me, and failing that, they'd keep me under surveillance. They're like Krazy Glue. Once they touch you, you're stuck. Arlene and I just want to be left alone."

"Then we've got a problem," Saul said. "I have to go to Gallagher and the priest, but I don't know what questions to ask. *You're* here to find the cardinal and whoever's trying to destroy the Fraternity. *I'm* here to find Erika and her father. I'm sure your search and mine have something to do with each other. I think the answers to your questions might help me answer my own. But if you won't let the Agency know you're involved, how can we both question the priest?"

25

Saul knocked on Gallagher's door. He heard the scrape of a lock being freed. In a moment, the door was opened, and he stepped inside, his nostrils feeling pinched from the smell of medication. He approached Father Dusseault, who was lying on the bed. The priest looked pasty. His broken nose had swelled. So had the bruised skin along his eyebrows. His jaw was puffy. The priest's black suitcoat had been removed, his shirt opened, his sleeves rolled up. Sensors attached to his chest and arms transmitted signals to portable heart and blood-pressure monitors that sat on a bureau shifted close to the bed.

Saul surveyed the rest of the room. The bathroom

door was open. The doctor and his assistants were gone. "Where—?"

"I sent them out to eat breakfast," Gallagher said. "What they don't hear won't burden them with something else to forget. I can have them paged in the restaurant if we have an emergency. They'll phone in an hour to find out when it's time to come back."

Saul turned again toward Father Dusseault, studying the IV that controlled the flow of Sodium Amytal into the priest's arm.

"He's still asleep," Saul said. "Does that mean he had a concussion?"

"No. In fact, he came around two hours ago. The doctor had to sedate him."

"But he can answer questions?"

"The monitors show he's at an ideal semiconscious level. He's primed to tell you anything you want to know."

"Good. Now I've got a favor to ask."

Gallagher shifted his weight. "You've had plenty of favors as it is. In case you've forgotten, this started with your promising to do *us* a favor if we let you come out of exile. But little by little, you've maneuvered us so we keep giving *you* favors. It's getting tiresome."

"One more. What's the harm?"

"I'll know when you tell me what you want."

"To be alone when I question the priest."

Gallagher stopped moving. "Jesus, you've got more nerve than—!"

"It's for your own benefit. If something goes wrong, if he *dies*, do you really want to be present when it happens? Do you want the Agency implicated in the death of a Vatican official?"

"Bullshit, Romulus. If he died, who'd know except you and me?"

"That's the point. Both of us would be one too many. You'd worry if you could trust me with what I knew if the priest didn't survive the interrogation. Maybe you'd decide I'm too dangerous a liability. I'm not anxious to sell my soul to the Agency again or have an unexpected

322

accident. So do yourself a favor and join the team for breakfast. Do *me* a favor by letting me take as many risks as I have to when I question the priest. I'll tell you everything I learn."

"How can I be sure of that?"

"Because I need you. I wouldn't have been able to come this far without your help. And with more help from you, I hope to go a lot farther. It's for sure he'll tell me things I can't follow up without the resources of the Agency. You have my word. You'll be told everything I learn about the Fraternity. All I want to know is what happened to my wife and her father."

Gallagher pursed his lips. "I know I'll be sorry for this. Your word?"

Saul nodded.

"You always played straight," Gallagher said. "It's one of the reasons I went along with you this far. I hope you haven't changed—because in that case you *will* have an accident. Two hours. After that, no matter what excuses you make, I'm coming back."

"You've got a deal."

Gallagher left. Saul waited long enough for Gallagher to have gone downstairs, then picked up the phone. He dialed as silently as possible, let the other end ring once, then hung up. He swung toward Father Dusseault. Two hours. He had to cram as much as he could into them. In a rush, he disconnected the sensors from the priest's chest and arms. He buttoned the priest's shirt but left the IV tube in his arm. Raising the priest off the bed, Saul grabbed the bottle of Sodium-Amytal solution and supported the priest toward the door. He managed to free the lock. Someone opened the door from the other side —Drew, who'd been alerted to hurry from Saul's room down to this one as soon as he heard a single ring on the phone. Wordlessly, Drew helped Saul bring Father Dusseault into the hallway, then gently shut the door behind them.

Silence was mandatory. It wasn't sufficient for Gallagher to have left the room so that Saul could protect Drew and Arlene from the Agency, because Saul was certain the room had electronic eavesdropping monitors. Gallagher was thorough. He'd want a record of the interrogation, a tape to listen to while he sifted through the information the priest supplied. In fact, Saul had counted on the microphones in the room to give Gallagher a rationalization for going downstairs. After all, from Gallagher's point of view, what difference did it make if he wasn't in the room during the interrogation as long as he had a recording of what was said? But if the interrogation had taken place in the room, Drew and Arlene would have had their voices on the tape, and Gallagher would next have interrogated *them*.

Saul felt exposed in the corridor, worrying that a guest or a member of the hotel staff would appear and notice Drew and himself supporting Father Dusseault. There wasn't any way to eliminate that danger. Saul heard the elevator rising and muffled voices behind a door. A lock scraped open behind him. He and Drew got the priest to his own door, opened it, and stepped inside just as a door came open down the hall and someone stepped out.

But by then Arlene was already closing his own door, locking it while he and Drew carried Father Dusseault to the bed. They set him down gently, placing a pillow beneath his head and stretching out his legs.

"Gallagher gave me only two hours."

"It's not enough time," Drew said.

"It'll *have* to be enough."

"What if Gallagher has a team listening to the microphones you think are planted in the other room?" Arlene asked. "When all they hear is silence, they'll know you're not questioning the priest. They'll warn Gallagher that something's wrong."

"I don't think there *is* a team," Saul said. "When Gallagher found out I'd kidnapped a Vatican official, he started worrying about his involvement with me. If this goes wrong, he knows he could lose his job. He's already concerned about the doctor and his assistants learning too much. He told them to leave before he sent for me. My guess is he doesn't have anyone listening to the microphones. The recording he hoped to get from the inter-rogation would have been for his ears only."

"Then at least we can count on the two hours we've got."

"Less than that now," Saul said. "We'd better get started."

Drew held up the bottle of Sodium-Amytal solution. Arlene inserted the needle from its tube into the valve mechanism of the tube leading into Father Dusseault's arm. Saul leaned close to the priest.

"We're your friends. You're safe. You don't have anything to worry about. Relax."

"Relax..." Father Dusseault's voice was faint, scratchy, as if his throat were dry.

"You feel at peace. Tell us everything we ask for. Hold nothing back. You can trust us."

"Trust you..."

Saul hesitated, trying to decide what his first question should be. There were many to choose from, but if he asked them at random, it would take too long to fit the priest's disparate responses together. He needed to construct a sequence in which the questions would lead logically from one to another.

But Drew intervened, going directly to the core of his own problem. "Do you know what happened to Cardinal Pavelic?"

"I killed him...cremated his body."

In shock, Drew glanced at Arlene and Saul.

"Why?"

"He found out what I'd done."

"What was *that*?"

"Told the Jews."

Saul stiffened. "Jews?"

Arlene asked, "What did you tell them?"

"About the Nazis."

The room became silent. Saul had the sense that a log was about to be overturned, a monstrosity revealed.

26

The revelation came slowly.

In 1941, as the result of an anti-Nazi coup that overthrew the pro-German government of Yugoslavia, Hitler determined to punish Yugoslavia so severely that no other nation would be similarly tempted to try to secede from the Third Reich. Its capital, Belgrade, was destroyed by massive aerial bombardment. The German army invaded, crushing all further rebellion. The country was subdivided, chunks of it annexed into Bulgaria, Albania, Hungary, and Italy. The greater portion became a separate Nazi puppet-state called Croatia.

Hell was in season. The newly installed Croatian government instigated a policy of racial and religious purification so brutal that even seasoned SS officers were appalled. A fanatical group of Croatians, called the Ustashi, became the government's instrument of purgation, hunting down Serbs, Jews, and gypsies. Victims were prodded to death in ponds; were made to kneel, their hands on the ground, while their heads were sawn off; had sharp sticks shoved down their throats; had drills thrust up their rectums; were disemboweled, set on fire, sledgehammered, trucked to mountaintops and thrown off cliffs, then blown apart by grenades. Those not killed where they were discovered endured the agony of concentration camps, dying slowly from starvation, dysentery, and exposure. The lucky ones were merely shot. At least six hundred thousand persons were slaughtered, perhaps as many as one and a quarter million.

Father Krunoslav Pavelic—born and raised in Yugoslavia—supported the Ustashi and their Nazi masters. Part of his motive was practical: to ally himself with the winning side. But part of his motive was also ideological: he firmly believed he was doing God's work. Racial matters aside, he applauded the elimination of all religions except Roman Catholicism. The Jews and the gypsies were heathen as far as he was concerned, and the Serbs —primarily Greek Orthodox Catholic—needed to be eliminated because of their break from the one true Faith. Not only did Father Pavelic support the Ustashi: he banded with them; he led them.

Church officials were unaware of Pavelic's personal holy war. But the inner circle did know about the massive Greek Orthodox murders in Croatia and knew as well about the even more massive Nazi slaughter of the Jews. With some exceptions, Church officials did nothing to try to stop the slaughter. Their rationalization was that, to protect its existence, the Church had to remain neutral. If Hitler won the war and if he'd perceived the Church as his enemy, he would destroy it just as he had Yugoslavia. "Pray and wait" became the Church's motto. "Survive these desperate times as best we can."

Following Hitler's defeat in 1945, one of the Church's methods of compensation was to assist refugees, particularly through the Red Cross. By then, Father Pavelic had been transferred from Croatia to Rome, where he arranged to be assigned to the Red Cross refugee program. From there, he secretly passed word through his contacts in the Ustashi that he would help defeated followers of what he still believed to be a just cause to escape retribution for what the Allies were calling war crimes.

He would do this for a fee—to assist the Church in its good works. The fee was the equivalent of the then considerable sum of two thousand dollars per fugitive. Only high-ranking Nazi officials were able to plunder enough to afford such a price. As a consequence, Father Pavelic's clients were among the most-hunted of war criminals, some of those directly responsible for the organization and perpetration of the Holocaust. Using Red Cross passports, Father Pavelic provided them with new identities and arranged for their safe passage to hiding places in South America, Mexico, the United States, Canada, and the Middle East. On occasion, he disguised his clients as priests, sequestered them in monasteries, waited until their hunters had lost the trail, and then used Vatican passports to expedite their escape.

But if his clients thought they'd heard the last of him

327

when they reached safety, they were soon surprised to learn that he'd kept track of them—where they'd finally settled, how they earned their living—and demanded a yearly bonus payment from them in exchange for his silence. Failing that, he threatened he would expose them. He took a risk, he knew. If his clients refused to pay and he had to inform against them, those he'd betrayed would no doubt implicate him in their escape. But it never came to that; his clients were too afraid of being punished to refuse his demands. He took another risk as well—that his clients would try to kill him rather than pay their yearly tribute. To protect himself, he made sure they understood that the documents about them were carefully hidden. If he were killed, a trusted associate would receive instructions about where the papers were, with orders to relay them to the authorities.

His clients acquiesced. At first, their yearly payment was the same as what they'd paid initially—two thousand dollars. But as they prospered, Father Pavelic increased the amount. In total, he'd received millions. The money was not for his own use. He wasn't venal. Every penny was given to the Church, to support the Faith. With the power that the money gave him, and with his talent for bureaucratic intrigue, he managed to attract supporters within the Vatican. Other Curia members, who'd discovered the nature of his activities during and after the war, found that they too had to support him, for unless he was promoted, he threatened to embarrass the Church by implicating it in his rescue of Nazi war criminals. Here, too, he took a risk—his loyalty to the Church was such that he would never have created a scandal about it. But his enemies weren't aware of his scruples, and along with his supporters, they did promote him. By the age of thirty-five, he was both a cardinal and a junior member of the Church's governing body. Five years after that, he became a senior member, one of those responsible for administering the Church's finances.

Saul, Drew, and Arlene learned all this from Father Dusseault. The priest's explanation wasn't coherent.

They had to assemble the puzzle on their own. But when this portion of the interrogation was completed, they knew that Father Dusseault, a member of the Fraternity assigned to the Vatican, using the cover of Cardinal Pavelic's assistant, had become suspicious about the source of some of the funds the cardinal was contributing to the Church. Through resources available to him as a member of the Fraternity, Father Dusseault discovered the cardinal's secret. Outraged by the cardinal's participation in the Holocaust and his manipulation of the Church, Father Dusseault determined to see justice finally done.

27

Saul leaned even closer to Father Dusseault. Drew and Arlene had been told much of what they needed to know. Now it was his turn. *Where were Erika and her father?* The priest's story about Nazis and Jews made him more convinced than ever that he was close to the truth.

"What did you do about what you learned? How did you seek justice?"

"By telling the Jews."

"What Jews? Who did you tell?"

"Mossad."

"*Who* in the Mossad?"

"Ephraim Avidan."

Saul's stunned reaction must have shown. Drew and Arlene looked at him in wonder.

Of course, he thought. They don't know about the cabin in the Alps that Erika and I visited. They don't know about the diary Avidan kept.

"Why did you choose him?" Saul asked.

"He'd been in a camp. . . . Wanted someone who'd act."

Saul understood. In recent years, Israel had been

329

much less assiduous in tracking down war criminals, preferring instead to create an image of restraint and balance, of being superior to the methods of its enemies. Vengeance had been replaced by politics and the due process of law. Impatient, Father Dusseault had used the resources of the Fraternity to find a Mossad operative who hated the Nazis for persecuting his family and himself as well as his race, whose background guaranteed direct reprisal in place of bureaucratic paralysis.

"But Cardinal Pavelic discovered what you'd done?" Arlene asked.

"Threatened me. Had to shoot him."

The cardinal's body had been cremated just as many of his victims had been, a prudent and appropriate method of disposing of the cardinal's remains. An investigation into the cardinal's disappearance was less dangerous to Father Dusseault than an investigation into his murder.

"Did you kill Father Victor?" Drew asked.

Saul started to ask who Father Victor was, but Drew stopped him with a gesture.

"Yes."

"Because he suspected you'd murdered the cardinal?" Drew asked.

"No."

"Then why did you kill Father Victor?" Drew asked.

"Discovered my attempts to destroy the Fraternity."

A further layer was revealed. The priest had come to despise the militant philosophy of the order to which he belonged, convinced that God wanted peacemakers, not warriors. As he'd felt obligated to cleanse the Church of Cardinal Pavelic's corruption, so he'd set out to excise the cancer of the Fraternity from the Church, sabotaging its operations whenever he could. When Father Victor, an investigator for the Fraternity, had become too suspicious, his quarry had been forced to shoot him during a late-night meeting in the Vatican gardens. The pistol had been equipped with a silencer. Nonetheless, its muffled noise had been heard by a guard who raised an alarm. Father Dusseault had to escape before he could dispose of the body as he had Cardinal Pavelic's. That explained why he'd chosen the greater silence of a knife when he'd gone after Drew in the gardens.

Saul was impatient. The priest had veered from what he needed to know. "Does the name Joseph Bernstein mean anything to you?"

"No."

"My wife followed you into the gardens. Did you have someone go there with you, as a backup? Do you know why she would have disappeared?"

"No."

Saul rubbed his temples. He stared at his watch. "We've only got twenty minutes before Gallagher comes back to the other room," he told Drew and Arlene. "It's not enough time. How am I going to find out—?"

The phone rang, harsh. Saul flinched in surprise. "If that's Gallagher..."

"He might have called his own room," Arlene said. "When he didn't get an answer, he called here."

"Maybe," Saul said. "But I don't think Gallagher would have used the phone. He'd have come right up. Besides, it isn't time for him to check in. He promised me a full two hours."

"It could be he had misgivings and changed his mind," Drew said.

The phone kept ringing.

"Maybe it isn't Gallagher," Saul said. "Maybe it's—" He didn't say Erika, but her name screamed through his mind as he reached for the phone. "Hello."

"Saul Grisman?" The voice belonged to a man. It was thin, with a faint metallic edge like a knife being sharpened on a whetstone.

"Yes."

"You must be distressed about your wife. No need to wonder any longer. We have her."

"*We?* Who the hell—?"

Drew and Arlene stood rigidly straight.

"You surely don't expect us to reveal our names," the voice said. "All you need to know is that we have her and she's safe."

"How do I know that?" Saul demanded. *"Let me talk to her."*

"Unfortunately, that isn't possible. She isn't with me at the moment, and even if she were, she's been sedated. But you can see her."

"How?"

"In fact," the voice said, "you can have her returned to you. If certain conditions are met. We'd like to arrange a trade. Your wife for the priest. You *do* have the priest, I hope. Otherwise there's no point to this conversation."

"Yes. I have the priest."

"We'd want to be sure of that. It wouldn't do to base your transaction on dishonesty. It would go very hard on your wife if you weren't completely honest."

"I told you I've got him!" Saul said.

"At six o'clock this evening, bring him to the Colosseum. In the last hours before sunset, the ruins will be crowded with tourists. Blend with them. Sit the priest down in the middle of the terraces on the northern side. I'll use binoculars from the opposite side to identify him. Make sure he's reasonably alert. I want to satisfy myself that he's capable of walking under his own power. But I don't want him so conscious that he'll make trouble. As soon as I'm sure you've brought the priest, I'll arrange for your wife to be placed across from you, on the southern terraces of the Colosseum. Bring binoculars, and assure yourself that she too is in satisfactory condition. When each of us sees what he wants, a man who appears to be a tourist will set a blue travel bag beside her and walk away. That will be the signal for us to make the trade. Approach your wife by circling to the right of the arena. I in turn will circle to your left. In this way, we'll never pass each other, and there won't be a risk of an unfortunate confrontation. Wait five minutes before leaving the Colosseum with your wife. I'd prefer not to rush getting the priest out of there."

Saul gripped the phone so tightly he thought its plastic would crack. "Agreed. At six o'clock."

"There *is* one further condition."

Saul began to sweat.

"In questioning your wife," the voice said, "I learned that she used to be an operative for the Mossad. Are they involved in this?"

"No."

"You'd say that, no matter what. I have to be sure. It's imperative—your wife's safety depends upon it—that you don't bring help with you when the transfer is made. No associates of any kind. That includes the man and the woman who were dressed as a priest and a nun in the Vatican gardens last night. We know what they look like. If we see them, if we suspect any sign of surveillance, any attempt to interfere with the transaction, your wife will be killed. When I leave with the priest, if I sense I'm being followed, I can still arrange for her to die."

Saul imagined a sniper hidden somewhere in the Colosseum, in two-way radio contact with the man he now spoke to. But he wasn't prepared for the tactic the voice described.

"A packet of explosive will be attached to your wife's back. I'll hide it under her jacket. The bomb will have a radio-controlled detonator whose electronic trigger will be in my pocket. As long as I'm within a mile of her, I'll be able to set the bomb off if I feel threatened. Don't fool yourself into thinking that all you have to do is remove the bomb from her and then betray me. The explosives will be held in place by a locked metal belt that's been wired in such a way that any attempt to remove it—by using metal clippers, for example—will blow her apart. Only when I'm out of radio range will the detonator be deactivated. Only then can the belt be safely cut off."

Saul felt as if insects had invaded his chest. "You seem to have thought of everything."

"That's why I've stayed alive so long. Six o'clock. Don't try to be clever. Just do what you've been told." With a click, the line was disconnected.

Saul set down the phone. He tried to keep his voice from shaking while he explained to Drew and Arlene.

Drew was briefly silent, assessing the information. At

once he spoke with resolve. "It's twenty after twelve. We've just got five minutes to take Father Dusseault back down to the other room before Gallagher shows up. You can question the priest for a while after that. But if he's supposed to be able to walk from the Colosseum, you'll have to stop giving him Sodium Amytal and let the drug wear off."

"That's assuming Gallagher agrees to surrender the priest," Saul said.

Arlene looked surprised. "You think he might not?"

"Gallagher wants to learn everything he can about the Fraternity. He won't be happy about the deal I made. Suppose he thinks he can infiltrate a surveillance team into the Colosseum? Suppose he decides the threat about the bomb is a lie and figures he can get the priest back after the exchange? I won't bet Erika's life on someone else's tradecraft. And something else—I'm not supposed to have moved the priest. How am I going to explain to Gallagher where I got the phone call? I'd have to tell him I brought the priest here so the two of you could help question him. He'd learn about you."

Drew glanced at Arlene. She nodded.

"Tell Gallagher," Drew said. "Your wife is more important than hiding us from Gallagher."

Saul felt a surge of warmth. His voice was choked with feeling. "I know how much your privacy means to you. I appreciate your gesture. Truly. More than I can say."

"It's not just a gesture," Drew said.

"But even if I did let Gallagher know about you, it wouldn't solve the problem. I still couldn't count on his keeping the bargain I made. I don't want his men at the Colosseum, and the only way I can guarantee they won't be there . . ."

"Is not to tell him?" Drew asked.

"We're going to have to steal the priest."

Drew committed himself immediately, reacting as if he and Saul had been working together for years. "Arlene, check the hallway. Make sure Gallagher isn't out there. Saul and I will carry Father Dusseault down the

334

fire stairs. Get the car. Have it waiting for us outside."

"But you'll be seen taking the priest from the hotel!"

"We'll pretend it's an emergency. We'll leave so fast no one'll have time to question us."

28

When Icicle heard a knock on the door, he stood abruptly. He'd been staring at the unconscious woman on the bed, brooding about Seth's behavior. To kill as an automatic choice, without sufficient reason, was a sign of lack of control. It wasn't professional. It wasn't... He *likes* it, Icicle thought. That's what bothers me. The gleam he gets in his eyes. It's as if he's having...

Sex? That realization made Icicle remember the near-fight he'd had with Seth to keep him from abusing the woman. Employing drugs or force to interrogate a prisoner was justified. But abusing this woman merely for the sake of self-gratification insulted Icicle's sense of dignity. Victims had a right not to be caused needless pain, not to be treated as objects.

Keep thinking about your father, he told himself. Nothing else... not the woman, not your principles... matters.

But he couldn't help noting that the conflict between Seth and himself was a replication of the lifelong enmity between their fathers. Was it happening all over again?

He checked the peephole, identified Seth, and freed the lock on the door. He felt uneasy about the packages Seth carried and the gleam in his eyes.

The gleam abruptly diminished when Seth glanced toward the bed. "You dressed her."

"She was shivering."

"Shivering?" Seth's gleam returned. "Since you feel so protective about her, I'm sure you'll be relieved to know that she'll be leaving us."

"What do you mean?"

"When you interrogated her, she told us her hus-

335

band's name and where they were staying in Rome," Seth said.

Icicle nodded.

Seth put the packages on the bureau. "I phoned her husband."

"You *what*?"

"I've made arrangements to exchange her for the priest." Seth opened the packages, revealing a fist-sized clump of plastic explosive along with a radio-controlled detonator and transmitter. There were batteries, wires, a metal belt welded to a metal box, a lock.

"Where the hell did you get—?"

"One of my contacts here in Rome." As Seth placed the explosive and the detonator in the metal box, he explained what he'd told the woman's husband.

Icicle's lips parted in astonishment. No wonder Seth didn't want to reveal why he was going out, he thought. I would never have agreed to the plan. "It's too risky. Despite what the husband promised, there's bound to be a surveillance team."

"With this bomb attached to her? If the husband loves her, he'll follow orders." Seth removed a blasting cap from his lapel pocket, inserted it into the explosive and wired it to a post on the detonator. He took the remaining wire, attached one end to a contact on the metal belt and the other to a second post on the detonator. "Once I put the batteries into the detonator and lock the belt, I've got a continuous electrical circuit. I'll close the metal box and wire the lid to the detonator. It's foolproof. If anyone opens the box to get at the detonator, the circuit will be broken. A switch on the detonator will engage another set of batteries that automatically triggers the bomb. The same thing will happen if someone unlocks the belt or snips it apart. Of course, the other way to detonate the bomb is by using this." He held up the radio-controlled transmitter.

Icicle watched him with loathing, troubled by a discrepancy between Seth's explanation and what he claimed to have told the husband. "Once you're out of radio range, the bomb can be dismantled?"

336

"No way."

"But you told the husband . . ."

"I lied." Seth slid the belt around the woman's waist and locked it. He inserted two sets of batteries into the detonator, closed the metal box's lid on the bare end of a wire attached to the detonator, and locked the lid. He smiled. "The only way to get this thing off her now is to blow the bitch up. How, my friend, do you feel about *that*?"

CRITICAL MASS

1

Toronto, Canada. 6:30 A.M. The sun had just risen. Exhausted, Joseph Bernstein told the taxi driver to let him off at the next corner. He'd directed the driver to one of the few decaying sections of the city. Soon to be purged by urban renewal, ill-maintained two-story houses lined the street. Bernstein paid the driver and gave him a tip neither so large nor so small that the driver would remember. The moment the taxi was out of sight, Bernstein tested his weary body's resources by walking one block south and two blocks east. He felt the way the worst houses looked. Lights were on in some of them, but he passed no one on the street, only a stray dog tearing apart a bulging plastic garbage bag. In the middle of the final block, he turned onto a cracked concrete sidewalk that led to a listing front porch. All the windows in the house were dark. An empty beer can lay on its side to the right of the top of the steps—the signal that everything was as it should be. He knocked three times on the front door, waited while a curtain was pushed aside, then stepped in when the door was opened.

Ephraim Avidan quickly closed the door and locked it, only then placing the Beretta he held into a shoulder holster beneath his rumpled suitcoat. "You had no problems?"

"Everything's on schedule. What about the others?"

"Upstairs asleep. We take turns, two at a time standing guard."

"No, I meant the *others*," Bernstein said. "Have you had any problems with them?"

"They take orders well." Avidan's mouth showed a trace of a bitter smile. "The sedatives in their food help."

"I want to see them."

"Your stomach must be stronger than mine. I despise them so much I try to see them as little as possible."

"I want to remind myself."

"As you wish." Avidan led him down a narrow corridor into a shadowy kitchen whose linoleum tile was peeling at the edges. He knocked three times on a warped plywood door, unlocked and opened it, then stepped back.

Bernstein peered down musty steps toward a concrete floor the color of a bullet. A pale light at the bottom revealed a tall, bearded man of about seventy who wore a thick pullover sweater and stared up anxiously, holding a Beretta as Avidan had. Seeing Bernstein, the man lowered his pistol.

When Bernstein reached the bottom, he put his arms around the man. David Gehmer was one of the most dependable, long-suffering members of the team. For the past four months, he—along with Gideon Levine—had endured without complaint the tedious, disagreeable task of acting as jailer. One by one, captives had been brought here from around the world—all told, eleven of them by now—imprisoned in the basement of this dilapidated house in Toronto. Yesterday, the other members of the team, having completed their tasks, had converged here as well and were asleep now in the upper floors of the house.

Bernstein scanned the large cellar. Its windows had been boarded over. Spaced equally apart, three bare lights dangled from the ceiling. White slabs of plastic insulation had been attached to the walls to minimize dampness. Nonetheless, the room felt cold and clammy. Bernstein understood why, even in June, David Gehmer wore a sweater.

The walls were lined with cots, eleven of them, upon each of which an old man lay covered with a woolen blanket. Some were awake, their eyes dazed by the lingering effects of the sedation in last night's supper. Most were deeply asleep. All were pale from lack of exposure to the sun. All were handcuffed. A chain led from each cuff to a ring bolted into the wall.

A few books and magazines lay next to each cot. Against a narrow wall at the far end of the room, shelves of plates and tinned food stood next to a small gas stove near an unshielded toilet.

"It's quite an assembly line," Bernstein said dryly. "All the comforts of home."

"By comparison with Auschwitz, this is the promised land," Gehmer said. "I shave each of them every other day. I cook all their meals. I make them take turns, cuffed to the sink, doing the cleanup. They're only allowed to use plastic spoons. I count the spoons after every meal. When they have to go to the toilet, I let them go one at a time, chained to the sink again. That's when they're allowed to wash up."

"Yes, you've organized them remarkably."

"They inspired me. These monsters had a special talent for organization, after all. Sometimes I remember so vividly I think I'm back in the camp. I want to..." Gehmer raised his pistol and aimed it at the nearest prisoner.

Bernstein touched Gehmer's hand. "Patience, my friend. We both have nightmares. But we won't have to endure them much longer. Soon justice will be served."

"Soon?" Gehmer spoke quickly. *"When?"*

"Tomorrow."

2

"Joseph surfaced again."

Misha Pletz, intent upon rechecking the plans for tonight's Operation Salvage, needed a moment before he realized what his assistant had said to him. "Surfaced?"

"Two hours ago."

"Where? Still in Washington?"

"No. Toronto this time."

"Toronto?"

"He contacted another of our operatives," the assistant said. "The same as before. He chose one of his former students. It was four-thirty in the morning there. Joseph showed up at the man's apartment, woke him, and gave him a message to relay to you. The operative had it coded and radioed here to Tel Aviv."

Misha held out his hand for the piece of paper his assistant clutched, but when he read it, he was baffled. "Two names?"

"Aaron Rosenberg. Richard Halloway." The assistant handed Misha a second piece of paper. "This is the operative's summary of the verbal instructions Joseph gave him. They're related to his previous message—the arms shipment he warned us was being sent to the Libyans to be used against us. Joseph says when you stop the shipment tonight he wants you to leak those names to the Libyans but not in a way that'll make them suspect it's a leak. He wants you to make it seem as if the two men accepted money from us in exchange for information about the shipment."

"But if the Libyans believe the leak, they'll want revenge." Misha stared at the paper in bewilderment. "We'd be setting them up to be killed. Why does Joseph want—?"

"Rosenberg and Halloway are the arms dealers responsible for the shipment."

"He wants to make it look as if they accepted money from and then doublecrossed the Libyans? He wants Rosenberg and Halloway punished by the people they were working for? Some crazy sense of justice? Why didn't Joseph give us these names in his first message? Why did he wait until—?" Misha paused; an explanation occurred to him. "Because he didn't want to give us time to check on them before we stopped the shipment? Is there another time limit we don't know about, another schedule Joseph is following?"

The assistant pointed toward the last paragraph of the report. "He made it a point of honor. The price for Joseph telling us about the shipment is we have to leak the names to the Libyans."

3

Saul waited anxiously with Father Dusseault in a recess of one of the middle terraces at the northern side of the Colosseum. The priest was able to walk, but he was still groggy enough to be passive, easily guided. He'd made no trouble when Saul had brought him here and sat him down. The many tourists paid no attention to the infirm priest.

Saul had arrived fifteen minutes early for the six o'clock appointment, and now it was ten minutes after. He used his binoculars to scan the opposite side of the Colosseum, worried that the exchange would not take place. As instructed, he'd come here alone with Father Dusseault. But terribly conscious of the sun setting lower, he cursed himself for disobeying one condition of the exhange by allowing Drew and Arlene to watch the Colosseum from the gardens of the Esquiline across the street. The Esquiline, one of the seven hills of Rome, was dominated by Nero's palace, the so-called Golden House, and the sightseers swarming through both it and the surrounding park made the chances of an enemy spotting Drew and Arlene highly unlikely. It had seemed prudent to take the slight risk.

But now he wished he hadn't permitted the violation. Because by twenty after six he was sure that something was wrong. The number of tourists began to dwindle. A woman with blue-tinted hair stepped in front of Saul, obscuring his gaze through the binoculars. Her overweight husband joined her, listening to her complain about the high-heeled shoes he shouldn't have let her wear.

Saul stepped to the right, to reestablish his view of the

opposite terraces. Scanning them, he suddenly froze the binoculars on a woman sitting on a walkway, her back against a wall. Saul had trouble steadying his hands on the binoculars. Erika? Even magnified, the woman wasn't distinct, her head drooping toward her chest. But her hair was long and dark like Erika's, and she seemed to be the same age, to have the same long legs and lithe body. What confused him was that this woman wore a green nylon jacket, which Erika did not possess.

Abruptly he remembered the voice on the phone telling him that Erika would wear a jacket to hide the bomb secured to her. When a man strolled over to her and set down a blue travel bag, Saul realized that the exchange was about to take place. With his binoculars, he tracked the tall pale man who'd left the travel bag and was moving to Saul's left. At once, the man stopped and raised his own binoculars, aiming them at Saul.

He's waiting for me to start circling in the other direction, Saul thought. He won't move until I do.

Saul didn't need encouragement. He left the priest sitting in the recess of the terrace and walked rapidly to the right. It took all his self-control not to run. For a moment, though, he almost faltered as the significance of something about the man occurred to him.

The color of his hair. *It was red.*

Dear God, had the voice on the phone belonged to *Seth*? The assassin, the son of a *Nazi* assassin, whom Drew and Arlene had described? If so, would his partner, the blond-haired Icicle, be in the Colosseum with him?

Saul didn't dare turn to scan the crowd. The gesture might disturb Seth into blowing Erika up as he'd threatened. Besides, at the moment Seth didn't matter. Nor did Icicle. Only Erika did. Rounding the curve of the Colosseum, approaching its southern side, he quickened his steps, his gaze focused anxiously on Erika. She continued to sit with her head drooped toward her chest. He hadn't seen her shift position. Had Seth reneged on his bargain? *Was Erika dead?*

He zigzagged through clusters of tourists, ignoring

their angry objections, too distraught to murmur apologies. He was thirty yards from Erika now, and she still hadn't moved. He started running. Twenty yards. No sign of life. He reached her. When he raised her face and saw her eyelids flutter, he sank to his knees, almost weeping with relief.

"Erika, it's me. It's Saul." He put his arms around her.

And froze when he felt the metal box under the back of the rainjacket. Moving his hands to her waist, he touched the metal belt that secured the box to her. Seth hadn't been bluffing.

Saul swung to stare toward the opposite side of the Colosseum. Seth had reached the priest, had lifted him to his feet, and was guiding him along a walkway toward an exit. The priest moved groggily. A few tourists glanced at him, but most were preoccupied with their cameras and the sunset-tinted ruins. At the exit, Seth turned toward Saul, raised his right arm, almost in an ancient Roman salute, his gesture ironic. Then Seth and Father Dusseault were gone.

Wait five minutes before leaving, Seth had instructed.

Five minutes it would be.

He turned to Erika, hugging her again. "It's Saul," he repeated. "You're safe." He kissed her. "I love you. We've got nothing to worry about."

4

Among shadows caused by sunset, Drew and Arlene watched from the Oppian Park to the east of Nero's palace. Their view of the Colosseum was impeded by the busy traffic on the Via Labicana, but even the frustration of an obstructed view was better than the greater frustration they'd have felt if they'd stayed away.

With only the northern and eastern curves of the Colosseum available to them, they probably would not see Father Dusseault and his captor, Drew realized. Still, the

Via Labicana was the most likely escape route, and for that reason, he concentrated less on the Colosseum and more on the street leading away from it.

He checked his watch. Twenty-five minutes after six. The exchange was scheduled to have occurred on the hour. Unless something had gone wrong, a no-show for example, they'd probably missed seeing Father Dusseault being led away.

All the same, Drew kept staring toward the opposite side of the street. If he still didn't spot the priest by seven o'clock, he and Arlene would go to a nearby phone booth where, by prearrangement, Saul would call to report.

He felt Arlene grip his arm. On the other side of the street, a priest—*Father Dusseault*—was being guided through a crowd of tourists emerging from the Colosseum. A gray Citroën veered from traffic and stopped at the curb. The priest was pushed inside onto the backseat, his abductor following. The Citroën sped away.

The pickup had taken no more than ten seconds, but even with the distraction of tourists and traffic, Drew had seen enough. There was no mistaking the red-haired man guiding the priest or the blond man driving the Citroën. *Seth and Icicle.* He bolted from Arlene's grasp, charging toward the street. Arlene ran after him. There was still a risk that Seth and Icicle had posted a surveillance team to watch for any attempt to follow the Citroën. In that case, if they noticed Drew and Arlene in pursuit, all the team had to do was contact the Citroën via two-way radio, and Seth or Icicle might make good on their threat to blow up Erika. But Drew was convinced that there wasn't a surveillance team. After all, Seth and Icicle hadn't arranged for help when they grabbed Medici, and the efficiency of that operation made Drew strongly suspect they trusted no one but themselves.

The Citroën was far enough down the street that he couldn't see it. That meant Seth and Icicle couldn't see Drew either as he darted through speeding traffic. He gestured frantically to a passing taxi. Arlene raced

345

across the street to him, reaching the curb as the taxi responded to Drew's waving arms. They scrambled inside.

Drew blurted instructions to the driver. If only we don't get caught in traffic, he worried. If only Seth and Icicle don't take a side street before I see where they turn. He wondered whether Saul had gotten Erika back and fervently prayed that his friend's wife was safe.

5

"What took you so long?" Driving, Icicle glanced quickly toward the backseat. "Did something go wrong?"

"I scouted the ruins before I showed myself. The husband followed instructions exactly. I couldn't be more pleased."

"Well, *I* won't be pleased till we get out of here. What if the other man and woman are hanging around?"

"Even if they are," Seth said, "they'll keep their distance. They know I can still use this." He held up the detonator. "All that remains is to question the priest. They wouldn't have abducted him unless they were certain he had vital information."

"But perhaps not the information we want."

"What reason would they have to question the priest, except to learn about the cardinal? He's the only outsider who knew where our fathers were. Once we find out why he disappeared, we'll know how the Night and Fog discovered our fathers." Seth grinned. "Yes, all that remains is to question him. But on second thought, perhaps not all. Pull over."

"We have to get away from here. Why do you—?"

"*Do it. Stop.*"

Icicle obeyed, halting at the curb. "Tell me why—"

"I can't resist the temptation." Seth peered through the Citroën's rear window toward the Colosseum. "Of course, I won't be able to see the explosion, but I'll hear

346

it." He shrugged. "The commotion among the tourists should be interesting." He flicked a switch to activate the radio-controlled detonator. A red light glowed.

"No," Icicle said.

Seth turned. "You still feel protective about her?" His eyes gleamed.

He's doing this to taunt me, Icicle realized. Not to punish the woman but *me*.

"What's the point? You told me you'd lied to the husband. In a while, when we're out of radio range, he'll think it's safe to disconnect the bomb without setting it off. Since she'll die soon anyhow, why kill her now?"

"Do I sense you hoping that the husband will find a way to remove the bomb without setting it off?"

"What would be the harm if he did? The drug kept her from seeing us. She can't identify—"

"The harm," Seth said. "is to my pleasure. Why should this woman, a stranger, matter to you?"

"Why should she matter to *you*? She isn't a threat to us. She doesn't have to die."

"But she does, my friend. To teach you a lesson. *Never interfere with me again.*" Seth aimed a finger toward the detonator.

Even then, Icicle might not have acted if it hadn't been for the cruel look Seth gave him. Rage broke Icicle's control. Like a tightly wound spring suddenly released, he flicked the switch to deactivate the detonator and yanked it out of Seth's hand. His movement was so forceful he ripped a flap of skin from one of Seth's fingers.

Seth's face contorted when he saw his own blood. "Give the detonator back."

"We've got too much at risk for you to delay. We'll settle this later when we get away from here."

"We'll settle it now."

In a blur, Seth drew a pistol. It had a silencer on the barrel, but even so, the confines of the Citroën made the muffled shot feel as if hands had slammed Icicle's ears. The moment he saw the weapon, he twisted away and took the bullet intended for his chest through the flesh of

347

his upper left arm. The projectile exited from his arm and slammed against the dashboard. Icicle ignored the shock of pain and lunged again, deflecting the pistol's aim before Seth could fire a second time. They struggled for possession of the gun.

Blood dripped from Icicle's arm. Despite his force of will, his weakened biceps were no match for Seth. Inexorably the pistol's barrel shifted toward Icicle's face.

Seth's lips curled. "I should have killed you before. The same as I did your father."

Icicle's eyes widened. *"Killed my father?"* Perhaps Seth had hoped that the statement would distract him, make him falter sufficiently for Seth to move the pistol the last few inches toward Icicle's face. If so, Seth miscalculated. Instead of faltering, Icicle screamed insanely and, with a savage burst of strength, he rammed the pistol back toward Seth's face, cracking the silencer against Seth's forehead. Seth's eyes lost focus.

Icicle scrambled over the seat, punching Seth's mouth. "You bastard, what do you mean you killed my father?" He punched Seth's lips a second time, mangling them. "Tell me!" he shouted, yanking the pistol out of Seth's hand. Just as he twisted it around to put his finger on the trigger, a taxi stopped behind the Citroën, its doors flying open. Icicle saw the man and the woman who'd been dressed as a priest and a nun in the Vatican gardens.

Seth struck Icicle in the stomach. Doubling over, Icicle felt Seth grab for the pistol, but Seth didn't get a firm hold, and the gun thumped onto the floor. Outside, the man and the woman were running toward the Citroën. With no time to do anything but obey his instincts, Icicle pivoted, grabbed the detonator off the front seat, shoved open the curbside door, and raced into the crowd. His wounded arm hurt terribly. He heard a muffled shot. A window shattered. Pedestrians scattered, screaming.

6

When Drew saw the gray Citroën stopped ahead at the side of the street, he yelled for the taxi driver to pull over. Through the car window of the Citroën, he saw two men struggling with each other. For an instant, he thought one of them was Father Dusseault, now sufficiently alert to put up a fight. But then he saw the blond and red hair of the two men grappling for what appeared to be a gun and realized that Icicle and Seth were trying to kill each other.

Their struggle was so intense, their distraction so great, Drew realized they wouldn't notice until he and Arlene were in position to overpower them. The taxi stopped. Drew darted out, followed by Arlene, racing toward the Citroën.

But Icicle's rugged face turned abruptly in their direction. His look of shocked comprehension was replaced by one of pain as Seth punched him in the stomach. In quick succession, Icicle grabbed something from the Citroën's front seat and lunged from the car just as Seth picked up an object from the rear floor, gaped at Drew and Arlene, who were about to reach the Citroën, and raised a pistol, firing.

The rear window shattered. Pedestrians screamed. Drew and Arlene dove to the street. Drew hadn't wanted to alarm the taxi driver by showing his handgun earlier, but now he pulled it out, prepared to return fire. The detonator, he kept thinking. Have to get the detonator. But he now identified the object that Icicle had grabbed from the front seat before rushing out of the Citroën. He could see the small rectangular control in Icicle's right hand as the blond assassin surged through the scattering crowd. At the same time, he noticed the stream of blood on Icicle's left arm.

Flat on the street, Drew shifted his attention back toward the Citroën, aiming at the shattered rear window. The moment Seth showed himself, Drew was prepared to pull the trigger. But Seth stayed low, charging out the open curbside door and racing into the crowd. Powerless, Drew couldn't shoot without hitting bystanders. He watched Seth escaping.

Or *was* he escaping? Seth didn't seem to want to get away so much as to chase after Icicle. The blond man ran along the Via Labicana and veered to the right, disappearing around a corner. Holding his pistol, the redhaired assassin sprinted after him.

What had happened to turn them into enemies? Drew wondered.

He stared into the Citroën. The priest was slumped across the backseat. "Arlene, get him out of here. Make sure you're not followed. Take him back to the hotel."

"But what about—?"

Drew shouted as he ran. "I'm going after them!"

7

The son of a bitch is coming after me! Icicle thought. Even when he's almost cornered, he still wants to kill me!

Icicle hadn't even been aware that he'd grabbed the detonator as he ran from the Citroën. The gesture had been reflexive. Only when he reached for the pistol wedged behind his belt beneath the back of his jacket did he realize that he was holding something in his right hand. The detonator. He switched it to his blood-smeared left hand, pulled out his pistol, and darted right off the Via Labicana.

He expected Seth to shoot at him, but not to kill, at least not right away. Seth would want to bring him down, disarm him, and make him watch the detonator being pushed. A few blocks away from the Colosseum, they would be able to hear the blast. Only then, having gained the maximum pleasure from his victory, would Seth kill Icicle and still have time to escape.

It didn't have to be this way! Icicle raged. *If it hadn't been for the woman, we wouldn't have argued! Seth wouldn't have told me he'd murdered my father! We'd be safely out of here! The woman means nothing to me! Why did I protect her from him?*

Another thought was equally distressing. Seth's arrogance, his pride and hate, had such control of him that, in taunting Icicle, he'd lost the chance to question the priest and find his father.

He's more insane than I imagined.

Racing down the side street, Icicle felt an excruciating jolt against the back of his right shoulder. The impact threw him off balance, twisting him to the right, almost shoving him to the pavement. Blood sprayed ahead of him. The muscles of his right arm refused to obey his mental commands; his hand opened involuntarily. His pistol clattered onto the sidewalk. Still able to make his wounded other arm respond, he clutched the detonator to his chest and ran with greater determination. But his loss of blood had weakened him. His vision blurred. His legs became wobbly. He hadn't heard the spit of Seth's silenced weapon. He didn't expect to hear it the next time either, but he had no doubt that Seth would aim toward one of his legs.

I'm too easy a target. Have to get off this side street. Find a place to hide.

Ahead, to his right, Icicle saw a structure that took up half the block and whose shadow filled the street. An ancient church! He rushed unevenly toward it. At that moment, Seth fired, his bullet missing Icicle's leg, smacking against concrete twenty feet ahead.

Arms throbbing, Icicle realized he was too exposed, too likely to be shot if he went up the steps to the huge main entrance to the church. He hurried forward, his face dripping sweat. In pain, he came to an intersection and veered toward the right once more.

But along this further street, he saw a side entrance to the church. A sign said St. Clement's Basilica. Seth rounded the corner, about to aim. With no other possibility of escape, Icicle lurched toward the church's small side door, mustering strength to shove it open.

Inside, he slammed the door and tried to lock it, but

351

there wasn't a bolt to slide into place, only a slot for a key. Whirling, he raced onward, finding himself in a massive chamber that stretched to his right and left. Frescoes of Christ and the apostles lined the walls. Two aisles were broken up by towering columns. A guide appeared, telling him that the basilica was closed to tourists after six-thirty. Icicle scurried past him, sensing rather than seeing the altar far to his left.

His impulse was to hide in what appeared to be the sacristy across from him, but the tour guide kept objecting to his presence, and when he heard the side door bang open, he knew that the guide would attract Seth to him.

I've got to find somewhere else to hide.

To the right of the sacristy, stairs descended. He started down them just as the side door slammed shut and Seth's footsteps echoed urgently after him. It was possible that Seth hadn't seen him, but he couldn't fail to see the trail of blood.

He came to a landing, turned right to descend another tier of stairs, and groaned not only from pain but also from desperation when he saw that he'd entered a long empty corridor. He heard Seth's footsteps coming nearer and rushed lower toward a door along the right side of the corridor. He entered yet another basilica.

The must of fourteen hundred centuries swelled his nostrils. Pale lights fought to dispel the darkness. But the ancient shadows couldn't hide him, not with the blood from his arms dripping across the floor. He staggered past faded frescoes depicting a Roman nobleman and his servants, all of whom had apparently been blinded by the aura of a holy man, and heard Seth's footsteps charging down the stairwell.

He stared toward the left of the altar toward an exit. *If I can get through it before Seth takes another shot at me, maybe I can find a way to surprise him. He's so confident, he might not expect me to attack.*

Quit kidding yourself. You don't have the strength. You've lost your pistol.

But I've got a knife.

He flinched as a bullet spattered pieces of fresco from a wall. Seth's footsteps rushed closer. But at once the tour guide entered this lower basilica, shouting at them. Seth shot the man. Hearing the body fall, Icicle could barely breathe.

By the time Seth aimed again toward the front of the church, Icicle had reached the exit to the left of the altar. He rushed through, hearing a bullet crack against a wall behind him, and saw only more stairs. Even older than the lower church that he'd just left, these stairs led down as well. There was no other choice—he had to follow them.

A landing. A turn to the right. He passed a sign that said Mithraeum and stumbled into an eerie underground structure that might have dated back to the birth of the Catholic Church. Directly below the altar of the lower basilica, the remnants of two Roman houses had been joined to form a temple, but the temple was, astonishingly, not Christian but pagan. Beyond two parallel stone benches that reminded Icicle of pews, there stood a statue of the Roman god Mithras. The center of the temple was taken up by an altar upon which another statue of the god—clean-shaven, resplendently handsome— performed some kind of sacred rite by slicing open the throat of a bull. A dog, a scorpion, and a serpent were trying to kill the bull before Mithras could complete the sacrifice.

In the time it took him to scan the temple, he realized he was trapped. He heard Seth scramble down the lower stairs and chose the only possible hiding place: behind the altar. His blood pooled on the ancient stone floor almost as if blood from the bull's slit throat were streaming off the altar down to him. Putting the detonator into a pocket, he used his more mobile left hand to withdraw a knife from a sheath strapped above his right ankle. He held his breath, wiped sweat from his face, quivered with pain, and waited.

Seth stalked into the temple. "Blood hides no secrets. I know where you are." His shoes scraped on the ancient stone floor. His shadow loomed over the altar.

Icicle peered up toward the red-haired man, whose punched lips were swollen, crusted with blood. Seth's eyes had never been brighter.

"The detonator." Seth held out his hand.

"I hid it before I came down here."

"Then you won't mind if I search you." Seth stepped closer.

Icicle squirmed backward.

"Give it to me," Seth said, "and maybe I won't kill you."

"You'll kill me, all right. But not until after you force me to watch you press the button."

"Our few days together have been like a long-term marriage, I see. You've learned to understand me." Seth stepped even closer. "Give me the detonator."

Icicle continued backward. "You'll have to take it."

Seth shook his head. "What I'll do is shoot you again, in the stomach this time, before I come closer. You'd live to see me press the button, but you wouldn't have the strength to attack." Seth raised his pistol.

Icicle's mind raced, desperate to think of a way to distract his opponent. "Did you mean what you said in the car?"

Seth hesitated.

"Did you really kill my father?" Icicle asked.

"Would I lie when the truth is so satisfying? Of course I killed him."

"Why?"

"It was Halloway's idea to bring you into this. I told him I didn't need help, but Halloway insisted. The trouble was, your father hadn't disappeared. Mind you, he might have been next on the list, but I didn't want to use up valuable time waiting for it to happen. So I got my hands on him myself." Seth's mangled lips formed a smile. "I did it at your dive shop in Australia. Used a silencer. Shot your father and your salesclerk while you were meeting with Halloway's emissary. I wrapped your father's body in a tarpaulin and loaded him into the trunk of my car. Did it in plain sight of everyone on the beach. No one paid attention. Does anyone *ever* pay attention?

354

Went back to the shop and set fire to it. Drove away. I might as well have been invisible."

Icicle wanted to vomit. "What did you do with the body?"

"Rented a boat. Took it out to sea. Let the sharks have a feast."

Icicle made a choking sound.

"The body had to disappear," Seth said, "to make it seem as if the Night and Fog was responsible. So you'd join us and help look for the rest of our fathers."

"What about Halloway's emissary? Why did *he* disappear?"

"I waited for him at his hotel. Identified myself. Took him for a drive. Shot him. Fed him to the sharks the same as I did your father. The theory was that if he too disappeared you'd think Halloway had something to do with the disappearances. I wanted to force you to seek out Halloway..."

"And when I did, like a fool I let both of you convince me you were innocent. I joined you."

"And proved of some help, I admit, when it came to grabbing Medici. But really," Seth said, "Halloway was wrong—I didn't need you. We could never have gotten along. Your father stole the woman my father loved. Your mother could have been *my* mother. *You* would never have been born. If my father's still alive, if I can manage to find him, I'm sure he'll be overjoyed to learn that I killed both his enemy and the *son* of his enemy. It's ironic, don't you think? Like our fathers, we fell out over a woman. Give me the detonator. I promise your death will be quick after you watch me push the button."

Loss of blood made Icicle sleepy. *Concentrate*, he told himself. *Don't let the bastard win.* "Your word?" he asked. "You'll kill me cleanly?" He raised his almost useless right arm to point toward the soft spot behind his right ear.

"You have my promise."

With the same arm, Icicle reached in his pocket and took out the detonator, holding it out to his enemy.

"Set it on the floor. Slide it over to me," Seth said.

"Too weak."

"I don't think so."

His heart sinking in despair, Icicle did what he was told, hearing the detonator scrape across the stone floor.

"Excellent." Seth stooped to pick up the detonator. He shifted his gaze from Icicle only for a second.

That second would be the only chance Icicle got. He whipped his agonized left arm from behind his back and threw the knife with all his remaining strength.

Seth jerked his head up. With a curse, his eyes fierce, he aimed. Not soon enough. The knife struck his throat, the blade entering his Adam's apple, splitting it. The tip made an obscene scraping sound against his neckbone. The handle's guard stopped against fractured cartilage.

Seth stumbled backward, his face twisting in shock, his skin almost chalk white in contrast with the crimson spewing from his throat. The massive trauma to his Adam's apple would cause swelling that would shut off the passage of air to his lungs, Icicle knew. He'd die from asphyxiation before he bled to death. But he wouldn't die instantly.

Icicle watched horrified as Seth squinted at him. You think you've won, his eyes seemed to say. But you haven't. I still have the strength to shoot you again. We'll *both* die. But not before you watch me do *this*.

Seth grasped the detonator and flicked the activation switch.

Icicle screamed, scrambling to stop him, but slipped and fell in the pool of his blood.

Seth staggered back out of reach and lowered a finger toward a button.

A shadow lunged from the stairwell, the man who'd been dressed as a priest in the Vatican gardens. The stranger yanked the detonator from Seth's grasp at the same time that he twisted the pistol away from him.

Seth turned toward his sudden assailant. Wheezing, he tried to remove the knife from his throat, but the stranger rammed the butt of the knife so the blade reentered Seth's throat. The impact made the knife twist sideways, widening the gap in Seth's Adam's apple.

Crimson gushed. Spastic, Seth lurched from the force of the blow. He fell against the statues on the altar, turned to grab them for support, slid down, and collapsed un-moving upon the floor. His blood trickled over the knife Mithras held to the throat of the bull.

Icicle had not yet adjusted to the sudden arrival of the stranger, who now flicked off the switch on the detonator and stalked toward him, aiming Seth's pistol. The stranger's expression was a combination of disgust and fury.

"Get me out of here," Icicle said, "before the author-ities arrive. We don't have much time. If you help me, *I'll* help you." Delirium made his thoughts drift. He fought to steady them. "I'll tell you anything you want to know. My father's dead. This isn't my fight any longer. Halloway has to be punished."

"Halloway. Who's Halloway?"

"For God's sake, get me out of here. The woman we kidnapped from the gardens. Seth rigged explosives to her."

"I know that."

"But her husband thinks he can safely remove the bomb if we're out of radio range. Seth lied. The bomb'll go off if the husband tries to disconnect the wires."

The stranger spoke urgently. "Can you walk?"

"I think so." Icicle almost fainted from pain when the stranger helped him up.

The stranger put his jacket over Icicle's shoulders. "It'll hide the blood."

Icicle leaned against the stranger and, through a haze, stumbled from the temple. The next thing he knew, he was in the subterranean basilica. He didn't remember going up the final group of stairs or crossing the upper basilica. He only knew that he was outside, that the last rays of sunset were blinding, that a police siren's wail was approaching.

"Walk faster," the stranger said, supporting him.

They reached a corner and turned in the direction op-posite to the siren.

At another corner, they turned again.

357

And again. Disoriented, Icicle had the sense of wandering through a maze. "I don't think I can stand up much longer."

"We're almost there."

A park to the south of the Arch of Constantine, Icicle saw. In the dimming blaze of sunset, tourists milled through the area, admiring the carvings on the monument. The stranger set him on the ground against a tree. Given the emergency, the cover was perfect, Icicle realized. As long as I don't bleed through the jacket he slipped over my shoulders, I won't attract attention.

"Stay here. I'll be back," the stranger said.

"Tell the woman's husband not to try to remove the bomb."

But the stranger had already disappeared through the crowd.

8

"Damn it, Romulus, I warned you not to jerk me around. Where the hell's the priest? I promised you two hours alone with him. I come back, and the room's deserted. Nothing's on the fucking tape recorder." Gallagher pounded a fist into his hand.

The station chief had been pacing angrily in the hotel room when Saul brought Erika back there. Saul had hoped to see Drew and Arlene, not Gallagher. He'd waited outside the Colosseum, expecting his friends to emerge from the park across from the ruins. When they hadn't come, he'd tried to call them where they should have been waiting at the prearranged contact site, a pay phone. But the first time no one had answered, and the second time a strident woman had asked if he was Luigi and why was he keeping her waiting. By then, it was after 7 P.M., the deadline for contact. Filled with misgivings, he'd decided that the hotel room was the only other place where Drew and Arlene would know they could get in touch with him. Besides, the hotel room would give him the privacy he needed to remove the explosives from Erika's back. Guiding her, he'd hailed a taxi and returned to the hotel as quickly as possible.

But now, in addition to his other pressures, he had to deal with Gallagher.

"The priest doesn't matter," Saul said. "I've got my wife back. That's all I care about."

"You're telling me the priest is gone because you traded him?"

"Yes! And I'd do it again! I questioned him, don't worry! I'll keep my bargain! I've got plenty to tell you! But not before I deal with this!" Saul slipped the rain-jacket off Erika, showing Gallagher the metal box attached to the belt at her spine.

Gallagher started. "Jesus Christ, it's a bomb."

Erika murmured something unintelligible; gradually the effects of the drug were lessening. Saul sat her on the bed and studied the apparatus secured to her. "I'll have to break the lock or cut the belt. But the belt's wired to the box. The whole thing—lock, belt, and box—forms a continuous electrical circuit."

"Then the bomb might be rigged to go off if the circuit's broken."

"Seth told me it was safe to take it off as soon as he was out of radio range."

"Seth? Who the hell is Seth?"

"I'll explain later. First I have to—" Saul reached toward the wires, stiffening when he heard a knock on the door. He swung his troubled gaze toward the sound.

Gallagher went to answer it.

"No! Wait!" Saul said. He suspected Drew and Arlene were in the corridor, and he didn't want Gallagher to see them.

"What's the problem, Romulus? Another secret?"

Gallagher opened the door; Saul's suspicion had been half-correct. Arlene stood out there, supporting the groggy priest.

"Who the hell are *you*?" Gallagher demanded.

Saul slumped into a chair.

Arlene held back for a moment, then acquiesced

359

when Gallagher tugged her and Father Dusseault into the room.

"Romulus, who *is* this woman?" Gallagher insisted, locking the door.

"A friend."

"That's not a good enough explanation."

"It's all you need to know. You've got the priest back. That's what you wanted, isn't it? Thank her. Don't ask questions about who she is."

Arlene brought the priest to the bed and laid him down on the side away from Erika.

"The priest back?" Gallagher said. "No, that *isn't* what I wanted."

"I wish you'd make up your mind."

"I don't want *him*. I want what he *knows*. After I learn about the Fraternity, the sooner I'm rid of him the better."

"He killed Cardinal Pavelic. He's been trying to sabotage the Fraternity. What's more, he can tell you where to find a dozen or more Nazi war criminals."

Gallagher's mouth opened in surprise.

Saul turned to Arlene. "I'm glad to see you again. When I couldn't make contact . . . How did you get the priest back? Drew? Where's Drew?"

"He went after Seth and Icicle," she said.

"Icicle?" Gallagher looked even more mystified. "Drew?"

Saul and Arlene ignored him.

"Your wife?" Arlene asked. "Is she all right?"

"Still groggy from being drugged. It doesn't seem as if they hurt her."

"She's beautiful."

"Yes." Saul felt tears in his eyes. "And smart and funny and kind. Strong, maybe stronger than I am—in all sorts of ways. I don't know what I'd do without her."

"Would somebody please tell me what's going on?" Gallagher said.

"After World War Two, Cardinal Pavelic helped Nazi war criminals escape from the Allies," Arlene said. "Over the years, he kept track of them. He blackmailed

them in exchange for his silence. His assistant"—Arlene
gestured toward Father Dusseault—"found out what the
cardinal was doing. Father Dusseault belongs to the Fraternity, but he hates what the order stands for. He used
his position in the order to try to sabotage it. He saw the
cardinal as a further example of corruption within the
Church. Not only did he kill the cardinal—he decided to
punish the war criminals the cardinal had been protecting."

"Punish them? How?"

Saul added to Arlene's explanation. "Father Dusseault gave the information to a Mossad operative whose
family had been killed and who himself had nearly been
killed in Dachau. The theory was that someone with so
terrible a grievance, particularly someone with his training and resources, would be a more reliable instrument
of punishment than trials that might take years."

"Punishment? Do you mean vengeance?" Gallagher
asked. "Did Father Dusseault hope the Mossad operative would kill the Nazis?"

Saul nodded. "I'm less sure about the rest of it, but
my guess is that the Mossad agent—his name was
Ephraim Avidan by the way—decided he needed help. I
think he went to other Mossad operatives who'd been in
concentration camps and organized a team. These operatives were old enough to be retired. Many of them were
widowers. They had the freedom, both politically and
personally, to do what they wanted. In Vienna, Erika
and I were given a list of men's names by our contact
with the Mossad. The men on that list matched the profile I just described. During the past few months, they all
disappeared. I think they were dropping out of the limited society they still had, preparing for their mission."

"Disappearing?" Gallagher asked. "It sounds like . . ."

"My wife's father," Saul said. "I think he's one of the
team."

The room seemed to shrink.

"What about the two men you mentioned—Seth and
Icicle?"

"Assassins. Sons of Nazi assassins. I think their fa-

361

thers are two of the war criminals the cardinal protected. If Avidan's team moved against their fathers, Seth and Icicle would want to know who was doing it and why. They seem to have decided that the cardinal was the key to the puzzle. If they found out why the cardinal disappeared, they'd find out why those war criminals became targets after so many years."

Gallagher gestured toward Arlene. "So how do *you* fit into this? Who's Drew?"

"No more questions," Saul said. "Erika's all that matters. *I have to get this damned thing off her.*"

That afternoon, he'd asked Arlene to buy the metal clippers Seth had claimed he'd need to get the belt off Erika once Seth was out of radio range. Now Arlene reached in her purse and gave them to Saul.

He pressed them against the metal belt and hesitated. "Arlene, maybe you, Gallagher, and the priest ought to get out of here. In case this thing blows up."

"If you think it's that risky, don't do anything."

Saul shook his head. "Suppose Seth isn't out of radio range. You said Drew was chasing him. Seth might press the detonator."

"Maybe we should all get out of here," Gallagher said. "I'll phone for an Agency explosives expert."

"By the time he got here, it might be too late." Saul studied the wires attached to the metal belt and box. "Unless . . . maybe. *Yes, it just might work.*" He hurried to unplug a lamp on a bureau. With sweat-slippery hands, he used the metal clippers to snip the cord from the base of the lamp and cut the electrical plug from the opposite end of the cord.

"What are you doing?" Gallagher asked.

Saul was concentrating too hard to answer. Gently, he pressed the clippers against the rubber insulation on the cord, nicked it two inches from each end, then peeled off the strips of insulation, exposing the wires. He went back to Erika and secured one end of the cord to a bare wire leading from the metal box to the belt. He attached the other end of the cord to a second bare wire leading from the box to the belt. He'd been afraid that the bomb would go off if he cut the belt and interrupted an electrical circuit. But now the lamp cord provided the same function that the belt did. In theory, he could now cut the belt, and the circuit wouldn't be damaged.

In theory.

"I think," Saul said, "that this would be a good time for all of you to leave."

Unprotesting, Arlene raised the priest from the bed. "Gallagher, let's take a stroll to the end of the hall."

"Romulus?"

Saul waited.

"Good luck."

"Thanks."

Gallagher grinned. "You're something else."

Ten seconds later, Saul was alone with Erika.

Aching with love, he pressed the clippers to the front of the belt and snipped it.

The phone rang precisely when he'd anticipated the explosion. The harsh sound jolted his nerves; his heart lurched.

"Shit!"

The phone rang again.

He tried to regain control, working with as much speed as caution would allow, removing the belt and the bomb from Erika's waist. Careful not to disturb the wires he'd attached to it, he set the apparatus on a chair.

The phone kept ringing.

He grabbed it.

"It's Drew! For God's sake, don't try to take that bomb off your wife! Seth lied! The bomb's rigged to explode if the belt's opened!"

Saul sank onto the bed and began to laugh. "*Now* you tell me?"

"What are—?"

Saul roared. He knew he sounded hysterical, but the release felt too good for him to care. "Everything's fine. The bomb's not on her anymore."

"How, sweet Jesus, did you manage *that*?"

Saul's laugh became one of affection toward his friend. Drew was the only person he knew who could make an expletive sound like a prayer. "With some help from a lamp cord. I'll tell you about it when I see you. But are *you* okay? Arlene said you'd gone after Seth and Icicle."

"Yes . . . Seth's dead. Icicle killed him."

"What?"

"Icicle's been wounded. If we help him, he promises to tell us anything we want to know."

At once Saul stood. "Where should I meet you?"

"The park south of Constantine's Arch. That's where I left Icicle. We'll be waiting along the Via di San Gregorio."

"Are you sure we can trust him?"

"Yes. He was the one who told me not to try taking the bomb off your wife. He didn't have to warn us. He didn't have to help Erika. When we talk to him, I think we'll get the last of our questions answered."

"I'll be there in twenty minutes." Saul set the phone back onto its receiver and hurried from the room toward Arlene, Gallagher, and the priest in the corridor. "Arlene, please stay with Erika. Take care of her." He ran toward the elevator.

"Just wait a damned minute," Gallagher said. "I'm not through with you. Where do you think you're going?"

"To meet a friend and bring back an Icicle. Tell your medical team we're going to need them again." When the elevator took too long to arrive, Saul rushed down the fire stairs.

9

Dusk and the chaos of headlights made Saul despair of noticing Drew and Icicle as he sped past Constantine's Arch, driving his rented car down the Via di San Gregorio. Pedestrians thronged the adjacent sidewalks. I should have asked Drew which side of the street he'd be on.

But Drew was suddenly ahead of him, his arm around Icicle as if holding up someone who'd drunk too much. Saul steered in their direction, hearing angry car horns behind him, and skidded to a stop at the curb. The instant Drew helped Icicle into the back of the car and shut the door, Saul sped away.

Icicle wore the jacket that Drew had been wearing this afternoon. The blond assassin's face was as pale as his hair. Blood soaked through the arms of the jacket.

"How badly is he hurt?" Saul asked.

"Shot in both shoulders. One of the bullets passed through. As much as I can tell, the other's still in him. He's delirious."

"Halloway," Icicle murmured.

"Who's Halloway?" Saul glanced back toward Drew.

"I haven't found out yet. Whoever he is, Icicle sure doesn't like him."

"Pay the son of a bitch back," Icicle mumbled.

"Why?" Drew asked.

"Sent Seth to kill my father," Icicle said.

"Why would Halloway . . . ? Is he an Israeli?"

Icicle laughed. "No."

"It doesn't make sense." Saul steered around a corner. "If Halloway isn't an Israeli, why would he be involved with the team that went after the Nazis?"

"Night and Fog," Icicle whispered.

"And how does *that* fit in?" Saul asked. "The Night and Fog was a Nazi terror tactic during World War Two."

"I wonder if . . . Could it be he just explained the Israeli team's method of revenge?" Drew asked.

Saul shuddered as he steered around another corner. "Using Nazi tactics against their enemies? Abducting war criminals and making their families suffer as Jewish families suffered during the Holocaust. *Erika's father is involved in this insanity?*"

"A passion for revenge," Drew said. "Because of the murder of my parents, I know all about hate. I *was* hate for many years. And I know when you borrow the tactics of your enemy you become your enemy. You learn to hate yourself."

Saul remembered the hate with which he'd stalked and killed his foster father to avenge his foster brother's death. But getting even for Chris hadn't brought satisfaction, only a terrible hollowness. "I've got to find Erika's father. I've got to stop him."

"Halloway," Icicle murmured.

"Who *is* he?" Drew asked. "If he isn't Jewish—"

"The Painter's son."

"Oh, my God," Saul said. "The Painter was the nickname for the assistant SS commandant at the Maidanek death camp. Day after day, he processed—that was *his* word, that was how he thought of it, a system, a *dis*assembly line—thousands of prisoners through the gas chambers and the ovens. At night, he painted idyllic scenes of forests and meadows."

"Was Halloway's father the assistant commandant at Maidanek?" Drew asked Icicle.

"Yes."

"Why did Halloway want Seth to kill your father?"

"To force me to join them. To make me think the Night and Fog had kidnapped my father."

"Where is Halloway now?"

Icicle didn't answer.

"If that bullet isn't removed, if he doesn't get a transfusion," Drew said, "we'll never get an answer."

"You're right. He'll die. And his jacket's soaked with blood now. We'll never be able to sneak him into the hotel. We need a safe house. Gallagher has to tell us where to meet his medical team." Saul stopped at the curb and scrambled from the car toward a phone booth.

But not before he heard Drew ask Icicle again, "Where is Halloway?"

"Kitchener. Near Toronto. In Canada."

10

Despite the sourness in his stomach, Misha Pletz swallowed yet another mouthful of scalding coffee and restrained his impulse to hurry down to the communications room in the basement of Mossad headquarters in Tel Aviv. It was only 11 P.M., he reminded himself. Operation Salvage wouldn't occur for another hour, and in the meantime its team was under orders to obey radio silence. Besides, I'd only get in the way down there, he thought. I've done my job. The plan's been checked repeatedly.

Nonetheless, he worried that the information Joseph had given him might be incorrect. Verification of the contraband, the time and place of delivery, and the identification codes had been impossible. With an informant other than Joseph, with a threat less critical to Israel's existence, Misha would not have risked acting. But under the circumstances, to do nothing was a worse risk. His superiors had reluctantly agreed with him.

The door to his office came open. Misha's assistant hurried in, his exhausted features flushed with excitement. "Romulus just made contact."

Misha's shoulders straightened. "I've been hoping. Where is he?"

"Rome."

"How did he get in touch with us?"

"Through the CIA." The assistant gave Misha a piece of paper with a number written on it. "He wants you to phone him as soon as possible."

The message was puzzling. When Misha had last seen Saul, the Agency had possibly been involved in an assassination attempt against him, and even if the Agency *hadn't* been involved, it had made Saul promise to stay away from them. Then why was Saul now using one of their contacts? Was Saul in trouble with them? Was this message a hoax?

But though puzzling, the message was also a double blessing. Not only was he anxious to talk with Saul and

Erika, but he felt grateful to be distracted from waiting for news about Operation Salvage. He picked up his safe phone and dialed the number. Trans-Mediterranean static crackled. At the other end, the phone rang only once before Saul's distinctively resonant husky voice said, "Hello."

"This is Sand Viper. Can you talk freely where you are?"

"I'm in an Agency safe house. They tell me the phone's secure."

"Are you in trouble?"

"With the Agency? No, they're cooperating. It'd take too long to explain." Saul's voice hurried on. "I've learned some disturbing things about Erika's father."

"So have I," Misha said. "Twice in the last two days he sent messages to me. I've had visual confirmation—he's alive. Tell Erika. Her father's alive, and he isn't being held captive. He wants to stay out of sight, though. He eluded two attempts to follow him. The messages he sent me—"

"About the Nazis?" Saul sounded surprised. "He actually told you?"

"Nazis?" Misha pressed the phone hard against his ear. *What are you talking about?*

"War criminals. That's why Joseph disappeared. He and Ephraim Avidan and the other former operatives whose names were on the list you gave us—they learned where war criminals were hiding. They formed a team and went after them."

Misha felt too astonished to speak.

Saul's voice became more urgent. "If Joseph didn't tell you, what was in his messages?"

"Even on a phone as secure as this, I can't risk telling you. He had information vital to Israel. That's all I can say. By noon tomorrow, I'll be free to explain."

"But tomorrow could make all the difference. Joseph might already have done things that'll haunt him for the rest of his life. For his sake, for *Erika's* sake, I've got to stop him. You said he disappeared again. Haven't you any idea where he is?"

"He keeps moving. His messages came from different countries. First the United States, then Canada."

"Did you say *Canada*?"

"Is that important?"

"Where in Canada?" Saul demanded. *"What city?"*

"Toronto."

"I thought so!"

"What's wrong?" Misha asked. "Do you know why Joseph would have gone there?"

"The son of one of the Nazis lives near there. The father was the Painter, the assistant commandant at Maidanek. The son's name is Halloway."

The name made Misha inhale as if he'd been struck. He wanted to tell Saul that Halloway was one of the arms merchants Joseph had revealed in his message. But he didn't dare discuss it until Operation Salvage had been brought to a close. When the team was safely back home, he'd leak information that would make the Libyans think Halloway was implicated in the mission, and then he'd be free—but only under guaranteed secure conditions—to explain to Saul.

"I have to hang up," Misha said. "I'll call you again at noon tomorrow. This is important. Don't do anything further. Just wait for my call. I have information for you."

Misha broke the connection.

11

A dial tone. Distraught, Saul set down the phone and turned toward the modest living room of this safe house, a farm on the outskirts of Rome. It had been converted into an emergency medical facility. Icicle, his skin almost the literal color of ice, lay on a foldout bed, a bottle of plasma suspended above a tube leading into his arm. The same doctor who'd attended to Father Dusseault had disinfected and now was suturing the wound in Icicle's left arm. He applied a dressing and bandaged it.

369

"Now comes the hard part," the doctor said. He assessed the readings on portable monitors. "His heartbeat's arrhythmic. His blood pressure's low. His respiration's... Keep giving him oxygen," he told an assistant.

"You think he might die?" Saul asked.

"With two bullet wounds, he tried for a record in the hundred-yard dash. Every move pumped more blood out of him. Die? It's a miracle if he doesn't. And he still has to go through the trauma of my probing for the bullet in his other arm."

"He can't die!"

"Everybody dies."

"But I still need information from him!"

"Then this is the time to ask him. Before I put him under. In fifteen minutes, even if he lives, he won't say anything till tomorrow night."

Conscious of the doctor and his two assistants, of Gallagher hovering tensely behind them, of Drew standing uneasily in an open doorway behind which Arlene watched Erika and Father Dusseault, Saul leaned over Icicle. He used a cloth to wipe sweat from Icicle's pain-ravaged face.

"Can you hear me?"

Icicle nodded weakly.

"They say you might die. But if you hang on, I guarantee once you're well they'll let you go."

"For Christ's sake," Gallagher said, "that promise isn't yours to make."

Saul pivoted toward Gallagher. "I'll promise anything if it gets me the answers I want. From the start, I told you this was personal. But it isn't just about my wife's father any longer. It's also about my wife. When she learns what her father's up to, she'll never forgive me if I don't do everything I can to stop him. Try to stop *me* and I'll..."

"What would you do to me? And what would that make *you*? Another version of her father?" Gallagher asked.

Saul hesitated, aware of the truth in what Gallagher

said. But his devotion to Erika made him press on. "No, there's a difference. This isn't hate. It's love."

"Maybe that makes it worse."

"Look, I'm sorry. I didn't mean to threaten you. But you've got to understand." Saul leaned over Icicle again. "Tell me what I need to know. Use all the strength you can manage. Live. And you'll go free. Or I'll die trying to protect you."

"A hell of a promise," Icicle murmured.

"Count on it."

Icicle licked his dry lips. "What...do you need to know?"

"In the car, as we drove here, you told me Halloway lived near Toronto. A place called Kitchener. Concentrate. How do I get to Halloway? *Where is...?*"

"Kitchener?" Icicle's voice was faint, like the rustle of dead dry leaves. "He lives"—a painful swallow—"just outside it. Highway four-oh-one...west of Toronto...eighty kilometers...exit number..."

Saul strained to remember every word.

12

Midnight. The Mediterranean. South of Crete, north of Libya. The captain of the cargo ship *Medusa* felt uneasy about the signal light flashing from the darkness off his starboard bow. His rendezvous with the Libyan pickup ship wasn't due until 3 A.M. It was three hours early, and he hadn't been alerted about a change in schedule. Since 11 P.M. he'd been maintaining radio silence, just as the Libyans were supposed to, lest enemies learn about the delivery. So if there *had* been a change in schedule, he wouldn't have been told. The important thing was that the signal being flashed to him was the agreed-upon code. He gave orders for the confirmation code to be flashed, waited, and relaxed when the Libyans flashed a further confirmation code. The sooner he got rid of his cargo, the better.

The smokestack of a ship loomed out of the darkness and stopped a close but safe distance from where *Medusa* lay still in the water. Boats disembarked from the opposite ship, their engines roaring. The captain told his men to lower rope ladders and ready the ship's crane to unload the cargo.

The pickup boats pulled up against *Medusa*. Men scurried up the rope ladders. The captain's welcoming smile dissolved when he saw that they wore masks, that they held automatic weapons, that they were subduing *Medusa*'s crew, forcing them into lifeboats. A pistol barrel was rammed against his head. He screamed.

Adrift in a lifeboat, he watched *Medusa* gain speed, disappearing into the night, with her one-hundred-million-dollars worth of machine pistols, assault rifles, plastic explosives, grenades, ammunition, portable rocket launchers, and heat-seeking missiles. Two members of the assault force followed *Medusa* in the long-distance speedboats that had brought them here. What he'd mistaken for the Libyan ship was actually a canvas silhouette of a smokestack that the marauders had hoisted above one of the boats. He suspected that a similar silhouette would be raised above *Medusa*'s deck to change her profile and make it difficult for pursuers to identify her. A new name would probably be painted over her own. By tomorrow morning, the pirates could reach a safe harbor. The captain touched his head where the pistol barrel had been rammed against it. He asked himself how in hell he was going to explain to the Libyans when they arrived, and blurted orders for his crew to row as fast as they could. To where? What difference did it make? As long as it was away from here. Away from the Libyans, who weren't renowned for their understanding and certainly not for their mercy.

13

Fully conscious now, Erika tried to overcome her confusion, to assimilate everything Saul told her: how he, Drew, and Arlene had joined forces, and what had happened after she'd been abducted. Bewilderment turned into shock as she listened to what they'd learned.

"A hit team? My father and Avidan and the rest... seventy-year-old men... disappeared because they're out for revenge against Nazi war criminals?"

"That might not be all they're doing."

"Worse?"

Drew helped Saul explain. "In the car, Icicle mentioned the Night and Fog. He didn't mean the Nazi Night and Fog. He meant... We think your father and his team weren't satisfied with punishing the war criminals they learned about. We think they decided to terrorize the *children* of the Nazis. To pay the fathers back in kind."

Sudden understanding gave Erika strength to stand from the bed. "But don't you see? If the point was to torture the fathers by terrorizing the children, the fathers must still be alive. Otherwise the vengeance isn't complete. The Nazis have to *know* their children are being terrorized. They have to suffer by realizing their loved ones are suffering. There's still a chance to stop my father's team before they kill."

Drew smiled. "Saul was right about how smart you are."

"If I'm so smart, why aren't I cheering my father on?" Erika asked. "Part of me *wants* him to get even."

"Part of me feels that way, too," Saul said. "Maybe that's why I'm so angry about trying to protect them."

"That's just the point," Drew said. "Part of you wants vengeance. But *only* part of you. I feel like an outsider —without a right to an opinion. *My* relatives weren't killed in the Holocaust. *My* race wasn't hunted and almost exterminated. But when I think about the SS, I feel so outraged I want to..." He sighed. "Some of them weren't even crazy enough to believe in what they were doing. They just complied with the craziness around them. To earn a living. To feed their families. If enough of the hypocrites had objected with sufficient force . . ."

"But the world isn't like that," Erika said.

"We are," Drew said. "That's why we refuse to condone Nazi methods being used against Nazis. Because we refuse to *become* like Nazis. Isn't that what the Nuremberg trials were about? Not vengeance but reason and law. Believe me, I want to see these war criminals punished. I don't care how old they are. They *must* be punished. Death in my opinion. An absolute crime requires absolute penance. But not by individuals, not on the basis of anger alone, not without the sanction of society."

"But how . . . ?" Erika faltered, reaching for the bed.

"Are you all right?" Saul hurried over and put his arm around her.

She nodded, anxious to ask her question. "How are we going to stop my father?"

"Toronto," Saul said. "Halloway lives nearby. Your father was last seen there. Do you feel strong enough to travel?"

"Even if I didn't, I'd say I did. For my father's sake."

"But *do* you?"

"Yes. Get two tickets on the first plane you can."

"Four," Drew said.

Erika glanced up quickly at him in surprise.

Arlene, who'd listened in silence, stepped forward. "I agree with Drew. Four tickets. We're coming along."

"But you don't . . ."

"Have to? Is that what you wanted to say?"

"It's not your problem." Erika gestured in frustration. "That sounds rude. I don't mean it that way. But he's not your father."

"Right," Drew said. "We're not obligated. All the same, we're coming along."

"You don't even know me."

"We will."

14

Joseph Bernstein sat alone in the dark living room of the house-turned-into-a-prison in Toronto. He tried to relax before the tension of tomorrow. A few minutes' quiet.

I'm seventy, he thought. Other old men...my comrades—sleep upstairs. Equally old men—my enemies—are our prisoners. Tomorrow, after more than forty years, I fulfill a vow I made in my youth. To avenge my family. To punish monsters as they punished me.

15

The Air Canada DC-10 landed in Toronto shortly after 2 P.M. Saul's body was still set for Rome time, where the sun would be setting, not blazing above him. He'd slept little the night before and felt exhausted. His legs ached from lack of exercise.

Arlene and Drew said they felt as he did. But Erika had an excess of energy. Concern about her father prompted her to take charge as soon as they passed through immigration and customs. She found a car-rental booth and twenty minutes later drove the group out of the airport complex, merging with Highway 401.

Traffic was considerable, most drivers ignoring the hundred-kilometer-an-hour speed limit. But Erika didn't want trouble with the police and, despite her impatience, maintained the legal maximum. The afternoon sun was oppressive. She switched on the sedan's air conditioner and stared straight ahead, oblivious to the farm fields that flanked the highway.

Saul watched the exit numbers and, fifty minutes later, pointed. "Here. Take this one."

He regretted that he hadn't been able to wait for Misha Pletz's phone call in Rome. Misha had insisted he had something important to say, and Saul had suspected the information was related to Halloway. But when it came to a choice between waiting in Rome or catching the earliest plane to Toronto, speed had dictated which decision to make.

"Turn here. To the left," Saul said.

Erika drove along a country road. Five kilometers farther, Saul told her to turn left again. The sun-bathed countryside was gentle hills, woods alternating with corn and pasture.

"We ought to be close now," Saul said. The blacktop road curved. He pointed to the right toward a gravel lane that led up through trees toward a sloping lawn and a mansion on a bluff. "I think this is it. The layout's the same as Icicle's description. There should be a . . . Yes, see the silhouette of a greyhound on the mailbox at the side of the road."

"Lots of people put decorations on their mailbox, and lots of those decorations are silhouettes of dogs," Drew cautioned.

"Icicle said there'd be a metal bridge around a bend past the mansion."

A minute later, Erika drove across such a bridge. "I'm convinced. It's almost three-thirty. Let's not waste daylight." She turned the car around and drove back across the bridge, stopping at the side of the blacktop. "Near the river, the abandoned car won't look suspicious. It'll seem as if somebody stopped to go fishing."

"I wish we'd been able to bring our weapons," Saul said.

"Through airport security? We'd still be back in Rome. In jail," Drew said.

"It's just a wish. But I'm going to feel severely underdressed when we get to that mansion."

"You never know. Weapons might not be necessary," Arlene said. "Halloway could be nothing more than a businessman."

"Don't forget his connection with Seth and Icicle. It's better if we anticipate trouble."

They got out of the car. On the opposite side of the road, woods obscured them from the mansion.

16

The woods were dense. Only on occasion did sunbeams pierce the canopy of leaves. Smelling fragrant loam, Drew followed a zigzagging game trail, stepped over a fallen trunk and started up a more densely wooded slope. He glanced back toward Arlene, admiring her graceful movements, her obvious feeling of being at home in difficult terrain. We'll have to go rock-climbing, he thought. Just the two of us in a wilderness for a couple of weeks.

When this is over.

He concentrated only on the present and climbed higher through the trees. At the top, he waited for Arlene to join him and touched her shoulder lovingly. Beyond the clearing, a break in a line of trees revealed the mansion to the right on the continuation of this bluff. Saul and Erika were ahead of them, crouched among bushes.

Even at a hundred yards, Drew could see a half-dozen armed guards in front of the mansion. Their attention was directed toward the entrance to the estate. Ten cars of different types were parked beside them. A man in a blue exercise suit strode out of the mansion's front door and stopped abruptly, appalled by what he saw. A truck arrived, raising dust as it sped up the gravel lane.

17

The previous evening, Halloway had felt so nervous about the impending munitions delivery that he'd decided to risk visiting his wife and children at the safe house in Kitchener. Three A.M. in Libya was 9 P.M. in Ontario, and allowing for the time required to transfer the arms from *Medusa* to the Libyan freighter and for the further time the Libyan freighter would need to get back to home port, he didn't expect to receive word about the transaction until the next morning.

Though he wasn't religious, he prayed that the mission would be a success, for he now shared Rosenberg's tense misgivings about the Night and Fog's possible discovery of the shipment. The enemy had learned so much with which to terrorize them that perhaps they'd learned about *Medusa* too. But Halloway couldn't warn the Libyans about the potential information leak. Assured of maximum punishment for sending a shipment that might have been compromised, he took the gamble of not alerting his clients and hoped that nothing would go wrong.

His hope was manifested by a toast at dinner. He raised a glass of wine and feigned a smile toward his wife and children. "I know you're confused about what's going on. The past few months have been a strain. You wish you were home. The bodyguards make you nervous. But sometimes international finance creates enemies. If it helps, I believe we'll soon see the end of the crisis. In the meantime, your patience and understanding have been remarkable." He sipped his wine and silently proposed another toast. To *Medusa*. To the satisfactory conclusion of a hundred-million-dollar agreement.

He noted that it was precisely 9 P.M., the time for the Mediterranean delivery. A bodyguard came into the dining room and handed him a telegram.

Halloway ripped open the side of the envelope and pulled out the message. He had to read it several times before he absorbed the impact of the words.

ALL PROBLEMS SOLVED. YOUR FATHER SAFE. RE-TURNING HIM TOMORROW. YOUR TIME THREE P.M. YOUR ESTATE. ICICLE. SETH.

Halloway exhaled, overcome with relief. For the first time in several months, he felt buoyant, liberated. True, he wondered why Seth and Icicle had sent a telegram instead of phoning, and why they'd sent the telegram here, to the safe house he'd told them about, instead of to the estate outside town. But after he phoned a guard at the estate and learned that a telegram had just arrived here as well, he felt reassured that Seth and Icicle had tried to contact him at both of the places where he'd probably be. They must have worried that a phone call, for whatever reason, would have endangered them. He instructed the security force at his estate to expect company tomorrow.

"Your grandfather's coming home," he told his children. With a beaming smile toward his wife, he departed from his usual abstemiousness and poured himself a second glass of wine.

By noon the next day, he felt so nervous he couldn't keep still. Protected by bodyguards, he drove out to his estate. A car had already arrived. Overjoyed, he rushed toward it.

But instead of his father, Rosenberg stepped out of the car.

Halloway froze in astonishment. "What are *you* doing here?"

"Your telegram."

"Telegram?"

"You didn't send one?"

"For Christ's sake, no!"

"But it's got your name on it." Rosenberg took the telegram from his suitcoat pocket.

Halloway yanked it away from him. His heart sank as he read it.

PHONE CAN'T BE TRUSTED. ALL PROBLEMS SOLVED. OUR FATHERS SAFE. ARRIVE TOMORROW. MY TIME THREE P.M. MY ESTATE. HALLOWAY.

"And you *believed* this?" Halloway crushed the paper.

"What was I supposed to do? Phone when you told me I shouldn't? Stay in Mexico when I hoped my father was here in Canada?"

"You stupid bastard, I received a telegram as well! The message was almost the same! *My* father was supposed to be here."

"Then you're as stupid as you think I am!"

379

"*They* did this!" Halloway pivoted toward the entrance to his estate. "They set us up!"

"*They?*" Rosenberg's knees bent. "The Night and Fog?"

"Who else would . . . ? They must be watching us right now!"

Halloway and Rosenberg retreated toward the mansion.

But Halloway pivoted again, hearing a car roar up the gravel lane. As guards rushed toward it, Halloway recognized Miller behind the steering wheel. "I told you not to come here!"

Miller's car crunched to a halt on the gravel. The angry architect surged from his car. "And I told you I was coming! You *knew* what my father was! You knew what *all* the fathers were! I tried to convince myself I'd only be sinking to your level if I came here and strangled you. But God help me, even knowing my father's crime, I wanted him back! And then you sent me this telegram! My father! You said he'd be here! *Where is he?*"

Halloway grabbed the piece of paper with which Miller gestured in fury. The message was the same that Rosenberg had received. "They're out there," Halloway cried. "I know it. I'm sure of it. They're out there."

"Out there?" Miller's anger rose. "What are you—? Out there? Who?"

"We've got to take cover. Quickly. Inside." Halloway scurried toward the front steps. He shouted orders to the captain of his guards. "Pull your men in from the perimeter! Protect the house!"

But at once he spun again, hearing a car roar up the lane. Oh, Jesus, he thought. Not another one.

18

It went on like that for the next two hours, cars rushing up to the mansion, men scrambling out, each clutching a telegram. From around the world, they'd been summoned. From Mexico, America, England, France, Sweden, Egypt, and Italy, they'd rushed to be reunited with their fathers, only to learn of the trick that had brought them to Halloway's estate. Sheltered in his study while guards watched the mansion, they raised frightened angry voices. They shouted, accused, complained.

"I'm getting out of here!"

"But it isn't safe to leave!"

"It isn't safe to stay!"

"What's supposed to happen at three o'clock?"

"Why was that time specified in the telegram?"

"What if our fathers *will* be returned?"

"What if we'll be *attacked*?"

The appointed time passed. Halloway heard another vehicle enter the lane. He rushed outside, hoping he was wrong about the Night and Fog, praying this was Icicle and Seth.

But instead of a car, he saw a truck. With wooden slats along its sides, a tarpaulin covering the top. It looked like . . .

Halloway shivered.

. . . a cattle truck.

God have mercy, he thought, filled with a sickening premonition. The threat was all the more horrifying because it was vague. But of this he was certain—the end had begun.

19

"What's happening down there?" Saul asked. Crouched beside Erika, Drew, and Arlene, he watched from the bluff as the truck approached the nine cars parked in front of the mansion. The man in the blue exercise suit gestured frantically to his guards, who raised their rifles toward the truck.

Drew's voice was strained. "We have to get closer."

"Now. While the guards are distracted," Erika said.

Beyond the bushes in which they hid, a waist-high barbed wire fence separated them from the lawn of the estate. Erika hurried toward it. There were no glass insulators on the posts; the wires weren't electrified. She didn't see any closed-circuit cameras. There might be hidden sound and pressure detectors, but need made her take the risk. She climbed a post, tumbled to the lawn, and crawled.

To her right, a hundred yards away, she saw the man in the blue exercise suit shouting orders to his guards, who aimed toward the cattle truck. It reached the top of the lane, approaching the cars parked in front of the mansion.

Impelled by a horrible foreboding, Erika crawled faster. She turned toward Saul, who was squirming through the grass in her direction. Drew and Arlene were farther to her left, spreading out so there'd be less chance of anyone seeing them.

With the sun on her back, she hurried toward a garden plot filled with tall orange snapdragons that would give her more concealment on the way to the mansion.

Abruptly she stopped. Two guards at the back of the mansion had scrambled toward the commotion in front. They joined their counterparts and aimed at the cattle truck, which had turned so that its hatch was pointed toward the group in front of the mansion.

She took advantage of the guards' preoccupation and hurried closer to the mansion. But on her left she saw a sentry. She crouched behind a shrub. The sentry, rifle at the ready, approached a shed, only to lurch back as if struck. He plucked at something on the side of his neck and suddenly collapsed. Baffled, Erika watched two elderly men emerge from behind the shed. One of them held a gun whose distinctive shape she recognized—it was used to shoot tranquilizer darts. Despite their advanced age, the men worked with surprising speed, dragging the sentry into the shed. One shut the door while the other grabbed the sentry's rifle. They hurried toward the back of the mansion and disappeared.

Erika's bewilderment increased when she looked to

her right, toward the front of the mansion, and saw an elderly man get out of the passenger door of the truck. The man walked toward the truck's back hatch and joined another old man, who'd gotten out on the driver's side and unseen by Erika had walked to the back. They braced themselves in front of the guards' rifles. With a mixture of fear and dismay, Erika crawled faster. Her heart pounded. Her premonition worsened. The elderly man who'd just appeared from the blind side of the truck was her father.

20

Rage had made him incapable of fear. Joseph Bernstein stopped at point-blank range from the rifles and turned toward Halloway. "Is this any way to welcome visitors?"

"Who *are* you?"

"I think you already know," Ephraim Avidan said. Standing next to Joseph, he lifted his hand toward the tarpaulin that covered the truck's back hatch. "Tell your guards to lower their guns." Ephraim yanked the tarpaulin to the side of the truck. The back hatch slammed down.

A bearded elderly man sat in the truck, aiming a machine gun. "Since munitions are your business, you're no doubt aware I've pulled back the cocking bolt on this weapon," he said. "You also know the devastation rapid-feed thirty-caliber bullets can accomplish. Even if someone shot me right now, my nervous reflex would pull the trigger. I'm aiming directly at your chest. Please do what my associate requested and order your guards to lower their rifles."

"If you need further incentive, look deeper into the truck," Joseph said.

Lips parted with apprehension, Halloway squinted toward the interior.

"Step closer. We want you to see every detail," Ephraim said.

Halloway took two nervous steps forward and paled when he saw what was in there.

Drugged, ashen, hollow-cheeked, the fathers were chained together, eleven of them slumped on the floor of the truck. An elderly man guarded the prisoners, pressing an Uzi against the forehead of Halloway's father.

"Dear God." Halloway clutched his stomach, as if he might vomit.

"Tell your guards to put down their rifles or we'll shoot the prisoners," Joseph said. He pulled a Beretta from a windbreaker pocket.

"Do it," Halloway said.

The guards set their rifles on the lane. Joseph searched them, found several handguns, and told the guards to lie facedown on the gravel.

"Why are you doing this?" Halloway asked. *"What do you want?"*

"Isn't it obvious by now?" Ephraim said. "We're here to discuss Nazi racial theories."

The large front door to the mansion came open. One by one, the other members of Halloway's group stepped out, their hands raised, their faces pinched with fear. Two elderly men holding Uzis followed them.

"Ah," Ephraim said, "the rest of our audience has consented to join us."

"I don't know what you think you're doing," one of Halloway's group shouted, "but—!"

"Mr. Miller," Joseph said, "please shut your mouth."

"You can't keep something like this a secret! You can't—"

Joseph struck him across the head with the Beretta.

Miller fell to the gravel. He moaned, clutching his bleeding scalp.

"Would anyone else like to say something?" Joseph asked.

The group stared appalled at the blood streaming down Miller's face.

"Very good," Joseph said.

Other old men, aiming Uzis, appeared from each side of the house.

"Did you restrain the rest of the guards?" Ephraim asked.

"The perimeter's been secured. We searched every room in the house."

"In that case, it's time to begin." Ephraim stepped toward the truck.

"Whatever you plan to do, it's wrong," a Mexican-looking man said.

"Rosenberg, don't presume to tell *me* what's wrong. You and Halloway are perfect proof that the vices of the fathers are inherited by the sons."

"What are you talking about?"

"The weapons you sold to Libya to be used against Israel."

"You *know* about—?"

"The weapons are now in Israeli hands."

Rosenberg gasped.

"It's only fitting that, even if you didn't intend to do so, you helped protect my race, the race your father tried so hard to destroy," Ephraim said. He reached into the truck and threw shovels onto the gravel. "Pick them up. All of you." He threw out more shovels. "We brought enough for everyone. We mustn't take all day about this. Efficiency is something your fathers always recommended. Teamwork. Organization."

"Shovels?" Halloway blanched. "What do you—?"

"Dig a hole, of course. A large deep hole."

"You're insane!"

"Were your fathers insane when they forced Jews to dig pits for the bodies of other Jews? Or is killing Jews a perfectly rational thing to do? Is it only insane when the executioners are executed? *Pick up the shovels.*"

Prodded by Uzis, the group stumbled forward.

"We'll dig the pit behind the house, out of sight from the road down there," Ephraim said. "I'm sure you're all wondering what we intend to do with *you* when the hole is ready. Will we force you to watch the death of your fathers and then shoot you just as your fathers shot those they ordered to dig burial pits? We offer you the same temptation your fathers offered their victims. Cooperate with us, and we'll let you go. Dig the pit—we'll be understanding. How much do you love your fathers? Many Jews were faced with that question during the war. If your father's going to die, is it a useless sacrifice to resist and die along with him? Or does it make more sense to cooperate with your persecutors and take the chance that you'll be spared? An interesting dilemma. If you refuse to dig the pit, we'll kill you. If you obey...?" Ephraim raised his hands, expressing a quandary. "Who knows? Experience what we did. It'll be an education for you."

21

Erika crouched behind a gazebo and surveyed the back of the mansion. The two old men who'd dragged the guard into a shed weren't in view anymore, presumably having entered a rear door of the mansion. But on the far side of the house, two other old men dragged a guard behind what appeared to be a long garage. They came back into sight, holding Uzis, and ran toward the rear of the mansion.

She looked toward Saul crawling behind her, held up a palm to warn him, and pointed toward the rear of the house. She couldn't see Drew and Arlene, assumed they were trying to circle the grounds, and hoped they would realize there were other strangers on the property.

At the rear of the mansion, the two old men had been joined by two others. They hurried inside the building. Erika forced herself to wait, to watch for an opportunity.

She was glad she had. The four men came back outside, aimed their Uzis toward the grounds as if making sure that the perimeter had been secured, then separated, two men running along each side of the house to join the group in front.

Now! She sprinted toward the rear of the house,

pressed herself against the back wall, and peered through a screen door toward shadows and silence. The instant Saul joined her, she opened the screen door and stepped inside.

She saw stairs on her right leading down to a basement. Ahead, three steps led up to a short corridor. While Saul checked the basement, she followed the corridor, smelling pot roast and freshly baked bread. The corridor opened into a large gleaming kitchen where two men, wearing servants' uniforms, lay motionless on the floor, a tranquilizer dart protruding from each neck.

She felt a chill on her own neck. When Saul returned from the basement, she proceeded through a swinging door toward another corridor, this one wider and longer, with landscape paintings on the walls. Though the paintings were beautiful, with a mystical quality of light, they filled her with horror because of the monster, Halloway's father, the assistant commandant of Maidanek, who'd probably created them.

On her right, she saw a dining room, on her left a large study where full ashtrays and empty liquor glasses showed that a large group had recently gathered here. But her attention was directed from the study toward the end of the corridor. The front door had been left open. Male voices—some angry, others pleading, a few disturbingly calm—drifted in from outside. *One of the voices belonged to her father.* Pulse pounding behind her ears, she eased along the corridor and hid against the wall next to the open door. Through a slight gap between the door and the jamb, she squinted toward the sunlit front steps where old men held middle-aged men at gunpoint.

Again she heard her father. The flood of excitement she felt at being close to him suddenly drained from her. Despair made her hollow. The conversation she heard was grotesque, as was the crunch of shovels being thrown onto gravel and the command to dig a pit behind the house. Restraining the reflex to be sick, she put a hand on Saul's shoulder.

22

As Ephraim described the pit that the sons would dig for the fathers, Joseph vividly remembered the pits that he and his wife had been forced to dig at Treblinka. In the absence of ovens, the SS had burned corpses in those pits, promising a reprieve to the Jews who shoveled the earth as long as their strength held out. Cooperate and live. Refuse out of loyalty to your fellow Jews and die in the gas chamber you could have escaped, be burned in the pit you refused to dig.

That terrible choice had threatened his sanity—the choice to live by disposing of the remains of his fellow human beings. Guilt had so consumed him, rage had so festered within him that to vent his agony he'd been prepared to do *anything*. Now that the moment had come, he didn't only remember Treblinka. He felt as if he were truly back there, the smoke of smoldering corpses swirling around him, the stench of charred flesh making him double over. But he had to force himself upright, had to keep working as the SS ordered more wood to be put on the corpses, more sacks of quicklime to be opened, more bodies to be carted from the gas chambers. Tears came to his eyes.

"Out!" he heard the SS scream. "All of you! Hurry! Faster! Jump, goddamn you! Out of the truck!"

Truck? But there *weren't* any trucks at Treblinka. The Nazis brought the prisoners in stockcars on trains. Why would a truck be at—?

He snapped from the nightmare of then to now, from Treblinka to Halloway's estate, and saw Ephraim's eyes bulging with hate.

"Out!" Ephraim shouted at the aged SS officers and whipped them with a rope, urging them faster from the truck. Chained together, the prisoners lost their balance as they did their best to descend in a hurry, falling on top of each other, chains rattling, frail bodies crunching on gravel. Jumbled together, they whimpered, squirming.

"No," Joseph said.

But Ephraim's shouts made his objection a whisper. Ephraim whipped the old men harder. "On your feet, vermin! Hurry! No time! Müller, you're an expert in what happens next! After the pit's been dug, we'll place a plank across it and make you stand in the middle! So when we shoot you, we'll know for sure you'll fall into the pit! We wouldn't want to waste time having to kick your body down if you fell on the rim! Efficiency, Müller! Wasn't that the motto? Organization! We mustn't waste time!"

"No," Joseph said again.

But again, amid Ephraim's shouts, no one heard him.

The sons were pale with shock.

"Aren't you going to try to stop us?" Ephraim asked. "Halloway? Rosenberg? Try to stop us! No? Are you beginning to understand how fear can rob you of your will? The SS used to say that the Jews deserved to die because they didn't resist being marched to the gas chamber! Well, now it's your turn! Resist! Show us how superior you are!" He whipped their fathers again. "On your feet! Damn you, hurry!"

Joseph watched Ephraim's hate-contorted face and felt sickened. It wasn't supposed to be like this. He'd expected to feel satisfaction, not disgust. Relief, not nausea.

Ephraim whipped the old men faster. "Soon you'll learn how it feels to see your sons dig your graves, to watch your sons being forced to watch you getting shot! You'll feel afraid, humiliated, debased!" Ephraim glared toward the sons. "And soon *you'll* learn how it feels to see your father killed, to stand helplessly back after you participated in his execution by digging his grave! Soon you'll learn how it feels to wonder if the obscene bargain you made will be honored, if you'll be killed or spared!"

The old men were being herded toward the back of the house, their sons prodded with Uzis, forced to carry shovels for the pit.

"Try to escape!" Ephraim shouted. "That's what *we* were tempted to do! We knew we'd be shot, and yet we kept hoping that something, *anything*, would stop the efficiency, stop the—!"

Joseph opened his mouth to shout again, "No!" But the word froze in his throat.

Because someone else, a woman, shouted it first.

23

Joseph swung toward the open front door of the mansion. The others spun with their Uzis. Ephraim drew his Beretta.

With dizzying astonishment, Joseph watched the woman step out of the mansion.

No! he thought. This can't be happening! I'm imagining it!

But he knew he wasn't. As the gravel beneath him seemed to tilt, he recognized beyond a doubt.

The woman was Erika.

Her face was flushed with anger. "No! You can't! This is wrong! It's *worse* than wrong! If you do to them what they did to you, to *us*, to our people, you make yourselves them! You destroy yourselves! This has to stop!"

"Erika . . ." Joseph murmured.

"You *know* this woman?" Ephraim asked.

"My daughter."

"*What?*"

A man and a woman rushed from the right side of the house, grappled with two members of Ephraim's team, and grabbed their Uzis. Almost at once, a man lunged through the mansion's open door, held a member of Ephraim's team in a stranglehold, and took his weapon.

Joseph felt a further disorienting sense of unreality. *The man at the open door was Erika's husband.*

"Saul?" he asked, bewildered. "But how did—?"

"It's finished!" Erika shouted. "There'll be no execution! We're leaving these old men with their sons! We're getting out of here!"

But Ephraim continued to aim his pistol at her. "No, *you're* going to leave! I've waited too long for this! I've suffered too much! Before I die, before *they* die, they'll be punished!"

"And it'll happen!" Erika rushed down the steps. "In the courts! Let the law take care of this!"

Ephraim scowled with contempt. "The law? Where was the law in Nazi Germany? I know what the law will do! Waste time! It'll give them rights their victims never dreamed of! The trials will take forever! And in the end, instead of being executed, they'll die peacefully at home."

"If you won't respond morally . . . !"

"Did the SS?"

"Then think about this! Kill them, and you'll be hunted for the rest of your life! You'll be caught and die in prison!"

"You're proving my point! The law would punish me more than them! And as for my life, it ended more than forty years ago!"

"Then you're a fool!"

Ephraim stiffened so abruptly Joseph feared he'd pull the trigger on his pistol.

"Yes, a fool!" Erika said. "By a miracle, you survived! But instead of giving thanks to God, instead of savoring life, you savored death! God granted you a gift, and you threw it away!"

Ephraim aimed toward Halloway's father.

"No!" Joseph yelled.

Erika ran to her father. "Tell him! Convince him! If you love me, make him stop!" She grabbed his shoulders. "Do it! For me! I'm begging you! Tell him these monsters aren't worth destroying your lives! You've got a grandson you've seldom seen! You could watch him grow up! You could learn about innocence and maybe even regain your own! You could be young again!" Tears streamed down her face. "For God's sake, do it! If you love me!"

Joseph felt a tightness in his chest that took his breath away. It was overpowering, frighteningly different from the pressure that had brought him here. Produced by love. not hate.

"Ephraim . . ." It was difficult to speak. "She's right." He sounded raspy, in pain, though the feeling was quite the opposite. "Let's get out of here."

Ephraim squinted down the barrel of his pistol toward Halloway's father. "It would be so easy to squeeze the trigger. It would be so satisfying."

"You didn't see yourself when you whipped them. You reminded me of the commandant of the work force at Treblinka."

"Don't compare me with—!"

"You aren't relieving my nightmares. You're bringing my nightmares back. I'm ashamed that my daughter saw us doing this. Ephraim, please, I know now what I want. To forget."

"And let them go?"

"What difference will it make? Killing them won't bring our loved ones back. It won't stop hate. But if you kill them, you'll be a part of hate."

Like Erika, Ephraim had tears running down his face. "But what's to become of me?"

Joseph took his gun away and held him. "With luck . . . both of us . . . we'll learn to live."

24

There were five of them now in the rented car. Drew and Arlene in front. Saul, Erika, and Joseph in back. As they drove from Halloway's estate, followed by the truck in which Ephraim brought away the rest of the team, Saul said, "Halloway won't dare call the police. He and the others have too much to hide."

Joseph nodded solemnly and turned to Erika. "How did you find me?"

"I'll need the flight back to Europe to explain."

"I'm afraid I won't be going back with you."

She paled. "But I assumed . . ."

"I wish I could." Joseph held her. "But there's much to be done. The operation has to be dismantled. Our escape procedures have to be cancelled. Besides"—Joseph glanced sadly toward Ephraim in the cab of the truck behind them—"my friends and I have a lot to talk about. To adjust to. It won't be easy. For Ephraim. For any of us."

"Then you have to promise you'll come to visit us, to see your grandson," Erika said.

"Of course."

"When?" she asked quickly.

"Two weeks."

"Thank God we got to you in time," Drew said.

"I wonder." Joseph brooded. "Ephraim was right about one thing. They'll die peacefully before they're punished."

"No. We'll contact Misha," Erika said. "We'll tell him what you found out. He'll force extradition. They *will* be punished."

"I want to believe that. But on the other hand . . ." Joseph smiled at something outside the car.

"What do you mean 'on the other hand'? Why are you smiling?"

"No reason."

He'd just seen a car go past. A big car. Heading toward Halloway's estate. It was filled with Arabs. Libyans, he was sure. Angry Libyans. About to demand an explanation from Halloway and Rosenberg about the hijacked munitions shipment.

Yes, Joseph thought and hugged Erika again, justice feels satisfying.

25

They caught a night flight back to Rome. Saul slept most of the way, but an hour before landing, he felt a hand grip his shoulder. Waking, he saw that Drew had just passed him and was motioning for him to follow.

Careful not to wake Erika, noticing that Arlene was still asleep as well, Saul unbuckled his seat belt and joined Drew where he waited out of sight in a narrow corridor between two rows of rest rooms.

"Before we landed," Drew said, "I wanted to talk with you."

"I figured we could do that in Rome."

"We won't have time. Arlene and I have to report to the Fraternity. We fulfilled our bargain with them. We learned why the cardinal disappeared and who was trying to sabotage the order. We're anxious to arrange for our freedom."

"Are you sure they'll stick by their agreement?"

"They'd better. What I wanted to tell you is I'm glad everything worked out for you and your wife. The way she stepped out of that mansion to face those Uzis—she's remarkable. Good luck to both of you."

"Erika and I couldn't have solved our problems without your help."

"And Arlene and I couldn't have made it without you and Erika. We're grateful."

"This is difficult for me to say."

Drew waited.

"At the start," Saul said, "I felt an instinctive friendship for you. Because of my dead foster brother. You don't only have the same background that Chris did. You even look like him."

"What do you mean 'at the start'? What's changed?"

"Resemblance to someone is a poor basis for a friendship. I want to be friends with you—because of what *you* are."

Drew smiled. "Fair enough."

They clasped each other's shoulders.

"There's something I want you to do for me," Drew said.

"Name it."

"Convince Gallagher not to look for us. Tell him we've had our fill of networks. We don't want to be recruited. All we want to do is drop out of sight. To live in peace."

"He'll get the message."

"And something else," Drew said. "We can't report to the Fraternity as long as the Agency has Father Dusseault."

Saul understood. If the Fraternity discovered that the priest was a CIA prisoner, the order would blame Drew and Arlene for jeopardizing its secrecy. Instead of gaining their freedom, Drew and Arlene would be killed.

"The last time I saw him, the priest was drugged," Drew said. "He doesn't know anything that happened since the night in the Vatican gardens. He doesn't know about you or that he's been questioned by the Agency. Tell Gallagher to learn what he needs to and then leave the priest near the Vatican. Father Dusseault will seek protection from the Fraternity, but after my report to them, they'll punish him for killing the cardinal and sending Avidan's group after the Nazis."

"And in time the Agency will go after the Fraternity. It shouldn't be hard to arrange," Saul said. "Gallagher's already nervous about keeping the priest. He's afraid of having exceeded his authority. What he wants is information without controversy about how he got it." Saul paused. "Will you keep in touch?"

"As soon as Arlene and I are free."

"Where do you plan to settle?"

"We're not sure yet. Maybe the Pyrenees."

"How about the desert? We'd like you to stay with us in Israel."

"I spent a year in the desert. It didn't agree with me."

Saul grinned. "Sure. I understand." His grin faltered. "It's just . . ."

"Tell me."

"I have a favor of my own to ask."

"Name it."

"Two weeks ago, when all of this started, our village was attacked. To get at *us*. We thought it had something to do with Joseph's disappearance. Maybe someone trying to stop us from finding out why he disappeared. The problem is, none of what we've learned is related to that attack. I'm worried that someone else is out there, someone with a different reason to want to kill Erika and me. I think they'll try it again."

Drew touched his new friend's arm. His eyes were hard with determination, yet bright with love. "We'll be there as soon as possible. After that..." He sounded so much like Chris. "I'd like to see the bastards try. Against the four of us? Let them come."

About the Author

David Morrell is the author of FIRST BLOOD, the novel that created the character Rambo. He is a former professor of American literature at the University of Iowa, where he lives with his wife and two children.

All books by David Morrell,
   including

THE BROTHERHOOD OF THE ROSE
and
THE FRATERNITY OF THE STONE

are available in bookstores,
or use this coupon to order by mail: